SUMMER
LIGHT

Luanne Rice

B A N T A M   B O O K S

New York   Toronto   London   Sydney   Auckland

ISBN 0-553-80122-8

Bantam Books are published by Bantam Books, a division of Random House, Inc. Its trademark, consisting of the words "Bantam Books" and the portrayal of a rooster, is Registered in U.S. Patent and Trademark Office and in other countries. Marca Registrada. Bantam Books, 1540 Broadway, New York, New York 10036.

PRINTED IN THE UNITED STATES OF AMERICA

For my niece, Amelia Onorato

Acknowledgments

With affection and thanks to Tracey Turriff, for taking me to the Hockey Hall of Fame and Maple Leaf Gardens, and for showing me even more of the warmth and beauty of Canada than I already knew.

Thank you, especially, to Rob Monteleone. Through years of watching Rob play hockey, I have become inspired by the mysteries of the ice, by the speed and competition and love and blood. Without Rob, I could never have known Martin.

SUMMER LIGHT

Prologue

THE LAKE WAS SO DEEP it had no bottom. When it froze, the ice was thirty feet thick. Mountains rose to the north, east, and west, thick snow covering every cliff and pine tree. Just before sunrise, the aurora borealis flashed across the northern sky. Without pausing to look up, the young boy strapped on skates and grabbed a shovel.

The temperature was five below zero. Inside, he had banked the kitchen stove with coal and firewood. The fire blazed, but it wasn't strong enough to warm the house. Martin was always cold, no matter that his mother gave him hot bread for breakfast, that she knitted him thick socks and heavy sweaters to wear.

Outside, the wind stung his cheeks red. It seared his lungs and froze his fingers. The cuts on his chest—new, raw, stitched with black thread—felt like a bear had clawed him, but nothing could stop him. He had school in a few hours, but first he and Ray were going to meet on the lake.

The sun broke over the eastern mountains, cracks of orange light shooting through the trees. Martin glided across the ice, pushing the shovel ahead of him, clearing last night's snowfall: two inches had fallen. Hearing the scrape of a blade, he looked up the lake and waved. Ray was shoveling fast and hard from his end.

The boys met and passed. As the sun rose higher, they cleared more of the area. Martin pictured the Zamboni at Maple Leaf Gardens, preparing the ice for his father to play. The crowd was cheering.

And now, the great Martin Cartier was about to meet the great Ray Gardner. . . .

They set aside shovels and found the sticks and pucks they had hidden under the old log. Martin's stomach growled. He hadn't had enough to eat last night, and this morning his mother's bread

hadn't risen right: The fire had gone out in the early hours, and the stove wasn't hot enough for baking. He had choked down half a slice to please her, trying to ignore the things she was saying about his father.

Martin's stomach rumbled louder, right through his heavy jacket. He knew Ray could hear it—it sounded just like a bear or a timber wolf—and he was embarrassed that Ray would know they didn't have enough money to stay warm or eat right.

"Ready?" Ray asked, pretending not to hear.

"Bien sûr," Martin said, grateful to Ray but giving him a deadly scowl, just like he'd seen the centers do it in the pros.

Their sticks clicked, Martin won the puck, and the race was on.

Flying down the ice, he heard their skate blades slashing. Clumps of snow whispered off the pine boughs onto the frozen lake. A family of deer nibbled the tops of tall grass sticking out of the snow. An owl flew low over the ice, chasing a field mouse.

Martin saw it all, even as he concentrated on the puck. The world went on around him, a thousand sights at a time, and all his focus was on the puck. They fought and tripped each other, hooking each others' ankles, hooting with joy. Martin was superhuman; he had the multifaceted eyes of a praying mantis; he was the greatest hockey player in the world.

Eyes in the back of your head, that's what you need, eh? That's what the real champions have. Martin could hear his father's voice. It was so clear, as if he was right behind him on Lac Vert instead of living it up in California. Driving for the goal, Martin imagined his father watching him now, watching him with pride. He left his best friend in a cloud of snow. He cocked his arm, aimed for the net, scored.

"Martin, what's that?" Ray asked, skating over.

"What's what?" Martin asked, grinning. He grabbed Ray in a bear hug, getting him in a headlock. "I beat you, that's what. Can't you take it?"

"No, that—" Ray shoved Martin away, pointing at the ice.

Drops of red led to one scarlet pool. The blood ran down his legs, over his skates, onto the ice. Bright red, it soaked through the thin snow and skate blade tracks.

"Nothing," Martin said.

"Merde!" Ray said.

Fumbling with the zipper, Ray undid Martin's jacket. Martin tried to fight him off, but he was shaking too hard. Ray threw down his gloves and unbuttoned Martin's shirt.

The slices were deep, and in the rough game, the stitches had come undone. Blood flowed from the crisscrossed cuts. The man had held Martin's neck with one hand, the knife with the other while his father had watched. "Pay," the man kept saying. "Pay, or I'll go deeper."

"What the hell?" Ray asked, looking into Martin's eyes. The air was so cold, their blood froze as they stood there. Ray took off his own jacket and pressed it against the wounds. Martin couldn't, wouldn't talk. He wouldn't tell a soul—not his mother, not his best friend—the details of what had been done to him.

And he never had—not one person—until he met May.

May, his only love. He had told her the whole story.

—◆—

He could see it now, the way it had been, the thing that had happened, that bright cold morning on Lac Vert. He could see as if it was right in front of him: every ice crystal, every pine needle, the look of wild competition in his friend's eyes. The scene was as clear as day.

Until he opened his eyes. He was lying in bed, sweating and tangled in the sheets.

"Martin, you cried in your sleep," May whispered beside him.

"I dreamed—" he began, then stopped.

"Tell me," she said. He could hear the anguish in her voice, and behind it the deepest love he had ever known. They had met at a strange, vulnerable time in each of their lives, and she had once told him they had specific things to give each other, things that no one else ever could. He was afraid, so afraid, that he had lost the power to give her anything.

"Of the lake," he said.

"What happened?"

"I could see."

May pressed her face against his chest. His scars no longer hurt as they once had, but they felt taut and hard as wire cables. Martin couldn't see her hand as she reached up to touch his face. He couldn't see their room, the window, the pictures of Lac Vert hanging on the wall, his only love lying beside him. He was going blind, and he couldn't see anything, except in his dreams.

Chapter 1

THE PLANE WAS CROWDED. As the passengers boarded, the flight attendant announced that every seat would be required, that people should stow all their belongings in the overhead bins or under the seats in front of them. May Taylor made sure her and Kylie's bags were out of the way, that Kylie knew she had to stay in her place and not bother the businessman in the aisle seat.

Takeoff was smooth, and the plane climbed through thin gray clouds into the brilliant blue. Until this year, May hadn't flown much—she had never had much reason. But Kylie's doctor in Boston had recommended that Kylie take part in a study at Twigg University in Toronto, with a group of psychologists focusing on clairvoyance and personality disorders.

May and Kylie lived with May's great-aunt in an old farmhouse on the Connecticut shoreline. May loved her daughter more than anything, but as she looked around the plane, she couldn't help noticing all the couples. The white-haired couple sharing the newspaper; the young professionals in his-and-her suits, talking on cell phones; two parents with their teenaged kids across the aisle.

May stared at the parents for a few minutes, wondering how it would feel to have someone to share the care of Kylie with: to travel with, laugh with, worry with. She watched the woman bend toward her husband, her hair brushing his shoulder as she whispered in his ear. His lips turned up in a wide smile, and he bowed his head, nodding in agreement.

May suddenly felt as if she'd swallowed a fishbone, and she quickly looked down. She had a sheaf of papers from Dr. Ben Whitpen at the Twigg University Department of Psychology to read, reports and observations and recommendations, all pertaining to Kylie. Upon landing at Logan, she would take them to Kylie's doctor on Barkman Street. After that, the long drive home

to Connecticut lay ahead. She stared at the letterhead, at the confusing and worrisome words swimming together, and the ache in
her throat grew worse.

"Mom?" Kylie asked.

"What, honey?"

"Big men."

Thinking Kylie meant the passenger sitting next to her, May
immediately leaned close to Kylie's ear. When Kylie got involved
with people, they sometimes got upset. And May could tell by the
man's expensive suit, his heavy gold watch, and the fancy briefcase
he'd placed in front of Kylie instead of his own seat, that he was
one of the ones who might get upset.

"The man's working," May whispered. "Don't bother him."

"No," Kylie whispered back, shaking her head. "In the special
compartment—really big men. Are they giants?"

May and Kylie were in the first row, but Kylie was staring
through the half-open curtain separating economy and business
class. Kylie was right: Several huge guys were sitting up there, talking to a semicircle of pretty female flight attendants. Their strength
was apparent in the size of their chests and arms, the breadth of
their shoulders. Some of them had logos on the sleeves of their
shirts, and May figured they belonged to some team or other. The
women were laughing, one of them saying she loved hockey and
could she have an autograph. May, knowing nothing about hockey,
turned her attention back to Kylie.

"They're just men," May said. "Not giants."

"Big, though," Kylie said.

"Yes," May said. "Big." She thought of the word "big," of how
it could mean so many things. Kylie's father was big—over six feet
tall. He was a lawyer in Boston, in one of the prestigious firms with
offices in a skyscraper overlooking the harbor—a big attorney. He
had seemed to love May until she told him she was pregnant, and
then he had told her he was married to someone else—a big problem. He sent her money every month, enough to feed and clothe
Kylie—but he didn't want to know their daughter. That made him
small.

The Department of Psychology was paying for this flight, with
an extra stipend besides. Even with Gordon's child support, life
away from home was expensive. Planes, hotels, and restaurants
were for other people, vacationers and business travelers with
someone to share the trip with. May felt a wave of loneliness.

Listening to Kylie humming beside her, May looked down. She

hadn't planned on motherhood, hadn't counted on anything as wonderful as Kylie coming from the worst experience of her life. Kylie was a fairy child, unique and odd but—if May could believe Dr. Whitpen—gifted instead of disturbed. May had been instructed to keep a diary of her visions, a blue notebook she filled with everything Kylie told her and with details May observed.

Right now, Kylie stared at the men up front with growing intensity, her eyes taking on what May called "the glow." She was seeing something. She bit her lip, to keep from blurting it out. Her eyes slid from May to the forward compartment and back again. Six years old, she was small for her size. Wavy dark hair fell to her shoulders, and velvet brown eyes gazed out from her creamy face, radiant as if lit from within by candlelight.

"Don't, Kylie," May said.

"But—" Kylie began.

"I'm tired," May said. "Look somewhere else. Draw pictures. I'll switch with you, and you can have the window seat."

Kylie shook her head and gave an exaggerated shiver, sliding low in her seat. She stared at the big men up front, her eyebrows knit together with fierce concentration.

"It's a baby one," she said, frowning as she clasped her hands in her lap.

"Kylie—"

As if feeling the intensity of Kylie's stare, one of the hockey players looked over his shoulder. He had the aisle seat, and as he turned May noticed a mischievous glint in his gray-blue eyes. A flight attendant stepped forward to yank the curtain shut. Blocked from view, their conversation and laughter were just as loud. Kylie stared as if she had X-ray vision, as if whatever she had seen was still there, in plain sight.

"Great," came an annoyed voice from the row behind. "Put the Boston Bruins on a plane, and watch the stewardesses disappear."

"They're screwing up the play-offs anyway," someone else said. "The Maple Leafs will finish them off tonight."

"The hell with hockey," a woman said with a laugh. "Just give me Martin Cartier."

"The hell with Martin Cartier," a man growled. "Just bring me a drink."

Kylie seemed oblivious to all the talk. Sitting between her mother and the stranger on the aisle, she was growing paler by the minute. May stuck the papers and her diary into a folder and snapped up her tray table. Her heart felt heavy, and her chest

ached. She watched Kylie stare at the curtain, her mouth moving in
silent words.

"Let's switch places, honey," May said, unsnapping her and
Kylie's seat belts. "It's springtime down there, and you can see the
new leaves. See all those fields? All the trees? We must be over
Massachusetts by now. See if you can count—" She paused, lifting
Kylie out of her seat and plunking her by the window. Kylie's skin
felt clammy, and May's heart was racing. The businessman let out
a loud exhalation as May kicked his briefcase out of the way.

"She wants her daddy, Mom," Kylie whispered, clutching
May's wrist. "She wants to kiss him."

"Count the barns," May pleaded, pointing out the window,
trying to find something to occupy Kylie, take her mind off the
hallucination.

"Oh, but she'll leave—" Kylie started, sounding sad. She swallowed, looking into May's eyes. May could almost watch her willing herself to obey, to stop whatever vision she was having and act
like a normal child—count the barns or sing her ABC's or look at
the Berkshires or ask to be taken to the bathroom.

Kylie had started seeing angels when she was four. She went to
nursery school and realized that she was the only child there without a father. A month later, her beloved Great-Granny—May's
grandmother Emily—died of a heart attack. Then, one fall day, on
a hike around the Lovecraft Wildlife Refuge, the two of them had
come upon a body hanging from a tree branch. All rags and bone,
the skull had grinned down like a decomposing witch. The police
later identified it as the body of a drifter, Richard Perry, who had
committed suicide.

Suddenly Kylie had started talking to herself. She would call
out in her sleep, cry all day at nursery school, speak in unknown
tongues to people May couldn't see.

The psychologist May had eventually taken her to had re-
marked on the timing: that Kylie had begun having visions right
after Emily Dunne—Kylie's great-grandmother, solid presence,
rock of the family—had died. At the same time, Kylie had come to
realize she was essentially fatherless. She felt abandoned by most
of the adults in the universe, the doctors said. Seeing the dead body
had been her breaking point, the catalyst for seeing ghosts. She
wanted a family, and the visions provided that.

May could understand. Having grown up in an extended, loving family, *she* wanted family too. Besides, she worked in the most

charmed profession in the world, with a legacy of magic from her grandmother and great-aunt.

But what if Kylie was schizophrenic, and not clairvoyant?

"She'll go," Kylie whispered, holding her mother's wrist, "before she gets to kiss her father. She'll leave if I don't pay attention—"

"Kylie," May whispered, her voice breaking. "Let her leave." If she wasn't so exhausted, frustrated, scared, and alone, she told herself, she would stand firm and tell Kylie in no uncertain terms that there was no one there, no one wanting to kiss her father, no baby angel hovering over the seats in business class.

———

Martin Cartier had his legs stuck out in the aisle, and every time one of the flight attendants passed, they braced themselves on his seat back as they stepped over. Two hours into the flight, he was being a jerk, blocking their way, but he couldn't help it. He had tried sitting slouched, straight, and sideways, but any way you cut it, the plane was too small.

Not just because of his size, which was considerable, but because of his energy. His mother always used to say he had a blizzard inside him, and Martin thought that might be true. He felt as if he'd swallowed a killer wind, with enough power to flatten cities and bury towns, that if he used it on the ice, he could destroy the other team. Martin's energy flew out his elbows and hips, slamming his opponents into the boards, bloodying the ice and sending people to the hospital.

Right now, the energy made him squirm in his seat. He felt prickles on his scalp, and once again he looked around. The flight attendant had closed the curtain, but peering through a crack, he saw the little girl staring at him, her pretty mother bending over to whisper something in her ear.

He played defense for the Boston Bruins, and they called him "the Gold Sledgehammer." "Gold," because of the name Cartier, and "Sledgehammer" because of the obvious: He always won his fights. He'd been named an All-Star ten times, won the NHL MVP twice, led the league in scoring twice. He was a tough and stalwart defenseman, winning the Norris Trophy two years running as the league's best blue-liner.

He wasn't mean, but if he drew aggression, he packed heat in his stick and fists. Fearless to his bones, he attacked back fast. He

was known for drawing the opposing team's leading scorer into the fray, bloodying him, and getting him sent to the penalty box. Wherever Cartier played, fans came in droves.

"Um, excuse me . . ." a female voice said.

Martin looked up. An attractive passenger was standing over him. She wore an elegant black wool suit with black lace showing under her jacket, and she had perfect legs in sheer stockings. High heels. White-blond hair curved over her long-lashed green eyes, and her lipstick looked red and wet.

"You're Martin Cartier," she said.

"Oui," he said. "That is true." It was only April, and already she had a tan. She wore large diamond stud earrings; the heavy gold chain around her neck had smaller diamonds in every link. She was talking about last night's game, which she had watched in her Toronto hotel room. Martin pretended to listen politely, but instead he found his attention drawn back to the woman and daughter several rows behind him.

The tan blonde was saying how unfair it was they had lost in overtime. She had watched him fight. Her fingers brushed his shoulder as she said how much she loved the physicality of hockey. Smelling her perfume, Martin thought of his elbow flying into the eye of Jeff Green, swelling it shut. The woman talked on, but Martin hardly heard her. Women with expensive blond hair and April tans came up to him all the time. For some reason, the sound of her voice made him feel as if he had the Arctic inside him: vast, frigid, and barren.

As the woman scribbled her home phone on the back of her business card, she was saying she loved hockey, never missed a Bruins game when she was in town, loved watching Martin skate, score, and nail his enemies. Martin had trained himself to keep his face neutral when people paid him compliments, and aware of his teammates watching, he accepted her card and tucked it into his pocket.

Touching Martin's hand, the woman told him to call. Thanking her, Martin settled back into his seat. He folded his arms across his chest, feeling the bruised rib where he'd caught a puck last night. He thought of his father, wondered whether he had watched the game on TV. Whether he'd seen Martin miss that easy pass. . . .

Feeling his scalp tingle, Martin turned around. The flight attendant was talking to Bruno Piochelle, leaning against his seat back, but Martin looked past her, through the crack in the curtain. The little girl was still watching him. Sitting in the window seat, she

seemed to be ignoring her mother, who was leaning over her to point at something on the ground. When the mother glanced up and saw Martin staring at them, she scowled.

For some reason, that made Martin smile. The mother looked ticked off at the very sight of Martin Cartier. The fact he was a big famous hockey player obviously made no difference to her. She looked slight and frazzled, no makeup and messy brown hair pulled back in a ponytail; she had one arm around her daughter, and it was clear from her expression that she just plain didn't like him on sight. Martin smiled at her, and when she frowned harder, he felt himself start to grin. He couldn't help it.

The fields looked like green blankets, and the rivers were blue scarves. New leaves sprinkled bare branches. Tiny towns looked like playthings: dollhouses, building-block factories, toy churches. Brick cities looked like pictures in books. Mommy wanted her to look out the window. They were up in the air, soaring and gliding like a bird, where it made no real sense for human beings to be at all.

Kylie only wanted to look at the man. He was a giant, no matter what Mommy said. His back was as big as a bull's; his hands were the size of bread loaves. When he talked, his voice carried back through the plane like the principal talking on the loudspeaker. Kylie was in first grade, and she didn't like school, but this big man's voice didn't scare her.

Because if he was bad or scary, what was the little girl doing so close to him? She was white and filmy, like all the angels Kylie saw. Her wings shimmered, like silk in the sky. She hovered around the man's head, the way hummingbirds circle flowers full of nectar. Her lips were puckered, and her arms were reaching out. Every chance she got, she turned toward Kylie, beckoning her to come and tell her father to hold still so she could kiss him.

"I can't. My mother won't let me." Kylie's lips were moving but her voice was silent.

"I need you," the little angel said. "You know how it is. When you want to kiss your father and you can't."

"Mine doesn't love me," Kylie told her. "Yours does, but you're dead. You and I aren't alike at all."

"We are, we are," the angel pleaded.

"My father doesn't love me," Kylie said again. She didn't re-

member her father. Mommy said he had gone away before Kylie was born. But Kylie was sure they had played together, that he had fed her bites of chocolate ice cream. She dreamed he was big and strong, that he sang with a deep voice and could fix anything. Kylie wanted him to come home. She couldn't imagine how her father could have stopped loving her, could just go away, and it made her stomach hurt so much, she had to hold her breath.

Kylie stared at the giant-father. Although he was so large, he was very handsome. He had bristly brownish-gray hair with blue eyes that looked so sad to Kylie she wondered why people seemed to be laughing every time he opened his mouth. The stewardess laughed, the other hockey players laughed, the pretty blond lady in the shiny black stockings laughed.

"If you don't help," the angel warned, "I'll disappear. I won't talk to you anymore."

"There are other angels," Kylie said.

"But I have something really, really good to tell you . . . help me or I'll go. I really will. . . ."

"I don't even know what you want me to do," Kylie pleaded.

"Stop talking," Kylie's mother begged. "Kylie, honey, there's no one there."

"Mommy, there is," Kylie whispered.

But when she looked back, the little angel was gone. The man was staring instead, peering through the crack in the curtain. Kylie almost jumped—his eyes were so big, and they looked exactly like the angel's. Looking up, Kylie saw Mommy frowning at the man. For some crazy reason, the man started to smile.

Kylie glanced out the window. Bits of fog were covering the ground, so she knew they were getting near the sea, closer to home. Just then, she heard a snap. It sounded like boys at school sticking their fingers in their mouths and making their cheeks pop. Conversations paused for a second, but nothing happened and people resumed talking. The plane's lights flickered once, but no one seemed to notice. The plane just kept flying, the engines buzzing.

"People are going to get hurt, aren't they?" Kylie asked her mother.

Mommy blinked. She stared at Kylie for a long time, her head tilted a little. Her eyebrows grew closer together, forming a small valley of worry between them.

"Plane crash," Kylie said.

"Kylie," her mother said. "Stop."

Kylie had seen crashes on TV—fire and smoke and people

screaming. Closing her eyes, she could see it now: All the people on this flight would be grabbing each other, crying for their mommies and daddies, trying to wish the plane back into the sky.

"I wish my daddy—" Kylie started to say. She would have finished with "was here," but her mother interrupted her with a firm hand on Kylie's upper arm.

"I mean it," Mommy whispered, her eyes bright and her voice scratchy. Tears puddled over her mother's lashes and spilled down her cheeks. Kylie watched the drops, wanting to kneel up and kiss them off. Her seat belt strained across her lap, and she couldn't get there. "I can't stand it," her mother said, wiping the tears herself. "I'm tired. I don't want to hear another word about angels, plane crashes, or your father. Do you hear me?"

Kylie watched Mommy's throat moving, as if a rock was caught there and she was trying to swallow it down. The more her mother wiped her tears, the faster they came. Kylie craned her neck for the girl angel up front, but she couldn't see her anymore.

"I have to go to the bathroom," Kylie announced.

Her mother exhaled. Very patiently, she undid her own seat belt, then Kylie's.

"I can go myself," Kylie told her.

"I'll take you," Mommy said.

"I'm big," Kylie insisted. Maybe if she did what that little angel had asked, helped her kiss her father, maybe she would save the whole plane. "I can do it."

"Okay," Mommy said.

———

May watched Kylie look back, then forward. Assessing the length of the line to use the bathroom at the rear of the plane, she— smart girl!—brushed through the curtain to use one up front in business class. Tilting her head, May kept her eye on her. She watched until Kylie had asked the flight attendant to open the door, and then she relaxed. She needed this moment to compose herself.

She talks to angels, May thought. She's only six, she's crazy, she's not clairvoyant at all, she's schizophrenic, she talks to dead people, she thinks the plane's going to crash. The reports and study documents felt heavy on her lap, and she knew if she could open the plane windows she would throw them right out. Let them flutter like propaganda down onto Boston's north shore. Forget taking them to the doctor's office; May would abandon that plan entirely,

drive Kylie straight home to Black Hall. She heard her own sudden sob, and she thought her chest would crack open.

Through her tears, May tried to see out the window. Below thin fog, the ground was getting closer. They had started their descent. May watched a flight attendant hurry past. Over the loudspeaker, the pilot was thanking everyone for choosing his airline, telling them the weather in Boston was cool and drizzly.

She remembered one time she and Kylie had flown here from Canada; her grandmother had surprised them by driving to Boston, to accompany them to Kylie's doctor. May had struggled to the gate with two carry-on bags, Kylie's stroller, and Kylie, to find her grandmother waiting there. Prescient herself, Emily had always sensed when her granddaughter needed her most. She had bumped people out of the way, helping May carry everything. May closed her eyes, trying to imagine her grandmother waiting for them today. She tried and tried, but she couldn't fool herself into thinking it would happen. She wasn't Kylie; she didn't see angels where there were none.

Craning her neck, she saw Boston Harbor and the coastline blanketed in thick New England fog. As the plane circled down, they were swallowed by it and May could see nothing more below. A sudden tremor shook the plane. The lights went off and on. Voices fell, stopped, then rose.

"Return to your seats," the flight attendant called, hurrying down the aisle. The plane seemed to wobble on its axis, gaining speed as it pulled to the left. Was it May's imagination, or did she smell smoke? Her heart began to pound, just before she spotted Kylie coming out of the bathroom. May saw her heading back up the aisle, heard the flight attendant tell her to hurry back to her seat. Kylie nodded, but then she immediately disobeyed.

She stopped in front of the hockey player. He was the biggest one, the man Kylie had told May was a giant, the one with the bright gray-blue eyes. Kylie stood in the aisle beside him, her lips and hands moving as she spoke rapidly, pointing at the sky. May leaned forward in her seat, trying to hear what Kylie was saying.

A sense of panic had swept the plane, the cold wash of fear showing on people's faces. But May noticed the hockey player smiling at Kylie, seeming to listen to every word she said. Glancing back, he caught May's eye. He smiled at her, raising his hand in greeting. May waved back, without knowing what she was doing. A flight attendant hustled Kylie back to her seat, and May buckled her up.

The plane lurched. This wasn't turbulence. May knew suddenly that they were going down. The lights flashed off, then back on. The flight attendant came running down the aisle, shouting for everyone to assume crash position. May put her hand on the back of Kylie's neck and pushed her head down. Tucking her own head between her knees, May held Kylie's hand.

People screamed and cried. May's heart was beating so hard, she couldn't breathe. Smoke swirled through the cabin, acrid and dark. The descent was steep at first, suddenly leveling off as the rushing air stopped whistling.

The impact was hard, but not much worse than a rough landing. The plane rolled to a stop. When she tried to unhook Kylie's seat belt, the buckle stuck. She tore at it in pure panic. It wouldn't give.

"Mommy," Kylie said.

May pulled harder, and the clasp jammed. With all her strength, she began to tug the belt itself. She felt as if she was losing it. Suddenly someone burst through the black smoke to crouch beside them. It was the big hockey player.

"I can't undo her seat belt," May wailed.

"Let me," he said.

His hands were steady as he unhitched the metal clasp. Kylie threw her arms around his neck. He grabbed May's hand and lifted Kylie into his arms. Shouldering down the aisle, he pulled them to the open door. People massed behind them, screaming and shoving.

Eyes stinging, May peered outside. The slide had deployed, and the flight attendant was directing people to kick off their shoes and jump.

"You two go." The hockey player tried to hand Kylie to May.

"No, don't put me down!" Kylie screeched in terror, clinging tighter and refusing to let go.

The man didn't hesitate again. Clutching Kylie, he wrapped his other arm around May. The three of them jumped onto the inflated yellow slide. The ride down took one second, and May felt her breath knocked out of her as she landed on the tarmac.

The man pulled her to her feet and away from the slide. Face to face, they stared into each other's eyes. They were far from the terminal building. Sirens rang out as emergency vehicles careened across the runways. Passengers poured down the slide, frantically searching for friends and family members as they hit the ground.

"Thank you," she managed to say.

"Oh," he said, and she saw his gray-blue eyes take on the same sweet and funny glint she'd noticed through the curtain in the plane. "Please don't thank me for anything. I had to—"

"Let's get away from the plane," May said.

"What's your name?" the man asked.

"May Taylor," May answered. "This is my daughter, Kylie."

"How did you know, Kylie?" he asked in a French Canadian accent.

"Know what?" May asked.

"That something was going to happen to the plane," the man said, holding Kylie's hand. "She stopped by my seat, asked me to help you when the time came—"

"The time?" May asked, staring at Kylie, who was gazing into the man's eyes.

"*She* told me," Kylie said.

"She?" the man asked.

"Your little girl," Kylie said.

The man dropped to his knees, looking deeper into her eyes. "My little girl's dead," he said.

The police cars and fire trucks had arrived, and emergency personnel came running to pull people away from the plane. A young police officer rushed up to herd everyone back. "Martin Cartier!" he exclaimed, stepping forward to grin and shake the man's hand. In a five-second burst he gushed about the Stanley Cup play-offs, Martin's game-winning goal, the likelihood of beating the Maple Leafs.

"You play hockey," she said.

"On the Boston Bruins," he said. "Are you from Boston?"

"Black Hall, Connecticut."

"And you fly into Logan instead of Providence or Hartford? That makes for a long drive, eh?"

"Well, Providence is closer," May said. "But the drive to Boston isn't too bad. We have an appointment in town. . . ."

Feeling suddenly exhausted, she knew that she was going to cancel it. Dr. Henry would have to wait to see Kylie's evaluations. May was going to drive straight home, put her daughter to bed, and take a hot bath.

But first, she reached into her pocket. Her fingers closed around a tiny glass bottle with a crumbling cork. A talisman, it was filled with white rose petals. May wondered how she could ever have doubted Kylie's gift. She had inherited a wedding planning business from her mother and, understanding that magic comes

from the most unexpected places, she had prepared the bottle and carried it for luck throughout Kylie's ordeal in Toronto.

"Thank you for what you did." She handed the bottle to Martin. "I hope this brings you luck in the play-offs."

He nodded, gazing at the small bottle in his hand. Hockey players just off the plane surrounded him, along with police and firemen and several women passengers. Martin Cartier looked up and held her gaze, even as she was being pushed away. His eyes were so bright and clear, ridiculously handsome across the tarmac. A woman had run over to be near him. She was svelte and expensive, dressed in jewelry and designer clothes.

The man reached out one enormous arm to push her aside. May wondered why, but then she saw him grinning at her. It seemed impossible, crazy on a magnitude worthy of the psychiatric department she and Kylie had just visited, but May thought he had just pushed the beautiful woman away so he could see her better.

Chapter 2

THE PLANE'S ROUGH LANDING WAS in all the papers. Someone had disabled the smoke detector to smoke in the bathroom, then thrown a cigarette butt into the trash. The fire had smoldered, then burst into flames. The automatic fire extinguisher had malfunctioned—a freak thing. And the flight attendants had hesitated just long enough for the air intake to fill with thin smoke, circulating it throughout the cabin and cockpit, filling the cockpit as the pilot had tried to land the plane.

The incident made even bigger headlines than it normally would because several Boston Bruins had been aboard—including their biggest star, Martin Cartier. A flying garment bag had banged his head, requiring that he be checked by the team physician; rescuing the woman and little girl, he had seared his throat and lungs from smoke inhalation.

The coach was all for keeping him on the bench, but Martin had said hell, no. Emergency landings were what separated the men from the boys. Martin had gotten hurt worse by sticks and pucks; he had experienced much more serious bludgeoning on the blue line than from crash-landing at Logan.

Driving his Porsche from Beacon Hill to the Fleet Center, Martin heard one sports-radio host talking about "the Cartier Curse." How Martin's wife Trisha had left him for that young shortstop from Texas. How his father—the great Maple Leafs star and coach Serge Cartier—was in prison on a gambling conviction. Not to mention the fact that no matter how gifted and industrious a player he was, Martin Cartier—unlike his father—had never led any team to a Stanley Cup victory. Worst of all, the tragedy with his daughter, Natalie. Now the bad-luck flight from Toronto—The Cartier Curse.

Thinking of Natalie, Martin's hands shook. He floored the gas

pedal, nearly clipping a truck as he turned into the player parking lot. Getting dressed in the locker room, he found the minuscule glass bottle May Taylor had given him after the plane crash. He thought of how her daughter had seemed to know about Natalie, and instead of setting the bottle aside, he stuck it into his pocket.

Martin Cartier burst onto the ice at the Fleet Center to a combination of standing ovation and loud boos, and he spent the next three periods protecting his team's goal from attack. Patrolling the slot, he aggressively harassed the Toronto Maple Leafs to keep them from scoring. Always fast on his skates, that night Martin Cartier was a blur.

Ray Gardner and Bruno Piochelle joined him at his flanks, and they set out to give Toronto nightmares. Martin was viciously rugged on offense, carrying the puck right to the net twice in the first period. He forgot his injuries, forgot the curse, forgot winning or losing, and a power he'd never felt before drove him to the net a third time—he had his first hat trick of the series.

The Bruins won 3–0, tying the play-offs.

After the game—which everyone had been predicting they would lose—Martin hit the shower and let scalding hot water pour over his body. He savored the victory, forgetting the negative talk, loving the win. If Serge Cartier had been watching from prison, he could have found no wrong in Martin's game. Maybe May's rose petals had brought him luck.

Ray Gardner, his best friend and teammate, caught up with him by the lockers. They'd been playing together for a long time, first in Vancouver, then in Toronto, and for the last two seasons in Boston. They had both been brought up in LaSalle, Canada, and their bond had been fast and hard: both had been only children with pro-hockey-playing fathers, raised mainly by their mothers in rural farmhouses. Their love for skating had been born on silent mountain lakes under endless skies.

"You greased them tonight, Martin," Ray said. "Bang, bang, bang."

"Merci, Ray."

"You sent him high ones," Ray said, and both men chuckled, picturing Martin's three shots whizzing by the Leafs goalie's head.

"Thought he was going to skate out of the net the third time." Martin laughed, still high from the win. He could see the whites of the goaltender's eyes, hear the thunk as the puck slammed into the right side of his helmet.

"Like a deer caught in the headlights." Ray grinned. "Couldn't get out of the way fast enough. You want to have dinner with me and Genny?"

"I want to catch some sleep," Martin said. "I'm getting old. Thirty-eight. I'd better retire soon. I want to win this year. It's time, eh?"

Ray nodded. He knew how much Martin wanted to win the Stanley Cup. All the other accolades seemed secondary, with that grand prize still eluding him. Shaking Ray's hand, Martin stuck the little glass bottle into his jeans pocket before heading out to his car.

Lying awake that night, he thought of Natalie, couldn't get her out of his mind. But he was picturing that little girl from the plane. Her liquid eyes, her insistent whisper: "Will you help us? No matter what happens, when the plane lands, will you help me and my mother?"

How had she known?

Rushing through the smoke, Martin had felt a deep compulsion directing him. He had run right past the open door into the smoke-filled cabin to find them, to grab the mother's hand and lift the child into his arms. He hadn't thought twice—it was as if he hadn't had a choice.

Fifteen minutes altogether in their company.

He couldn't get them out of his mind—the girl or her mother. Was it the child's similarity to Natalie, the way she had guessed he'd had a daughter? The mother's beauty? Martin shook his head hard. He didn't know why he was thinking these things.

For so long, he had left people alone—especially women with kids. Hockey groupies came around, and he dated them—he wasn't proud of himself, that was just the way things were. He had wanted no part of nice women with little girls. Life was dangerous, and the only place his world felt safe was on the ice.

But then he'd see Ray with Genny, or he'd get tired of talking to his dates about the same meaningless garbage, and he'd imagine a different kind of connection. He'd imagine really caring for someone, wanting the best for her, trusting her enough to tell her his hopes and dreams. In his fantasy, she would care for him, too. She'd hold him at night, tell him he wasn't alone.

He kicked off his covers, rolling onto his back to stare at the ceiling. With all the women he had ever met and dated, all the beautiful models and famous actresses, Martin Cartier found himself obsessed over a woman he didn't know. He couldn't stop picturing her face—those guarded eyes, that brilliant smile, her messy

reddish-brown hair. He wondered how far Black Hall, Connecticut, was from Boston. And then he fell asleep.

The barn stood in the midst of an orchard. Three miles from Trumbull Cove, bathed in the seaside light that had attracted artists to this part of Connecticut for a hundred years, the land was bright with mountain laurel and dark with granite ledges.

Four cars were parked under the apple trees, and inside the barn, the bride and her mother and bridesmaids milled around, talking as they looked at pictures.

May's grandmother, Emily, had built this barn with her husband Lorenzo Dunne, but she had run the wedding-planning business—The Bridal Barn—with her only daughter, May's mother Abigail. Their books, diaries, and photo albums lined the shelves built into the barn's silvered wood walls. A yellow cat skulked along the floor, guarding against mice.

Standing by the window, May talked quietly to Tobin Chadwick. May's oldest and still-best friend. Tobin had stayed in Black Hall after getting married; she had started working at the Bridal Barn the year her youngest son started school. She was small and strong, with dark hair and a ready, wonderful smile. She and May loved to bicycle together through hilly back roads, staying in shape by racking up the miles, racing on the straightaways.

"Start with Toronto," Tobin said. "Or start with the plane crash. I can't believe what a day you had yesterday."

"It was eventful." May rubbed a bruise on her elbow.

"What did they say—the doctors?"

"They tested her," May said. "They showed her two cards, one red and one blue, then mixed them up and put them facedown on a table and told her to say which was which. Over and over again."

"Sounds more like a casino." Tobin frowned.

"That's how it felt," May said. "They had her try to predict number sequences, first on paper, then on a Ouija board. She didn't miss any—not even one! Then they handed her a pen and told her to write with her left hand—"

"She's right-handed."

"I know. They called it 'spirit writing.' "

"Did she contact any spirits?" Tobin asked with a slight smile. She sometimes seemed not to know what to think. To most people, even Toby, it seemed bizarre that a renowned university would

have a department devoted to psychic phenomena, even stranger that May's daughter would be part of a study there. To May, with her background of herbs and roses and love spells, it was less so.

"Well, not at the university," May said. "But on the plane—"

"What happened?"

"It seems she knew there was a problem with the plane before anyone else. She says she saw an angel. She walked right up to one guy," May said, gazing into the middle distance, remembering the look in his eyes. "And asked him to help us when the time came. She told him his daughter told her to—"

"His daughter?"

"She's dead." Glancing over at the bridal party, May saw that decisions were being made, that the women had found pictures they liked in the books. The bride waved at May, and she waved back. Her stomach lurched as she thought of Kylie: what if it wasn't family magic, but schizophrenia?

"She's so imaginative, May," Tobin said gently. "That's all it is."

"She talks to people who aren't there."

"So did your grandmother, to herself, anyway. And remember when we were kids? How whenever we read books about kids with imaginary friends we wished we had them?"

"We had each other," May said.

Tobin hugged her. "She doesn't belong in a study," she said. "You know that. She got freaked out, finding that body at the Lovecraft."

"I know," May said.

"I'd have nightmares if I found that, and she was only four." Tobin shivered. "I'm surprised they're not studying you. You were there—you saw it, too."

"I did," May said. Closing her eyes, she saw the grinning skull, mouth open as if to implore them to do something. Kylie had dreams about death's-heads, all begging her to help them. May opened her eyes, looked at Tobin.

"She's going through a phase," her best friend continued. "It's a little lonely out here in the country, no girls for her to play with. I should have had daughters instead of sons."

"I knew it was your fault," May said. "The doctors want to see her again in July. They want me to continue keeping that journal of her sightings."

"She'll outgrow it all. You'll see."

"Or maybe she'll become an actress or writer—when they use their imaginations, no one says anything," May said.

"That's right," Tobin agreed.

But then the bridal party began moving toward them and it was time to get back to work. Dora Wilson, the bride-to-be, introduced everyone to May: her mother, her best friend Elizabeth Nichols, and two old friends from college.

"May, will you please talk some sense into her?" Dora's mother called. "She wants a Friday night wedding, and I keep telling her it's impossible. Half the family will be flying in from Cleveland, and the other half will be driving up from Baltimore. A lovely afternoon ceremony—"

"Mother," the bride said shakily. "You know I want a candle-light ceremony. I always have. I—"

"They're outdated," Mrs. Wilson said, waving her hand. "They're so boring—people had them in the seventies. Are you afraid of daylight? Because I promise you, no one, not one soul will guess your age. May has a marvelous makeup artist; I saw what she did for Shelley Masters. So did you—and we both know Shelley's older than you are!"

May glanced at Tobin, and exactly like a well-seasoned team of cops they split up the pair. While Tobin took Mrs. Wilson, May went over to Dora.

Starting out, May had thought she would be hired mainly by young women, unsure of their own taste. Instead, she had found many of her clients to be thirty-five or older, established in their own careers. They came in carrying briefcases and cell phones. Dora Wilson, today's bride, was forty-one. A successful business-woman, she wore an Armani suit and Prada shoes. She had expen-sive hair—cut and color by Jason of Silver Bay—and a worked-out body. But like most new clients—almost to a woman—she looked to her mother when the important questions were asked: number of attendants, nighttime or day, church or not.

"I think she's right," Dora said as May walked over. "Saturday afternoon would be better. More practical."

"No." May looked Dora square in the eye. "She is wrong."

"But the relatives are coming from far away—"

"She is wrong," May repeated. She held Dora's gaze and re-fused to look away. Dora blinked, as if trying to resist hypnosis. "It is your wedding. You will be the bride; your mother already had her chance. You have dreamed of a candlelight ceremony your whole life."

"But I might have made a mistake. The more I think—" Dora began.

May gazed at Dora. Today she wore jeans and an L.L. Bean sweater—navy blue with white dots resembling stars. "Know what my mother used to tell me at times like this?"

"What?"

"Don't think more. Think less."

"Less? My God, there's so much to think about, so many details!" Dora said, her voice rising. "When I sell a house, believe me, I don't tell the buyer to think *less*—there's the contract, the appraisal, the inspection . . . a wedding's even more complicated!"

"Less, Dora," May said quietly. Her own head had been spinning with worries about Kylie, memories of the hanging man, comments the psychologists had made. But as she thought of her mother, she felt a little of the tension slip away. Across the room, Tobin was talking firmly to Mrs. Wilson, her voice and eyes steady.

"We have to plan, make *lists*," Dora said almost hysterically. "How do you expect me to plan without thinking?"

May sat very still. She cared about this middle-aged bride so much. She wanted to find a way to help her do this. Suddenly May found herself thinking of the hockey player.

Their hands had brushed when he'd picked up Kylie, and his blue eyes had seemed to look straight into her heart. No man had helped May like that in a very long time. Wanting to support Dora now, May thought of Martin Cartier's eyes and cleared her throat.

"With your gut," May said. "With your heart." She reached out and touched Dora's breastbone. Her hand was steady, and she could feel the warm energy flowing from her fingertips into the trembling bride. Dora was brash and sharp, and all her forty-one years showed in the lines around her thin mouth. But at that instant the years fell away, and she looked about sixteen and very vulnerable.

"You have always dreamed of a candlelight wedding," May said.

Dora gazed at May, and her eyes suddenly flooded with tears. "I have," she whispered back.

"Then you will have one."

"But my mother . . ."

"Breathe," May said, hearing her mother's voice.

"But she—"

"Breathe," May said. "And then tell her no."

"They're divorced," Dora said, the tears starting to fall. "My father lives in Watch Hill with his second wife. I don't have any sis-

ters—I'm her only daughter. She wants me to do things a certain way, she has dreams too, I don't want to disappoint her . . ."

"I know," May said quietly.

Dora hugged her, but May hardly felt it.

Turning, she walked across the open barn. She locked herself in the bathroom and turned on the water in the sink. It ran hard and fast, loud enough to drown out the wedding party's voices outside. She made the water hotter, leaning over as she breathed in the steam. She envisioned the mist washing away the knots inside herself. Her mother had always told her to believe in her own power, to know that magic was an everyday thing.

Don't be an escape artist, her mother had always told the brides: Don't hide in wine, shopping, exercise, or work. Stay awake, present, and connected. When May raised her head, she saw the mirror clouded with steam. Clearing a window with the heel of her hand, she stared into the eyes of a burned-out wedding planner. She wished she could conjure her mother's spirit, take comfort in one of Kylie's visions.

People were talking just outside the bathroom door. Their voices drifted through the heavy wood, into May's consciousness. Dora and her mother were making up; the wedding would take place on a Friday night, after all.

May closed her eyes. What so many brides hoped: that the perfect dress, the perfect day, the perfect man would add up to the perfect life. Those had been May's own dreams once. She had fallen in love, hoping to get married. So much for her own power, the magic of love! Sometimes she felt she could choke on her own bitterness.

But then she thought of Kylie. Love hadn't passed May by; it had just come in a different package. She dried her face, then walked out of the bathroom. Tobin walked over with an armful of pink roses, Aunt Enid trailing right behind.

"Are they for Dora?" May asked. Sometimes men would send flowers to their brides-to-be at the Bridal Barn, a gesture May found incredibly romantic.

"Not exactly," Enid said. She was May's grandmother's youngest and only surviving sister, with similar blue-white hair, light blue eyes, and gentle manners that disguised a deep curiosity for what went on in other people's lives.

"They're for you," Tobin told her. Some of the bridesmaids had gathered around, and they leaned closer to see who May was getting flowers from.

May read the card: "Thank you. We won. Martin Cartier."

"The guy from the plane?" Tobin asked.

"Yes," May said.

"Martin Cartier?" one of the bridesmaids asked. "*The* Martin Cartier?"

"He's a hockey player," May said.

"I know who he is," the bridesmaid said. "He's the handsomest athlete alive."

A black barn cat rubbed May's ankles, making her shiver.

"How do you happen to be getting roses from the handsomest athlete alive?" Mrs. Wilson asked.

"But of course she would," Aunt Enid said, eyes half-closed like a knowing cat.

May held the bouquet, letting herself be surrounded and swept away by the deep and musky smell of roses. No one had sent her roses in a long, long time, and the scent mingled with some forgotten memory and made her throat ache.

"You and I need to go for a long bike ride," Tobin said.

"As soon as everyone leaves." May was smiling as she smelled the roses.

Chapter 3

BOSTON WAS A SPORTS-LOVING town, and the papers were filled with articles as the Bruins advanced in the play-offs. May had never really followed hockey, but now she found herself buying the *Globe,* reading about Martin, checking the scores. On Saturday afternoon a week later, with clients milling around the Bridal Barn, she and Tobin kept the radio tuned low to the game.

"What's that sound?" the bride's mother asked, frowning. Mrs. Randall was a Black Hall matron wearing a knit suit and Ferragamo shoes, with a sense of decorum that didn't include sports radio in the wedding salon.

"The Bruins game," Tobin answered.

"The last time we were here, you had that beautiful music playing—you know, the Irish girl."

"Loreena McKennitt," Aunt Enid said. "I'll put her on." She started to put in the CD, but May grabbed her wrist.

"They're up three-two with two minutes to play," she said. "We have to stay tuned."

"Darling, this is the Bridal Barn. Your mother always said we're selling them a mood, not just a wedding. If they want Loreena McKennitt—"

"Her mother never had her life saved by Martin Cartier," Tobin said. "Fire me, but this is the play-offs."

"She's right, Aunt Enid," May said.

"Atmosphere is everything in the wedding business," Aunt Enid said darkly, walking away.

But the Randalls signed a large contract for the dress, flowers, ceremony, and reception, and the Bruins won, so everyone was happy. "The Bruins beat the Toronto Maple Leafs," the announcer said. "Martin Cartier scored the winning goal, and Boston will be

one game closer to playing the Edmonton Oilers for the Stanley Cup."

"Martin, Martin," Kylie said, chanting along with the crowd on the radio.

"Martin?" May asked, smiling at Kylie's using his first name and pronouncing it the French-Canadian way: Mar-tan.

The telephone rang. "Bridal Barn," Aunt Enid said. She listened for a moment, looking pleased and wise as she passed the phone to May.

"Hello?" May said.

"We're winning the play-offs," Martin Cartier said in his French accent. "Your rose petals—they brought me luck."

"I know, I heard."

"Really? You follow hockey?"

"I started to recently," she said. "Are you calling me from the ice? You must be—the game just finished."

"I'm in the locker room."

"Wow," May said. She pictured him in his uniform, surrounded by his teammates. She could hear them in the background, laughing and shouting. Her own teammates—Kylie, Tobin, and Aunt Enid—stood in a silent semicircle, not even pretending not to listen.

"Did you get my roses?" he asked.

"I did," she said. "They were beautiful. I wanted to thank you, but I didn't know where to call. How did you find me?"

"May Taylor in Black Hall, Connecticut," he said. "It wasn't hard."

"I didn't remember telling you, with everything going on around the plane. I wanted to thank you for that, too."

"How's your daughter?"

"She's fine. How about you?"

"I've been on four planes since," he said. "It only catches up with me at night, when I dream."

"Me, too," May said. She'd had nightmares since their flight from Toronto, her eyes stinging and throat searing as the smoke enveloped her and Kylie, with no way out. . . . Kylie's dreams had been of the angel she had seen on the plane, a solemn white-winged being hovering over her father's head. May had dutifully recorded the incident in her diary. Thinking of that now, she glanced over at Kylie.

"Maybe we can talk about it sometime, eh?" he said. "Can I call you again? Maybe have dinner?"

"I don't know," May said. "This is the wedding season. I have a pretty busy schedule. . . ." she trailed off.

"*Bien*." He sounded disappointed. "Right now I have to catch another plane. We're heading to New York for the next series. Wish me luck."

"Fly safely," May said.

"I meant hockey," he said.

"That, too," she replied, feeling let down and not exactly knowing why.

With no more clients expected that day, May asked Aunt Enid to watch Kylie for an hour while she and Tobin took a bike ride. The oaks and maples were covered with new leaves, and the chestnuts were just starting to flower. Violet shadows spread across the winding roads as the two friends rode single file through the valley.

They rode up Crawford Hill, shifting into low gear for the long climb. May followed Tobin, keeping pace as they passed the abandoned mill, Childe's Orchard, and the pine hollow. This land had hardly changed at all over their lifetime, and she wondered how many times they'd ridden their bikes along this same route. When they turned onto Old Farm Road, where they knew there wouldn't be any traffic, Tobin fell back so they could ride side by side.

"What did he say?" Tobin asked. After so many years, the friends could practically read each others' minds.

"He asked me out to dinner."

"Was that the part where you mentioned your incredibly busy schedule?"

"I didn't put it like that—"

"You were laying the groundwork to squirm out," Tobin said. "I knew the instant you said the words."

"At least I don't eavesdrop," May said, starting to pedal harder. Surging ahead, she felt sweat rolling between her shoulder blades. Her chest burned, but not only from exertion. She felt like crying but didn't know why.

"Forgive me," Tobin said, catching up. "But it's not every day my best friend starts filling the Bridal Barn with the sounds of rinkside mayhem instead of mood music. You've got me wondering."

"Wondering what?"

"You know what," Tobin said.

"Let's get an ice-cream cone," May said. They wheeled down the backside of Crawford Hill, past the white churches in town, and no matter how fast Tobin pedaled, she couldn't keep up. May skid-

ded, turning into the sand parking lot of the ramshackle Paradise Ice Cream stand, nearly wiping out.

The two women ordered their favorite cones: maple walnut dipped in chocolate sprinkles and vanilla straight up.

"Why won't you admit it to me?" Tobin asked kindly as she licked her cone. "You like him."

"There's not much maple in this batch," May said, closing her eyes.

"What's so bad about liking him? Would it kill you to have dinner together?"

"We went through something big together," May said, catching a drip before it hit her shirt. "He helped me and Kylie off the plane."

"And you like him."

"I hardly know him."

"Okay, we can put it another way. You *think* you like him—"

"That's not a smart idea," May said. Closing her eyes again, she kept licking her cone.

"You've gotten *too* smart over the years," Tobin said quietly. "You've learned how to think instead of feel. That's your trouble."

May's eyes instantly filled with tears; Tobin's words were true. She thought of Gordon Rhodes, Kylie's father. She had been in love with him from the very beginning, and when they'd conceived a child together, she had rocketed into happiness she'd never even dreamed of before. She had been wide open to life and love and commitment and passion, and then Gordon had told her he was married. Separated, but married.

"I date," May said. "I have plenty of dates."

"No kidding," Tobin retorted. "With Mel Norris and Howard Drogin, the two men in Black Hall most unlikely to give your heart a palpitation. Ever since Gordon, you've gone completely for safety."

"Kylie's second doctor," May said. "Cyrus Baxter, that psychiatrist from Boston. I had dinner with him once."

"And when he asked you again, you switched her from the study at Mass General to the study in Toronto."

"Dr. Henry says the Toronto study is better." Tears were streaking down May's cheeks. "That's why I switched her. Dr. Baxter had nothing to do with it."

"Oh, May," Tobin said.

"You know I wouldn't let my feelings dictate where Kylie gets help."

"I know that."

"For all I know, Martin Cartier could be married," May said.

"He's not," Tobin said.

"How do you know?"

"I checked."

May's eyes widened as her friend shrugged apologetically. Tobin had dark hair and wide bright eyes. She gazed out from under her bangs, as if she thought May might be angry.

"What did you do?" May asked.

"I called the Boston Bruins publicity office and said I was a wedding consultant doing a magazine piece on married hockey players, and that I was thinking of including Martin Cartier. Once the guy stopped laughing, he let me know I was out of luck, that Martin is considered practically the most eligible bachelor in the NHL."

"What's he doing asking me out to dinner?" May asked.

"He knows a good thing when he sees it," Tobin said.

May stared down at her sneakers. She was a single mother who had made some mistakes, and her dual mission in life was to raise Kylie right and to help other women have the weddings of their dreams. It had been a long time since she had entertained dreams of her own, much less imagined how it might feel to be rescued from a burning plane and sent roses by the most eligible bachelor in the NHL. Long gone were her beliefs in family magic and love spells working for her the way they did for other women.

"You've got maple walnut on your chin," Tobin said, licking her thumb and wiping the drip off May's face.

"Thank you," May said.

"Don't mention it."

"First you check up on my hockey player, now you're cleaning off my face. . . ."

"Well, I do it because your father would want me to," Tobin said.

May glanced over to see Tobin's expression. Growing up, the two girls had been like sisters, sleeping over at each other's houses, going camping and to the movies and the beach with each other's families. Jokingly, Tobin had sometimes called May's parents "Mom" and "Dad," and May had done the same with Tobin's.

May blinked, listening. "My father," she said after a minute.

"He's not here to look after you himself, and I know he'd want the total lowdown on any Boston Bruin chasing after his daughter," Tobin said.

"So you found out for him."

Tobin nodded, taking her last bite of vanilla. "And your parents wouldn't want you riding around Black Hall with ice cream all over your mug either, so I did what I had to do. We've probably ruined our dinners, eating these."

"I won't tell your kids if you won't tell mine," May said.

Shaking on it, the two women climbed on their bikes and headed home down the winding roads.

Five nights later, he called again.

This time, May had found herself hoping he would. She had stayed up late, to watch some of the game before going to bed. The Bruins had won; they'd be going to meet Edmonton in the finals. The sportscaster was ecstatic, and May realized that she was, too. She waited for a while, and she was just about to doze off when she heard the phone ring.

"Did I wake you?" he asked.

"No, not quite," she said. "Congratulations on making the finals."

"You heard?" he asked, sounding pleased.

"Yes, I and most of New England. You are certainly the man of the hour."

Martin chuckled, and May thought she heard voices in the background.

"Is someone there?" she asked.

"Yes. I'm with the team. We're going out to a restaurant to celebrate."

May pictured the happy athletes surrounded by beautiful women like the one on the plane, and she thought of what Tobin had said: that he was the most eligible bachelor in the NHL. She'd been crazy, thinking whatever she had been thinking. She and Martin were worlds apart. He was rich and famous, and he could have any woman in the world.

"What are you doing?" he asked.

"Getting ready for bed," she said.

"Why don't you come to New York, eh?" he asked. "It's just two hours. You could hop on the next train, be here by midnight."

May laughed nervously. He sounded serious, but she knew he had to be kidding.

"I wish you would," he said.

"My party dress needs ironing," she joked. "And my daughter's fast asleep."

"How is Kylie?"

"She's great."

May heard someone call Martin's name as he quickly covered the phone. Bits of muffled conversation came through, something about a limousine, some friends, a restaurant near East Twentieth Street.

"You have to go," she said when he came back.

"They're waiting for me," he said.

"Okay." Her heart was pounding.

"Did you ever feel that something was meant to be?" he asked.

"Like what?"

"I can't explain it," he said. "Ever since I saw you on the plane . . ."

"You mean after the crash, when you came back to help us?"

"No, before that," he said. "When I turned around and saw you sitting there. I knew I had to talk to you, but I just didn't know why."

"A mystery." May tried to laugh.

"For now," he said. "I know you said you're busy, but will you have dinner with me tomorrow night? I'll be back in Boston, I can jump on ninety-five and be there by seven."

"Okay," she agreed, prodded on by a vision of Tobin. "I will."

When May hung up, she found that her hands were shaking. She started to call Tobin, to tell her about the conversation and to joke that Martin Cartier remained the NHL's most eligible bachelor, with dinner invitations and romantic talk about how things were meant to be. But instead May just sat very still in her bed, listening to night birds and locusts in the meadow, wondering how anyone could ever know what was meant to be, whether it was possible to find out.

———

Twilight the next night was cool and peaceful, and the music of a thousand tree frogs filled the air. The sky was lavender with several stars already showing. Kylie sat on the top rail of the old fence, watching for Martin's car. Mommy had told her he was coming, but she wouldn't believe till she saw him with her own eyes. Overhead, a plane flying high above left a white trail like a magic chalk mark. Kylie followed it with her eyes, watching it pass, knowing that her great inspiration had happened in the air.

Now she heard a car engine. Coming fast from the main road, it sounded loud and powerful. Breaking out of the trees into the field, the car sped along the lane and stopped short in front of Kylie. Balancing on the rail, she leaned down to look into Martin's face. The car was a black convertible, very small, and Martin was alone in it.

"Hello," Martin greeted her. "It's the young lady who spoke to me on the plane."

"I asked you to help and you helped," Kylie said. "Are you coming to pick up my mother?"

"Yes. Am I near your house?"

"It's over there." Kylie pointed toward the hollow across the meadow. "If you give me a ride, I'll show you."

"*Bien sûr*. Hop in." Martin reached across the seat to open the passenger side door. As Kylie scrambled in, she felt her heart beating very fast. She had to say the right things, to make everything happen the way it was supposed to.

"My mother looks pretty tonight," Kylie said.

"Yes, I imagine she does," he replied.

Sometimes Kylie saw things other people didn't. At night, she swore she saw her great-grandmother walking through the house, lighting her way with a candle. She saw the winged ghost of her puppy Tally, who had been hit by a car. On the plane she had seen an angel, and sometimes she sensed the spirits of children who had died. But mostly she saw quiet things, signs that were visible to everyone.

Like an expression deep in a person's eyes, or the hint of a smile behind someone's mouth, or a wish shimmering in the air just above the person's head. For a long time, Kylie had seen a wish floating around Mommy, and the strange thing was, she saw the same wish glowing like a halo around Martin. It had to do with loneliness, with finding someone. Kylie felt it herself.

"Do you believe in evil spirits and good angels?" she asked, testing him.

"Well, I'm not sure. . . ." he said.

"Because they're everywhere."

"In stories, you mean?"

"No," Kylie said. "In real life."

He laughed as if he understood. "Maybe I do. I meet evil spirits on the ice," he said. "My opponents on the other team."

She nodded. Although she didn't know what "opponents" meant, she felt satisfied. There was good and bad in the world, and

for the job Kylie had in mind for Martin, she wanted someone who knew wicked and wonderful when he saw it.

"I like your car. It's like a spymobile in the movies," she said.

"It's a Porsche," he told her.

"Yes," Kylie said, feeling the wind blow her hair out behind her. She had never been in a car with the top down before, and she had to agree: It was a lot like a porch. Like sitting out under the stars with her mother and Aunt Enid, the crickets singing in the tall grasses, the stars coming out above. "I like your porch," she said.

"I'm glad," he said with a wide smile.

"My mother's prettier than any bride," she said.

He glanced over, but he didn't say anything.

"Any bride that ever was," Kylie said.

The restaurant was dim and romantic, halfway down a country road behind the old stone abbey. Salt breezes blew though the open windows, the warm night air enveloping them like a silken shawl. No one seemed to recognize Martin. Perhaps it was because they were so far from Boston, or perhaps it was the type of place he had chosen—too quaint and old-fashioned to be frequented by serious hockey fans. He had found it listed in a guide of shoreline restaurants.

They ate filet of sole with tiny spring peas and white truffle pasta, and they drank water instead of wine because Martin was in training. They seemed nervous together, and neither had yet mentioned last night's phone call. May told herself he'd been kidding, that his words hadn't meant anything. This was just a first or maybe only date, nothing at all extraordinary.

But her body was saying otherwise: her heart was racing, and her cheeks felt hot. Her hands wouldn't stay still, and every time she looked into Martin's eyes, she had butterflies in her stomach.

"I'm glad you were free tonight," he said.

"So am I," she said. "Did you have a good time last night?"

"Maybe a little too good." He sounded embarrassed. "The team went out to celebrate."

"Sounds fun," she said.

They told each other the basic facts of their lives: that May was single and Martin's marriage had been annulled, that she lived in Black Hall and he had a town house in Boston, that she planned weddings and he had played hockey since he was a child.

"Did you grow up on that farm?" he asked.

"Yes and no," she said. "Yes, I grew up there, but it was never a farm. My grandmother built the barn to house her business—she was a wedding planner. One of the first, she always said. She considered herself an artist, and I guess I do, too. She always said it takes creativity to plan the perfect weddings, even more to make a marriage last."

"So, you're wedding-planning artists?"

"She said so. And Black Hall *is* home to lots of artists."

"Why would you need a barn for that profession?" he asked. "A store, I can imagine. Or an office."

She smiled, sipping ice water. "You think we just help people pick out dresses."

"No, I don't know," he said. Then he smiled, as if she'd caught him. "Yes, I guess I do. Pick out dresses, the cake, things like that. But I suppose that's like thinking hockey's just a game."

"It isn't?" she asked innocently.

He shook his head, ready to explain, then saw she was kidding him. She liked the feeling of teasing each other, as if they were talking around their real reason for having dinner together. It felt half like a game, half like a mystery they weren't ready to solve yet.

"Tell me about the barn," he said.

"We grow our own herbs," May said. "Our own roses."

"I know."

"That's why we're having dinner tonight, isn't it?" she asked, laughing. "Because my roses brought you luck, and you want me to give you more."

"Maybe," he said. "Maybe that's why. But keep talking. Tell me more."

May told him about making beeswax candles from the bees they raised, about drying herbs and making sachets and perfumed oils, about supplying the brides with homemade products for love and luck, how she still had her grandmother's tattered book of potions and recipes.

"We like the big space for designing ceremonies, rehearsing processions, trying on gowns. My mother collected old gowns, and once a year we hang them from the rafters, every one—" May loved the tradition; it was one of her favorites. She could tell Martin was really listening, hanging on every word, and she suddenly felt embarrassed.

"Do you like barns?" she asked.

"Yes. I grew up on a farm in Canada, and we had plenty of

barns. My grandfather flooded one once, and we had the first in-door rink in my part of the province. So we both had innovative grandparents. . . ."

"You lived with your grandfather?"

"My mother, and my father's parents, yes. After my father left."

"He left?"

"To play pro hockey," Martin said. "He was a great player. A great role model for me, when all I wanted to do . . . He taught me to skate before I could walk. But that was a long time ago."

"He's still alive?"

"Yeah, but we don't speak. Never mind about him. What about you? You lived with your grandmother?"

"Yes," May said. "My parents died when I was twelve. A truck hit their car. Moving so fast they never saw it coming. At least, that's what my grandmother told me, what I've always wanted to think . . ."

"Things happen fast." Martin covered her hand with his when he saw the tears in her eyes. His own face was filled with emotion, as if all his features were connected straight to his heart: his eyes, his mouth, his jaw.

"They missed out on seeing a great girl grow up," Martin said, holding her hand.

"Thank you. That's what my friend always says."

"Your friend?"

"Tobin Chadwick. We were inseparable then, and she's still my best friend. She knew my parents well; I can't explain why that means so much to me."

"You don't have to. I have a friend like that—Ray Gardner. He's like my brother, always has been. He knows the whole story, inside and out. I don't even have to talk—he just knows. We're teammates now."

May touched her glass of water, felt the icy drops with her hand. She saw the shadow pass across his eyes, the darkness she had seen that first time.

"I lost my daughter, just as you lost your father," he said. "I have many regrets myself."

"You can tell me." May was watching his eyes.

"I have the feeling I can."

May waited.

"Some things are meant to be," he said steadily, using the words he'd said on the phone last night.

Her hands were trembling, and she didn't reply.

"There was a connection I can't explain," he said. "I looked back and saw you. And then your daughter came over, spoke to me. She knew about Natalie."

"Natalie?"

"My daughter."

"Kylie's very imaginative," May said, not wanting him to have the wrong idea. "She's extremely sensitive; she picks up on things. Maybe she overheard you talking about Natalie."

"I don't talk about her."

"Or maybe she saw you looking at a picture . . ."

Martin pulled out his wallet. He placed a photo on the table between them, a color snapshot of a bright, smiling little girl with curly hair and one tooth missing in front.

"Did you have it out on the plane?" May asked. "Even for a second?"

"Someone gave me a business card," Martin said, frowning. "I might have put it in my wallet."

"Kylie probably saw Natalie's picture." May gazed at the girl's face. "She's beautiful."

"Merci bien."

"I don't want to disappoint you," May said. "If you've been thinking Kylie has some connection to your daughter. She's very sensitive—she sees things other people don't. I've been taking her to some psychologists in Toronto. See, we had this traumatic thing happen once. We found a body on a nature hike."

"A body?"

"A man who had hanged himself. She's very curious about death," May added.

"She knew the plane was going down," Martin said. "She asked me to help you."

The waitress came over to clear their plates away. May's heart was beating so loud she was afraid Martin and the waitress would hear. For reasons no one understood, her daughter saw angels. How could she give him the alternate explanation: that Kylie hadn't known about the crash, that she had just been looking for a suitable father-figure, that she'd wanted a father her whole life, that May had never quite managed to provide her with one?

"I think she just liked the way you looked," May said. "She probably wanted you to help us with our bags."

Martin laughed. He stared at his daughter's picture for a moment longer, then replaced it in his wallet. "Carrying your bags

would have been easier," he said. "Would you still have given me those rose petals?"

"Yes, I probably would have," May said, glad to stop talking about Kylie.

"They brought me luck, those petals. I want to thank you, but I also want to ask you for a favor." He grinned, as if he wanted May to think he was kidding, but she could see he was completely serious. May kept her expression steady. She felt shaken up by their time together—by a million strange emotions racing inside. She was close to the edge, and she didn't know what she'd see if she leaned a little closer.

· "What would you like?" she asked calmly.

"A few more," he said. "Don't tell my teammates; they'd have me on the bench so fast . . . but I'm an old man in the NHL, and this might be my last real shot at the Stanley Cup. It's crazy, I know."

"Crazy?" May laughed. "I work in a world where standard operating procedure is something old, something new, something borrowed, something blue. I meet with doctors who study the supernatural. A few rose petals don't seem weird to me at all."

"So you'll give me some?"

"Yes," she said. "I have some back at the barn. I'll give them to you when you drop me off."

"D'accord," he said. "That's a deal."

An hour later, after taking the long way back, Martin followed her into the old barn. He felt intoxicated by the smells of hay, lavender, honeysuckle, and roses. He had thought the scent was coming from the countryside, but when May stopped short, he realized it was coming from her neck. She led him through the darkness with owls and nighthawks calling from the rafters above.

"Do the owls scare the brides?" he asked.

"The birds are quiet during the day," May said. "And the brides almost never look up. Sometimes I find piles of fur, shells, and bones on the floor, and I make them into little wedding amulets to bring the brides luck."

"Owl throw-up," Martin said. "Very romantic, *non*?"

"I'll give you one." May opened a heavy glass door and led him into a dark, humid greenhouse. Grow-lights glowed darkly over rows of new shoots. "For luck."

Martin tried to control his breathing. He wasn't known for the sensitivity he showed to people, especially women, but in talking about his mother and grandfather earlier, he had felt something ancient awakening in him, the part of him that knew and cared how people felt. Then the conversation had started veering too close to Natalie, and Martin had felt the ice come sliding down.

But this time, he felt something different: He wanted to tell May more. He had the feeling he could trust her, that he would be telling her things for a long time to come. Walking beside her, he wondered whether she could read his mind. Maybe clairvoyance— or whatever she wanted to call it—ran in her family.

"Here are our off-season roses," May said, standing among the pots. "We have a beautiful garden outside, but it doesn't bloom till June. My grandmother was a great gardener. She experimented with different varieties, and we all have our favorites." Crouching down, she took shears and snipped off a very full and perfect bud.

" 'We all'?" Martin asked.

"My grandmother, mother, great-aunt, Kylie, and I."

"Whose favorite is that one?"

"Kylie's," May said.

He nodded, but she wasn't looking. He watched her peel the petals from the rose one by one. She laid them on a rough wood table, and then she took two small silver trays from a pile on a high shelf. Uncorking a blue bottle, she poured a small amount of oil onto one tray. Martin smelled the oil, and it made him think of being lost in a deep forest. It reminded him of being a child, of hiking dense mountain trails, of mulched leaves, new grass, life, and death. The bones around his eye sockets ached and the arthritis in his ankle throbbed, and he could hear May breathing.

She worked in the dark, in the purple glow of the grow-lights and the sparkle of starlight coming through the glass hothouse roof. He took a step closer, standing nearer to her body, but she gave a sharp look over her shoulder.

"*Pardon,*" he said.

"I have to concentrate," she said. "I want my hands to be steady."

Using an instrument that looked like ivory forceps, May lifted each rose petal, carefully rolled it in the oil, then set it on the second silver tray to dry. Martin's mother was a good photographer, and watching May reminded Martin of the darkroom, how his mother would use tongs to move the negatives from the vat to the drying rack.

A clock chimed ten, and Martin checked his watch: In nine hours, he would be on a plane to Edmonton. The Porsche would get him to Boston in less than two hours, but he should already be home, if not in bed then watching training tapes of the Oilers. What was he doing in this woman's greenhouse, watching her dip rose petals in oil? What did any of this have to do with hockey, with the Stanley Cup?

"What do they do?" he asked. "You said you give them to people for luck. How do they work?"

"They just do," she said, continuing the ritual.

"It's late," he said, feeling increasingly nervous, wondering what he'd gotten himself into. "I believe they work, they did already, but—"

"But how?" she asked.

"Yes. That's what I want to know. I should get going. I have a plane to catch—"

May opened a creaky drawer and removed a small leather pouch. In it she inserted the white rose petals, along with a small ball of fur, claws, and a tiny backbone. "Owl throw-up," she said, grinning as she used his phrase.

"Merci." His heart was racing, as if he were already late.

"How it works . . ." she said. "Well, it's simple. My grandmother grew this rose, I picked it, and it's Kylie's favorite. The owl pellet is to remind you that life is very short, that you must shoot for the stars every chance you get. The leather pouch is . . . more masculine than lace. So the guys won't laugh at you." She smiled, and Martin tried to laugh.

They stood close together, the grow-lights under the tables casting shadows upward into their faces. Martin's heart was pounding, and he forgot about the roses, the greenhouse, tomorrow's game, the guys on his team. He took May into his arms, and kissed her hard. He saw stars as he held her body close, feeling her respond as she kissed him back.

"What were you saying?" he asked after a long time, when she stood holding him tight and gazing up with eyes that made him feel he was melting at his core. He felt like a teenager, someone who hadn't kissed a thousand women, who had never before fallen in love.

"I have no idea," she said.

"Do you mind if I kiss you again?"

"Not very much at all."

This time he leaned against the rough wood bench, pulling her

into his body. He felt passion unlike anything he'd ever experienced before, and he heard the words come out of his mouth: "You know how I asked you if you believe certain things are meant to be?"

"Yes."

"Do you?" he asked.

"I'm not sure," she said. "How could we know?"

"Because I have proof."

"Proof?"

"Yes." Martin said, holding her closer. "It's happening right now, to us."

"We're meant to be?" May asked.

"We're supposed to get to know each other. I'm supposed to court you, and we're supposed to figure out what we have in common."

"Looking at it that way, it doesn't make sense," May said. "I hardly know anything about hockey, and you don't seem like the flower garden type. I'm raising my daughter on a farm in Connecticut, and you're a jet-setting sports star in Boston."

Martin held her tighter, shaking his head. "None of that makes any difference," he said.

"How can you say that?"

"Because this is meant to be. I took one look at you on the plane, and I knew."

"Knew what?" she asked softly, as if her mouth were too dry to quite say the words.

"That you're the one."

"But how can you know?"

"The same way you do," he said. "Because it's true."

Chapter 4

WITH GAME 1 OF THE Stanley Cup finals about to be played on the fast ice of Edmonton, Martin sat in the locker room of Northlands Coliseum. The trainer had just finished taping Martin's ankles, knees, and wrists, and he was distractedly thinking about May and when he'd see her again when Coach Dafoe walked over. Hands in his pockets, he stood by the bench.

The coach had an easygoing demeanor, calling the team "his boys," inviting some of them home for Sunday dinners with his wife and kids, but he was also the most focused coach in the NHL. He had known both of Martin's parents, having played with Serge Cartier on the Montreal Canadiens when they were both young men. Balding and paunchy now, Coach Dafoe had dark eyes that reminded Martin of a shark's—they never blinked, and they missed nothing.

Clearing his throat, he looked Martin straight in the eye.

"This is it, Martin."

"I know," Martin said.

"We've asked a lot of you all season, and we're going to do that again tonight."

Martin nodded, but he didn't speak. He had been playing hockey a long time, and it was every player's dream to make it to the finals. This year he and the Bruins had taken each other all the way. He knew he was their "star," that expectations were higher for him than anyone. His stomach jolted, and when he closed his eyes, he could almost imagine it was his father standing before him instead of Coach Dafoe.

"You've had a few days off now," the coach added.

"A chance to rest," Martin agreed. *And to fall in love with May.* He wouldn't let the other thought materialize: *to get nervous about the series.*

"That's good." The coach crouched down, still looking Martin square in the eye. He talked about Martin's deadly shot, how there wasn't another player on the ice who could score like him, how tonight Martin should fight the urge to pass the puck to his teammates.

"If Ray's in the clear—" Martin said.

Coach Dafoe shook his head. Martin's mother's early coaching had had one flaw: She had stressed good sportsmanship, and she'd taught her son to pass whenever possible. He passed flawlessly without appearing to cock the stick, fooling his opponents and sometimes his own teammates.

"When in doubt, shoot," Coach Dafoe said.

"But Ray and Bruno—"

"This could be your year," Coach Dafoe reminded him. "The Bruins' year."

"I know, Coach."

"We don't know how good we are yet. That's what we're going to find out tonight. During the playoffs, I was watching you hard. You know I was. I didn't like that critical occasion when you missed practice . . ."

"I told you—" Martin said, but the coach stopped him.

"Whatever you told me, the fact is you missed practice, and for three games straight you lost your concentration. For us to win, I need you to combine your defense and your offense, and I need you to lead this team. It's a simple fact—you're the dominant factor, and when you're distracted, so is everyone else. Wherever you went, it took you out of your game."

Martin looked down at the floor. During the play-off series in New York, he had rented a car and driven upstate. The countryside had been white under a springtime ice storm, snow covering branches laden with apple blossoms. Coils of razor wire glistened silver in thin sunlight; the brick prison walls were black under a coating of ice. Deep inside sat Martin's father, a man who skated like the wind, who had won three Stanley Cups, to whom Martin hadn't spoken in seven years.

Martin had sat in the car, staring at the prison. He had driven north from Manhattan, wanting to absorb some of his father's greatness—he'd just sit outside, taking whatever he could through the walls. He had wanted a spark, something extra to bank the fires of competition he had burning inside himself at all times. But that first time up, Martin felt nothing.

Later in the series, with the Rangers having their way against the

Bruins, Martin felt dead inside; the fires were out. Down 3–0, Martin had driven back up to the prison in Estonia. This time he was going to go inside, see the old man and lay things to rest. The snow and ice had melted, but Martin just sat in the same spot outside the prison walls, their bricks red now in the sun instead of slick black.

"You got your edge back in Boston," the coach was saying. "Whatever happened in New York and Toronto, you beat it at home."

Martin nodded, his face impassive. He had met May, that's what had happened. He had saved her on the plane, and now he had fallen in love with her. He held the leather pouch in his left hand. Unable to get what he'd been after from his father, he had gotten it from a stranger. Inspiration, connection, divine intervention, love at first sight: the extra edge. His blood pounded just thinking about it.

"Four days' rest," the coach said, his hand on Martin's shoulder, "and fourteen years of restlessness. You want to win the Stanley Cup. It's time."

"Yeah." Martin's throat felt tight, and he felt the tundra winds building inside him. Not even loving May could stop them.

"Nils Jorgensen wants to nail you."

"I know." Martin pictured the Oilers' goalie, one of his few true enemies in the NHL—the man who had fractured his skull and smashed his left eye socket three years ago.

"He wants to make it personal," Coach said.

"It *is* personal," Martin muttered.

"Your father'll be watching, you know."

"I figure he probably will."

"And your mother will, too."

Martin bowed his head. He wouldn't let himself admit how much he wanted this win. He had lived and breathed hockey his whole life—it was as much a part of him as his heartbeat. His parents had brought him to this moment, but his father was in prison and his mother was dead. This was a part of him May might not ever understand; he wasn't even sure he'd want her to.

"I believe in heaven," Coach Dafoe told him. "They're up there."

"They?" Martin asked, looking up.

"They're up there right now, my mother and yours, rooting for us. Yelling, stamping their feet. Your mother used to make a real racket, watching the games."

Martin nodded. If his mother was up there, so was Natalie. He felt the leather pouch. Suddenly Coach's words began to make

sense. Maybe May was some sort of angel, a messenger from his mother and daughter. *Four days of rest and fourteen years of restlessness:* fourteen years of playing pro hockey without winning the Cup. He had won countless trophies, been voted MVP twice during the regular season. He had made it to the play-offs ten times, never before to the finals.

"Remember what I told you," Coach Dafoe said, his black eyes shark-stern as he backed away.

"When in doubt, shoot," Martin repeated. "Don't let Jorgensen win."

"That, and don't disappoint our mothers."

———

The first night Boston played Edmonton, Tobin's husband and sons were busy readying a car for the soap box derby, leaving Tobin on her own. So she rode over to the Taylors', to watch the game with May and Kylie on May's bed with the television turned up.

"Are you following the puck?" Tobin asked.

"There it is." Kylie pointed at the screen.

"Everything moves so fast," May said.

"You can say that again." Tobin laughed, and May knew she was referring to what she'd been told about dinner with Martin. Her husband and sons were into fishing and car racing, not hockey. So Tobin learned the lingo along with May and Kylie: penalties, right wings, blue line, center ice, the crease. May kept her eyes on number 21—Martin Cartier—and she felt thrilled.

One, two glides, and Martin was in full flight, skating and slamming his way across the neutral zone and into Oilers' territory. Skates clicking, blades slashing, the tympanic thump of bodies against the boards.

"I wish I was there," May said.

"I'll bet you do. Look—the camera's on him. He's staring straight into it."

"Right at us," Kylie said sleepily.

"I wonder if his father's watching," May said.

"His father?" Tobin asked.

"Sounds like they have a complicated relationship," May said.

Kylie snuggled against her half asleep, as she tried to stay awake long enough to see who would win. But her eyes were so drowsy, they were closing fast.

"In what way?" Tobin asked.

"They don't speak."

"That sounds straightforward," Tobin said. "Not complicated at all."

"But it's his father," May said, watching the TV.

Tobin laughed. "He'd better be careful, what he tells you. Little does he know how you feel about fathers."

"Oh, now you're my analyst?"

"Always." Tobin laughed again, but then the crowd went wild, and she and May turned their full attention to the game.

"What happened?" May asked.

"Something with Martin," Tobin said, as they watched him skate across the ice with his fists pumping overhead.

"He's a lightning rod," one of the announcers exclaimed as Martin scored his first goal of the night.

"The Gold Sledgehammer," the other said as Martin slammed into one of the Oilers, knocking him to the ice as he nailed the puck with his patented slap shot. "Cartier's got the body of a heavyweight boxer and the killer instinct to match," the first announcer added.

"The Gold Sledgehammer," Tobin said admiringly.

"Killer instinct," May said, watching him lock eyes with Nils Jorgensen, the Oilers' star goalie.

The announcers explained their rivalry. In one of hockey's most famous fights, Martin and Nils had tangled hard, with Nils's nose being broken and his face needing substantial repairs. In retaliation, three seasons ago, Jorgensen had clocked Cartier, leaving him with a pulverized eye socket requiring surgery to repair a detached retina. Such was hockey, but when May saw the scars on the goalie's cheeks and chin, she felt chilled to think Martin had done it and had it done back.

Once the TV camera zoomed in on Martin's face, and May thought she had never seen such intensity in human eyes.

"They hate each other," Tobin said.

"They do, don't they?" May was shivering.

"Wow, May."

"I know."

"That's a look we don't see every day. Martin hates Jorgensen with a passion. Should I be worried about you?"

May had been staring at the two faces on the TV screen, thinking that emotions worked in two directions: that if Martin hated Jorgensen, the feeling was probably mutual.

"Worried about me?" May asked, surprised by her friend's question.

"A guy who can look like that," Tobin said. "Who can fight another person, let himself get so wild . . ."

"To me he's so gentle, Tobin," May said, remembering his kiss.

"But he has it in him." Tobin stared at the screen. "You can see it, can't you? He's violent."

"Not to me," May insisted.

"I wonder if he can control it," Tobin said. "When something makes him really angry."

May thought of the owls in the barn, how they'd narrow their eyes and dive-bomb their prey, and that was how Martin looked to her at that moment. The idea of giving him rose petals seemed ridiculous, embarrassing, but as she slid farther down the bed, she was thinking *it was meant to be. . . .*

"You're not saying anything," Tobin prodded.

"Gordon was a lawyer," May said quietly. "He went to Harvard. He's a partner at Swopes and Bray, and he belongs to the University Club. There's no one more in control than Gordon. Is there?"

"No."

"And no one has ever hurt me more," May said.

"I know," Tobin admitted.

"Martin won't hurt me."

"Are they winning?" Kylie mumbled, suddenly coming slightly awake.

"Yes, two to one," May said.

"Where's Martin?"

"There," May said, crouching forward to touch his figure on the screen.

"Martin skates fast," Kylie said. "And he can skate backward."

"He can," May said, not taking her eyes off him.

"You can say that again," Tobin said, letting May know she was on her side.

Hockey had never meant anything to them. No team sports had. As girls, May and Tobin had played tennis, gone swimming and bike riding. They had hiked around Selden's Castle every summer and cross-country skiied the Black Hall fields every winter. But now, watching Martin Cartier slam the puck at 101 MPH high into the net, May wondered what she had been missing.

He went in, skating back and forth, moving as if he loved motion, darting forward and falling back, teasing the other team, receiving and passing and shooting for the goal in one fluid motion.

Then doing it again from the other side. It was like dancing and fighting, all at the same time. May was mesmerized but she felt afraid of the impact—those scars on the Edmonton goalie's face.

"Go, go," Tobin cried.

The crowd was screaming, and the announcers were yelling. May watched the clock ticking down. She had dug her fingernails into the palms of her hands as she heard them say ". . . pass intercepted by Cartier, he takes it, he turns, he shoots . . ."

"They won!" May said.

"Oh, boy," Kylie yelled.

"The Bruins," the announcer went on, "have won Game One, beating the Edmonton Oilers by the score of three to one, with a hat trick by the amazing Martin Cartier. The unpredictable, volatile, amazing Martin Cartier. What do you think, Ralph? Is the Cartier Curse broken? Is this Martin's year to go all the way and win the Stanley Cup?"

"I sure hope so, and I know all the Boston fans are saying the same thing back home. After a less-than-brilliant season and playoffs, Martin Cartier tonight showed himself to be—"

"What's the Cartier Curse?" Tobin asked.

"I think it has to do with how long he's been trying to win the Stanley Cup."

May turned off the sound, wondering about the Cartier Curse. They sat very still, May's arm around Kylie, watching the TV screen. The camera showed wild shots of the crowd, the dejected Oilers, their furious goalie Nils Jorgensen, the jubilant Bruins.

"That was incredible," Tobin said, yawning as she climbed off the bed.

"Thanks for watching with us."

"Better than listening to John and the boys revving the engine every ten seconds. You think hockey's rough, try letting your kids turn the garage into a lab for their homemade car."

Outside, the night was warm. The windows were open, the white curtains fluttering in a light breeze. The air was scented with meadow grasses and wildflowers, a world away from the ice and violence of a hockey game. As May stared out at the old wedding barn, illuminated yellow in the white light of a half-moon, she could hardly believe that he had been right here, in her barn, just two nights ago . . .

The telephone rang.

"I'll get it," Tobin said, lunging past May. "Hello?"

May sat quietly, holding Kylie, listening.

"Well, congratulations on winning the game," Tobin said, and May knew it was Martin. "The Gold Sledgehammer himself. I've heard so much about you . . . that's right, Tobin. How did you . . . really, she did? . . ." Tobin grinned, her gaze sliding to May.

"Let me speak to him," May said, holding out her free hand.

"We go back a long, long way," Tobin said. She listened silently, as if Martin was going on at length. May's pulse kicked over, wondering what he might be saying. Tobin's expression was sharp, amused, but as May watched, it softened. "Oh, I'm glad to hear that," Tobin said after a long while. "Very glad."

Handing the phone to May, she said, "It's for you. I'll put Kylie to bed, okay?"

"Thanks," May said, taking the phone.

"You have a good friend," Martin said.

"I know," May agreed. "She came over so we could watch your game. You were great."

"Thank you."

"You won!"

"Actually, *we* did," he told her.

"Yes, the Bruins—all of you," she said, correcting herself.

The connection was scratchy, as if he was calling from a portable phone. In the background, May could hear men's voices laughing and shouting. She pictured the locker room, or what she imagined of a locker room, filled with victorious hockey players.

"I don't just mean the team," he said.

"Then—"

"You and me, May," he said. "You were with me out on the ice. I don't know how or why. I just know it's true."

May's heart pounded. She thought of being with Martin in the game. She imagined flying down the ice with him, helping him win, keeping him safe. "That's because of the rose petals," she said. "That's what they're for."

"Well, they worked."

This wasn't May. It wasn't May at all to be holding her breath, straining her ears, just to hear someone at the other end of the line. May had been shut off for so many years. She had stopped believing in this kind of connection for herself. It might be possible for the brides she worked with, but not for her.

"I'd better go," he said. "I'll call again, when we get back to Boston, eh?"

"I'll keep watching you," May promised.

"Tell your friend and Kylie I said *bonne nuit*."

"I will."

"*Bonne nuit* to you, May."

"Good night, Martin."

Then May stood in the dark, holding the phone as she gazed out at ghostly cats hunting around the moonlit barn, closing her eyes to keep his voice in her mind.

Boston won the opener, but needed a double-overtime goal from Ray Gardner to take Game 2. Game 3 also went into overtime, and this time the Oilers won it 2–0, Nils Jorgensen brilliantly blocking every shot Martin made.

Back in Boston, Martin's ankle was killing him. An old knee injury flared up. The trainers wouldn't leave him alone, trying every treatment known in New England and some imported from ancient China. Ice, laser, massage, acupuncture. The Oilers took Games 4 and 5, and the Bruins won Game 6, tying the series. Martin thought of his father in the brick-red prison, watching every mistake he made. Bowing his head, he cringed, blocking the thought from his mind.

Coach Dafoe found a picture of Martin's mother in an old hockey yearbook, and he pasted it next to a snapshot of his own mother and taped it to Martin's locker. Ray Gardner's wife was going to Mass every morning to pray for victory, and Jack Delaney said his daughter had lost a tooth and left the tooth fairy a note asking for the Bruins to win instead of her customary dollar.

Martin talked to May after every game. He wanted to invite her to the Fleet Center, to watch in person, but caution prevented him. He needed every bit of concentration to focus on winning the Cup. Every bit of focus, every molecule of strength, had to stay in his brain and bones.

When he was younger, he'd invite women to watch him play, and he'd get off on showing them his stuff. But May was different. He didn't need to show off for her, and now, with so much riding on this postseason, he didn't quite trust himself to think of May and win at the same time.

After midnight, sleepless after losing to the Oilers, Martin questioned his plan. With all the other guys relying on prayers, teeth, and dead mothers, Martin didn't feel quite so strange about the rose petals, and he considered the possibility that he was screwing up his chances, keeping May away. He called her house.

"I want you there, you know?" he asked. "But I'm thinking it might be a distraction."

"A distraction how?" she asked, disappointed.

"See," he said. "I need to keep my eyes on the puck."

"I'd stay out of the way," she said.

"Even so, I'd know you were there."

"It's okay. I understand," she said, sounding hurt.

"You don't," he said.

"I promise I do." Her voice was cool.

During their lunch break, May and Tobin left Aunt Enid with that day's bride and her mother, taking their sandwiches out to a tree behind the barn. There in the shade, they ate their lunch and listened to a chorus of birds singing in the branches.

"You're upset," Tobin said.

"I am. I can't help it."

"Because he's back in Boston and didn't invite you to watch him play?"

May nodded, staring at her sandwich. "He says he wants me there, but he thinks I might be a distraction. It reminds me of Gordon going on business trips, never wanting me along."

"Because Gordon wasn't going on business trips," Tobin reminded her. "He was going home to his wife."

"I know," May said. "Telling me he had deals in Hong Kong and London, when he was actually reconciling with her."

"Martin's not lying to you," Tobin said.

"How do you know?"

"Because you can watch him on TV. You know he's where he says he is."

"Then why doesn't he want me there?"

"Maybe because of what he said—he's afraid you'll distract him."

"I think he knew I was upset on the phone last night." May stared at the Bridal Barn, shaking her head. "Relationships are so complicated. I'm barely getting started, and I can't stand myself."

"Gordon really worked you over."

"That's not Martin's fault."

"Then tell him the next time you talk. Wish him luck and mean it."

"I do," May said miserably.

But Martin didn't call that day, and she realized she didn't have a number for him. She watched the game on TV, saw Martin win Game 6 with a blast from the slot high into the cage, electrifying every person in the Fleet Center, shooting them to their feet in a roaring ovation. Nils Jorgensen lunged after him, restrained by his teammates. May saw Martin meet his eyes, and she saw the rage boiling between them.

She wished he would call her, but he didn't.

In a blue concrete room stinking of sweat, stale cigarette smoke, and smuggled-in alcohol, a crowd of men thronged around the TV, cheering and jeering loudly, in almost equal measure. The Bruins had just taken Game 6. The cell block was built of concrete and steel, so the men's voices were hollow, crashing echoes. Pucks of sound, the old man thought, slamming against the walls.

"Fucking killer," one man said, watching Martin Cartier. "He's one of us, sure as shit."

"Bruins suck, the Rangers should've taken it from them—"

"Harsh, man—Cartier's boy is harsh."

"Next time I'll use a hockey stick, do more damage."

"Your boy's a stone killer," someone said, laughing as he stuck his face directly in front of Serge's. "You like that, don't you?"

"I like it fine," Serge growled.

"He's a hero, man," someone else said. "A national fucking hero."

"No Canadian's a national hero. This is the USA!"

"He's gonna cop the Stanley Cup!"

"Hey, old man—whadda you think of that?"

"He's not gonna cop it tonight," Serge said roughly, staring at his son's face on the TV screen. He could almost feel the beautiful, crisp cold rising from the ice. He breathed the frosty air and thought of the north woods. "Don't count on that which hasn't happened yet. Get back to me tomorrow."

Game 7 was about to start, and all around the country, hockey fans were tuned in to the action in Boston, Massachusetts. One hundred miles south in Black Hall, Connecticut, May and Kylie were again watching the TV in May's bedroom. Violet, the black

house cat, lay curled at their feet. With a big wedding on Saturday, May was surrounded by drawings, photos, lists and the menu.

"Why can't we go?" Kylie asked, frowning. "I want to go to the game. We're special to him."

"It's better to watch from here," May said. But inside, she was wondering whether they were special to him after all. He hadn't called in two days. May had been busy with work and Kylie, whose dreams had been bad last night, of tiny mute creatures trying to tell her something, flying around her head like a thousand white moths. May had recorded the details in the diary.

The telephone rang, and May answered, expecting to hear the bride or her mother or the caterer.

"Hello?"

"What are you doing?" Martin asked.

"Watching you," she answered, gripping the phone as she watched the Bruins starting to skate out. "Why aren't you on the ice?"

"They're calling me," he said. "I just have a minute."

"Oh—" She was speechless, as if she'd had the wind knocked out of her.

"Tonight," he said, taking one very deep breath.

"This is it."

"Are we going to win?" he asked. "We are, aren't we?"

May laughed nervously, wondering why he was asking her. "Yes," she said, because she knew that was what he needed to hear. But she didn't necessarily mean the Stanley Cup.

"You don't sound sure," he said.

"Something my mother always said," May told him, "is that it isn't whether you win or lose, but how you play the game." The words were out before she could stop to consider she was saying the old saw to a pro hockey player about to play the national championships.

"I've heard that before." Martin laughed. "I just don't do it very well."

"Neither do I," May admitted. "I was a jerk the other night."

"Why? Because you wanted to come? I wish you had."

"You do?"

"*Oui.*"

"Martin's going to win," Kylie chanted. "Martin's going to win."

"You'd better get out on the ice." May could see the team taking practice shots.

"I still have the bottle you gave me."

"With the rose petals?"

"Ssh." He laughed. "My teammates might hear."

"Wouldn't want that." May laughed back.

"I love you, May," he said, stopping her heart.

"Martin," she said, shocked.

"Just one more thing," he said, trying to laugh, sounding as if his voice was very dry.

"What's that?"

"If we do win," he said, "I'm going to ask you to marry me."

"Now I *know* you're kidding me."

"You think I'd do that?"

"I don't know what to think," she said, incredulous.

"Yes, you do, May Taylor," he said. "You just don't want to believe it."

"You're standing there at a hockey game," she whispered.

"What's the difference where I am?"

May thought of the rose petals, talismans of love, and when she looked at Kylie and saw her daughter staring at her with total intensity, she wondered whether this could possibly be happening.

The camera panned across the crowd: she caught sight of a beautiful blonde holding up a sign: "Cartier Rocks." Two girls wearing halter tops stood by the ice, shivering and screaming "Martin!" May blinked.

"Okay. Enough. Not over the phone," he said. "I'll see you later."

"Yes," May said, still staring at the screen, but no longer smiling. At the rink, a bell rang and a blast from an air horn sounded.

But he had already hung up, because suddenly she saw him on her TV screen, the ruggedly handsome blue-eyed muscle-man. Everyone in the Fleet Center saw him too: They jumped to their feet, cheering. May held her daughter, staring at him. There wasn't an ounce of excess baggage on his six-foot frame, and she found herself wondering where he'd put the rose petals.

"He means it, Mommy," Kylie said sleepily.

"Means what?" May asked, glancing quickly down.

"What he said. He wants us to be a family."

May stared at Kylie. There was no way she could have heard Martin's end of the conversation. Was it another sort of vision? She reached for the diary, to record Kylie's words, but then she put the book down. Some visions were too deep to be dissected.

The old man had done it himself, won the Stanley Cup three times, for two different NHL teams, so he watched the game with a certain nostalgia and some definite opinions. Dafoe couldn't coach worth shit. The old man could read his lips, and the only things Dafoe seemed to say were "concentrate" and "discipline." What about "shoot"; what about "get the puck to Martin"?

"Shoot," Serge growled under his breath. "Shoot the damn thing."

Martin cocked his right arm and gunned straight at the net. Jorgensen blocked the shot. Ray Gardner got the puck, slowing Martin down.

"Give it to Martin, *idiot*," Serge said. God, he hated Dafoe's coaching style. Having coached in the NHL himself, Serge could bet Dafoe was talking out of one side of his mouth, telling Martin to shoot, out of the other telling the team to take their time setting Martin up right. When Martin didn't need setting up—he just needed feeding.

"Got money on the game?" one of the old-timers asked.

"Shut up," Serge said.

"Your kid's old," someone else put in. "Too old to win the Stanley Cup. He's about to get his ass kicked."

"If I were Nils Jorgensen, I'd cut off his balls."

"What balls?"

"Hey, man, can't say the Sledgehammer lacks balls. Can't say that."

"But he's old for hockey, man."

"Seriously, Serge—got money on the game?"

Serge no longer heard them. Crouched over, he just stared at the screen. The voices boomed around him, echoing off the concrete blocks. The prison guards stood nearby, as interested in the game as anyone else. One of them asked Serge if Martin had called him, asking for any pointers. Serge's lips thinned.

"You hear me?" the guard asked louder. "Did Martin call his daddy?"

Serge narrowed his eyes, focusing on the TV. His heart felt small and hard, dry as a ball of tar in his chest. Martin hadn't called or visited in a long, long time. That was Serge's private business, and no one needed to know. The cell block sounded like a raucous locker room, the din ricocheting off the walls. The guard tapped Serge hard on the shoulder, but Serge just stared

harder. The old man wondered whether Martin listened to his coach.

"Concentrate," Dafoe's lips seemed to say. "Discipline."

Serge ignored the other world around him, concentrating on the game. The Bruins and Oilers were tied, 1–1.

—

Martin was skating for his life: that's how he felt. He had scored one goal, but Jorgensen had managed to block all his other shots. Edmonton had scored again, putting them up 2–1, and Martin could read victory in his enemy's eyes, all his scars bending into a big smile.

He could hear the Boston fans screaming for a goal. They were throwing things on the ice, and the police were out in force. Looking into the stands, Martin saw signs: the Cartier Curse; Double or Nothing: Cartier Loses. Martin thought of his father, wondered whether he was watching from prison.

God, let me win. The prayer came out of nowhere. He wanted to do it for May, for himself. Martin heard the fans jeering. He thought of all the news stories about his father's gambling on his own team, throwing the game, letting down the sport. Serge Cartier, the great NHL forward, three-time Stanley Cup winner. CARTIER TURNS GOLD INTO JAIL, one headline had read.

Martin wanted to set the name right. He wanted to prove to his father he could do it, he wanted to prove to the world the Cartier name was still worth something in hockey. Even in the twilight of his career, Martin wanted his father to be proud of him. But then he thought of Natalie, of how his father's gambling addiction had taken her life, and he heard himself moan.

It came from deep inside himself, and it was so loud the whole stadium heard. Martin sounded like a wild animal. Trying to focus on the goal, Martin took the puck from Ray. The clock ticked. He went charging down the ice, cutting in from the right wing as he neared the cage.

"Shoot!" the crowd yelled.

Shoot, Martin told himself. Jorgensen faced him with hate in his eyes. Shoot, Martin thought. He pictured his mother watching, like Coach said. He saw Natalie's face. He heard his father's ratchety, low voice: Shoot. He couldn't do it. Passing to Ray, he came around again.

The crowd saw his hesitation and started to boo. The fans' frus-

tration and fury sounded in their yells, the rink resounding with discordant and hostile echoes. The clock ticked faster. Martin steeled himself, catching Ray's eye. The team was setting him up. "Concentrate!" he heard Coach Dafoe shout.

Martin saw a grizzled man with prison pallor; he heard a little girl crying with fear on a balcony in Toronto. He thought of his mother dead, but instead of seeing her in heaven, he saw her cold in the ground. He pictured May, radiant and alive. Concentration impossible, Martin caught Ray's pass and aimed it at the goal.

Nils Jorgensen blocked the shot.

The buzzer sounded; the score was 2–1.

Martin's skating would be clocked at 29.2 MPH; the slap shot at 118.2 MPH. That's what the record books would have read, immortalizing the moment, if Martin Cartier had won the Stanley Cup for the Boston Bruins.

Except they had lost.

May's voice hurt from yelling, but suddenly she stopped. Kylie had been jumping wildly on her bed, but now she dropped to her knees as if someone had cut the string holding her up.

"Mommy, he didn't get it into the net."

"No, he didn't," May said.

"Did they lose?"

"Yes, honey."

"Oh." Kylie stared at the screen, her face solemn.

Together they watched the TV, the close-up shots of angry Boston fans firing cups and wadded-up programs onto the ice. The camera showed the jubilant Oilers piling onto Nils Jorgensen, hoisting him into the air and carrying him on their shoulders. Panning across to the Bruins, it showed their faces in shock and anger and disbelief.

When the camera found Martin, his eyes were blank. His face was craggy and weathered, as if he had been playing in the snow and wind instead of under the lights of an indoor stadium. But his blue eyes looked empty; they reminded May of a dog she had known once, kept inside a cage most of the time.

"Oh, Mommy," Kylie breathed.

"Oh, Martin," May whispered, tears coming to her eyes.

"Why does he look like that?"

"I think because he wanted to win so much."

"But you always tell me it's how you play the game."

"I know. It is . . ." May began, and then she stopped. Because there were things about sports and men she didn't understand, a need to win that she had never really had. Kylie was tired, and she wanted to go to sleep. May read her a story, listening all the while for the telephone.

He'll call, she thought. *He can tell me about what happened, how bad he feels, and I can listen.* She thought of the things she would say to him, words to soothe and comfort, to give him hope. In the back of her mind, way back behind Martin's disappointment over the Bruins' loss, were his words: that he was going to ask her to marry him.

It wasn't until an hour later, once Kylie was in bed and the moon had circled around the yellow barn and painted the fields and greenhouse with silver light, that the phone rang.

"They lost," Tobin said. "He must be devastated."

"He hasn't called."

"Guys have to lick their wounds alone," Tobin told her. "It's the way of the world."

"He asked me," May began, wanting to tell Tobin about what Martin had said. But some things were too private to tell even a best friend. So she bit her lip and let the words trail away.

"He'll be back," Tobin said. "Just give him time. When John got passed over for promotion, he went fishing alone for a week. He couldn't even look me in the eye until he got right with himself."

"What am I doing, starting something like this?" May asked. She thought of Howard Drogin, how he always called when he said he would, how he never seemed overly disappointed when May said she had other plans.

"You deserve more of a life," Tobin said, "than planning other women's weddings and hauling your daughter to psychologists."

"She's only had one bad dream since the plane crash," May said. "Only seen angels once. But tonight she mentioned something Martin said—she couldn't possibly have heard it—"

"She read your eyes, your expression," Tobin said. "She does it all the time. Any special power Kylie has—if you want to call it that—comes from her connection with you."

"We're so close," May agreed.

"You've had to be," Tobin reminded her. "You're both mother and father to her. She adores you. She reads your mind because she knows you so well."

"I'll put that in the diary," May said. "When we head up to Toronto in July, I'll tell the doctors your theory."

"Good."

May laughed. "My notebook isn't getting fuller these days. I think they might be disappointed. Kylie's psychic activity has slowed down."

"Maybe she doesn't need any imaginary friends right now."

"Why?"

"Maybe because her mother's been happier."

But when she hung up the phone, May didn't feel very happy at all. The rose petals hadn't worked, after all. May felt sorry that Martin hadn't called, but not only for herself, for him: She would have liked to give him comfort.

She would have liked that so much.

Chapter 5

"THE BRUINS *LOST*," MICKEY AGNELLI hissed into Kylie's face.

"Yeah," Eddie Draper said. "You said they were going to win for sure."

"I didn't say for sure," Kylie whispered, standing by the drinking fountain in the hallway of Black Hall Elementary. She glanced from side to side, wishing a teacher or a big girl would come. Here she was, a first-grader surrounded by third-graders, with no one to help her.

"You said Martin Cartier had special powers," Mickey said.

"Yeah, the power to *lose*," Eddie added.

"And you said Martin Cartier was going to come to school," Nancy Nelson put in. "So where is he?"

Kylie cringed. Although Martin hadn't said he would come to her school, Kylie had been sure he would. He was her friend, and she had been so sure her wish—all of their wishes were going to come true. From the first minute she had seen him on the plane, something about his eyes had made Kylie think he needed them as much as they needed him. She had picked him out to be her daddy, asked him to help them when the time came.

And now four days had passed, and he hadn't even called Mommy once. He had dropped out of their lives as if he'd never been in them. Kylie's stomach ached, just thinking about it.

"Yeah, where is he?" Mickey demanded.

"Not that we'd want him," Eddie said. "The Bruins should trade him for Nils Jorgensen."

Kylie felt her shoulders growing together in front of her chest, as if she could fold herself inside a pair of wings. She didn't like people talking about Martin like this, even if he'd stopped calling, even if her wish wasn't going to come true.

"Martin Cartier is a loser," Mickey taunted.

"Lost the Stanley Cup," Eddie said. "Know how big a loser you have to be to lose the Stanley Cup?"

"Don't call him a loser!" Kylie cried.

"LOSER!" Mickey shouted.

"A big, stupid, dumb one," Nancy added.

"Stupid and dumb are the same thing," Kylie told her. "So maybe you're talking about yourself."

"You're a loser, too," Mickey said. "For lying about him. You don't know Martin Cartier, and he never was coming to school. And he sure didn't win the Stanley Cup. Come on, guys—let's leave the first-grade baby alone."

Kylie's eyes flooded as she clenched her fists and watched the three older kids run down the hall. They all had fathers. She knew, because she'd seen them at the Shoreline Fair. Everything they had just said to her stung, but one part in particular bruised her ribs and made her hug herself. She wished the angels would come. She wished they'd surround her with their soft wings and be her friends.

"I didn't lie," she said to the empty hallway. "I do know Martin Cartier. I do."

—

Martin went underground. He was in his house, in the middle of Boston, but he might as well have been in a cave. Shades drawn, phone unplugged, beard growing. They had lost the Stanley Cup again, and nothing was going to change it. He slept for two days straight.

The first day, he dreamed of the lake. The ice was smooth and black; you could see fish frozen beneath its surface. Trout, bass, pike. Martin skated like pure spirit, the silver blades barely scratching the ice. He was free, light, unencumbered. But he had to get somewhere; the wind at his back was pushing him toward a person he couldn't see.

The second day, he dreamed of skating faster. Lac Vert spread before him, its serpentine path carved into the mountains of Canada. Tall pines shadowed the dark ice, and Martin knew the person he sought waited just beyond the next bend. Who was it? The closer he got, the farther away the person seemed. His mother? His father? Natalie? The ice began to melt around his feet.

Waking tangled in the sheets, his heart was racing. God, who was it? Lying back, he faced the truth: He had lost the Stanley Cup

again. He had let everyone down. He was alone in the world, even in his dreams. The ice had been melting, the lake about to swallow him if he couldn't get to her.

"Her?" he said out loud.

And then he knew.

Of course, it was May. She had been there, waiting for him. In the dream, he had nothing in his hands, nothing in his pockets. He had only himself.

That was all May wanted. She was good and kind, and he'd felt an overwhelming connection with her the minute they'd met.

Martin had felt himself sinking, the ice melting around his ankles. May had been just around the corner, waiting for him. If only he could get to her, maybe he could be saved. His throat caught, thinking of her little girl.

Maybe they all could be saved. Pushing himself up on one elbow, he stared through his darkened bedroom and thought about facing the light of day.

The month of May was a busy time for weddings, for couples who wanted to get married under arbors of wisteria, with bouquets of fresh-picked violets and lilies of the valley, but a slow time for wedding consultants: The planning was long done. May spent most of her time in the garden; it wasn't uncommon for her to greet the few bridal parties for the first time with grass-stained knees and dirt under her fingernails. But these last days, May's heart hadn't been in her work.

Four days after the Bruins' loss, after Martin's last call, May knelt in the rose garden scattering coffee grounds around the roots of an old white rosebush. Every rosebush had a history, told to May by her mother, grandmother, and great-aunt. This one had been planted in 1946, the year Emily Dunne had built the barn. It had nearly died in an early frost that first year, but Emily and Enid had kept it alive by wrapping it in a scrap quilt made from their father's old shirts. Abigail had lovingly fed it rose food.

"Give that one extra coffee," Aunt Enid told May now, coming over to supervise.

"Like this?" May asked, spreading out half a cup.

"Twice that," Aunt Enid said. Her hand shook with a slight palsy, and as she reached out she had to lean on May's shoulder to steady herself. May's grandmother had claimed that roses liked

coffee, that they grew taller, fuller, and brighter when fertilized with the morning's grounds. The smell of loam and French roast mingled in the warm air, making May miss her mother more than ever. She must have sighed, because Aunt Enid looked over.

"What's the matter, honey?"

"Nothing, Aunt Enid."

"I don't believe you." Then, as Tobin came over, "Will you see what you can do with your friend?"

"I'm trying, Enid," Tobin said, putting her arm around the old woman.

Aunt Enid had once been five-five, but age had curved her spine and reduced her height by four inches. She had close-cropped white hair and pale blue eyes, and she was dressed in her favorite gardening clothes: a pink housedress, an old canvas jacket, and knee-high green rubber boots that had once belonged to her sister.

"Oh, honey," Aunt Enid said. "Is it the hockey player?"

"The who?" May asked.

"Nail on the head," Tobin said.

"Kylie told me he'd been calling, and then—" Aunt Enid stopped herself.

"Kylie liked him," May murmured.

"Oh, and that's the reason," Tobin said.

Aunt Enid reached into the pot of old coffee grounds and let them run through her gnarled fingers. She did that over and over, and then she spread them carefully around the roots of the old white rose.

"Missing someone's a funny thing," Aunt Enid said. "It overtakes you, doesn't it? You can't figure out where it begins and where it ends."

"She can't," Tobin said, and May felt her gaze on the back of her head.

"Will you two please stop?" May asked. "Page Greenleigh is coming with her mother in a little while. I'd better get washed up."

"You could call him," Aunt Enid suggested.

"That's a fine idea," Tobin agreed.

May looked through the rose bush at her aunt. The suggestion was Bridal Barn heresy: Emily Dunne had always maintained a man's greatest fear was being trapped—"lassoed," she called it. In her famous list of "musts and musn'ts," calling men was at the head of the musn'ts. As if reading May's mind, Aunt Enid went on.

"Men can hurt, too. He lost the championship," Aunt Enid reminded her. "Maybe he needs someone to talk to."

"That sounds right to me," Tobin said.

"What about men needing time to lick their wounds?" May asked.

"Enough's enough."

"He knows he could call," May said.

"I've never thought of you as prideful before." Aunt Enid picked a Japanese beetle off a glossy leaf, holding it loosely in the palm of her hand to release into the rose-free field. "But it seems you're putting your own feelings ahead of someone who might really need you right now."

"Aunt Enid's right," Tobin said.

May didn't reply. She spotted a second beetle, its shell glimmering like a murky rainbow in an oil slick. Taking it from the rose's stem, she tapped the hard shell, the size of a cherry pit, with her fingernail. May's own shell felt hot and hard in the morning sun, as she thought about how long she had lived with it on, wondered how it would feel to take it off.

Over the years, Tobin had tried to set her up with John's brother and his cousin and men he knew from work. Barb Ellis had taken her on a ski weekend to meet a friend from Vermont she'd known was perfect for May. Carol Nichols had arranged a blind date with a guy she'd known in graduate school, an oceanographer in Woods Hole. Dutifully, May had gone along. But she was now thirty-six years old, and she had never once felt about anyone the way she did about Martin.

Very slowly, May stood up straight. She walked into the greenhouse, to the telephone on the north wall. Martin had never gotten around to giving her his number. Calling the Boston Bruins organization, she got a receptionist, then an office manager, finally the team publicist. Explaining herself, May heard the man's skepticism.

"Remember that plane crash?" May asked. "He saved me and my daughter. He really did. Kylie, my daughter, asked him to help us, and the thing was, we became friends. He and I had dinner, just before the finals started, and I gave him—" she stopped, her mouth dry.

"I'm sorry, ma'am," the voice said. "But we're not allowed to give out the players' numbers."

"But we're friends," May argued. "We really are. I'm sure a lot of people tell you that, but in this case it's honestly true."

"Uh-huh, but even so, I'm not permitted . . ."

May leaned her head against the cool glass wall. A pair of swallows crisscrossed the air overhead, building a nest in the greenhouse eaves. May felt her chance slipping away.

"Please," May pleaded with the man on the phone. Suddenly she knew she *had* to get through to Martin. If she could have climbed through the wire and seized his number, she would have. "You have to tell me."

But the man had hung up. May walked slowly back to the rose garden and resumed her work. Aunt Enid glanced over, but she didn't ask what had happened.

"You didn't get him?" Tobin asked.

"No."

"Damn," Tobin said. "Maybe I could try. I could—"

"Sssh," May said, digging in the garden. "Okay, please?" Her friend walked away.

When Aunt Enid went into the barn for some bonemeal, to supplement the coffee grounds, May bent over and put her face close to the earth. She felt damp warmth rising in waves, and she closed her eyes. "I can't believe this is happening to me," she said to her knees.

She had fallen in love. She, who had been foolish in love once and totally self-protected ever since, had—almost without noticing—just given her heart to a man who had disappeared. Last night, writing in Kylie's dream diary, she had been shocked to find herself writing about Martin.

Page Greenleigh, her mother, and her sister came and left, and May returned to the garden. The air grew hotter, and bees swarmed the roses. The sound of an engine made her look up. It was a car on the road, coming fast. The louder the engine got, the faster May's heart began to beat. She was wearing an old straw hat and a faded yellow sundress. Her hands were covered with dirt again, and she had coffee grounds under her fingernails as she watched Martin Cartier driving his Porsche through the field.

May peered across the tall grass. Pushing herself up, brushing her hands off, she stood. She tried to smile, but she couldn't stop her chin from shaking.

Tall and strong, he came toward her. He wore a white shirt tucked into jeans, a blue baseball cap, and sneakers. His right cheek was bruised, and he had stitches under his left eye. As he got closer, he took off the baseball cap.

"Hello," she said.

"I was taking a ride," he said.

"All the way down here?" she asked.

"I like the salt air," he told her. "Here in Black Hall."

May found herself staring at Martin's feet, but she felt his hands on her shoulders. Suddenly she found herself looking into his eyes. He seemed momentarily unsure of how his body worked, and as he reached for her, he fumbled his baseball cap and dropped it onto the ground.

The kiss took May's breath away. Martin held her tight, and she held him back. The day was balmy, on its way to being hot, and they were surrounded by the powerful scents of tall grass and white roses. May would never again smell spring without thinking of Martin.

"I didn't think I'd see you again," May said.

"Honestly?" he asked.

"I didn't know." She shrugged, standing back.

"I lost," he told her.

"That didn't matter to me."

"I screwed up. I—"

"You were wonderful," she said. "Like a tiger out there. I never knew a person could skate so fast, then go straight for the jugular . . ." May didn't know what she was saying, how to describe her impressions of his game, but as she talked, she felt some of the tightness leave his body. He didn't say anything, but as she looked into his eyes, she felt him listening.

"I saw your face," she said. "The camera showed you up close. I felt as if I was right there."

"I'm glad you weren't—to see me lose."

"But you nearly won."

He pulled back slightly. The bruises were purple and yellow, the stitches an angry black line.

"Nearly doesn't count in hockey."

May didn't know what to say to that.

"I choked. I had a clean shot, and I gave it away. Passed to Ray—Ray Gardner. My mind was racing. It was the Stanley Cup, maybe my last chance. I thought of my father. He's—" Martin's face twisted as he thought about it.

"You didn't want to let him down?" May asked, guessing. She had read the papers. She knew his father was in jail.

Martin snorted. "I just didn't want him to see me lose. Letting him down was beside the point."

May frowned, listening.

"He's old," Martin went on. "He's . . . I told you. We're estranged. We haven't seen each other in years."

"He's still your father."

"I'm different from you," Martin said. "There's nothing sentimental or nice about me and my father." His accent was thicker than usual. He seemed very uncomfortable, talking about his father, about losing the game. May remembered the last four days, wondering where he had been, and she couldn't manage to smile.

"I didn't come to talk to you about my father," Martin said, holding her hand.

"No?" May asked.

"Our first fight." Martin grinned, and he looked so disarming, May started to smile. "Forgive me?"

She nodded, laughing.

"I had the rose petals in my pocket," Martin said. "I kept hearing you say: 'How you play the game . . .' "

"You thought of that while you played?" May asked, laughing again at the idea.

"I did." Martin laughed. "It didn't help."

"Rose petals aren't magic."

"They were for a while." He stroked her hand. "They really were."

May looked down at their hands. She couldn't tell him that many brides accepted her rose petals expecting their marriages to be blessed, to be in love forever, never to fight or drift apart. She didn't want to tell him that some of those brides were now divorced, hated the men they had once loved more than the moon and stars, were now married to other people.

Instead, she told him, "Kylie will be glad you came back."

"She will?"

"Yes," May said. "She had a lemonade stand yesterday, right over there by the fence. She hit up every bride who drove in, but I know she was hoping for you. She missed you." She didn't tell him about Kylie's bad dreams returning, about Kylie screaming in her bed last night about the angel on the plane trying to tell her something.

"What about her mother?" Martin asked, stepping closer.

"I missed you, too."

"I want to marry you."

"Martin," May whispered, her face turning red.

"May," he said softly.

"We just met a few weeks ago."

"I told you. It's meant to be."

Meant to be . . . what did that mean? May's pulse was racing, but her thoughts were cool. They were so different: She had a young daughter; he traveled all the time. May's feelings had been horribly hurt during the last four days of not hearing from him. She looked him straight in the eyes.

"I'm flattered beyond words, really. This has never happened to me before," she said. "But the thing is, I come with a daughter. You're very romantic, and my mother and grandmother must be playing trumpets right now, but honestly, I can't play around like this."

"Play around?" he asked, frowning.

"Well, yes."

"Do you think I would do that?"

"You might not mean to," she said. "But you don't know me—us—very well. You'd suddenly have a ready-made family, and it's one of the more unusual ones around."

"Unusual how?"

"Well, I've been single a long time, like my whole life. And Kylie's very . . ." She searched for the right word. "Magical."

"Do you think I do not know that, eh?" he asked, suddenly breaking into a grin, as if the whole dilemma had been solved. "She takes after her mother. Rose petals in a bottle—that's unusual. You inspire her."

"Thank you," May said.

"*Bien sûr.* You are the most magical woman in the world."

"You should have met my mother and grandmother," she said, laughing.

"But you will tell me about them, no? I'll meet them through you. I know how important they are to you, May. I hear, by the way you talk about them. Your family will be my family."

"I've always wanted that," she whispered.

"Have it with me," he said. "What are we waiting for?"

"To know each other!"

He smiled, taking her face in his hands. "I think we do already. The important parts, eh? In here." He touched his heart.

Suddenly May thought of all the brides: all the proper Black Hall girls with long courtships, marrying boys they went to prep school with, men they'd met through their college roommates or sailing friends or law partners. She thought of brides who did everything by the book—correct and proper and eternally boring—and May began to smile.

"Tell me," he demanded.

"I might be crazy," she told him.

"Yes, probably," he said, making them both laugh. "But so am I. Terrible, the way my mind goes. You're all I could think about, all through the play-offs. What's the word for it—obsessed? But in a good way."

"Good obsessed?" May smiled.

"Mais oui." He touched her face, cupping her cheek with his hand. "I couldn't get you out of my mind."

"And you think that means we're meant to be?"

"Don't you?" he asked, stepping closer.

"I'd like to think that." She suddenly felt her heart starting to pound.

"Then think it," he said. "I'll prove it as time goes on."

"How?" she whispered.

"By loving you, May."

May kissed him. His eyes widened with surprise, but then he wrapped his arms around her and held her tight until they'd had the chance to calm down. When they stepped back, May was dismayed to feel an ache deep in her chest.

"I told myself over and over not to hope for this," she said.

"You did?"

"This kind of thing doesn't happen to me."

"Strange you should say that," Martin said. "Because it did."

"I noticed."

"I brought something for you." He was frowning slightly as he began to go through all his pockets. Once he'd reached into each of them, the frown grew deeper. But then he had it, and a great smile wreathed his entire face. Pulling a ring out of his front pocket, he started to slide it on her finger. The move was very smooth and romantic, but May was so nervous, she flinched, and the ring fell into the freshly turned dirt.

"Oh, dear," she said. "Here, let me get that." Kneeling down, she started to paw through the soil, but Martin gently grabbed her wrist.

"Let me." Digging it out of the dirt, he stayed on his knee and slipped it on her finger. Looking directly into her eyes, he said, "May, will you marry me?"

She put her hand over her mouth and felt frozen. The seconds ticked by, until she could finally speak.

"I need some time," she heard herself say. "Not just for me, but for Kylie."

At first he looked stunned, and she thought she had pushed him away. She'd lose him now entirely; he'd take his ring and leave. He looked so vulnerable kneeling there, and she felt so sorry to have hurt him. But she had to take care of herself and Kylie; that's how it had been for so long.

"Martin, I'm sorry," she said.

"Well," he said, a wry smile coming over his face. He rose to his feet, brushing the soil from his hands. "I'm going to have to court you."

"I don't mean it like that."

"I'll do it right, May. I won't let you say no again."

"I didn't say no this time," she said quietly.

"But you're not ready to say yes."

"I just want to know you better. I'm not asking for a courtship—you make it sound as if I want hearts and flowers, things like that—"

"Well, want them or not, that's what you're going to get. May Taylor, I already lost the Stanley Cup this spring. I'm not going to lose you, too."

—

The bouquets began to arrive the next morning. As if they didn't have a garden full of flowers, window boxes full of petunias, the Bridal Barn began to fill with bunches of white roses.

"He must have called every florist in Connecticut," Aunt Enid said.

"How did he find them all?" Kylie asked, scrambling around, noting the logos for Sea Flowers, the Silver Bay Greenery, the Black Hall Wildflower Shop. "Mommy, he must like you a lot."

"Yes, he must, dear," Aunt Enid said. "I know that no price can be placed on affection, but these roses cost quite a bundle."

"I didn't mean he had to send me flowers," May said, thinking that she had only meant to learn more about him, but secretly thrilled to be treated in such a special way. Twelve bouquets with a dozen roses each had arrived so far, with another florist's van pulling down the drive even now.

"May, you throwing a whole bunch of weddings this week?" the delivery man, who came here often, asked as he unloaded two large white boxes. "Either that, or some fancy bride's going crazy, buying us out of white roses."

"No, they're for her!" Kylie exclaimed. "Every single one!"

That night Martin picked May up at six, and they drove into Silver Bay. After thanking him for the roses, May felt surprisingly shy, as if she was on a first date. She'd ask Martin a polite question; he'd give her a pleasant answer. "Did you have a good day?" "Yes, did you?"

Catching themselves at it, they began to laugh.

"We sound like two people in one of those language classes," he said.

"Yes, where you learn how to speak more stiffly than anyone ever does in real life," May laughed, remembering high school French. " 'At what time does the large department store close tonight?' "

" 'It has closed already, madame.' " Martin played along. " 'Owing to an infestation of mosquitos.' "

"Quelle horreur!" she said.

"Ah, you speak French!" he exclaimed, grabbing her hand to kiss it.

"Not much, though," she said, glowing as he refused to release her hand.

They strolled down the docks, past the fishing and scallop boats, past the weathered shacks, their gray shingles covered with old lobster buoys. Stopping in the stores, they said hello to May's friend Hathaway Lambert at the Cowgirl Rodeo. They ate clam rolls at Ollie's Fish House, sitting at tables covered with red-and-white-checked vinyl tablecloths.

People began to recognize Martin. Drifting over from the bar, they asked him to sign their cocktail napkins. He signed a few, then asked that he and May be allowed to finish their dinner in peace.

"Does that happen all the time?" she asked.

"Pretty often," he said. "Sometimes they tell me what I did wrong in the last game. We're far enough from Boston to not be getting too much grief over the Cup. But it comes, believe me."

May listened while he talked about the Stanley Cup. How his father had been one of Canada's greatest players, how he had taught Martin and Ray how to play. May waited for him to talk about how he felt about his father, what he thought about everything that had happened, but Martin veered into another area.

"We learned to play on Lac Vert," he told her.

"What's that?" May asked.

"Oh, the most beautiful place on earth," he said. "Wait till you see it, May . . ."

He described the deep water, reflecting tall mountains and

green woods. "It's incredible. We call it Lac Vert, 'Green Lake,' because of the color. It's as if another world lay below, filled with pines, oaks, maples, trees of every shade of green. In winter, when the lake freezes, the colors darken almost to black."

"You love it there." She was struck by the look on his face.

"More than anywhere else," he said. "It's my home, and I'm going to take you there. You'll love it, too."

Sitting at Ollie's, May had a vision of the lake. Just as if Martin had taken her hand, led her to the water's edge, she saw the vista spreading out before her. The mountains, the crisp northern sky, the clear green water.

"I'm sure I will."

"When can we go?" he asked.

But before she could answer, the waitress brought the bill, Martin paid it, and it was time to go. They had ice-cream cones at the Sandbar, then climbed into Martin's car for a ride through the hills behind Silver Bay, past the big old abbey, down Old Farm Road toward the Connecticut River and Black Hall.

Holding his hand, May found herself telling him about herself. She had him drive through town, and she pointed out the stone elementary school she had attended long ago and Kylie did now, her high school, the white church famously painted by Black Hall artists, and from which had been married many Bridal Barn brides.

"Dating back a long time," he commented.

"The church? Actually, it burned in a fire and was rebuilt about a hundred years ago," she said.

"No, the Bridal Barn," he said. "Your family business. You come from a long line of strong women, no?"

"I do," she agreed. "My grandmother was a real visionary. It wasn't easy to sell people on the idea of planning weddings. But she had a gift, and she said if we don't use what's given to us, it dries up and blows away." May paused, thinking of other men she had known. "Does the idea of strong women bother you?"

Martin laughed. "Not at all, and I know what I'm talking about. You should have known my mother. Lac Vert is beautiful, but winter doesn't get any tougher than we have it there. My mother kept us going on no money, hauling wood by herself to keep me warm while I slept, getting me to school no matter how bad the ice or snow. We were broke half the time, but that never stopped her from buying me new boots or jackets—"

"But your father," May began, thinking of Serge playing professional hockey. Certainly he must have provided well for his family.

"One thing you'll learn about me," Martin said, "is that I take more after my mother than my father—thank God. We don't need to talk about him. This night is too special."

May wanted to talk about him, but she let the subject drop. It was time for Martin to drive her home. Aunt Enid didn't like to stay up too late, and May wanted to get home to Kylie. But they stopped on their way, beneath the Holden Bridge.

The big bridge spanned the Connecticut River, and its lights sparkled like a sunken city in the slowly moving water. May pointed up, showing Martin the catwalk two hundred feet overhead, which she and Tobin had crossed the night of their high school graduation.

"Strong *and* brave," he said.

"And stupid," she added. "I'd die if Kylie ever did something like that."

"You probably came down here with your boyfriends." Martin slid his arms around her, kissing her in the shadow of the bridge. Melting into his arms, she let him kiss her long and tenderly, and when they stopped she was glad that he seemed to have forgotten, that she didn't have to tell him no, she had never done this before, never parked down here with anyone else besides him.

———

They drove down the dirt road behind Firefly Beach, sat in the sand, and listened to the small waves. May pointed east, toward the labyrinthine marshes of the Lovecraft Wildlife Refuge, and she described the frightening experience of finding the body of Richard Perry—despondent, he had hanged himself from a tree—there with Kylie.

"That's when her visions started?" he asked.

"Soon afterward," May said.

"Is that the right word for them? Visions?"

Whenever they talked about Kylie, she felt an extra degree of concern. Her daughter was precious beyond words, and she had already been hurt by others, including her own father. "Yes," May said carefully. "That's what they are."

Martin nodded. "I understand that."

"It's unusual," May went on. "Most people wouldn't understand. Her teacher called them 'hallucinations.' But she's not schizophrenic. . . ."

"Of course she's not. What do teachers know?"

"If Kylie hadn't had one on the plane, if you didn't already know about it, I'm not sure I'd be talking about it now. We try to keep them secret—"

"If that's what you want, I won't say a word. But, May, I'd be proud of them."

"Why?" she asked, turning toward him.

"Because she's a great girl. As sensitive as her mother and grandmother and all the rest of your strong magic-women. She's just another in a long line."

May let herself smile. She had the blue notebook in her hand-bag. Sometimes, filling it out, she felt filled with a sense of dread. People feared what they didn't comprehend, and there was so much about her daughter that she didn't understand. To have someone to talk to, someone who saw Kylie in the same wonderful light she herself did, made her feel happy and grateful.

"Thank you, Martin."

"Anytime," he said, gazing at the water, shaded with currents and ripples. The sun was setting, casting violet light on the break-water and big rocks. "Now, tell me about this water, eh? Is it the sea? I spend so much time skating I don't even know my geogra-phy. Canada's one thing, but New England is totally foreign to me. What is it, the Atlantic Ocean?"

"No, it's Long Island Sound."

"But it's salt?" he asked.

"Yes." She smiled. "It's like an arm of the sea. The Atlantic's right over there—" And then she explained how Long Island Sound was more gentle than the open ocean several miles east, that her father had taught her to swim and sail here when she was a little girl. Throwing stones into the water, May described the way her father had held the boat—a Dyer Dhow, a sailing dinghy—steady until she had climbed in.

Then he had pushed them off, stepped over the stern to take the helm and show her how to sail. He had handed her the tiller, shown her how to trim the sheets.

"Every step of the way." She stared out at Orient Point, a brushstroke on the horizon. "He was always so patient with me."

"He sounds like a good father," Martin said.

"Oh, he was. I got scared once, when the wind came up and the boat nearly went over, and I threw the lines at him, screamed for him to take the tiller. He did, just as calm as anything. He never made me feel sorry or embarrassed for needing to take it slow."

"I hope I never do that." Martin's voice was serious and low,

and May snapped her head to look into his eyes. She hadn't realized what she had done, asking him to wait. Her father had been
her role model, the man she would always judge all men against.

"I love you," she heard herself say to Martin Cartier for the
first time.

He swept her into his arms, pulling her closer as he kissed her.
The breeze was soft. It stirred her hair, moving the tall beach grass
in a constant whisper. May felt Martin's body against hers, and she
imagined sailing with him on a calm sea. This would be a perfect
time for it: not too rough, not too windy. She would feel as secure
as she did on dry land.

May would even feel safe enough to bring Kylie: her truest test
for any situation. She could imagine being in a boat with Martin
and Kylie, holding the tiller, trimming the sails, heading out into
the Sound, wherever life wanted to take them.

The next afternoon, they went for a long, leisurely bike ride.
May had packed a picnic lunch, and they had eaten it in a wide
meadow overlooking the Connecticut River. Heading home, they
rode along country roads, past vast farms dotted with granite boul-
ders, stone walls separating one property from the next. Red barns
and dairy cows were everywhere. The houses were Colonial, Geor-
gian, or Federal, painted mainly white or yellow.

"It's pretty here," he commented.

"We call that color 'Black Hall yellow,' " she told him, "because so many of the houses around here are painted it."

"You love this place, no?"

"Yes."

"Would you ever be able to move from here?" he asked.

She rode in silence for a few seconds. Just last night she had
lain awake, thinking the same thing. Her roots were deep here.
The history and legends had become part of her own story. She re-
lied on Aunt Enid for so much, and she wanted Kylie to know
where she came from, who her people were.

"It would be hard," she admitted. "But I think I could."

"I don't think I'd ever be able to ask you to," Martin said.

May glanced over. Was he taking back his proposal? He hadn't
mentioned it in the days since he had first asked, and although she
still felt relieved not to be pressed, she had almost started to wonder whether she'd imagined it.

"I could commute," he said.

"Commute?"

"If we could just spend the summer at Lac Vert," he went on, "I'd give up Boston in a minute. We could live here, in Black Hall. I'd drive to work, straight up three-ninety-five to the Mass Pike . . ."

"You're still thinking about . . ." she began.

"Oh, yes," he said. "I am."

Martin was like no one she had ever known before. He was so determined, yet very gentle. They rode along the quiet lane, side by side, until they came to a junction with a much busier road. May held the handlebars, her feet planted on the ground. Traffic whizzed by.

"Are you sure you want to go this way?" he asked.

"Just for a little while. I want to show you something."

Nodding, Martin got on his bike first. He wheeled across the busy road, watching over his shoulder as May came right behind. They rode single file behind the painted line, with May's heart beating faster with every turn of the pedals.

She wasn't even sure why she was doing this. Aunt Enid would never understand. Tobin would, but May didn't plan to tell her. Something was happening inside herself that made her want to move faster, to get this part over with, to tell Martin about the most important secret in her life.

A steady but sporadic stream of vehicles passed by, the drivers mostly workmen and local residents. Vans, sedans, and station wagons. When one huge dump truck rattled past, May felt shaken inside. They passed a pond on the left, a farm on the right. The road curved, granite ledges rising on both sides.

"Here." She stopped, her eyes fixed on the road.

"What is this?" he asked, looking around. His eyes were filled with anticipation; May had shown him so many beautiful places, the high points and garden spots of her beloved Black Hall. But this was not one of them.

May climbed off her bike, and Martin followed suit. Leaving the bicycles leaning against a crumbling stone wall, Martin laid the backpack on the ground. She walked back to the road, with Martin close behind. The traffic rushed by so close, she could feel the hot wind and exhaust in her face.

"This is just a busy road," he said.

"It's not just a road," she said quietly.

"What, May?"

"My parents were killed here."

"Here?"

She nodded, staring at the spot. The truck had hit their car head on, spinning it off the road and into the rock ledge. They had been killed instantly, and for years, on the school bus, May would come through here and think she heard them calling her name.

"Their blood was on that road," she said.

"How long ago?"

"Twenty-four years." Maybe she and Kylie weren't different at all. Seeing ghosts and angels, hearing voices . . . forget the magic of roses and herbs. The real similarity lay in how they listened for the dead, opened their hearts to ghosts.

"You lost them so young."

"Much too young!" she said, her chest hurting. She felt wild inside, as if she had to explain this to Martin so he would understand. What had happened to her parents on this curve had made her who she was, carved out the parts of her she didn't comprehend and couldn't get away from.

He tried to hold her, but she stepped back, away from the traffic.

"Everything looks one way, but it isn't," she said. "I'm strong, like you said. I'm there for my daughter, every minute, every day. I run my family's business, I help other women have the weddings of their dreams . . ."

"You're all those things."

"But I'm something else, too." She gazed at the pavement. She could almost see that dark blotch—blood or oil, she'd never been sure—that had been there for months after the accident. How she had prayed for the snow and rain to leave it alone, to never wash it away.

"What, May?"

"I lost part of myself here," she told him.

"That's understandable, for you to think that way. You were a young girl, from a close family. Losing your mother and father—of course you feel as if you lost some of yourself."

May shook her head. "No, Martin. That's not it. Not all of it, anyway."

He waited, watching her lift her eyes.

She wasn't seeing him at all just then, but her father. His face was as handsome as ever, with those high cheekbones and straight nose and laughing hazel eyes.

Hiking along the Connecticut River to Selden's Castle, he had

carried his baby daughter in a backpack. He had taught her to sail, to read the sky and tell the weather. Although she had loved being in the barn with her mother and grandmother, the outings with her father had been more special than anything.

Tobin had loved him too, and she'd been with May that last day. Two twelve-year-old girls, wanting to go to the store with May's parents for candy. In a hurry, May's father had told them they couldn't come.

May took a deep breath. "When my father died, I was angry with him. It was something stupid, just the kind of fight parents and kids have every day—he wouldn't let me go with them to the store."

"He saved your life."

"I know that now," she said. "But when he walked out the door that day, I hated him. Really, Martin. I was that mad. In a dumb, twelve-year-old rage. He said 'I love you,' and I didn't even turn around. He wanted to kiss me, and I wouldn't."

"You didn't mean anything by it."

"No," she agreed. "I know he'd forgive me, deep down."

Martin didn't reply. Did he think she was a fool, carrying this around all this time? May felt embarrassed, as if she wasn't sure why she'd brought him here, why she had told him this. All she could do was keep trying to explain. "It's everything to me," she said.

"What is?" he asked as a car hauling a boat trailer whizzed by.

"Sometimes I think I've lost the way to connect."

"You?" he asked, incredulous.

"Yes. As if I lost it that day—here, with them."

"May," he said seriously, pulling her toward him. "I think you connect better than anyone I've ever met."

"I bring other people together, help them get married." Tears welled up as she pressed her head into his chest. "But sometimes I think that what I know most about is missed chances."

She thought of her father's back as he walked out the door. She thought of the men she had chosen, of the disappointments she had brought to herself and Kylie. Although Martin had said she was strong, deep down May felt afraid. Fearful and hollow, as if all of her courage had leaked onto this small patch of road, twenty-four years earlier.

Silently they walked back to their bikes. The rock walls cast long shadows across the road, and they rode along with even greater caution than before. May started off leading the way, but

once they reached a straight stretch, Martin pulled alongside and rode beside her as long as he could.

Thcy passed fields through which they could observe the river flowing by, clear light slanting through tall trees. May's throat ached with the beauty and emotion of the day. When they got to the Bridal Barn, they turned up the dirt road and cut behind the gardens.

Climbing off her bike, May started to show Martin where to put his, when he stopped her. Taking her in his arms, she let the bicycle clatter to the ground.

"You think about missed chances," he said.

She held him, not speaking as she waited.

"Well, I'm not going to let you miss this chance." Martin held her even tighter.

"What?" She stepped back so she could see into his eyes.

She saw him digging in his pocket. He had the box open, the ring out, before she could protest. They were standing in the same spot as before, just over a week earlier. "Wc'll try this again. May, will you marry me?"

May looked from the ring into Martin's blue eyes. His nose and cheeks were speckled with road dust; dried grass clung to his shirt from when they had had their picnic. This time she didn't hesitate.

"Yes," she said.

Martin put his arms around her again. His eyes were wild with emotion, and suddenly May realized she had never wanted anything so much in her life. She stood on her toes and kissed him very hard. Longing rushed from her head down her spine and made her dizzy.

"I'll make you so happy," he said when they stopped kissing.

"I believe that," May said. "And I'll do the same for you."

"We'll have a wonderful life," he promised. "Here, Boston, Canada. Kylie will love Lac Vert. Wait till you see it."

"I can't wait."

"We'll never leave Black Hall," he said. "We'll live everywhere."

"We can do that." May was smiling.

"Do what?" Aunt Enid asked, and then they realized that they had an audience.

"Oh, wow." Tobin was standing in the open doorway of the yellow barn. Aunt Enid hovered just behind her.

"You must be Tobin," Martin said.

"You must be Martin."

"Aunt Enid," May said. "This is Martin Cartier."

"We were just talking about you . . ." Aunt Enid shook his hand.

"Enchanté," Martin said, "to meet you both."

"Where's Lac Vert?" Tobin asked.

"Canada," he told her. "My home."

"You're not taking her to Canada, are you?" Tobin asked, linking arms with May.

"Part of the time there," May said. "And part here."

"Where's Kylie?" Martin looked around. "I have something to ask her."

"Not home from school yet," Aunt Enid said. "Now where, when, how many guests . . . my, I don't know where to start!"

"Take it slow," Tobin suggested. "May looks like she's about to levitate."

"Oh, I wish your mother and grandmother were here," Aunt Enid said to May, wiping her eyes. "This is a wedding they would love to plan."

Chapter 6

MOMMY'S WEDDING DIDN'T HAPPEN IN the usual way; at least not the way that she and Aunt Enid and Granny planned for other brides.

When Kylie came home from school that day, Mommy and Martin told her they were getting married. They met her at the bus, and together they walked through the field, and when Martin said, "I feel as though I should ask someone for your mother's hand in marriage, so I'm asking you," Kylie threw her arms around his waist and said, "YES!"

Later, when she was alone, she did a little dance to a song she wrote: "I'm going to have a father, I'm going to have a father, we like him a lot, he likes us, too." Kylie tended to dance often, as a way of getting somewhere slightly faster than walking, and her step looked like something between skipping, waving with both hands, and stepping on a bug. But she wasn't allowed to talk about the wedding at school because Mommy and Martin weren't ready to tell the world yet.

Kylie told her other friends, the ones who came to her at night. Her dreams were filled with angels and ghosts. Kylie told them all: Mommy was getting married, she was going to have a daddy.

At night, Mommy went out with Martin or stayed home sketching bridal gowns. Kylie had watched her doing this for other brides forever, and at first, Kylie was very excited to see her doing it for herself. Tobin seemed pleased, but not as much as Aunt Enid: She kept leaving picture suggestions on Mommy's desk—of dresses that would look beautiful, veils that seemed just right for Mommy's face.

But Kylie began to notice that all Mommy's sketches were winding up in the trash. "Don't you like that one?" Kylie would ask. "Too formal," Mommy would answer, frowning, or "too

fussy." Kylie was beginning to worry that Mommy didn't like any dress, that maybe she didn't want to get married at all.

After they'd been going out a month, one Saturday night in mid-June, they were waiting for the Chadwicks to come over, when Kylie found out the truth. She was sitting between Mommy and Martin on the front porch watching lightning bugs in the field.

"There's another," Kylie called, counting lightning bugs. "And another. Eleven, twelve, flying over from Firefly Beach."

"Wait till you see the fireflies in Canada," Martin said. "My mother used to tell me they were stars come down to earth. When we go there, I'll show you."

"When will we go there?" Mommy asked.

"Whenever you want." Martin tried to pull Mommy closer. He was holding her hand behind Kylie's back, and it felt so good, leaning back into their arms.

"Whenever?" Mommy asked, looking over Kylie's head, her eyes shining like those earthbound stars Martin had mentioned.

"Yes," he said. "If Tobin won't mind too much."

"I think she'll understand," Mommy said. "We'll come back eventually, right?"

"Eventually." He laughed.

"Let's elope there," Mommy said.

"Elope?" Kylie asked. "What's that?"

"It's getting married without a wedding planner," Mommy told her, and Martin laughed again. Mommy turned so her back was leaning against the porch rail and she was facing Martin, leaning forward with excitement. "It's doing the important part and leaving out the rest."

"The rest?" Martin asked. "But that's what you do, isn't it?"

"It is," Mommy agreed. "And sometimes it seems incredible. To help someone plan the rest of her life with the one she loves . . . it's great. But calling the church, choosing the readings, deciding on the invitations, having programs printed, choosing attendants, buying a guest book . . ."

"A guest book." Martin started to grin.

"Does that sound like us?" Mommy was grinning back.

"What else happens when you plan?"

"I choose my gown, I have fittings, I get to practice my hairstyle with my headpiece."

"Headpiece?" Martin asked. "We wear those in hockey."

"I don't feel like having fittings," Mommy said, climbing across

Kylie to sit on Martin's lap. She kissed him lightly on both cheeks. "I don't feel like wearing a headpiece."

"No?"

"Yesterday I spent two hours with a young bride, trying to decide whether to wrap the stems of her bouquet or not to wrap them. Whether to use pink or ivory satin ribbon. Whether to leave them bare. Peony stems showing or wrapped? Two hours." Mommy giggled, kissing Martin again. "Usually I'm patient, mostly I can listen to brides all day, but yesterday all I could think about was you. Just you."

"Are you going to wrap the stems of your bouquet?" Martin asked, and Kylie liked the way he smiled as he teased Mommy.

"I don't care about my bouquet," Mommy told him. "I only care about you and Kylie."

"We could elope," Martin said, agreeing now, and Kylie watched him hold her mother as if she was the lightest, most precious thing in the world. Kylie wanted to climb up on his knee too, but she was too entranced, just watching. "I could take you to Canada, to LaSalle, and show you the mountains and lake where I grew up."

Just then, the Chadwicks pulled up in their old station wagon. The boys—Michael and Jack—jumped out and ran right over to the porch, their parents right behind them. Mommy and Tobin hugged, and then they introduced Martin to John and the boys.

"My friend goes to all the Bruins games." Jack was staring at Martin with huge eyes.

"You play hockey?" Martin asked.

"Yeah, sometimes," Jack said.

"Me, too," Michael chimed in.

"Well, we'll have to shoot the puck around some," Martin said. "You play, John?"

"In high school," John said, his eyes almost as big as Michael's. Kylie had noticed how weird people acted around Martin. Just because he was famous, on TV, he was still a normal person. Kylie liked how happy he seemed around her mother; he had lost that air of loneliness he'd had when they'd first met him.

"Fishing's his sport," Tobin said, sitting on the top step. "He brings me fish to cook every summer night. When he's not building a race car."

"I go for trout," John said. "Mainly."

"We'll have to have you up to Lac Vert."

"Lac Vert?"

"Where I grew up in Canada," Martin explained. "I kept the family cabin. We're just talking about—"

"A trip up there," Mommy said, her eyes shining. She was looking straight at Tobin, and Tobin gazed back.

"When?" Tobin asked.

"For the summer," Martin said.

"We're thinking about eloping." Mommy touched Tobin's shoulder. "I wanted to tell you first."

"Congratulations." John shook Martin's hand.

"You mean really elope? No guests at all?" Tobin looked as if she might cry.

"Just me, Martin, and Kylie." Mommy's voice was small, and Kylie watched Tobin look away.

"That's the way to do it," John said.

"I loved our wedding," Tobin said.

"But you didn't love our mothers fighting over the guest list, the food, the church. You didn't like my uncle getting drunk and fighting with your dad's friend."

"I loved having May as my maid of honor." Tobin's eyes were glittering.

"I loved being your maid of honor," Mommy told her.

"You're not having any attendants?"

Mommy hesitated.

"You're not," Tobin said, as if she could read Mommy's mind.

"I'm thirty-six," Mommy said. "I don't want a big wedding."

"Thirty-six isn't old," John protested. "You make us feel old."

Martin was holding Mommy in his arms, but Kylie watched her ease away, moving closer to Tobin.

"You know, if I had anyone I'd have you," Mommy said softly.

"It's not just that I won't be in your wedding." Tobin was now crying openly. "I'm not even invited."

"Oh, Tobin . . ."

"Maybe we should change our minds." Martin looked worried. "If we'd known it would hurt you . . ."

"I should have told you when we were alone," Mommy said. "Talked to you about it."

"Boy," John said, handing Tobin his handkerchief. "Wonder what you must think of us. We meet you for the first time, and it's the waterworks."

"I don't want you to change your mind." Tobin honked as she blew her nose. "And I'm not the waterworks."

"I've already changed my mind," Mommy said. "If it's okay

with Martin, we'll have a normal wedding. Will you be my matron of honor?"

"No," Tobin said, blowing harder.

"What?"

"I said no. You're eloping. I'm giving you something borrowed to pin to your dress, and that's about it."

"Tobin—"

"Honey," Martin said, pulling Mommy closer to him. "She's giving you what you want."

Now it was Mommy's turn to be the waterworks. Starting to cry even harder than Tobin, she buried her face in her best friend's shoulder. They clung to each other, sobbing hard. The Chadwick boys slunk away, embarrassed by all the tears. Kylie sat with Martin, and the strangest thing happened: She had a vision of her mother and Tobin when they were young, her age, best friends sitting on these same steps.

"It is what you want, isn't it?" Tobin asked, kissing Mommy's cheek. "To elope?"

"It is."

"Then do it."

"Really?"

"I give you my blessing." Tobin kissed Mommy again, and then she leaned over to kiss Martin.

"That means a lot to me."

"She doesn't have parents anymore," Tobin said. "Think of me as their stand-in."

"Then your blessing means even more to me," Martin said.

Kylie saw the look in Tobin's eyes, as ferocious as a mother bear's as she whispered: "Take care of her."

"*Toujours*—always," Martin promised. "Both of them."

◄━━

Over the next days, Tobin put May at ease about eloping. Not only did she forgive her for it, she came to believe it was a good plan. Summer was one of the Bridal Barn's slowest times. Proposals occurred in summer, planning began in September. Tobin and Aunt Enid could cover the business while May went to Canada.

"You haven't told Aunt Enid yet, have you?" Tobin asked.

"No," May confessed. "As hard as it was to tell you, I can't even imagine telling her."

"She'll be crushed," Tobin agreed.

"The look in her eyes—I can see it now," May said, shaking her head to dispel the vision. "Now I know why girls climb down ladders to avoid telling their parents."

"Are you planning to climb down a ladder?"

"Help me tell her, will you, Tobe?" May glanced at the house.

"You want me to tell her for you?"

May shook her head. "No, I know you can't. And I know she'll try to talk me into doing it the Bridal Barn way."

"How true that is. But you have a respite—she's taking a nap right now. Okay, let me see the ring." Tobin grabbed May's hand. "I've been dying to get a better look."

May couldn't help it: She felt proud. After years in the wedding business, she had a practiced eye for diamond rings, and Martin had given her a beauty: platinum, with one large emerald-cut diamond flanked by tapered baguette diamonds, all dancing with fire.

"Holy shit," Tobin exclaimed. "Nice rock."

"Thanks."

"The tide has changed," Tobin said, laughing. "Spoiled brides, eat your hearts out."

"What do you mean?"

"Oh, May," she said. "You know. All these years, you've been so humbly serving the rich brides of the shoreline. Unmarried May, the wedding planner. Not that they looked down on you, but you made it possible for them to feel, well, one-up."

"I know," May said, remembering some of the condescending looks and comments, the big rings and lavish budgets, the stories of how they'd all fallen in love.

"This is delicious." Tobin was grinning as she tapped the ring. "I can just imagine Page Greenleigh's face. Can't you stick around, just till she has her final fitting?"

"Don't tempt me." May laughed.

But Tobin's expression was serious again. "Maybe I just don't want you to go at all."

"You mean marry Martin?"

"No, I want that for you, May. I do. I'm a little worried it happened so fast, but I also think it's the coolest love story I've ever heard. It will be fantastic for business. Once word gets out that you married the number one bachelor in the NHL, brides will be lining up for miles. We'll have to market your rose petals. No, it's not that."

"Then what?"

"I don't want to lose you," Tobin said. Tears pooled in her

lower eyelids, and May watched as they spilled over. "Marriage changes everything."

"It won't change us," May said.

"Sure it will."

"Yours didn't change us."

"Because we were too young to know better. When John married me, we were all kids, and you were part of the package. Now we're all entrenched. John and I are confirmed Black Hall lifers; you're marrying a guy who might decide to play on a team in Oregon."

"I don't think Oregon has a hockey team."

"Well, California, then. Manitoba. Vancouver. Far away."

"I know," May said.

"He's taking you to Canada for the summer."

"Yes, he is."

"We've never spent a summer apart before," Tobin said.

"No, we never have." May's throat was tight.

"The truth is, my fine friend, that this is just the beginning. He's got a whole life story, and so do you, so do we. John and I got to write our life story together. But you and Martin are joining together mid-book. You know?"

"But what you're forgetting, Tobin," May said, wiping her face with her shirt sleeve, "is that you *are* my book."

"I hope so," Tobin said as May pulled her close in a hug and Aunt Enid walked in.

Although Enid appeared refreshed from her nap, she had bed wrinkles and pillow hair on her left side. With Tobin giving her silent encouragement, May led her aunt into the office, closing the door.

"What is it, dear?" Enid asked.

"I have something to tell you."

Enid smiled. Touching her fingers to her lips, she waited.

"You know Martin and I are getting married."

"Oh, yes, May," Enid said, coming around the desk. "You deserve so much happiness. It was such wonderful news."

"Thank you." May put her arms around her tiny aunt.

"I've got my work cut out for me," Enid said, breaking away and grabbing her clipboard.

"Um, there's one thing—"

"Now you just sit back and be the bride while your auntie goes to work. Never before has Black Hall seen a wedding like this. We'll pull out stops we didn't know we had."

"Aunt Enid, no stops."

The older woman laughed, as if May had just told a good one. Portraits of Emily and Abigail smiled down, and Enid pointed at them, still chuckling.

"Honey, they'd let me have it if I didn't go all out! This is the Bridal Barn, and you're our precious flower! The day you came home from the hospital—I can remember as if it were yesterday! Your mother, your grandmother, and I stood around your white bassinet . . ."

May closed her eyes. She could remember the bassinet—white wicker; she had used it for Kylie—and she could almost remember the moment. Three eager, loving faces smiling down as she gazed into her brand-new world; they *were* her world.

"And we showered you with orange blossoms and rose petals. Your mother said a prayer, and your granny said a poem, and I tickled your toes. It was our little ritual, to make sure you led a blessed life."

May smiled, thinking of her odd and wonderful family, of the small ceremonies they held at important times. She was certain she could remember that early introduction to rose petals.

"So if you think I can possibly let you get married without a bang-up Bridal Barn special, I assure you Em and Abby would never forgive me."

"Aunt Enid," May said, taking her hands. "We're eloping."

Enid gasped, wobbling as if about to faint. May helped her to a chair, encouraged her to put her head between her knees.

"Good God," Aunt Enid said. "I'm getting old. For a second I thought I heard you say you're eloping." The look in her eyes was hopeful. May nodded gravely.

"I did."

"May, no."

"It's what we want."

"Was it his idea?" As if somehow that would be easier to take.

"No, it was mine."

"But *why*?"

May drew up a chair beside her. "This might sound strange. But we have so much love for each other, we don't need all the rest. The planning, the guest list, the expense . . ."

"But I can do all that for you," Aunt Enid said.

"I know. You're so good to me, Aunt Enid. You always have been. I feel so lucky, as if I've always had an extra mother."

"Oh, May." Enid grabbed her hand. "You've been just like my daughter."

"Please understand—you've taught me so much. You, Mom, and Granny, I've planned a hundred weddings with you—more, even! I have all that experience, all those memories inside me."

"The Trowbridge wedding at the Congregational Church, the Paul James party at the Silver Bay Club . . ."

"Martha Cullen's wedding last fall, Caroline Renwick getting married at Firefly Hill last Christmas . . . surprising everyone, just like me," May said. Her mind filled with pictures: roses, ivy, satin, lace, yards of white tulle, mothers and fathers, sisters and brothers, tiny flower girls, brides and grooms.

"I have it all inside," May said. "Every wedding we've ever planned."

"That's why we should have one for you."

"Martin and I want to do it our way."

Enid took a deep breath.

"You're sure?"

"We are."

Nodding solemnly, Enid pulled herself up. She walked across the room, so she was standing between the two portraits on the wall. Although she was so short her head barely came to the lower part of the gilded frames, she stood in line with Abigail Taylor and Emily Dunne.

"Then we give you our blessing."

"Thank you, Aunt Enid."

Enid raised her index fingers, pointing up at the two women immortalized in oil paint. May lifted her gaze, staring into the eyes of her mother and grandmother. The portraits had been done by Hugh Renwick, the great artist from Firefly Hill, a few miles down the coast, as a gift after his daughter Clea's wedding. Keeping it in the family, with Hugh long dead, last winter Caroline had had a Bridal Barn wedding. The seasons and generations went on, as Aunt Enid stood silently pointing at the paintings.

May had been raised to be polite and grateful, and she knew what Enid was waiting for.

"Thank you, Mom," May said to the portrait of her mother. "And thank you Granny," she said to the painting of her grandmother.

The time was getting closer, and in spite of eloping, there were still plans to be made. May chose a dress from the barn attic and she bought a dress for Kylie. And just before she left, Tobin gave her a box to open.

"You didn't have to get me a present," May said.

"It's not a present," Tobin told her. "It's something borrowed."

Her fingers trembling, May pulled the wrapping off the small box. Opening it, she found a small ring inside. It was Tobin's class ring from sixth grade graduation at Black Hall Elementary. May had had one just like it, but she'd lost it long ago.

"It's so tiny," May said.

"Try it on your pinky," Tobin suggested.

May did, and it fit. The gold was smooth and worn, the black stone extremely scratched up.

"We've been through so many ceremonies together," Tobin told her. "We don't need one more."

"Oh, Tobe, thanks for seeing it that way," May said, telling herself both Tobin and Aunt Enid were now convinced.

"You're marrying Martin, and I couldn't be happier for you. I'll be with you in spirit."

"You always are, Tobe," May said. "You always have been."

May's mother and grandmother had told her to always follow her gut. So, on Kylie's last day of school, May packed their bags and kissed Aunt Enid and Tobin goodbye.

Martin had loaded up his other car—a white Jeep—just before noon, and by one o'clock on a brilliant June day, they had picked up Kylie and were heading west on the Massachusetts Turnpike.

"Poor Aunt Enid," Kylie said, once everyone had settled down.

"I think she understands." May glanced doubtfully over her shoulder as if she might see her aunt standing there.

"She never had children of her own?" Martin asked.

"No," May said. "In a way, I'm it. She never married, never left Black Hall. We're very close."

"Are you sure you don't want her to come?"

May nodded. "Well, we said small," she said. "I thought you, me, and Kylie."

"That *is* small," Kylie said.

"My mother said certain love is too pure for a big wedding. That when you have love like that, you have to be quick and simple."

"Like a perfect slap shot." Martin laughed. "Quick and simple. I like that."

They all laughed, but May couldn't stop looking out the Jeep's back window, as if watching for a small, humpbacked woman with white hair to catch up to them, waving madly all the way.

Soon the lovely rolling Berkshires surrounded them, rounded hills covered with green, valleys spreading north and south, lakes and reservoirs reflecting the blue sky.

They stopped in Stoneville, so Kylie could have her last after-school snack as a first grader at the Red Hawk Inn, and Martin bought her a rag doll from the gift shop next door. He bought May a soft black wool shawl, because he told her the nights in Canada were chilly and she would need something besides him to keep her warm.

Back in the Jeep, they veered north. They drove for hours, and Kylie saw the first signs for Canada just as the first stars were coming out. The sky was deep blue, as soft as a mantle of dark cashmere. It draped over the low hills, covered the fields and barns and woods. Approaching the customs station, Martin slowed down. He pulled out his identity card and asked May for her and Kylie's passports.

"Martin Cartier!" the customs agent exclaimed as he looked into the car. His face lit up like a young boy's, and his reaction alerted his colleagues to come hurrying over. They pushed papers into the car, begging Martin to sign them for their sons, their brothers, their sisters, their nephews. Martin did so quietly. The men spoke French, and he answered them in kind.

May felt proud of Martin—the way he signed autographs so humbly, in stride, exhibiting low-key confidence with such good nature. This was her first brush with Martin's fame since that night at Ollie's Fish House. She noticed the men peering inside the car, trying to get a look at her, and she gave them her biggest, most glamorous smile.

"Why did they do that?" Kylie asked from the backseat when they were driving again.

"Hockey is very popular in Canada," Martin explained. "Some of those guys have been watching me play practically my whole life."

"Why were you writing things for them?"

"That's called signing autographs," May told her, turning around. She watched Kylie getting sleepy, clutching her new doll. "They asked Martin because they like him so much."

"Mickey and Eddie don't believe Martin's my friend," Kylie said. "Because he's so famous."

"Oh, I'm your friend." Martin watched Kylie in the rearview mirror. "You send those boys to me. I'll show you how to hip-check them into the boards."

"You will?" Kylie asked, a look of devilish joy filling her eyes.

"Absolument," Martin promised. And as he used his native language, driving toward his boyhood home, May watched a more peaceful expression of bliss spreading across his face. He reached across the front seat to take her hand, and May felt it too, radiating throughout her body. Martin was going home, and he was taking her and Kylie with him.

They arrived in the middle of the night, and May had the impression of a bumpy road, the scent of pine, the Milky Way blazing over mountain peaks. Martin carried Kylie into the guest room, where she and May would sleep until the wedding. Both he and May were fighting back killer desire, but she was touched and a little amused by his old-fashioned determination to stay apart until they were married. She definitely would have tried to talk him out of it if she weren't so tired from the long drive.

Kylie woke up at first light.

"Oh, my God," she called, downstairs already. May got out of bed and oriented herself. They had slept in one of two small bedrooms upstairs in a rustic bungalow. Brushing aside the curtain, May saw nothing but deep woods. But when she'd pulled on her robe and walked downstairs, she saw picture windows opening onto the most beautiful scene she had ever seen.

Kylie stood on a small front porch beside Martin. Together they were gazing over a long lake twisting through the mountains. The rising sun painted every rock ledge gold, and the lake itself was deep, dark blue. Swans glided across its surface. Pine trees grew down to the water's edge, where twenty white-tailed deer were scattered, drinking. Two long weathered barns stood in the shadow of one sixty-foot cliff.

"Bonjour," Martin said, holding May.

"It's beautiful." May was awed.

"It's my lake," he told them. "Where I learned to skate."

"When you were my age?" Kylie asked.

"Younger. The year I learned to walk."

"I want to learn to skate," Kylie announced.

"You will," Martin promised.

"The deer are so close," May said. "And there's not another house—anywhere!"

"It's private," Martin agreed.

"You should get married right there." Kylie pointed at an old gazebo nearly hidden from view by pine trees, rustic and delicate, made entirely from birch branches and wood. "Or there," she said, pointing at a small dock jutting into the lake, a small rowboat tied by a line. "Or inside," she called, running back into the house.

"Or here on the porch." Martin gently kissed May's lips.

"Or anywhere at all," May said, touching his face.

"Do you like it here?" Martin asked.

"I love it." May had never been anywhere so peaceful and beautiful; Kylie's rapture made her so happy she could barely speak.

"It's my home," he said. "It always has been."

"This is where you lived with your first wife?" The words just jumped out before she knew they were coming.

"No," he said, looking surprised. "Then I played for the Blackhawks, and we lived in Chicago."

"But—" May began. She had a million questions about Martin's past. But when it came to second marriages, her mother had always counseled the brides to leave the past in the past, not to ask questions they didn't want to know the answers to, never to invite old loves into new marriages.

"Don't, May. Let's not talk about anyone else today. Just us."

"You're absolutely right." She saw pain furrow Martin's brow, and she thought guiltily of Natalie: his daughter must have loved it here. As much as Kylie did, or more.

He led May inside, and they made coffee on the old black stove. May looked around, noticing the great stone hearth, the natural wood walls, the stunning black-and-white photos taken by his mother. He told her how his father's father had built the house, raising his own family here and taking Martin and his mother in after Serge had left them to play for the Maple Leafs.

Hockey memorabilia was everywhere: Martin's first stick, his face mask, pucks signed by his idols, photographs of him skating and scoring from the age of three upward. The sofa back was lined with

small pillows done in needlepoint and cross-stitch by Martin's mother, depicting hockey sticks, a lake scene, a small rabbit, and the gazebo. May wandered through as if the house were a museum, as if everything in it had things to teach her about the man she loved.

"Kylie," Martin called, after they were all dressed. He stood in the doorway holding a bag of bread he'd taken out of the freezer.

"What's that for?" she asked.

"For the swans' breakfast."

"Mommy and I feed swans at Firefly Beach," she said, her eyes shining.

"Well, come on. We'll go down and feed ours. The Lac Vert swans. Let them know we've come home." Lifting Kylie up, he put her on his shoulders. May's heart swelled to see the expression in her daughter's eyes as she took the bread he handed her.

"And when we're done," he said to May, drawing her close, "I'll take a ride into town. Maybe I can find someone who'll issue a marriage license today."

"Aren't there rules? Residency?" May asked. "Blood tests?"

Martin's eyes took on that mischievous glint, and he gave her the sexy half-smile she'd first noticed on the plane. "They might bend the rules a little," he said. "Because my grandfather used to be mayor and, *eh bien*, because once in awhile it doesn't hurt to be Martin Cartier."

May burst out laughing, and Martin looked embarrassed but kept grinning.

"I can't help it," he said. "It's just that in Canada, we really do love hockey."

"The swans are hungry," Kylie reminded him, holding onto his ears.

He nodded. And the great Canadian hockey star Martin Cartier headed down the bluestone path to the gently sloping banks of Lac Vert, his shirttails hanging out and the pocket of his jeans torn slightly off, to show Kylie Taylor the proper way to stand near enough the lake to throw bits of bread past the big swans to the babies but not close enough to fall in.

Gazing after them, May found herself wishing Aunt Enid was there to watch them, too.

Martin arranged almost everything. In this part of Canada, people spoke mostly French, and since May spoke only English,

the bureaucratic details of elopement were beyond her language skills. So, while Martin obtained the license and found the officiant, May and Kylie set to work baking the cake and decorating the gazebo.

Kylie, as flower girl, took her title and duties very seriously. The morning of the wedding—the Saturday after arriving in LaSalle—she walked through the side yard picking every flower she came across. Daisies, buttercups, gentians, and black-eyed Susans went into the basket she held on her arm. May stood at the kitchen window, mixing butter-cream frosting and watching her daughter, the sweet smell of yellow cake drifting on the breeze.

Later they sat on the dock braiding the flowers into crowns for each of them. They made bouquets of violets and lilies of the valley, and they hung them from the gazebo's birch rails. Martin had disappeared in the Jeep on a mysterious errand, but May was just as glad: even though she was eloping, she knew it was bad luck for them to see each other before the wedding.

"Mommy?" Kylie asked.

"What, honey?"

"Is it really a wedding if it's not in a church?"

"Yes." May smiled. "Are you worried?"

Kylie shrugged as if she wasn't at all, but then she nodded. "I want it to be real."

"It will be real, Kylie."

"I like him, Mommy. You do, too, right?"

"I love him."

"I can tell. When you're with Martin, you smile so much."

"Didn't I smile before?"

"Not enough," Kylie said in a low voice. "Would you be marrying Martin if it wasn't for me?"

"Wasn't for you?" May asked. The lake had been hidden by early morning mist, but suddenly the sun burned through, turning the surface blue and gold. May squinted, holding her hand over her eyes. "What do you mean?"

"I brought you together," Kylie said, her voice almost too low to hear. "I wanted a father, Mommy. I wanted one so much, and when I saw Martin, I wanted *him*. I picked Martin out on that plane ride and asked him for help."

May stopped braiding daisy stems. The memory flashed in her mind: Kylie stopping to speak to Martin, smoke filling the plane, Martin rushing to their seats.

"How did you know we'd need help?" May asked.

"She told me."

"Kylie . . ."

"I can't help it. I'm not lying. You asked me, and I'm telling you the truth. The angel girl."

"Are you sure you saw an angel girl, Kylie?" May asked, always wishing for a simple explanation of why Kylie seemed to take her family's magic to a different place. "Then it wasn't a picture?"

"What picture?"

"The one Martin carries in his wallet."

Kylie stared at May. She started to speak, but then she shrugged. "Maybe," she said.

May dropped all the flowers on the dock and pulled Kylie into her arms. Kylie clung to her as she always had, like a little tree monkey. May had the same overwhelming sensation she felt every time she smelled her daughter's hair, felt her arms around her neck. "You don't have to tell me what you think I want to hear," she said.

"I know."

"You sometimes do that with the doctors, don't you? You're so smart, you figure out the answers they want before they're finished asking the questions."

"I don't want any more doctors," she said.

"I know," May said, reading her eyes, the only place Kylie was never able to fool her.

"What will I call him after the wedding?" Kylie asked, quickly changing the subject.

"Well . . ."

"Will I call him Martin?" Kylie asked. "Or something else?"

"Like—" May began, but Kylie jumped out of her lap as if she had suddenly turned shy, too embarrassed to go on.

"Mommy, I found a doll in a cupboard."

"Honey, you shouldn't be going through other people's things."

"I wasn't. I just wanted to see if anything scary was inside, but there wasn't. Just a little doll with yellow hair. She's old, or at least, she's not new. There's jelly on her dress, glitter on her face. And she's missing one shoe. Whose is she?"

"Martin's daughter's," May said quietly, watching Kylie's reaction carefully.

She sat down next to May, hands on her knees, staring into her eyes. "She died," Kylie said.

"Yes, she did."

Kylie tilted her head. She looked more thoughtful than surprised, not at all upset. "We would be sisters?" she asked.

"Stepsisters," May told her.

"Sisters," Kylie said firmly.

"Well, almost," May said, not wanting to get too technical.

"Like you and Tobin."

"Her name was Natalie."

"Natalie," Kylie said. She picked up a handful of daisies. "Can
we make a crown for her? Her dolly can wear it—"

May gazed at her. Their dealings with death had been disturb-
ing so far. Kylie had been bereft when May's grandmother had
died. And then they had come upon Richard Perry's body while
hiking around the Lovecraft. One researcher had suggested that
Kylie might have second sight, but May didn't believe in such
things. She wanted to keep Kylie as far from the subject of death
as possible.

"I don't think so," May said.

"Why not?"

"Because," May began, and wished she could leave it at that.
"I know Martin misses Natalie very much. It might make him sad
to see you playing with her doll."

"Please, Mommy," Kylie said. "I won't play with her—we'll just
make the crown so she'll know."

"So the doll will know?"

"No, Natalie. My almost sister," Kylie said. "I want her to know
I love her. Like Aunt Enid still loves Great-Granny, like you love
Tobin."

"Well, I don't see why not." May started to weave together a
new bunch of stems, amazed by her daughter's sense and kindness.
It's really true, she thought as she braided: Love doesn't stop just
because a person dies. Natalie and Martin's mother will be with us
today, and so will my parents and grandmother. She had a sharp
pain in her heart thinking about Aunt Enid, alive and alone in
Black Hall.

Just twenty minutes later, when the third daisy crown was complete and Kylie had run into the house to put it on Natalie's doll,
Martin's Jeep pulled into the yard and Tobin and Enid climbed
out.

May left the flowers where they were and ran up the hill. Martin stood there holding their bags, grinning when he saw the smiles
on May, Tobin, and Enid's faces.

"Your aunt needed an escort, so I volunteered," Tobin announced.

"She did," Enid said tearfully. "She didn't want me to travel alone."

"I'm sorry, Aunt Enid," May cried, embracing her aunt.

"You're Emily's granddaughter." Aunt Enid wiped her eyes. "When was I ever able to talk you into anything?"

"How did you both get here?" May asked.

"Martin flew us up. Then he drove all the way to Quebec City to fetch us," Tobin explained. "I was planning to fly straight back home, I really was."

"I talked her into coming," Martin said, holding May. "I know you wanted to elope, but the closer we got, the sadder I could see you getting."

"Thank you, Martin." May reached across her aunt's shoulder to take his hand. But Aunt Enid eased her arm down.

"Don't touch each other," she said, sniffling. "It's bad enough luck to see each other before the wedding. Don't go making it worse by having physical contact. Of any kind. Emily would say the same thing. So would Abigail."

"I'm so glad you're here," May said, kissing her. Turning to Tobin, she added, "You, too."

"Are you sure?"

"Positive."

"The family should be together." Martin's voice was lower than usual, and he wasn't smiling. In spite of her aunt's admonition, May walked over to him.

"I have my aunt and best friend," she said, "and I think you should invite someone. It'll be an unconventional elopement—lots of people."

"I wish Natalie were here!" Kylie exclaimed. "We could both be flower girls, and . . ."

Martin stiffened. His face changed completely, as if he'd been attacked. His eyes narrowed, and he grimaced.

"Stop," he said. Everyone looked shocked.

"What's wrong?" Kylie asked, frowning.

"Don't talk about Natalie," he said.

"Martin—" May began.

"She's been gone a long time," Martin said quietly. "It's better that we don't talk about her, okay?"

"Kylie didn't mean anything," May said softly. "I understand your pain, but Kylie's so happy, excited about the wedding . . ."

"I'll show Kylie pictures someday," Martin said, getting himself under control. "I'll tell her about . . ." he paused, unable to say the name. "About Natalie."

"I just wish she was here." Kylie's lip was trembling.

"I know you do," May said.

Martin's back was stiff, his shoulders hunched up to his ears. Despite what she had said, May was upset, shaking with the desire to get him alone, to tell him he couldn't speak to Kylie like that. She was just a child, eager to fit into Martin's life, and his words and tone had crushed her.

But Martin must have realized his mistake. She watched him bend down, hug Kylie, and tell her he was sorry. She saw Kylie relax and smile. Then, while Kylie showed Aunt Enid and Tobin the lake, Martin turned to May.

"I didn't mean to sound so angry," he said.

"You scared Kylie," May told him.

"I know. I saw her face. I'm really sorry—it's just that I hadn't expected her to mention Nat, and I overreacted."

"Okay," she said, hugging him. She shivered, and she knew she was feeling bridal jitters. Second thoughts about something that was happening very fast. For the first time in several days, she had misgivings about the quickness of this marriage. She suddenly felt very glad that Tobin had come.

Of course it was natural that Martin would find it hard to talk about Natalie at a time like this: when she should be here, part of the family, celebrating their new life together. Martin was reticent, where May wanted to talk about everything. They would have to work on a compromise.

"Listen, there is someone I want to call," Martin said, steering everyone back to the wedding plans. "Ray Gardner. It's time you met him and Genny—you'll love her. Time I introduced my family to them."

—◆—

"I have something to ask you," Martin said, checking his watch. He was on the phone to Ray, who lived with his wife and kids several miles north on the opposite shore of Lac Vert.

"Go ahead," Ray said. "As a matter of fact, you want to come over? I'm just having some coffee."

"No time," Martin told him. "Can you and Genny be witnesses at my wedding?"

Ray dropped his coffee mug. Martin heard it shatter as Ray spit out his mouthful of coffee. "Your what?"

"It's a long story. *Oui ou non*? I need to find witnesses."

"Can't be too long. I saw you three weeks ago and you were lonely and miserable. *Oui*."

"Hurry over. I want you to meet the most beautiful girl in the world."

Chapter 7

THE CEREMONY TOOK PLACE AT TWILIGHT. The gazebo was festooned with garlands of laurel, daisies, and honeysuckle, and Aunt Enid and Kylie had made a hundred paper boats fitted out with emergency candles and set them floating on the lake's smooth surface. Father James Beaupré looked solemn in his black robe, as Aunt Enid and the Gardners stood on either side of him. Martin, wearing his gray suit, was the first to see them coming.

Kylie led the procession down from the house. She wore a pale yellow dress, and she held a basket of wildflowers. As she walked, she dropped buttercups on the path, stopping in her tracks to watch Tobin coming behind her—in spite of everything, she was matron of honor, after all.

And then came May.

May wore her wedding dress, an even paler yellow cotton sheath, so creamy in shade it matched her grandmother's pearls, which she wore at her throat. She had found it in the Bridal Barn's attic, the place where her grandmother had kept the most beautiful old gowns.

It was very modest—high at her throat and down below her knee—but when she looked at Martin, she felt herself blush. Kylie and Tobin walked May straight to Martin, watching as each took the other's hand. Father Beaupré began the ceremony. He spoke English with a heavy French accent. There was no wind, but as the sky grew darker, a slight chill crept into the air. May instinctively took a half-step closer to Martin, just to feel his warmth.

Eloping meant many things, and May couldn't help thinking of them as she stood beside the man who was about to become her husband. Eloping meant no long guest list, no carefully chosen readings, no organ or brass quintet or soloist, no big church or fancy reception, no veil or train, and no calligraphied place cards.

On the other hand, it meant their best friends being present, candles on the lake, stars in a dark-lilac sky, night owls calling down the mountains, Tobin sniffling nonstop, Kylie's wildflower crown slipping over one eye, Genny Gardner gently adjusting it as if she'd known Kylie her whole life, and the simplest wedding vows May had ever heard.

"Do you, May, take this man, Martin, to be your lawfully wedded husband, for better, for worse; for richer, for poorer; in sickness and in health; as long as you both shall live?"

"I do," May said, gazing past their clasped hands into Martin's blue eyes, staring long and hard to let him know that she was making him a promise—before God and nature and the priest and the people they loved most—that she would keep until they both died.

"And do you, Martin, take this woman, May, to be your lawfully wedded wife, for better, for worse; for richer, for poorer; in sickness and in health; as long as you both shall live?"

"I do," Martin said without smiling, with such passion and conviction in his eyes and tone that May knew they'd be together forever.

They stood facing each other, the simple words ringing across the lake, the mountains echoing them back, time standing still.

"*Mes enfants,*" the priest said, blessing them in French, English, and Latin, making a sign of the cross with his right hand. A wind blew up from nowhere, skittering across the lake and making Aunt Enid's candle-boats rock on small waves. Daisies and violets scattered out of Kylie's basket, landing on the surface.

"I now pronounce you husband and wife," the old priest said, once in French and then, for good measure, in English.

Martin held May's face between his two hands and stared long and hard into her eyes. She had the feeling he was trying to tell her something without speaking, a message too deep and important to be spoken out loud. May was doing the same thing. Reaching up, she traced his cheek, his ear, the back of his head. His eyes were filled with fire. *Forever,* she was thinking. *I'll love you forever.*

"You may kiss the bride," the priest said, just as Martin slid his arms around her, cradled her against his body, and kissed the bride.

~

Everyone moved onto the front porch for cake and champagne. They gave Kylie a glass of ginger ale, and when the grown-ups raised their glasses, she raised hers, too. She listened to every-

one laughing and talking, the music playing from an old stereo in the living room. The Gardners seemed wonderful, and Kylie enjoyed hearing them exclaim about how happy they were for Martin, what a huge surprise to learn he was getting married.

Genny stood by Mommy's side, asking her questions, calling her a brave woman for joining the ranks of hockey wives. Tobin stood close, wanting Genny to know that Mommy already had a best friend. Martin introduced Ray to Aunt Enid, telling her he had been his best friend since childhood, that they had skated to school together on cold winter days.

"And still skating together!" Aunt Enid exclaimed in that sweet, beaming way she had that Kylie loved so much.

"We're lucky," Ray said.

"Yes, you are," Aunt Enid agreed. "Just as May's lucky to have a friend like Tobin. They've known each other since first grade."

"Really?" Genny asked, smiling.

"Yes, we used to walk home together," Tobin told her. "We'd be in school all day, then we'd play till our mothers called us home."

"It's still the same," Aunt Enid said. "They work together all day, then disappear on their bikes. Right, Kylie?"

"Right."

"So lucky . . ." Genny said.

The priest was very old, and his black robe smelled like mothballs. He had to leave early, but first he leaned down and made the sign of the cross on Kylie's forehead. When he did, he looked straight into her eyes as if he could read her mind.

"How old are you?" he asked.

"Six."

"I thought so." He nodded.

"Martin and my mother are married," Kylie said, although she was actually asking a question.

"Yes, they are."

"Even though that isn't a church?" she asked, looking down toward the gazebo.

"Yes," the priest assured her; he might have laughed at her question, but Kylie liked him for taking it seriously. "Even so."

"That's good." Kylie was so relieved she felt dizzy. "For me and Mommy."

"I have known Martin for a long, long time," the priest went on. "He made his first communion at my church. He has been at my church for . . . for other things, as well. This is good for him, too."

When the priest walked over to say good-bye to Martin and Mommy, Kylie slipped away, down the steps and back to the gazebo. Only when she was sure she was out of sight of the porch did she reach into her basket, under the flowers, and pull out Natalie's doll. Martin had looked very mad before, and she didn't want that to happen again. She fixed the crown of flowers on the doll's head, then turned her facing out toward the lake.

The night was very dark. Fish jumped out of the lake, making quiet splashes. The sky above the mountain peaks glowed with stars. Down here, fireflies twinkled in the pines and tall grasses. Kylie felt breathless, holding the doll. Something was about to happen, even more amazing than the wedding. She knew, she knew, she always did. . . .

Scanning the opposite shore, she saw a little girl all dressed in white, with gossamer wings and shining white shoes: the angel she had seen on the plane. As Kylie watched, the girl opened her arms. Kylie opened hers back, as if she could hug the child across the water. But a hug wasn't what the girl wanted.

"The doll?" Kylie asked, and the little girl nodded.

Kylie crouched down to place the doll in the basket. A rag doll, she had a simple painted face. But Kylie kissed her anyway. She would have liked to keep the doll, but she knew she shouldn't. If you have a sister, you don't take her toys to be your own.

Taking the basket down to the water's edge, Kylie set it adrift. The basket tilted from side to side, righted itself, and sailed swiftly, as if carried by a current, to the child across the lake. Kylie watched it go, and she saw the angel girl standing still, her arms still open, waiting for it to come.

"Are you sailing toy boats?" came Martin's deep voice.

Kylie was so surprised, she nearly fell into the lake.

"Well," she began. "Sort of. I—"

"Father Beaupré told me you might be here," Martin said.

"He's nice," Kylie said.

"He told me you're happy about the wedding. That your mother and I are married."

"I am," Kylie whispered. She was so happy, she couldn't even speak in a normal voice.

"Don't worry that it wasn't in a church." Martin put his hand on her shoulder. "This is my church, it always has been: nature, the outdoors. I'll take you rowing on the lake, Kylie. When it freezes over, I'll teach you to skate. Would you like that?"

"Yes," she said, staring up at him. "So much."

"Do you see the fireflies?" he asked.

Kylie nodded, and she remembered what he had told her once before. "They look like stars."

"Come down from heaven," Martin said. "That's what my mother used to say."

"Heaven," Kylie repeated.

"I have a daughter in heaven." Martin was staring across the lake. His gaze was hard and strong, and he was looking straight at the tiny girl standing there. She was flapping her wings, and Kylie knew she was about to fly away. Kylie's heart started pounding, because she wanted so badly for Martin to see Natalie: that Natalie was right here, on Lac Vert, that she had come down to earth with the fireflies to see her father's wedding and meet her new sister.

"Natalie," Kylie called, but Martin thought she was talking to him.

"Yes, Natalie," he said. "Your mother told you."

"Natalie!" Kylie called louder.

"I'm the reason you see angels," Kylie heard the little girl say. "There's something I have to tell you."

"Tell me?"

"It has to do with my father," Natalie said. "He needs you to help him."

How? Kylie wondered.

"People can be blind, not only with their eyes," Natalie said. "They can be blind to love, to the truth."

"I miss her," Martin said, looking so sad as he stared right at, right through, the shimmering white angel across the lake. "That's why I got upset before."

"She misses you, too," Kylie said, trying to concentrate on both things at once.

"Your mother said," Martin began, crouching down, "that you wanted to know whether you should call me Martin or something else."

"Something else . . ." Kylie said, her throat so choked up she could hardly say it.

"Watch and listen," Natalie said. "He needs you."

"You can call me Daddy," Martin said, holding her hands. "If you'd like. That would make me very happy."

Daddy, Kylie thought. The word sounded so beautiful in her mind, so right and so wonderful. She had never called anyone by that name before, never had a daddy before, never said the word

except when talking to her dolls. Thinking of dolls, Kylie looked across the lake for Natalie.

She was gone.

All that was left was a shimmer of white on the water, as if the entire Milky Way was reflected in the lake. Hordes of fireflies had gathered there, flying in a cloud, following something back across the water's surface. When it arrived, Kylie could see it was the empty basket.

Natalie had taken her doll. There was nothing left in the basket except a white feather, as if from one of the swans that lived on Lac Vert.

"Daddy," Kylie whispered.

And Martin picked Kylie up as if she were his own daughter, and he wrapped his arms around her just as her mother came looking for them, came walking straight into Martin's embrace. Standing by the old gazebo where they'd just had the wedding, Kylie watched the two grown-ups and knew she finally had the father she'd dreamed of for so long.

Chapter 8

THE HONEYMOON WAS HOT AND LAZY, clear summer days spent on the banks of Lac Vert. It began with their wedding night, after Kylie had gone to bed and the Gardners had driven Tobin and Aunt Enid back to the airport. Martin had lived here for many years, and the residents of Lac Vert were fiercely protective of his privacy. He assured May that no word of their marriage would leak out, no reporters would spoil their honeymoon.

It was their first time as man and wife, their first time together at all. Getting undressed in the bathroom, May's fingers shook as she unzipped her dress. She had bought a new peach silk negligee, but suddenly she realized she had left it in the bedroom, where Martin now waited. So she pulled on his old white shirt, hanging behind the door.

Walking along the upstairs hall, she saw that the bedroom door was ajar. Shadows were dancing on the ceiling. As May entered their bedroom, she saw Martin lying on the old iron bed. She had been intending to grab her tissue-wrapped nightgown and hurry back to change into it, but as she passed the bed she saw his bare chest and shoulder gleaming in the light of one blue candle. He took her wrist and held it.

"Where are you going?" he asked.

"I have to change—"

"Come here," he said, easing her down onto the bed. She sat on the edge, but then he pulled the sheet back and helped her climb under. Their eyes were shining, face to face, as he started kissing her softly.

"Stay," he said. "You don't have to change."

"I do. I want you to always remember—"

"Remember this night? I will, May. You don't have to worry about that." His hands traced her shoulders and upper arms, mas-

saging her back as he kissed the side of her neck. May shivered from his touch. His body felt so hard and strong under the covers, and she wanted more of it. She pressed against him instead of pulling away, and she knew that nightie wasn't going to get worn tonight.

"I can't believe it," she said. "That we're here together, married . . ."

"May Cartier," he said, smiling and kissing her. "Or are you going to stay May Taylor?"

She shook her head, feeling his arms around her. "May Cartier," she said. "It'll take some getting used to, though. I've used Taylor my whole life."

"This is what I want to get used to," he said, kissing her throat, the spot between her collarbones, her breasts. "Being with you."

The candlelight brought wildness to the room, the way the flame flickered and danced. Who needs a hundred candles? May thought. One is amazing. Just as their simple ceremony had been filled with intense power and grace. Now Martin held the sides of her body as she arched her back, reaching toward him, touching the side of his face.

His expression was tender, but his arms were bands of iron. His stomach was as hard as marble, and one part of her felt awed and amused to be looking, as it were, under the jersey of the Bruins' biggest star. Hiking up on one elbow, she felt his muscle and smiled at the way he rolled his eyes. Teasing him, she pressed all the way up his arm.

"The Gold Sledgehammer . . ." She kissed his chest. "Now I know the real meaning."

"May," he said, trembling under her lips, her tongue.

"How do you get muscles like this?" she asked. "Do you work out all year round?"

"From now till September, not at all," he said, laughing.

In the candlelight, May could see various scars. On his chin, over both eyes, the left side of his head, behind his right ear: she could imagine all the flying pucks and sticks striking his beautiful body. But across his chest, the scars looked different and mysterious: two long vertical lines, straight down the middle, and an X directly over his heart. She had been teasing, but at the sight of those scars she felt cold inside.

"What happened?" she asked.

"Don't, May," he said, his eyes closed.

"Tell me, Martin. They look—"

But he didn't give her a chance to finish. He rolled her onto her back, and kissed her hard. His intensity exploded. He whispered her name, holding her against him as if he needed her more than anything.

May held him tight. She felt him inside her, their eyes locked together, moving in rhythm. Every surface of him was hard as ivory, but at the same time they were melting together. She stared at him with passion and trust, her new husband, and she knew this was what she had been missing all these years. Not because he was a hockey star, not because he was the strongest man she'd ever touched, but because he was Martin, her husband, the man she had been waiting for her entire life.

—

True to his word, Martin taught Kylie how to row and swim in the lake. Although she had swum in pools and on the beach, she had always been afraid of the grass and leaves hiding in muddy lake bottoms. Martin told her the easiest way was to walk out on the dock, hold on to the wooden ladder so she wouldn't have to touch the mud, and lower herself straight into the water.

May sat in the gazebo, watching them. The sun was hot, so she stayed covered with sunscreen, one of Martin's shirts, and a big hat. She had sketched every detail of her wedding, so she would have it forever. Now, she drew her husband and daughter on the dock, in the old rowboat, their heads bobbing in the blue water.

"I'm touching stringy stuff with my toe," Kylie called out.

"It's just grass," Martin told her. "It won't hurt you."

"It feels scary, like witch's hair." Kylie scrambled into Martin's arms. He was treading water, holding her up.

"Mental toughness," he said, gazing into Kylie's eyes. "That's what you need more of, just like a hockey player. Don't let it get to you. Tell yourself it's just grass, not witch's hair. Over and over. Let me hear you say it."

"It's just grass, not witch's hair," Kylie repeated. "It's just grass, not witch's hair."

May laughed, scribbling notes in her journal so she would never forget the day her husband gave his best pro-athlete, NHL-training advice to Kylie. Her daughter said the words over and over, and May watched as she let go of Martin slowly, easing herself back into the lake.

"It's just grass, not witch's hair, it's . . . It's WITCH'S HAIR!"

she yelled out as soon as her toes touched the wispy strands, scrambling back into Martin's arms, making him laugh out loud.

———

The three of them set out one morning to row to an island in the lake. It was sunny and bright, and May had packed a picnic lunch. She sat in the stern, and Kylie rode lookout in the bow, while Martin sat in the middle, pulling on the oars. His oars never seemed to touch the water. They would slice in without a splash and send the boat gliding forward.

Around every bend, white-throated loons swam and dived. Deer grazed along the shore, fleeing into pine groves at the sight of the boat. Twenty minutes passed, then half an hour, and Martin just kept rowing. As the sun rose higher, he slowed down to pull off his shirt. May trailed her fingers in the lake, watching rivers of sweat pour down his bare chest, wishing they were all alone.

With Kylie up front, occupied with spying wildlife, Martin and May teased each other in low voices. May wore a blue bathing suit, and she had pulled the straps down to tan her shoulders. Her eyes kept darting to the strange scars on his chest, hidden in his curly hair, but he was so handsome and sexy she nearly forgot about them.

"In your wildest dreams," May said, "did you ever imagine honeymooning with a six-year-old along?"

"It makes things interesting," Martin replied, giving May a passionate look.

"An island?" May asked. "A private island? That's where we're going?"

"*Mon Dieu*, May. You look good in that bathing suit."

"A private island . . ." May tilted her head back and closed her eyes as she imagined spreading out their blanket, taking off their clothes, making love . . .

"Fish!" Kylie yelled, so excited she jumped up and nearly fell in. "Huge, gigantic fish! Look, Mommy and Da—!" She stopped herself from saying "Daddy."

"Sit down, honey," May called.

"We're just about over the old trout hole," Martin said, glancing over. "This is where the great-granddaddy of the lake lives. Those are his lieutenants."

"A trout army?" Kylie asked.

"Yes," Martin said. "Led by the biggest rainbow trout you've ever seen. Ray and I have tried to catch him our whole lives."

"You never have?"

"Once," Martin said. "But he got away."

"He wouldn't get away from me," Kylie said, peering into the dark, still water.

"I'll take you fishing here some morning. Have to get up early, though. Before dawn."

"Okay, I'll be ready," Kylie said. But then she spotted a black bear eating berries on the shore. Two cubs emerged from the brambles. Kylie squealed, pointing, and Martin held her to let her know she was safe. May stared at his bare arms, his wide shoulders, and she thought of the night before.

But her passion took in so much more than just the physical: She loved the way Martin talked to Kylie, how he seemed to enjoy playing with her. May loved how they were all becoming a family together. By the time they got to the island, Martin and Kylie were starving. May set up the picnic, and she tried to eat, but she was just too happy. All she could do was lie back, feel the sun on her face, and wish for their honeymoon never to end.

On the way back, with the sun sliding behind the north ridge, the air turned cool. Both May and Kylie had gotten more sun than they were used to, so Kylie slept in the bottom of the boat while Martin rowed home.

"Wouldn't you like me to row for a while?" May asked.

Martin just smiled, shaking his head.

"Don't you think I can?" she asked.

"You can, but you don't have to," Martin said. "I want to take care of you, May. Is that bad?"

"No." She felt a lump in her throat, and tears sprang to her eyes. It had been a long day, and she was tired, but her feelings were deep and more complicated than that.

"What is it?" he asked, reaching out his leg to touch her toe with his.

"It's been such a long time since I've felt . . ." she began, the tears running down her cheeks. "My father took care of me. He was everything to me—to both of us, me and my mother. I've never really had anyone take care of me since he died."

"Not even Kylie's father?" Martin asked in a low voice.

"Especially not him," May said. "He wanted no part of us."

"He's a fool."

May nodded, wiping her eyes as she gazed down at her daugh-

ter, sleeping in the bottom of the boat. Curled up on a pile of sweaters, she was perfectly still. "Look what he's missing," May whispered.

"Where is he now?"

"Boston. The checks come straight from his law firm. Never a personal note or call."

"Some fathers aren't worth the name," Martin said, gazing with even deeper tenderness at Kylie.

"Are you talking about your father?"

Martin nodded as he rowed. "It wasn't always that way. At the beginning, he was the best. He taught me to fish and skate right here. Taught me to row this very boat. But then fame and fortune began to matter more, and he chose them over us. Me and my mother."

"In a way that might hurt more," May said.

"How do you mean?" Martin asked, the oars gently splashing the water's surface.

"To love someone so much, and to have him taken away," May said. She knew from experience, having lost her own father.

"He wasn't taken away," Martin said. "He *went* away. That was his choice. Not everyone in life has good motives."

"Martin." She was staring at the scars on his chest. "What happened to you? Was it something to do with your father?"

"Please, May. Don't ruin a perfect day," he said, frowning as he grabbed his shirt and put it on. "That story has no business in this boat, with you and Kylie. Okay, May? Leave it alone."

The warmth had left his eyes, and he started to row harder, getting them home as fast as he could.

Two mornings in a row, they wakened with an uneasiness between them. They'd have great sex, and while May kept hoping for Martin to start talking, he kept jumping out of bed for his morning run. Then he'd tell her to sleep late while he took Kylie out fishing for the great-granddaddy trout. Lying in bed, she listened to them getting ready downstairs. Kylie was so excited, she talked nonstop.

May tried to appreciate the bond growing between her husband and daughter, but why did she feel Martin was using it to avoid spending too much time alone with her? Fishing with a six-year-old was much easier than opening up to her mother. Kylie, for her part, was being cautious: she had yet to call Martin "Daddy."

After a long bath and two cups of coffee, May took a walk through the house. She hadn't seen Natalie's doll since the wedding, and she wanted to make sure Kylie had put it back where she'd found it. The doll seemed to have disappeared, but every time May entered a room, she saw something she hadn't noticed the time before. Family pictures, a collection of fossils, an old leather-bound Bible, embroidered pillows on the back of a sofa, framed photos of the lake and mountains. Today she found a basket of knitting—a red sweater half-done—by an armchair in the living room. Crouching down to look more closely, she was surprised by a voice.

"That was Agnes's," said Genny Gardner. She stood in the doorway, holding a glass jar.

"Oh, hi!" May said, standing up.

"I brought you some strawberry jam that I made yesterday, and I was going to tell you about the great aphrodisiac qualities of Lac Vert strawberries, how all honeymooners should eat them, but let's face it—it's just an excuse to barge in!"

May smiled, watching Genny throw up her hands, as if she'd just been caught in the act.

"I saw Martin and Kylie fishing on the lake, so I knew you'd be home alone. I've been dying to come over and talk to you. In fact, I promised Tobin I'd stop by and make sure you were getting along all right."

"I'm glad you did," May said. "It felt so strange, meeting Martin's best friends for the first time at our wedding. We should have given you a little warning. Tobin said she could have used about six months' notice. Was Ray shocked?"

Genny laughed. "Surprised at first, but very happy for Martin. I thought it was wonderful. The most romantic wedding I've ever been to."

"Really? Thank you," May said, beaming. "Would you like some coffee? And toast for the jam?"

"Sure." Genny followed May into the kitchen and took out the coffee while May rinsed out the pot. Then she set the jam on the table and started opening a drawer for a knife, but May watched her stop herself. Although she must have known where everything was, she wanted May to feel like it was her kitchen. May appreciated the gesture, and she let Genny know with a smile.

"Agnes was Martin's mother?" May asked, settling down across the pine table.

"Yes," Genny said. "She was a wonderful lady. Ray loved her

almost as much as his own mother, and that's saying something. It's such a shame she died before meeting you. She would have been happy to see Martin settled down."

"I thought Martin said she had died a few years ago."

"She did. Oh, you mean because her knitting's still there?"

"Yes," May said.

Genny smiled. Petite, with short blond hair and wide gray eyes, she had a deep warmth about her. "Martin can't bring himself to put it away," Genny said. "That's what I think. He's tough as nails, the scourge of the NHL, but he misses his mother very much. She loved needlework of all kinds, but she also coached him and Ray when they were young, and she held him together after—God, after all of it."

"Do you mean after his daughter died?"

"Especially that," Genny said. "But in a way, everything was all tied together. The divorce, Serge going to prison. Martin almost lost his mind. He disappeared into the woods for two weeks, and Ray honestly didn't think he'd ever come out."

May had so many questions. She wanted to know everything, but from Martin himself. So she just poured the coffee and listened to Genny talk.

"Agnes was solid as a rock. Hockey mothers, hockey wives—you'll see."

"She was a hockey wife, too, right?"

"Yes, married to Serge. Poor Serge—he made some bad mistakes and hurt himself and everyone else. Martin hates him, you know."

"I know."

"That wasn't always the way. Martin totally idolized him as a child. He was so proud—to have a father who could play like Serge! Both Martin and Ray worshiped him. Just imagine living in the sticks out here, reading about him in the papers, having all their friends talk about him."

"But imagine Martin waiting for him to come home," May said, aching for her husband as a child.

"That, too," Genny agreed.

"Loving his father that much," May said, remembering what she'd said in the boat, "must have made the disappointment much worse later. When he felt Serge had let him down."

"Serge let *hockey* down," Genny said. "His team, the fans, Canada. He liked to gamble, but it wasn't until he bet against his

own team and got caught that the trouble really started. He let down the whole NHL."

"That's not half as bad as letting down his son."

"Oh, Martin's lucky to have you," Genny said, nodding. "I'm glad you see him this way."

"What way?" May asked.

"As a real person. An ordinary man who used to be a sweet little boy. Most of the world sees him as the Gold Sledgehammer, the great star defenseman, the sexy killer who loves to fight. At least, most of his other women saw him that—" Genny stopped herself abruptly. "I'm so sorry, May."

"That's okay." May served the toast to Genny, opening the jar of strawberry jam. "Well, we both have pasts. I know he was married before. Plus yesterday he got a sackload of fan mail, and I couldn't help noticing all the envelopes with women's handwriting."

"You'll have to get used to that," Genny said. "Even Ray gets plenty, and he's never been voted 'sexiest athlete alive.' Plus, he's been married to me for fourteen years."

"You must think I came out of nowhere," May said. "Marrying Martin so quickly."

"We're thrilled," Genny told her. "I've known Martin nearly as long as Ray has. I grew up in Ste-Anne-des-Monts, up the valley from here. They were great skaters even back then, and we joke that I was their first groupie. Then they joke that they were mine, too—I skiied in the Olympics."

"Another great athlete." May was impressed.

"Years and years ago."

"You've been together forever," May said.

"And that's why I'm so glad you've come along," Genny told her. "I'm tired of worrying about Martin all by myself. And sitting at games with no one to talk to. Just wait till the press hears about you, though. They won't leave you alone."

"They won't care about me," May said. "I'm just a wedding planner who fell in love."

"With Martin Cartier," Genny said. "Just wait and see."

May laughed, but right now she wanted to take the chance to speak to Genny about Natalie.

Just then, she heard voices outside. The screen door creaked open, and Kylie came running in. Martin was right behind her, holding the rods, looking worried.

"Mommy, I caught a fish. He wasn't the great-granddaddy," Kylie said, her face pale. "But he was pretty big."

"Where is he?" Genny asked, smiling.

"Kylie wanted to let him go," Martin said. "So we did."

"Fishes have families too." Kylie sounded upset. "It was okay to catch him as long as I let him go, right, Mommy?"

"Right, honey."

"She put her hands over her ears," Martin said. "She said the crying was so loud."

"It stopped, though." Kylie stared up at May with worried eyes. "As soon as we put him back in the water. He had speckles everywhere. He swam away, straight back to his kids."

"You heard the fish crying?" Genny asked, smiling. "What an imagination!"

Kylie stared at May. "Don't take me to the doctor again. I don't want to go. He doesn't believe me, but you do, right? You believe I heard the fish crying?"

"I do, honey."

May hugged Kylie, her sensitive girl. As a child, May had never liked killing bugs, even mosquitos. The last time she'd taken Kylie to the psychologists, she'd felt Kylie was treated like a specimen. What was the truth?

"I'm glad we let the fish go," Kylie said.

"So am I," May told her.

All of May's anxieties dissolved in the heat and light of summer on Lac Vert. The Gardners' daughter Charlotte offered to baby-sit Kylie overnight at their house up the lake, and May said yes. The three of them—Martin, May, and Kylie—spent the day fishing and picnicking on the island, Martin and May looking forward to their first honeymoon night all alone. Rowing north on the lake, toward the Gardners' house on the far shore, they felt sunburned and happy.

"Is she sleeping?" Martin asked, looking down at Kylie, who was curled up on the picnic blanket in the stern.

"Out cold," May said, smiling. "She's having so much fun, she's knocking herself out."

"That's what growing up on a lake will do for you. Everything's an adventure," Martin said. "When you're six, anyway."

"Or thirty-six." May touched his toe with her bare foot.

"Careful, woman." Martin grinned. "Don't get me going."

"Okay, okay," May said, pretending to be disappointed. "Tell me about being six and having adventures."

"You know, snapping turtles in the mud, the fox family in the dead tree, panther tracks that turn out to be Ray's father's dog, the fish that grows a little every time he gets away . . ."

"I think that's the guy Kylie's been after."

"Yes, she likes to fish—as long as we file down the hook and let him go. She's got the knack for a real good fish tale. An excellent imagination on her, just like her mother. You would have been great growing up here, fit right in. What'd you look like at six, May? Let's see . . ."

Feeling Martin stare at her, May began to blush. She ducked her head, but he stuck one oar under his arm and reached over to tilt her face up.

"Freckles," he said. "Definitely freckles. And braids, right?"

"Right."

"Let me see." Martin watched her separate her hair into two pieces, start to twist the strands on the left. She was halfway done when he stopped her with a kiss. "I love you, May. I wish I'd known you all our lives, since we were six."

"So do I," she whispered, wondering about his secrets. They started to kiss, but just then Kylie stirred, waking up slightly. She seemed to be having a dream, and she tossed and turned, crying out. Martin drew back, smiling ruefully, letting May tend to her.

"Are you sunburned, sweetheart?" May asked.

"Oh, what happened, what happened?" Kylie mumbled.

"Nothing, Kylie," May said steadily, wanting to bring Kylie awake slowly.

"Yes, something bad!"

"Sweetheart . . ."

"Natalie!" Kylie cried out, rubbing her eyes.

Glancing up, May saw that Martin looked shocked, his smile gone, the color draining out of his face. He stared down at Kylie.

"Sssh," May said. "You're dreaming, honey. It's just a dream . . ."

"What happened to her?" Kylie asked, the words tearing out in a sob.

"Kylie," Martin said. "Don't cry. Please don't—"

"Did she drown in the lake?" Kylie wept, staring up at him. "Is that what happened to her?"

"No, Kylie." Martin suddenly sounded tired. His shoulders let go, and he seemed to rest for a moment on his oars, staring out at the mountains. As if feeling the chill, he reached back for his shirt. As he pulled it on, once again May noticed the maze of scars on his

chest. She shivered, drawing Kylie closer. "She didn't drown," Martin said.

"I want to call you Daddy," Kylie cried. "But I can't until you tell me what happened to her. I can't, I can't."

May held her breath. For an instant she was afraid Martin wouldn't say anything more, that he would leave Kylie wondering what had happened to his daughter. Kylie was trying to stop crying, drawing her breath in deep gasps. May encircled her with her arms, needing Martin to answer the question—for May as much as for Kylie.

"Martin," May said, her eyes pleading. "Tell her."

He opened his mouth, his eyes washed in pain. He stared at Kylie, as if he wanted to find the words to explain, but when he spoke, the feeling drained out of his eyes.

"Martin?" May asked, her heart racing.

"I don't . . . I can't talk about Natalie," he said, and his eyes were cool and his voice was steady. "I'm sorry. She didn't drown, though. Okay, Kylie?"

"I'm not calling you Daddy." Kylie was sobbing against May's knee. "She told me to, she said I should . . ."

"Who told you to?" May asked, afraid to hear, cradling Kylie against her.

"She did," Kylie cried. "Natalie."

"Natalie didn't tell you anything," Martin said angrily.

"She did!"

"Take that back, Kylie," Martin yelled. "Natalie's dead!"

"Martin, stop that," May said, grabbing his arm. "You know she sees—"

"So help me," Martin began, then bit down on the rest of his words.

"She did tell me. I don't care whether you believe me, but I'm not calling you Daddy," Kylie sobbed. "I'm calling you Martin forever."

"I'm sorry about that," Martin said, but his eyes looked blank, like a man locked inside himself, and he didn't try to change Kylie's mind. Pulling hard on his left oar, he changed direction. The light coming through the pines on the west shore was now in May's eyes. Martin was rowing them home instead of to the Gardners', and no one in the boat said another word the rest of the way.

Chapter 9

GENNY CALLED TO ASK WHERE they were, and May said that Kylie had had a bad dream, that May didn't want to let her spend the night away from home. Her chest hurt, thinking of how extremely quiet Martin had been ever since Kylie had asked him about Natalie. But she just told Genny she'd talk to her tomorrow, and that they'd plan another time for Charlotte to baby-sit.

That night, Martin's silence seemed deeper than ever. He barely said a word. When May looked into his eyes, she hardly recognized him. His face was a mask, blank and expressionless. May cooked steak with baked potatoes, but he said he wasn't hungry. She and Kylie sat at the kitchen table alone, and May forced herself to eat so Kylie would.

"Can we talk?" May asked when she'd done the dishes and put Kylie to bed. Martin sat in the living room, a magazine on his lap, staring straight ahead. Waves of energy were pouring out of him, so strong May thought he could probably move furniture with it.

"Nothing to talk about," he said.

"Kylie talks to angels. Remember on the plane? When she knew we were going down?"

"That's just in her mind," Martin argued. "You told me she saw the picture in my wallet, that it planted an idea."

May nodded. "Natalie's picture, yes. I believe that real events are springboards for Kylie's dreams and fantasies. You know that diary I keep? It's about Kylie. I write down everything she tells me."

"I know," Martin said. "I've seen you."

"Some of it's about Natalie."

"She doesn't even know her."

"That doesn't matter," May said steadily. "She's very real to Kylie. Kylie considers Natalie to be her sister."

"May, stop," Martin said. "She hears the fish crying, too. She's creative, that's all."

"It all has to do with families," May explained. "It always has. 'The fish have families too.' Remember she said that?"

"I'm not ready for this," Martin told her. "I want to bury the past, eh? Just dig a big hole and shove it all inside. I know you worry about Kylie: I see you writing in that notebook. But, please, May—leave me out of it. Me and Natalie. I don't talk about her or the past. The past is separate."

May stared at him. "I think you've got it wrong," she said, suddenly furious. "It's connected now, not separate at all."

He banged through the screen door, and May watched him start running down to the lake and disappear around a bend. Her heart was pounding. She needed someone to talk to. She knew marriage was private, that a couple should solve their own problems, but suddenly she grabbed the phone and dialed Tobin's number.

"It's me," she said when Tobin answered.

"How's the honeymoon?"

"Over before it began," May said. "I'm so mad, I swear I feel like—"

"Whoa, tell me what happened."

"Martin just ran out of here." She took a huge breath.

"What happened?"

May told her about Kylie asking about Natalie and Martin's reaction. "He told me he'd like to bury the past. He doesn't want to talk about his daughter, and Kylie keeps dreaming about her."

"That sounds like Kylie," Tobin said. "Her imagination has been piqued, and her dreams take shape."

"You know her so well," May said, feeling grateful to Tobin, outraged at Martin. "I should have married you, goddamn it."

"We've known that all along. But, listen—Martin will know her soon. You're going to hate to hear this, but give him time. That's the best marriage advice I know. You have to get used to each other."

"He took off at a dead run, just to get away from me."

"So run in the opposite direction. Remember when John and I were first married? How much overtime I put in at the Barn?"

"I thought you were saving for a down payment."

"That, too. But we needed space so we wouldn't fight all the time."

"You were each other's first real loves," May said, wishing that

was true for her and Martin. "Neither of you had ever been married before, you didn't have kids with other people. You were right about the book being half written."

"What do you mean?"

"We both have so much baggage," May told her. "Even though I wasn't married to Gordon—"

"You have the scars to show for it."

"It drives me crazy that he won't talk to his father," May said, thinking of real scars.

"Because you wish you could talk to yours."

"And that he won't tell me about Natalie."

"Give him time," Tobin repeated, lowering her voice to sound old and wise.

May laughed.

"I'm glad you called me. I've been afraid you're bonding too much with Genny Gardner. She's nice, isn't she?"

"Very," May said.

"Is she becoming your best friend?"

"I already have one of those," May said.

"Try to talk to him alone," Tobin advised. "When running in the opposite direction fails, try coming together. One way or the other, I know he loves you and deep down wants to talk."

"How do you know?" May asked.

"It's John's best-kept secret," Tobin said. "But he wants me to know everything."

———

That night, Martin slept on the couch. By dawn, when he hadn't come to bed, May felt hollow inside. She went about her day, trying to concentrate on the jobs in front of her. After Martin stayed up late again, watching TV and falling asleep, May knew they were in trouble. Calling Genny, she asked if Charlotte could watch Kylie so she could have some time alone with Martin.

When she got back from taking Kylie to Genny's, she found him sitting out in the backyard, hands gripping the arms of the old birchwood chair, staring at the lake. He didn't look up at her approach, even though her shadow fell right across his face. May stared down at him, her heart pounding. She saw the veins pulsing in his temples. He was scowling, and she hadn't even spoken yet.

He had been running: He wore shorts and a T-shirt, and he was soaked with sweat. His arms and legs gleamed with it, and his hair

was pushed back from his eyes. Ever since the fight, all Martin had done was run and row and pummel the punching bag hanging in the barn. She had heard him last night, pounding the bag as if he wanted to kill it. The sound had filled May with fear, and she had lain awake until he had stopped.

"You're leaving me," he said. It wasn't a question, and it brought May up short.

"Are you kidding?" she asked.

"I'm acting like an animal, I know it," he said.

"If you know it, then I don't have to tell you," she replied.

"Leave me alone, eh?" he asked.

She didn't say a word, but she looked down at his face. Martin stared out over her head; his jaw and eyes had grown hard over the last two days. Crickets hummed in the tall grass behind the barn. The sky was purple over the lake and blue-gold above the mountains. Swallows dipped in and out of the shadows, catching bugs. Fish rose to the surface of the lake, snapping at low-cruising flies.

May's gaze fell on Martin's hands. They were grasping the chair arms, each finger tense and digging in. The veins on his hands and wrists were blue, raised and surrounded by golden hair. His knuckles were bruised from punching the bag. Leaning forward, she kissed the purple knuckle of the index finger of Martin's right hand. Then the middle finger, then the ring finger.

"May," he growled. "Stop."

She didn't. She kissed the knuckle of the little finger of his right hand and then the thumb. Shifting around Martin's sweaty knees, she started on his left hand. She sensed the tension draining out of his fingers, out of his arms.

"Leave me alone," he repeated.

"I can't," May said, because now she had gotten to the ring finger of his left hand, to his wedding ring. Kissing his knuckle, she licked the gold band. She thought she heard him groan, and then she felt his right hand on the back of her head.

"What are you doing?"

"We have baggage," she said. "That's the whole problem."

"Baggage?"

"Don't you hate the word? It sounds like something you'd hear on a talk show. Like two big suitcases filled with the past. You have one and I have one."

"I'd like to kick mine off a cliff," he said, staring across the lake.

"The thing is," she said, "I don't think that would work. It would find you. You can't ditch it just because you want to."

"So what do I do?"

Purple shadows had spread all the way up the mountains, into the sky. This far north the summer sky stayed light long into the night, clear and radiant with particles of gold dust. The evening star appeared in the luminous sky, and up the lake a loon screamed.

"I want to help you," May told him.

"When it comes to this, to her, no one can," Martin murmured into her neck.

"Natalie," May said, because Martin hadn't said her name.

May pushed back slightly, leaving just enough space between them so she could look clearly into his eyes. They were bruised and troubled, almost to the point of panic. But they weren't angry anymore.

"I'm sorry for how I've acted," he said. "It's been bad, and I know it. But I've never gotten this close to anyone before, at least not since she died. When I think about her, when her name comes up, I go crazy. When it's during the season, I just take it out on the other team. On the ice, that's easy."

"But it's summer," May said. "And there's no ice."

"No, there's not. And there's you and Kylie."

"Yep."

"In summer, usually I do what I did today, yesterday, the day before. Work out till it's time to sleep. I'm tired, May. Can we—" He sounded better, as if his old spirit was coming back, and May knew he was going to suggest going inside, eating dinner, heading upstairs.

"Let's stay out here," she said.

The sky was bright and dark at the same time, and May could feel Martin shaking. Dragging the other chair closer, she sat.

"We were divorced, her mother and I," Martin began. "Trisha lived—lives—in California, Santa Monica, and Natalie came up to spend the summer with me. Trisha was glad. She never gave me any trouble about having Nat. She liked the freedom, but it wasn't only that. She knew Nat and I weren't about to do without each other just because she had another thing going."

May listened, staring up into the endless sky.

"It was seven years ago, July, hot and muggy. Natalie was six then. I'd screwed up my knee that season, really bad, and I'd had surgery in Detroit before coming up here. One day I was riding

bikes with Natalie, stupid the doctor told me, and I don't know— my knee just went out. So I was back in the hospital, the so-called one right down the lake in LaSalle."

"Natalie was with you?" May asked, knowing how scared the little girl must have been, remembering how upset Kylie had felt the time May had cut herself on a broken glass and had to get stitches at the Coastline Clinic.

"Wouldn't leave my side." Martin grinned.

"Loyal daughter."

"To the point of stubbornness. They took me to Toronto, to a better hospital and a top knee guy."

"At Twigg University?" May asked, picturing the familiar brick buildings.

"Near there," Martin said. "Hockey players are his specialty. Trisha wanted Nat to come right home, but we said forget it. I'd be laid up for a week at the most, and she'd be reading to me when I got bored just sitting still."

A fish jumped in the lake, and the rings spread out collecting starlight and the strange golden shine spreading down from the darkening sky. May listened to the splash recede and waited for Martin to go on.

"My father lived in Toronto," Martin continued. "Pretty near the hospital. We weren't on great terms back then, but it was better than when I was a kid. Took me a long time to forgive him enough to let him come watch me play, when that's all I ever wanted anyway. He was a bastard to my mother, and what the hell—I took myself seriously as man of the family. But he never stopped trying. Kept sending those cards and letters, and when he found out he had a granddaughter, he was relentless. Doted on Natalie like mad. Went to visit her every chance he got."

"All the way to Santa Monica?" May asked.

"Yep. And she loved him. Gave him the benefit of the doubt I never could. He was her grandpa, the guy who built her a life-size playhouse with a real doorbell and a refrigerator for her snacks. To Nat, he could do no wrong."

"She brought you back together? You and your father?" May asked, thinking that was how family was supposed to be: love and different generations building over and healing the rifts of the past.

"For a little while." Martin's voice sounded dangerous.

"He took care of her while you were in the hospital?"

Martin nodded. A mosquito buzzed close to his head, and he caught it in one hand. The loon called again, but when Martin

slammed his hand down on the arm of his chair, the entire lake fell silent. "He took care of her, and he killed her."

The blood in May's body began to burn, and she felt every hair on her skin stand up. "No," she heard herself say.

"He's a gambler," Martin said. "You know that, right? That he's in prison for betting against his own team, for hiding assets so he didn't have to pay taxes?"

"He didn't kill Natalie," May whispered, because the idea was so unthinkable, so much worse than anything she had imagined.

Martin began to take off his T-shirt.

The sky glowed, as if somewhere deep inside the night there was a candle giving forth rich blue light. It bounced off the mountain walls, turning the pine trees golden green, making every rock surface shine. Martin's chest was bare now, and every muscle seemed defined by the strange light. The hairs glistened, and underneath them May saw the bizarre pattern of crisscrossed scars.

"Gamblers owe money," Martin said. "They all do, one way or another. They might win for a while, but that doesn't last forever. When I was ten, some guy my father owed money to wrote on my chest with a knife. He did this."

May traced the scars with her fingertips, tears streaming down her cheeks.

"My mother found out and said my father could never see me again. He moved out that night and he kept his word. Never saw me again until I was grown up, playing pro hockey."

"They're so deep," May cried, feeling the scars thick as ropes across Martin's wide chest.

"He said he'd changed," Martin said. "That that stuff was in the past. He was an old man, he said, a grandfather. All he cared about was family—me and Natalie. We were all he had. He was just an old man."

"When you were in the hospital—" May suddenly felt the night go cold. The sky's glow shut down, and they could have been anywhere—in Black Hall, at the beach—instead of beside a lake ringed with mountains. The sky was pitch black now, dotted with ordinary stars.

"I knew," Martin said. "That's the part I can't forget or get over. I'd experienced it myself, what my father's greed could do. I knew he'd owed money once, and what made me think he didn't owe it again?"

"He owed money?"

"Big money. A fortune. Enough to make him bet against the

team he coached. Enough to make someone come after him and—"

May blinked, suddenly glad the light was gone. She couldn't see Martin's scars anymore, and when she took her fingers away, she couldn't feel them either. She was shaking, and when Martin spoke, she could tell by the sound of his voice that he was, too.

"Hockey stars make a lot of money," Martin said. "You wouldn't know it from this house, but we do. Coaches, too. My father was a rich man. In ways besides money, but money was what mattered that day."

"What day?" May asked.

"The day they came to collect my father's debt," Martin said.

"And he had Natalie with him?"

"He lived in an apartment by Lake Ontario. A big shiny place, where other famous people lived. It was always getting pointed out by those paddlewheel tours. Nat got such a big kick out of that. She'd be playing on the terrace, and she'd hear some garbled microphone voice saying 'And that's where Serge Cartier lives . . .' as the boat cruised by." He stopped, and then, as if it were an afterthought, added, "She was on the terrace that day."

May heard the loon cry out, far up the lake, its call throaty and insane.

"The guy held her upside down, over the railing," Martin said.

"No," May whispered.

"She must have been scared, eh? But she didn't show it. Even when he brought her back in, put her down safe. She ran straight to my father. Hugged him hard. With everything they put her through, she was worried about him—knew he was in big trouble."

May had thought Martin was going to say the man had thrown Natalie over the side, and she felt herself relax almost imperceptibly. She had been holding her breath, and she started to breathe again.

"My father wanted her out of the way. Says he thought the guy might try to hurt her again. So he pushed her—not hard, he says. *Still* says. She hit her head on the corner of a table, but she jumped right back up. No harm done."

"Then—" May began, confused.

"She came home with me. Stayed the last two weeks. She told me about the bad guy and the terrace railing, but she never said a thing about her grandfather shoving her. I called my father, told him he was out of my life again and this time forever, and he's the

one who mentioned Natalie hitting her head. I didn't think anything of it—I was too busy hating his guts."

Martin was breathing hard, as if he had just run a race.

"Her eyes looked a little cloudy, but I told myself that was because she was crying. She always did when we were about to say good-
bye. She was scheduled to fly back to her mother that next day."

Martin's groan shook the night. It sent the night birds flying,
their wings slapping the surface of the lake. May held his hand, crying silently beside him.

"She died that night."

"Oh, Martin."

"In her sleep."

"God," May whispered.

"They did an autopsy. She'd had a concussion, and a blood clot
had formed. She had a cerebral hemorrhage. My father called that
night, taking all the blame, crying that he'd never meant for it to
happen."

"Of course he didn't."

"The blame was mine," Martin said, gripping the chair arms
again. "For trusting the son of a bitch in the first place, and then
for not getting her checked out."

"It wasn't your fault."

"I tried telling myself that for a long time. I hate my father so
much, it's almost possible to believe it's all his. Sometimes I forget
he's doing time for racketeering and tax evasion, not murder."

"Blame never helps," May said, thinking of how her parents
had died, how for so long she had wanted to blame the truck driver,
hate someone for taking her parents away.

"It might not help," Martin said. "But it's there. So you can see
how I couldn't tell Kylie what she wanted to know. I couldn't tell
her how I put my own child in danger, then failed to get her help.
Just hearing her say Natalie's name, I went crazy."

"You're not crazy," May said. "You're grieving."

They had been holding hands, and now they embraced hard, as
if they had one skin between them, and she felt his heart pounding
against hers. He was crying, but he didn't want to let her know. His
shoulders heaved; she held him the best she could.

The wind picked up. Leaves rustled overhead, and pine boughs
brushed the rocky sides of the mountain. More stars had come out,
and now milky galaxies flowed overhead.

"Kylie would be scared of me if she knew what happened to
Natalie," he said.

"We tell the truth to each other, Kylie and I," May told him. "It's how we've always done things."

"And we will tell her the truth—together. But she'll be scared. I worry for her, May. You think I don't, but I worry a lot. I see you writing in that blue notebook."

"The diary."

"Keeping track of her dreams. I don't want to be the cause of more nightmares for her. I know she thinks about Natalie being dead. And she died in a horrible way."

"I'm so sorry. Thank you for thinking of Kylie," May said.

"I do. She's my stepdaughter. You said yesterday that everything's connected. Everything and everyone."

"I believe that's true," May said, and Martin held her. But she found herself thinking about the other person in the story, still as alive and as connected as any of them, the man Martin never talked about: his father.

Chapter 10

As their time in Lac Vert drew closer to its end, every day seemed more important. Summer seemed shorter this year than it ever had before. On their last day, Martin asked Kylie if she wanted to take an early morning row out to the fishing hole, to see if they could find the great-granddaddy trout.

"Sure," Kylie said, with a certain reluctance dating back to the very bad dream-day, out in the boat, when Martin had yelled so loud. Although there had been hikes, rows, and picnics since then, Kylie had mostly made sure her mother was along, too. But today she was eager to go with him. Lately he had been as nice as he'd been at the beginning.

"Come on, then," Martin said, grabbing the oars, rods, buckets, and filed-down hooks. Kylie dug worms in the old potato patch while Martin loaded the rowboat. Her feet were bare, and the dirt wedged up between her toes.

They headed straight out, gliding over the smooth water. A rippling V formed behind them as the oars dipped and rose. Kylie leaned back in the old wooden boat and smelled summer: lake water, dried mud in the bottom of the boat, pine needles sparkling on the trees. Loons and swans swam along the shore.

Martin didn't speak, so neither did Kylie. She stared at him and wondered what made people get lines around their eyes and mouth. Absently, she touched her own smooth face. Martin saw what she was doing and smiled. But he just kept rowing.

When they got to the fishing hole, Martin baited their hooks and they dropped their lines in. When the sun came out from behind the trees, Martin pulled two caps out of the bucket. He stuck one on his head and held the other out to Kylie.

"Put this on," he told her.

"What is it?" She held the cap in her hand. Navy blue felt, with

a blue-jay insignia, it was identical to Martin's, only smaller. The felt was worn, the leather strap in back slightly curled. Holding it, a slight shock went through Kylie's fingers, and she knew that the hat had belonged to Natalie.

"A baseball hat," he said.

"But you play hockey."

"True," he said. "But a hockey helmet would be pretty hot out here on the water. In summer, we wear baseball hats."

"This was Natalie's?" Kylie asked, staring up at him.

"Yep, it was." Martin squinted as he cast his line again.

Kylie thought back to that day, when he'd yelled at her in the boat. Soon afterward, he and Mommy had told her why: He missed Natalie so much, he sometimes got upset when he thought about her. Then Mommy had told Kylie how Natalie had died, that she had tripped and hit her head while visiting her grandfather, that Martin hadn't known how serious it was and hadn't taken her to the doctor in time to save her. And he felt very, very bad about that.

"Why are you letting me wear it?" Kylie asked now.

Instead of answering, he just squinted and frowned harder, staring at the lake's surface as if he could see every trout swimming below.

"Martin?" she asked.

"So the sun won't be in your eyes," he said finally.

"Oh." Kylie nodded as she jammed the hat onto her head. His answer made perfect sense; the sun was getting higher, and Mommy didn't like her getting too sunburned. Martin smiled to see her wearing it. He reached out, adjusting the peak.

"*Voilà*," he said.

"Thanks, D—" Kylie said. For the first time since he'd yelled, she had nearly called him Daddy. But she held the word in. "Thanks, Martin," she said instead.

"You're welcome, Kylie," he said.

Was it Kylie's imagination, or did he look disappointed? No matter; they both got on with their fishing. Martin wasn't mad anymore. Kylie felt peace in the boat, coming from Martin, especially when he looked at the hat on her head. It was almost as if, by looking at the baseball cap, he was able to see Natalie.

"Oh, wow," Kylie said suddenly.

"What?" Martin asked.

Natalie stood on the eastern side, dressed in cool white, her wings flapping up a storm. Kylie moved over to fish off the boat's left side, and she never looked away from Natalie.

"I love my father," Natalie said, her lower lip wobbling.

"I know," Kylie whispered.

"Just seeing him makes me remember how much."

Kylie listened and stared, but she couldn't talk in a normal voice because Martin was there, fishing off the other side of the boat. She wouldn't take her eyes off Natalie for a second.

"He gave you my cap," Natalie said.

"Do you want it?"

Natalie bowed her head and began to cry. Her answer didn't seem to be yes, but it wasn't no either.

"Please tell me," Kylie said.

"He gave me so many things," Natalie said. "It used to be so much easier, when I thought things were what mattered."

"Don't they?"

Natalie shook her head. "I'm trying to tell you . . . you're learning. But boats and toys and even that cap aren't very important compared with love."

Kylie laughed. "Of course they're important! I can touch them and see them."

"Some things you can't see with your eyes," Natalie said, starting to fade. "Help Daddy to understand."

"What?" Kylie asked as Natalie disappeared. How could she say the cap was not important? Hadn't it made her cry?

Kylie wondered if the cap would float across the lake. She took it off her head, dipped it in the water. Letting go, she watched it tilt like a small boat, then quickly fill and start to sink.

"Whoa, you lost your cap," Martin said, reaching out to grab it.

"Sorry," Kylie said.

"I didn't feel the breeze come up," he said, drying off the cap, securing it on her head. He gave her a funny look, as if maybe he suspected something.

"My head was hot," Kylie said, scanning the shore. "I wanted to get it wet."

"We'll go for one last swim when we get back to shore," Martin said, starting to row for home. Standing under the pine trees, Natalie materialized. Kylie thought of what she had said about things you can't see with your eyes. Just then, Natalie blew Kylie a kiss, and confused, Kylie blew one back.

———

Leaving Lac Vert that summer meant saying farewell, after one final dinner at the Gardners', to Genny and Ray, Charlotte and

Mark. The Cartiers didn't want to leave, and the Gardners didn't want to say good-bye. But while Tobin and Aunt Enid had been holding down the office, May knew she had to get back to work.

Martin had decided to drive to Toronto with them for Kylie's July appointment, and continue on to Connecticut from there.

They took their time, driving along the St. Lawrence River, staying in small towns along the way. In Toronto, Martin pointed out the hockey and baseball stadiums. He told them about the Hockey Hall of Fame, where all the great players were immortalized. May tried to listen, but all she could think about was the little blue notebook in her purse.

Finally they arrived at Twigg University, a campus of wide greens and ivy-covered brick buildings north of the city.

Dr. Ben Whitpen's office was in the Psychology Department, in an old building with leaded glass windows. The hallways were dark and cool, the classroom doors made of heavy oak. Martin stood there blinking, trying to focus.

"Don't be scared." Kylie was holding Martin's hand. Helping him seemed to make her forget her own unhappiness at coming here. "I was the first time."

"I'm not scared," he said. "But it's dark in here."

"Not that dark," Kylie said.

"Are you okay?" May asked, watching him rub his eyes.

"My eyes itch," he told her. "It's hard to focus. Maybe I got something in them."

"Do you want to wait outside?" May asked. "Kylie and I will meet you afterward."

"Maybe I will," he agreed. "I'll go check out the hockey rink. See you back here in, what? An hour?"

"Make it two," May said.

It seemed strange to May now, coming in from a bright summer day to this gloomy place, with a notebook filled with her daughter's bad dreams. While Martin went out, May and Kylie climbed one flight to the Dream Research Lab and opened the door.

Dr. Whitpen greeted them. Dressed in jeans and an untucked polo shirt, he looked more like a graduate student than a doctor with a big research grant. Leading Kylie straight to the toy box, he told her to make herself at home while he talked to her mother.

Other doctors sat in small cubicles, working on computers or talking on the phone.

May followed Dr. Whitpen into his office. Watching Kylie through the door glass, she passed him her notebook.

"More angel dreams," he said, reading. "Good, you included the incident on the plane. She heard noises, smelled smoke before anyone else. Approached a man, asked him for help when the time came. Said his daughter told her to—his daughter?"

"She's dead," May told him.

"Ahh." Dr. Whitpen raised his eyebrows. He continued reading. "Mute angels in a dream, surrounding her head like moths. Interesting. Natalie's doll, wanting to bring the doll to the wedding. Wedding?" he asked, looking up.

"I told you I got married," May said.

"Oh, yes, that's wonderful. Best wishes."

"I married the man on the plane."

"The man Kylie approached?" Dr. Whitpen seemed shocked.

"Yes," May said. "We fell in love. It has nothing to do with what happened that day." As she spoke, she felt protective of her relationship with Martin.

"It's an unusual story," he commented.

"I know," she agreed. "But we're here to talk about Kylie. As I told you on the phone, I'm not as worried as before. Maybe I've made a mistake, taking her to so many doctors. As if she's a curiosity, with something wrong with her."

"You were very upset when we first met," he reminded her.

"I know," May said, remembering how desperate she had felt. "I'd taken her to that group in New York, and all it took was one person mentioning schizophrenia . . ."

"Kylie's not schizophrenic," Dr. Whitpen said sharply, with certainty. "But you were troubled about more than that."

"We had just found that—" May recoiled from the memory. "That body. Just a bag of bones, really. A skeleton held together by rags, old clothes, just rattling in the wind. I'll never forget it. I know Kylie won't, either."

"She dreamed about it every night at first—and then she started seeing angels," Dr. Whitpen said, consulting his notes. "Her second encounter with death very soon after losing her great-grandmother."

"She's so sensitive and caring," May said. "She can't stand seeing things hurt. When she and my husband caught that fish this summer, she said she heard it crying. She stares when she sees an-

imals killed on the side of a road, and she asks me about parents and babies left behind."

"That was her concern about the hanged body—Richard Perry," Dr. Whitpen said, reviewing the chart. "About the family left behind." He looked up. "The investigation revealed that he'd been a suicide, right? A loner in trouble with the law. Parents out west, no wife, no kids."

May nodded. "Kylie made his parents a sympathy card."

"I remember," Dr. Whitpen said.

"She's compassionate," May went on. "And she has an amazing imagination. I'm inclined to think that explains the rest. Or enough of the rest. I think we're going to stop coming after this visit."

"If that is your wish, I'll respect it. Although I hope you decide to continue," Dr. Whitpen said. "Let me talk to her, okay? Get a feel for how things are going from her perspective. I'd like to ask her about the mute angels in her dream."

Carrying the blue notebook with him, Dr. Whitpen led May back to the play area. He took out the deck of cards, and Kylie watched him. She shuffled, then he did. The deck went down on the table, and he cut it in half.

"Top card," he said.

"Red."

He checked: red.

"Again," he said.

"Blue."

Dr. Whitpen showed her that she was right, and she clapped her hands. They went through the whole deck. Kylie got three wrong. He started from the top, but she seemed bored and wandered over to the dollhouse.

He crouched on the other side, joining in as Kylie arranged the doll family, their pets, and their furniture. May sat back, watching Kylie fly the girl doll around the house like a bird.

"Who's that?" Dr. Whitpen asked.

"Natalie," Kylie said.

"Her doll, you mean?"

"No, Natalie. My sister."

"What's she doing?" Dr. Whitpen asked, watching Kylie move her arms up and down.

"She's talking."

"With her arms?"

"Maybe," Kylie said.

"Can't she speak?" Dr. Whitpen asked, and May knew he was referring to the mute angels.

Kylie smiled at him, as if he'd just told a good joke. "She doesn't need words with me," she said. "I understand her."

"What's she saying?"

" 'Help me,' " Kylie said in a voice not her own.

"What kind of help does she need?" Dr. Whitpen asked, leaning closer.

"I'm not sure. She doesn't want her hat. And some people can't see with their eyes," Kylie said, looking as if she might cry. Placing the doll back inside the playhouse, Kylie let them know the game was over. She ran to the low table where paper and crayons were kept, and she began to draw.

"Your mother got married," Dr. Whitpen said, following her.

"I have a father now." Kylie was drawing fast and hard. "And a sister."

"Natalie," he said.

"That's right!" Kylie beamed with pleasure to hear him say her name.

"What does she look like?"

"Pretty." Kylie started drawing again. "With wings and a white dress."

"Like the other angels you've seen?"

Kylie shook her head. "No one looks like Natalie. She's real."

"The others aren't?" Dr. Whitpen asked, smiling.

"No, but I love her, and that makes everything *more* real," Kylie said, looking him in the eye. "I don't know the others' names, and I do know hers: Natalie Cartier."

May watched her go back to work, drawing pictures on the white paper. Dr. Whitpen stood up, came to sit beside her. He raised his eyebrows. "Natalie Cartier? You married Martin Cartier?"

"Yes." May had known Martin was famous, but somehow she hadn't expected his name to mean much to the researcher. "You're a hockey fan?"

"Not much of one. I know the name for another reason. His daughter died a tragic death."

"You know about it?" May asked.

"Everyone in Canada does," he said. "Her grandfather was responsible. He was a great player himself, and he became involved with criminals. He caused Natalie's death indirectly, later went to prison for fixing games, hiding money. It was a national scandal."

May watched Kylie, to see whether she was listening, but she was drawing furiously, talking out loud to herself. The picture took shape: the lake, the gazebo, pine trees, a girl, a cap floating in the water.

"Martin doesn't talk about him. Or about Natalie."

"At all?"

"Hardly at all. It's too painful for him. Why?"

"That might explain why Kylie picked Martin out in the first place—there might be a connection," he said, sounding excited.

"What kind of connection?" May asked, bristling.

"The terrible death, the father's inability to face it—"

"What are you saying? That Martin married me because Kylie's clairvoyant?" May stood up. "He didn't even want to come inside. He's on campus right now—he came into this building with us and wanted to go right out. He wants no part of this."

"Ms. Taylor—I mean, Mrs. Cartier," Dr. Whitpen said. "Please. Sit down. Forgive me, that's not what I mean at all. Please."

Not wanting to upset Kylie, May lowered herself into the chair again. She watched as Kylie drew mountains around the lake, clouds in the blue sky, one big fish under the water's surface.

"What, then?" May asked.

"Your husband might not be aware of anything. He probably isn't. It's Kylie I'm thinking of."

"Kylie?"

"Your daughter is gifted."

"We knew that already." May's heart was racing. She wanted to leave and not come back. Martin would be waiting downstairs. She'd leave the notebook with Dr. Whitpen, let him make whatever he wanted of it.

"Of course, but—"

"I've had enough of this," May said. "Cards, dolls, keeping track of her dreams. Kylie's gifted, I agree. Our whole family believes in magic—a certain kind, anyway. As long as Kylie's not ill, not schizophrenic."

"No, she's not. But she's not like anyone in your family either. She sees through the veil."

"The veil?" May had never heard this before.

"Between worlds," Dr. Whitpen said. "This world and the next."

May sat very still.

"What made you take that trail at the Lovecraft the day you

and Kylie came upon the hanging?" he asked. "You had to hike through some deep woods to get there. The body had been hanging there a long time. It wanted to be found."

"No," May said.

"Kylie told you, didn't she? She picked a trail and told you she wanted to take it."

May closed her eyes, remembering the day. It had been cool, autumn leaves falling all around. Kylie had grabbed her hand, pulled her through thick brambles, down a twisted path to the clearing where the body hung. Richard Perry, the loner from California, dealing drugs in Worcester, with no family around to wonder where he was, to worry when he didn't come home.

Dr. Whitpen went on. "Kylie was drawn to Martin because Natalie has something to tell her. Something she wants her father to know."

"I don't believe that."

"Maybe it's about Natalie's grandfather. Maybe it's about the way she died. Maybe it's a message, or even a warning, for the living—for Martin himself."

"I've been very open to your ideas. But this is too much." Rising, May waved at Kylie. "Come on, honey," she said. "We're going home now."

"The veil is thin, Mrs. Cartier," the doctor said. "So thin any one of us can see through it. That scares most people, and they have to look away. But not Kylie—she'll keep looking whether you help her or not."

"Come on, Kylie," May said, her blood pounding, taking her daughter by the hand. Suddenly Ben Whitpen seemed like a mad scientist, suggesting that she and Martin were together for such a far-fetched reason. Her ego felt very bruised. Fumbling, she grabbed her bag and headed for the door. Kylie looked surprised, but she didn't resist. May saw the notebook on the floor beside her chair. Hesitating, she snatched it up and stuck it in her bag.

~

The bride business was back in full swing within minutes of returning home. Tobin brought May up to speed, handing her six new client files.

"Wow, you've been busy," May said.

"Just proving we can do it without you if we have to."

"Well, I'm back now."

"How's married life treating you?" Tobin asked.

"Great." May grinned, trying to show that everything was wonderful. She didn't mention Natalie, Martin's father, the study in Toronto. After her last call, she'd felt guilty for confiding too much. Weren't certain things supposed to stay secret in marriage? Now Tobin would be judging Martin, remembering everything May had told her about their fight.

"Really?"

"Yes. We're staying in Black Hall till hockey season begins, and then we're moving into Martin's house in Boston. On Beacon Hill."

"Beacon Hill, way to go," Tobin said. "You're in the big time." May frowned.

"That's a joke, May."

"I know," she said, waving. "It's just, we're so happy. The lake was wonderful, we're so lucky to have each other. I can't wait to move into Boston."

"To Beacon Hill," Tobin reminded her.

May went straight to her desk, to catch up on work and get away from the awkwardness she suddenly felt around her best friend. It made her uncomfortable, not knowing where to draw the line on what to tell her and what to keep private. Could she tell her what Dr. Whitpen had said without divulging too much about the Cartiers?

Later that morning a nurse from a Dr. Hall's office called, to confirm Martin's appointment on Tuesday and to remind him to bring his X rays. Puzzled, May said she'd pass on the message. Tobin glanced over, but May didn't say anything.

When Martin came home from working out that night, May told him about the call.

"Oh, yeah," he said. "Just my usual physical. The team wants to make sure I'm still worth the money they're paying me, eh?"

"That's all it is?" May asked.

"A physical, *c'est tout.*"

"But she mentioned X rays."

Martin laughed. "I play hockey, eh?" he said. "I've had so many X rays, I glow in the dark. Come on, let me take you upstairs. I'll show you."

"I've seen—" May began, falling into his arms. They kissed, and then he pulled her onto the sofa.

"I'll tell you what we really have to worry about," he said, nuzzling her neck. "Reporters. I think they're on to us—the word has

been leaking out, and I think the story of our marriage is about to break. We're so lucky that the people at the lake respect our privacy. They let us have a great honeymoon."

May had a strange gut feeling that he wasn't telling her the whole truth, that he was trying to distract her from asking about the doctor. But there was no reason for him to lie to her about X rays, about a team physical. He was a pro hockey player, after all. Injuries and doctors' visits were everyday things.

But deep inside, she knew there was something Martin wasn't telling her. She would have liked to call Tobin, to confide her fear, but it seemed that talking about it might make it real. Instead she went to check on Kylie, and stood there staring at her sleeping child.

—

Lying beside May later that night, Martin listened to her steady breathing. She had seemed anxious since the visit to Toronto. He had thought returning home would settle her, but if anything she seemed more worried. Tonight, though, they had made love, and she had finally fallen asleep in his arms. Wanting to be sure, he watched the rise and fall of her chest. Then he climbed carefully out of bed.

He went into the bathroom and closed the door. Turning on the light, he checked his face in the mirror. So many scars, from all the times he'd been smashed by sticks and pucks. Leaning forward, he tilted his head to examine the side of it. He had a slight dent, just above and behind his right ear.

The X rays in question, that the stupid nurse had called to remind him to bring, had been taken during the summer.

During the previous season, in a game against Chicago, a puck had split his head open. Concussion was obvious, and he'd missed the next two games. Against the doctor's advice, he'd played the third. No problems for the rest of the season.

But then, one morning while he was fishing with Kylie, the headaches had started. Splitting, pounding, making him see double. He'd blamed it on the bright sun, a skipped breakfast, the stress—wonderful though it was—of being newly married. That night May had wanted to talk about something—Natalie or his father—and Martin had snapped at her. The next day he'd blamed his bad behavior on the headaches.

Then they had gone to Toronto. He had intended to accom-

SUMMER LIGHT

141

pany her and Kylie upstairs, to the doctor, to give them his support. But as he stepped inside the building, everything had gone dark. His vision had faded to black, and he'd thought he might pass out. Standing in the hallway of that old building, Martin had felt as if he was going to die.

So he'd done what came naturally: drove down to the nearest hospital for a quickie exam. A lifetime of hockey injuries had gotten him very used to emergency rooms, X-ray machines, doctors and nurses. The thought of telling May didn't even occur to him— or maybe it did. She'd just worry, want to come with him, make more of it than it was.

Strange thing, coincidence—the Toronto hospital was the same one he'd been to for knee surgery while Nat had stayed with his father. Déjà vu, he'd thought the whole time he was getting checked out.

This time, the film had picked up a hairline skull fracture. No big deal—it would blend in nicely with all the others. The hospital had sent him home with the X ray, suggested he take it to the team doctor. Whose dumb nurse had decided to be helpful and leave the message with May.

The weird thing was, he thought as he turned out the light, his head hardly hurt at all anymore. He had hung on, and the pain had passed. That always seemed to be the way. Complaining had never done him any good. He didn't believe in whining about his problems, never had. Being married wasn't going to change that—he didn't want to inflict every stupid hurt on May.

Past or present. Ever since she'd heard the truth about Natalie and his father she had seemed content to leave it alone. That was good. In Martin's opinion, the deeper that business was buried, the better. Telling her stories about his family couldn't make anyone happier.

The summer had seen many betrothals. May listened to stories all day long. She took copious notes. Often her best wedding ideas sprang from tales about proposals and engagements. One woman told of a flight to Italy, how she and her boyfriend had planned a week in Positano. At the airport, after they had placed their luggage on the conveyor belt and passed through the security gate, alarms went off. When the guard asked her boyfriend to empty his pockets, he refused. More security was called, and as they were

pulling out the handcuffs and the young woman was panicking, he dropped down on one knee and took a small box from his pocket.

Other travelers gathered around. "He's proposing, he's proposing," the woman heard them say, and then their voices faded. Her boyfriend took out a diamond ring and asked her to marry him.

"I said yes," the woman, whose name was Jean Wesley, told May. "I couldn't believe it; I was in shock. He had wanted to wait till we got to Italy, but the ring set off all the alarms. We want a Valentine's Day wedding."

Smiling as she made notes, the phone rang. Tobin answered, and May heard her talking to someone in a friendly tone. She laughed, and then hung up. Gesturing to May, she stood by the window.

"That was your husband," Tobin said.

"Didn't he want to talk to me?"

"He's driving out—the onslaught has begun."

"The what?"

"The press knows about you. They're on the way here now."

—————

The trucks stayed a respectful distance away, which was to say they kept off the rose beds and herb gardens. Reporters swarmed around, while techs ran around with cameras, microphones, and lights. People were shouting, wires being dragged over green grass and stone walls.

Just another day at the Fleet Center or Madison Square Garden or Maple Leaf Gardens, Martin thought. But this was May and Enid's meadow, their peaceful home. The statement should have been made anywhere else, but the vultures had already picked up the location and landed.

"All this, just because we got married?" May asked, a slight furrow of worry between her brows.

"If you have any secrets, now's the time to tell me," Martin told her.

"I know them all," Tobin laughed.

"Talk to me later," Martin said.

"I can't believe this is news," May said. "Our wedding. Our elopement."

"Other women want him," Kylie intoned.

"Well, they can't have him." Tobin raised her eyebrows at May over Kylie's head as everyone chuckled.

"They wouldn't want me if they knew me," Martin said to Kylie. "Only your mother was blind enough for that."

"Blind as a bat." May closed her eyes tight as she leaned in to kiss Martin. Although the news conference wasn't supposed to start for ten more minutes, a blizzard of flashes went off and a torrent of shutters snapped.

"Are you mad at me for blabbing?" Kylie asked anxiously.

So proud to have Martin as a stepfather, Kylie had gone up to everyone saying her new name was "Kylie Cartier," that Mickey and Eddie hadn't known anything when they'd called her a liar last May. Her lunch aide's sister worked at WBTR and had called in the story. It had taken off like wildfire.

Martin smiled down at her. While the grown-ups leaned on a stone wall, Kylie sat cross-legged at their feet. She wore Nat's old blue Blue Jays hat Martin had given her their last day at the lake, and it hurt him slightly less every time he saw her wearing it. "*Mais non*," he said. "We're not mad at you. Not even slightly."

"Who told you other women want him?" May asked.

"Kids on the bus. It came on the radio on my way home from school. The big girls were saying it, and then our bus driver—Mrs. Patterson?—pretended to cry. She says the only thing that keeps her going is Martin's poster on the wall in her bedroom."

"Her husband ought to rip it down," Martin said.

"She made me promise to get your autograph," Kylie said. "So did Mickey, and Eddie, and Jeff, and Austin."

"Can I have it, too?" Tobin asked.

Martin smiled, shaking his head.

But by then Pete McMahon, the Bruins spokesman, had finished briefing the press, and the moment had arrived. Lights blared from above, even though the sky was clear and bright. Martin put his right arm around May and his left hand on Kylie's head. He swallowed, his throat already parched. Although he had faced the media a thousand times, he had never felt so nervous or uneasy.

"Ready, Martin?" Pete asked, walking over. "And you, May?"

"I might need to kill you later," Martin growled.

Pete laughed. Martin's shoulder muscles rippled, exactly the way they did when he felt the urge to slam an opponent into the boards. But Pete was a good guy. Publicity was his job, not his fault.

He and Martin had huddled together on this, coming up with a strategy to face the media. In a Stanley Cup year, Boston was rab-

idly protective of its hockey stars. Pete had told Martin one tabloid had headlines set to call May "The Cartier Gold Digger," and Martin had suggested Pete warn the editor to kill the tag or prepare for a new face. Martin wanted Pete to make the statement for them, but Pete suggested that by giving the press one fair shot at May and Kylie, they might head off future intrusion.

So Martin had agreed.

"All set, sweetheart?" Martin asked.

May nodded, looking nervous and excited. Martin scowled at Pete and nodded. Walking in front of the cameras, Pete straightened his tie and raked his hair back. The newscast would be carried live on certain Boston stations, and one producer began counting down. "Four, three, two . . ."

"On June seventeen, 2000, Martin Cartier married May Taylor at his lakeside home in the Laurentides, just north of Quebec, in Canada. It was a quiet, private ceremony attended only by family and close friends. They, along with Ms. Taylor's daughter Kylie, welcome you now, and will be happy to answer your questions."

"Cartier, Mommy," Kylie said.

"I know, honey," May whispered. She sounded suddenly terrified, and although she was talking to Kylie, she was staring into the wall of cameras like a deer caught in the headlights.

"But he called us Taylor, and now we're Cartiers. Right?"

"Right, Kylie," Martin said firmly as the entire crowd of reporters began to laugh, as Pete gave a desperate head shake and mouthed, "I'm sorry."

"I don't think it's funny," Kylie said, frowning.

Now the questions came hard and fast.

"Martin, how did you meet?"

"Mrs. Cartier, what did you say to get him to notice you?"

"What time was the wedding? Who exactly were the guests?"

"When you say 'family,' was Serge Cartier aware of the ceremony? What was your father's reaction? Did he send his good wishes? Have you introduced your bride to him yet?"

"Do you think your performance in the Stanley Cup finals was adversely affected by your imminent wedding plans?"

"For any wedding planner, this had to be the coup of the century! How'd you pull it off?"

"Why the rush to marry? Why the secrecy?"

"Ms. Taylor, do you feel you made him lose the Stanley Cup?"

"A rumor has surfaced regarding rose petals. May, can you explain—"

S U M M E R   L I G H T145

"Her name is 'Mrs. Cartier,'" Martin said, his voice so forceful that many earphoned techs swore and ripped off their headsets.

"I'm sorry," the reporter said. A smarmy jerk with hair too dark and perfect for his age and the light wind, he smiled and continued, "Mrs. *Cartier,* can you explain the story circulating in Boston now, that you gave Martin 'rose petals'"—he might as well have been saying "Spanish fly"—"to carry during the play-offs?"

Martin wondered who had leaked the rose petals—had to have been someone on his own team. His back muscles trembled as he prepared to loosen the teeth in the reporter's head, but May answered sharply, "When you love someone, you want to help in any way you can."

"Help him fall in love with you, you mean?" the reporter asked.

"No, not exactly, although I was happy that that was the outcome," May said directly, every inch of her shining as she smiled.

"Then you *did* intend—"

"She just answered you," Martin said through clenched teeth, ignoring Pete's wide-eyed warning gaze from the sidelines.

"To slip him a love potion?" the reporter continued.

"Mommy's a wedding witch," Kylie said proudly. "She makes people fall in love."

Shutters whirred, and the crowd of reporters snickered and scrawled. They had just gotten what they wanted, Martin knew. They were looking for a way to bash May and Kylie had inadvertently given it to them. Not realizing, May beamed. She hugged Kylie from behind, rocking her back and forth.

"Enough, everyone," Pete told them. "Thank you for coming."

"Yes, thank you," May called graciously.

The reporters ignored her. They laughed among themselves, hurrying off to file their stories. Martin watched May and Kylie holding hands, positive that they'd done a great job. They had, but they didn't understand that now the whole world would be waiting for the marriage to fail. People didn't want their sports stars to fall in love forever: They wanted them to live fast, date movie stars, crash and burn.

"We did it!" May threw her arms around Martin. "That wasn't so bad."

"You were beautiful," he said, gazing into her eyes.

"And Kylie." May was laughing. "Wasn't she funny?"

"Very," Martin said.

Kylie had danced over to Aunt Enid, and Pete seemed to be

steering them and May into the house, away from the reporters. Martin knew how bad she would feel if she knew what she'd done, that she had opened a door to the headline he already knew was going to appear tomorrow.

"How did it go?" Tobin asked.

"She was charming," Martin said. "The trouble is, they're not."

"They'd better not hurt her," Tobin said, gazing at the reporters. "I know how they take people's words and twist them. May didn't set out to catch you."

"I know that."

"She never even set out to fall in love. She's been so busy taking care of Kylie, trying to live a good life. I hate how much she's been hurt." Tobin's eyes sparkled with tears. She turned to Martin, her gaze intense.

"I hate that, too," he said.

Tobin nodded. Wiping her eyes, she chucked his arm with her fist and walked away. Martin watched her for a minute before turning back toward the media trucks.

He had planned to drive into Boston early tomorrow, to see the doctor, but now he changed his mind. He would stay here, by May's side, all day long. His wife would need support when she saw what they wrote about her. Having seen their treatment of the death of his child, the imprisonment of his father, Martin Cartier knew that the press sharks out there would consider his second marriage anything but sacred.

Chapter 11

H EY, OLD MAN," the bald kid said. "Seen this?"
     Serge stood there reading a purloined racing sheet. After
Sunday's knifing over a choice of TV programs, the cell block's
cable had been cut off and papers hard to come by. Serge didn't
look up, but he knew who was talking. New youngster on the unit,
in for selling drugs—what else was new? Flexing his biceps, Serge
made his face passive.

     "Seen all I want to see of you," Serge said. "Buzz off."

     "No, man," insisted the kid, whose name was Tino. "You
wanna see this."

     Serge had his eye on Talisker, a frisky two-year-old everyone
had written off after his loss in the Burnham Stakes. Racing was
not Serge's game of choice, but in here he grabbed what he could.
Scanning the page, he tried to ignore the kid long enough for some
peace and quiet. But the tabloid headline came slamming into his
vision:

CARTIER SECRET WEDDING BLUES

     "What the hell?" Serge dropped the racing sheet.

     "Your kid got married," Tino told him. "Married some gold-
digger bitch who put a spell on him." He rattled on as if he was the
reporter himself, all about the woman getting Martin to marry her
using rose petals and love spells, how the fans were blaming her for
distracting Martin and making him lose the Stanley Cup.

     "He's got another Trisha on his hands," Serge muttered, start-
ing to read the story.

     "Got alimony, child support waiting to happen," Tino com-
mented. "Got me plenty of that. I know."

     "Shut up," Serge said. "Get lost."

"Why're you talking to me like that? Didn't I just bring you good news?"

"Go smoke crack," Serge told him. An athlete all his life, he had no patience for strong young men who wrecked their bodies and minds with chemicals. Anyone in for drugs was off his list, and they were all in for drugs.

"I'm clean," the kid protested, sounding hurt.

"Yeah, for the last ten minutes. Now leave me alone."

Folding up the tabloid, Serge walked down to his cell. He lived on the skid row block, home of bone-breakers, wife-stranglers, subway-knifers. No one cared that he had thrice skated to Stanley Cup victories, that he had been wined and dined by senators and prime ministers. Serge didn't care himself. He was in prison, with the violent and incorrigible, right where he was supposed to be.

Lying on his bunk, he again opened the paper. Hands shaking, he looked past the story to the accompanying photo. There was Martin. Jesus, Serge thought. My son, my son. He looked old and young at the same time, Serge's towhead turning gray—gray!—his face getting lined—too damn old to be playing hockey, killing his body—but robust youth and fire still alive in his vivid blue eyes.

Martin had his arm around a woman. Pretty, very pretty. Nothing at all like Trisha—soft in every way Trisha was hard. Looking almost shy, as if she didn't like the cameras pointing at her, but Serge knew that was probably part of the lie, one segment of her act. But staring at the picture of his new daughter-in-law—May, her name was—Serge wasn't sure.

Later, in the dining hall, an inmate named Buford Dunham glanced over his shoulder. Buford laughed, staring at the picture.

"What's funny?"

"Just wondering what's her act," Buford said.

"She's no act. I know an act when I see one," Serge said, ignoring Buford's comment as he examined May's open face, her happy eyes.

"You should. You lived one yourself. A hockey player by any other name's just another asshole into the loan sharks. The press kissing your ass in one room, Joey the Cheese threatening to break your legs in the next."

Serge was silent. Buford had worked for organized crime, and he knew what he was talking about. His favorite line was "You pay when I come, you pay on time." He said it for everything from the morning paper to extra coffee at night.

"They eloped. True love, how nice," Buford said.

But Serge barely heard. He was staring at the little girl in the picture. May's daughter Kylie, the story said. *Out of the mouths of babes,* the reporter wrote, *came the truth—that her mother had been plotting this marriage for some time, casting a New Age net around the Gold Sledgehammer to make him fall in love with her.*

Kylie was wearing Natalie's cap. Serge put his finger on the picture. He would know that old hat anywhere. Serge had wangled a pair of caps—one for Natalie and one for Martin—from his friend John LeGrange, third-base coach for the Blue Jays, and sent them off on baseball season's opening day. Martin must have given Kylie the hat.

"She's no act," Serge repeated.

"What?"

"He wouldn't have given the kid Nat's hat if her mother was an act."

"What're you doing, turning sentimental? Maybe we should rent a Jimmy Stewart video tonight. I'll make the popcorn, you mix the martinis."

Serge couldn't take his eyes off the family picture. He stared so long, his eyes filled with tears. He wished the photo weren't so grainy, that he could see their faces better. Natalie's hat, he thought. What a nice hat. It fit Kylie well. It looked good on her.

"Looks good," Serge said out loud. "Fits real nice."

"Either quit talking like you have Alzheimer's, or shut up."

"Shut up yourself," Serge muttered, but only under his breath. He had a healthy, unholy respect for this inmate. Buford had been in the same line of work as the man who'd come to call that last day Serge had seen his granddaughter.

That last day, Serge thought, that last day. If only he could get it back. If only Serge could do that last day over again. He stared at the picture until it blurred entirely. Natalie was dead. That fact would never change, and Serge knew it was his fault. Now Martin had a new family Serge would never meet.

And Serge knew that was his fault, too.

⌒

Hockey practice had started, but the Cartiers were safe in Black Hall until the regular season began. The press was in a feeding frenzy, so May wanted to stay as far away from the arena as she could. Her telephone rang so often—new clients, strangers saying

variously supportive and hateful things, reporters requesting inter-
views—that she hired an answering service just to take messages.

Genny sent a letter of support, along with a big basket of Lac
Vert apples and a jar of apple butter. May baked a pie and served
the apple butter with English muffins every day, and just knowing
Genny had experienced the same kind of publicity made the ordeal
easier.

Kids at school had started treating Kylie differently. Some who
had never paid attention to her before now wanted to be her best
friend. She had been invited to birthday parties for kids in third,
fourth, and fifth grade, girls and boys she didn't even know. Other
kids teased her for helping May cast spells on Martin, to get him to
marry her.

But the worst happened one day when Kylie came sobbing into
the barn, straight off the school bus into her mother's arms. The autumn day was golden, the color of dried wheat, with summer's last
heat making it possible to still wear short-sleeved shirts and jeans.

"We didn't put spells on Martin, did we, Mom?" Kylie cried,
her arms around May's waist while Tobin stood there watching.

"No, honey, we didn't."

"He would have married you anyway, right?"

"That's what he says," May replied.

"What's a basket?"

"Well, you know." May smiled, confused. "We've made them
ourselves, soaking the reeds and weaving them."

"But when it's about a person? When it's about me?"

"I don't know," May said, feeling chilled. "What did they say?"

"That I'm a basket without a real father." Kylie's lip was quiv-
ering again, and May heard Tobin draw in a deep breath. "That we
only want Martin for his money."

"Who told you that?"

"A big kid, Joseph Newton. He's in fifth grade, and he said his
father told him."

"Oh, it's not true, Kylie. Not true at all."

May sat with Kylie for as long as it took for the sobs to stop,
until she climbed off May's lap and wandered away to look for
Aunt Enid. Tobin stepped forward, pulling a chair close to May.

"He called her a bastard." May was shaking.

"I heard her," Tobin said quietly. "Are you okay?"

"I've protected her all this time," May went on. "No one has
ever known our story, and now the papers are printing it. They
know about Gordon, they know I never got married. . . ."

"They should know you're the best mother around," Tobin said. "That you've always put Kylie first, that Martin Cartier is the lucky one—"

"Thanks, Tobe." May wiped her eyes. She swallowed hard, wanting to spill all her feelings, her fears and anxieties. Her life was changing so fast; suddenly her story was everywhere, strangers judging her for her past and present.

"There might be one silver lining," Tobin said, her eyes glinting wickedly.

"What's that?"

"Well, if the press is after you, they're probably after Gordon, too. I can just see the hallowed halls of Swopes and Bray, swarming with reporters and cameras and microphones."

"That is a truly lovely image," May said, closing her eyes. She was glad Tobin had veered off into humor, because she was still so upset she didn't know what to do.

Later that night, May held Kylie, waiting for sleep to come and the moon to rise. Sitting on the edge of Kylie's bed with the lights out and the barn cats sprawled across the quilt, she heard Martin's car in the driveway. After talking to Aunt Enid downstairs, he came up the stairs two at a time and burst into the room.

"What happened today?" he demanded, standing in the doorway.

May slipped away from Kylie; together, she and Martin walked down the hall to their room.

"Someone called her a bastard," May told him. "Kylie didn't understand the word, but she got the meaning."

"Who?"

"Some fifth-grader. His father told him, and if you only knew what I'd like to do to his father—"

"I'll annihilate him," Martin said, pushing her down onto the bed. "I'll send the little creep into the boards so hard, he'll leave his teeth in yesterday. Seriously, what's his name?"

"The boy is Joseph Newton, and his father is Patrick."

"Bad news," Martin said, grabbing the phone and paging through the local phone book. He snapped the buttons, letting out a deep breath.

When the phone was answered, he didn't waste time with pleasantries. "Patrick Newton? . . . This is Martin Cartier . . . Yeah, you are a fan? . . . Well, let me tell you why I am calling. I have a child in your son's school, and it comes to my attention that Joseph

called her a bastard . . . That's right—the word was bastard . . .
Kids'll be kids, you say?" Martin's voice was rising in anger. "Listen, Mr. Newton, where I come from, kids learn garbage like that
from their parents . . . They learn to build themselves up at the expense of others too small to defend themselves, eh? . . . That's
right, I'm blaming you. And if I hear that it happens again, I'll do
more than blame you . . . Good, I'm glad to hear it. I don't want to
hear of Kylie being hurt again."

He hung up the phone and faced May.

"Thank you," she said.

"He's a reasonable man, after all," Martin told her.

"For a minute, I thought you were going to go over and beat
the hell out of him."

"So did he," Martin said, his eyes hard.

Within a few weeks, once the shock of Martin Cartier's sudden
marriage had worn off, the press's and town's attention turned to
the Boston Bruins' prospects for another shot at the Stanley Cup.
Martin came home every night with his ankles hurting, knowing he
didn't have more than a season or two left in him. May rubbed his
back, saying one season was all he needed.

The papers started playing up the rivalry between Boston and
Edmonton, between Martin Cartier and Nils Jorgensen. One afternoon, Martin caught a practice puck in the eye, and he had a
shiner and six new stitches. The doctor examined him. He suggested Martin see an eye specialist, have some tests done.

But Martin ignored the suggestion. Hockey was rough; injuries
were to be expected. His vision wasn't 20–20 anymore, and he
didn't want to hear anything bad. If he could see well enough to
skate, that was enough. Denial worked fine: It had gotten him
through concussions, torn retinas, broken bones. Still, it hurt for
him to read, so the next morning he asked May to read him the
Globe's article about the Cartier-Jorgensen rivalry.

"You don't really hate him, do you?" May asked from across
the breakfast table. "The writers are just being sensational, as
usual."

"Uh, no." Martin sipped his orange juice. "They've got it right."

"But why?"

"Let's see. Let me try to nail it down to one reason. Because
we're both fierce competitors and both of us hate to lose?" Martin

asked, his purple eye squinting like a pirate's as he grinned. "Oops, another reason: because I once rearranged his face with a hockey stick?"

"Martin," May said, shivering.

The fact was, she hadn't yet experienced an actual hockey season with Martin, and she couldn't imagine how she'd feel about him heading into the fray, the violence, game after game. She gazed from his hands to his face, counting all the scars, lingering on his swollen right eye.

"I'm a shark, and he's steak," Martin said, spreading apple butter on his toast.

"It's that personal?"

"Mais oui."

"With all the other players, or just Jorgensen?"

"Mainly Jorgensen."

"You *really* hate him?" May asked.

Martin wiped his fingers on his napkin and took her hands in his. "May," he said. "Hockey season is starting soon."

"I know," she said. "I'm afraid, and I don't know why. Hate is such a strong word."

"I really hate him. I can't explain it, but I do. Almost as much as my father."

May felt chilled by his words. She thought of her own father, how he had walked out without a final kiss or word from her. She wondered whether Martin could so easily say he hated Serge if his father weren't still alive, if he didn't still have the chance to make peace.

"I wish you didn't." May stared at his black eye. "And I can't explain that, either. I want you to win—all your games, the Stanley Cup, everything. But I wish it all wasn't so violent."

"It's what I do," he said, holding her hands. "Play hockey."

"The season hasn't even started yet," she said. "Would you think I was the biggest idiot alive if I asked you to promise to be careful?"

Pushing their toast and coffee aside, Martin pulled May onto his lap and started kissing her in the autumn sun. He often stopped whatever he was doing to kiss and hold her, but May sensed more intensity than usual. Smoothing her hair, running his hands down her back, whispering in her ear, Martin said, "No one's ever asked me that before, May. Not once in my entire life."

But when the season actually began, in the opener against Montreal, May was on her feet beside Genny, amazed by the thrill of it all. Cheering their lungs out, they watched from a special box right on the ice, so close to the players they could hear their breath as they skated by. Kylie had stayed home with Aunt Enid to watch the game on TV, and when the camera zoomed in on the wives' reaction, Genny reminded May to wave.

When the Eastern Conference Championship banner was hoisted over the stadium, to celebrate last season's amazing effort, May and Genny both felt so proud they had tears in their eyes. Trying to catch Martin's eye, May saw him staring down at his feet.

"He's refusing to acknowledge it. He's still disappointed they didn't win the Cup," Genny explained, "and he won't be happy until he sees a Stanley Cup banner hanging up there."

"Ray looks happy," May commented, watching Genny's husband smile and cheer.

"Ray's different from Martin," Genny said.

May knew the basics: puck, shot, goal. And she'd learned a few terms during last season's play-offs. But she still had a whole new language to learn, and Genny explained it to her: slap shot, penalty box, red line, in the slot, hat trick.

"Hat trick?" May asked.

"Three goals by the same player in the same game. What your husband's on his way to getting if he keeps playing like this. Aahh!" Genny said, wincing as Martin slammed an opponent right into the boards in front of them, grinning at May as if he were a big cat laying a mouse at her feet.

When an opponent jammed his stick into Martin's side, May gasped. "Hey, umpire!"

"They're called officials in hockey. Or line judges or refs," Genny told her, smiling. "Besides, don't worry. Martin'll give it right back to him."

Which Martin did, pounding his body into the same guy just as he'd cocked his stick to shoot the puck. The Montreal Canadien went flying onto the ice, skidding backward on his bottom like a little kid on a pond. May raised her fists, shouting just as loud as any other Boston fan.

Martin Cartier put on an amazing show. He skated like a comet, fast as a fireball. Blocking shots, stealing the puck, making impossible passes, aiming straight, scoring goals that sent the entire crowd flying to its feet. May had known she was married to a professional athlete, but until tonight, she hadn't really known

what that meant. Her husband wasn't a mere human: He was a wizard who could fly through the air on ice skates.

Martin scored once in the first minute, got penalized for fighting four minutes later, scored a penalty shot—all in the first period; in the second, he sustained a bloody nose and went to the penalty box for hooking; with Martin off the ice, Montreal scored two goals in quick succession. Coming back, Martin blocked his thirtieth shot of the game just as the clock ran down on the second period.

As the Bruins skated off the ice, May found herself thrilled and breathless; the palms of her hands were raw from digging her nails in, her voice raw from yelling.

The Zamboni came out and made the ice smooth. While music thumped from speakers overhead, May watched the big square machine slide over the rough ice, melting the grooves and freezing it into glass. Kids hooted and hollered, trying to get the players' attention. They stood huddled around Coach Dafoe, planning how they'd break the 2–2 tie and win.

"He's telling them to give the puck to Martin," Genny told her, studying the scene. "He's saying no matter what, regardless of what your man is doing, get the puck to Martin."

"You know so much about hockey," May said.

Genny broke out laughing. "No, that's what he always says. Every game! Martin's our star, but, wow, May—he's outshining even himself tonight. 'Cause of you, you know. How's it feel to have your husband showing off for you?"

"Not bad." May said, so happy she couldn't stop smiling.

"Okay, okay!" Genny called, stamping her feet. "We're ready, guys! Come on out and win this game—put these babies to bed!"

"Come on!" May shouted just as loud. "Go Bruins! Let's win!"

Just then, a crowd of young women came over to the box where May and Genny were sitting with several other wives and girlfriends. May felt her stomach tighten. Martin had warned her to expect comments and catcalls, to throw her shoulders back and ignore it all, and so far she had. But here were four gorgeous women—just like the blond-model type May had seen talking to Martin on the plane that first day—storming the box.

"Hang tough," Genny muttered. "Incoming."

"Excuse me," the tallest blonde said, rapping on the Plexiglas.

"Yes?" Genny asked as she opened the door a crack, doing an admirable sentry imitation with a frostiness May hadn't imagined her capable of.

"May Cartier?" the blonde asked.

"This box is private," Genny said, standing between May and the intruders.

"I know, forgive us." The blonde was smiling sheepishly now, holding out a card. "I just wanted to give her this. It's . . . well, it's just a message from me and my friends. We're big Bruins' fans, and we just thought—"

"I'll give it to her." Genny closed the door firmly behind her. Turning to May, she handed her the large white envelope. May held it for a moment, trying to decide what to do. Her heart was pounding, and she knew she was afraid of what the card said.

"Maybe I'll wait till later," May said. Play was about to resume; she didn't want to ruin the rest of a great game by reading something that would upset her.

"Why not open it when I'm with you?" Genny asked. "We'll just laugh it off together."

May nodded. Tearing open the envelope, she pulled out a greeting card. It showed golden wedding bells in a white church steeple, and the message read: *Best wishes on your recent marriage. May your years together be long and filled with the blessings of love.* It was signed: *Mary Truscott, Doreen O'Malley, Amy Jenckes, and Carolina Grannato.* Then, in tiny perfect handwriting, the following P.S.: *Dear Mrs. Cartier, My fiancé and I got engaged in August. I read about you being a wedding planner, and I'd really like you to plan our wedding. We're thinking about April. I'll stop out at the Bridal Barn soon. My aunt had a Bridal Barn wedding fifteen years ago. It's a small world! Congratulations on your marriage—Go Bruins!*

"Wow," Genny said, reading over May's shoulder.

"Another lesson in 'benefit of the doubt.'" May smiled.

"No, I was thinking, wow, May's lucky to have . . . the Bridal Barn."

"You mean my career?" May asked, when Genny didn't go on.

"It's sad, but I was going to say 'a life.' Maybe I meant 'an identity.' I don't know . . ."

"You have those," May said, surprised by Genny's serious tone.

Genny stared at the ice. The players were starting to skate out, but her expression was soft and thoughtful, as if she were far away from the Fleet Center. "I'm mainly Ray Gardner's wife," she said. "Mrs. Right Wing on the Boston Bruins. I love my husband, I have a terrific life. I'm not complaining—it's been great."

"And now I'm Mrs. Gold Sledgehammer," May said.

Genny shook her head. "You're more than that. It's obvious. No groupies ever stopped by the box to hand me a nice card. . . ."

"Maybe if they tasted your apple butter they would. Or your strawberry jam. Or if they knew what a great person you are."

Genny laughed. The players were milling around, and the crowd's tension filled the air. As Genny started to focus on center ice, with both teams getting settled on either side of the red line, May stared at her.

It was great to have someone to share hockey with. It was so new and extreme, and Genny was happy to show May the ropes. At the same time, May felt a pang, deep down, because she felt herself edging away from Tobin. Her life was changing at the speed of light, and she didn't know how everything fit together.

"Can you stop by this week?" May asked. "At the Barn? I'd like to show you around, tempt you to let us sell your wares. And my aunt and Tobin would love to see you again."

"The Bridal Barn? I'd love to!" Genny flashed May a brilliant smile just as the teams began to face off.

"Good," May said, turning toward the ice.

A horn sounded, the puck dropped, and the official's whistle signaled the start of third-period play. Boston got the puck, Ray passed to Martin, and bang—Martin scored his hat trick. May screamed her lungs out as Martin skated by and planted a big kiss on the Plexiglas.

His lip marks were there all through the rest of the game. Martin shot again and again, scoring goals four and five. The crowd chanted and pounded the bleachers. The scoreboard flashed Martin's name and stats, and then—to May's amazement—it showed wedding bells. Right in the middle of the third period, with six minutes left to play, the scoreboard began flashing "MAY! MAY!"

"Listen," Genny said, grabbing May's hand as the crowd took it up.

"May, May!" they chanted.

"Oh, no!" May laughed, blushing as the call grew louder. She ducked her head, but the crowd just kept calling her name, turning it into a rhyming cheer: "May, May Cartier . . ."

"You've won them over," Genny told her.

"I can't believe it . . . after what they were calling me last month," May said, hoping Tobin was watching TV.

The crowd kept up the racket as Martin scored an incredible, heart-stopping sixth goal.

"Believe *that*," Genny said.

This time Martin bowed as he skated by the box, and May bowed back with Genny holding her hand, welcoming her to the

real and superheated life of a wife in the NHL. Her emotions over-loaded, she thought of her parents, what they would think if they could see her now. And then she wondered, just for a moment, about Serge: whether he was able to watch the game from prison, whether he was proud of his son.

May stared at the ice, and she did manage to watch the last few minutes of the game, but her eyes kept returning to her husband's lip prints on the scarred old plastic, wishing that everything she had at that moment—familiar and new—could go on forever.

Chapter 12

THE DAY WAS COLD AND cloudy, with a fine dusting of snow on every roof and field. Wearing old leather boots and a down jacket, May showed Genny around the property. It was mid-November, and they found themselves talking about the upcoming holidays, traditions, parents, and in-laws.

"Tell me about Serge," May asked.

"Oh, Serge," Genny said. "He's a complicated man."

"Did you know him well?"

"When I was young. He adored Martin, recognized his amazing talent right away. He'd coach him from morning till night, and often Ray and I got to play along. He was Martin's idol."

"Really?"

"Yes. It was one thing when Serge was living at home, commuting to play in Montreal. But then he got traded to the Maple Leafs and soon afterward, everything changed. The assault on Martin happened, and then Serge and Agnes broke up, and after that he never came back anymore. He turned his back on Martin."

"But it wasn't Martin's fault," May said, thinking of her relationship with Kylie's father, how it always seemed to be the children who suffered most for their parents' troubles.

"Of course it wasn't. But Martin didn't believe that. He started playing hockey harder, with a vengeance, as if he thought that might win his father back. He made Ray practice with him, with Agnes coaching the two of them out on the lake. . . ."

"Serge missed all that."

"Don't feel too sorry for Serge. He was a celebrity before hockey players were seen that way. Between seasons, he lived the real high-life in Los Angeles, Las Vegas—we'd see him in magazines, his arms around models. He only came back into Martin's life once Martin left home and joined the NHL himself."

"Once Martin was out from under Agnes's wing."

"Exactly. Serge is legendary around Lac Vert, though. Kids idolized him—for being such a great player himself, then for having a son like Martin."

"Martin never talks about him," May said, thinking back to the summer, to those awful nights when Martin had slept on the sofa. "Only once."

"No, I know," Genny agreed. "Martin wrote him off the day Natalie died."

"I wonder if someone can really write off his father," May said, low and thoughtfully. "No matter how much he thinks he wants to."

The Bridal Barn tour progressed. May couldn't help trying to see through Genny's eyes, wishing she had come earlier—with the herbs and flowers in bloom, the old white roses climbing up the side of the barn—to see the place at its best.

They walked into the barn, decorated for autumn with thick sprays of bayberry and bittersweet. Bright, gnarled squashes and gourds lined the old stalls and cross-beams. Owls slept in the rafters, shadowed from the bleak white light slanting through the skylights.

Tobin, finishing up with a new client, glanced over from her desk.

"Oh, this makes me homesick for Canada," Genny said, waving to Tobin. "I can smell the wood. It's cold outside, but you have these nice heaters going."

"Our biggest expense," May told her. "Keeping this big place warm all winter."

"Martin must feel like home here," Genny said.

"I think he does."

Walking through the great space, Genny touched the silvery barn board and tarnished brass hooks, examined the wide-plank floors, found the hole in the wall where the owls flew in and out. Carrying a pile of manila envelopes, Tobin walked over to meet them by the hay ladder.

"I've seen you on TV, at the games," Tobin told Genny, "but it's good to see you in person."

"Good to see *you*." Genny leaned over to hug her.

"You and May are so famous."

"Against our will," Genny laughed.

"Want to have tea with us?" May asked.

Tobin shook her head, glancing down at the envelopes.

"Thanks anyway. I'm in the midst, and I'm not sure how long this will take. See you later. Nice to see you again, Genny."

"You, too," Genny said.

Climbing the ladder into the hayloft, Genny tapped May's shoulder.

"Is Tobin okay?"

"I think so." But May felt Tobin's distance. For one thing, Tobin and May had always been jealous of outsiders, other women seeming to threaten their friendship. But beyond that, their relationship was changing in other ways and they both knew it.

"It's a big adjustment," Genny commented. "Seeing her old friend on TV, in magazines."

"It's a huge change for me."

"The NHL looks glamorous to outsiders," Genny said. "If they only knew."

"Martin's away half the time, recuperating from injuries the rest. We've hardly had a chance to get to know each other."

"Sometimes it's lonelier being married than not," Genny agreed. "You love someone, but he's hardly ever there. And when he is, he's obsessed with the last game or the next game."

"That's it." May was relieved to have Genny to talk to, but feeling guilty for holding the same things back from Tobin.

They ambled through the hayloft, filled with old gowns hanging from the rafters. Organza, taffeta, silk, and satin swished as they walked through. Some were nearly museum pieces, but toward the back were newer styles, as well as a collection of bridesmaids' dresses. As in Emily's time, they stored them up here, out of view, except for the once-yearly showing. But May wanted to show them to Genny.

"Oh, Genny, I haven't seen you since the wedding." Aunt Enid came over as they climbed down. "Welcome to the Bridal Barn. How are you? Ray and the kids?"

"Fine, Enid." Genny hugged her back. "Deep into the hockey season just like May."

"I thought I'd make tea before the three o'clock clients get here. Want some, Aunt Enid?"

"No, you girls go ahead. I'm just answering mail. Trying to keep warm by the space heater, and it's only November. Look at me in this getup—I hope I don't scare the brides away."

Aunt Enid got cold easily, and she was wearing her habitual fall-winter dress: wool leggings and a thick turtleneck under a gray flannel jumper. Glancing down at her own scruffy jeans and boots,

May had to smile: It was a wonder brides seeking stylish nuptials wanted to come anywhere near the place.

"We're pretty casual around here," May told Genny as they headed for the back room.

"That's what people love, I bet. You have this elegant raffishness about you."

"Ragged, maybe," May said, plucking the frayed sleeve of her old canvas jacket.

"No, *raffish*. Like a shy country girl with a sophisticated secret. Martin told Ray your smile reminds him of the Mona Lisa."

"You're kidding." May turned on the kettle.

"No," Genny said. "Up at Lac Vert, right at the beginning."

"She's so mysterious," May said. "I'm nothing like that."

"That's what you think." Genny regarded her. "You look, I don't know, 'knowing.' Wiser than your years. But no one ever really sees themselves the way others do."

Mulling that over, May set out the tea things. From a pine cupboard she withdrew a bone china pot decorated with cabbage roses and two cups painted with violets and blue ribbons, and set out a plate of biscuits and the last of Genny's apple butter.

Sipping their tea, May showed Genny her grandmother's famous wedding scrapbooks. There were weddings in cathedrals, churches, lighthouses, yacht clubs, penthouses, rose gardens, grandmothers' houses, and onstage at the Silver Bay Playhouse.

Genny talked about her own wedding to Ray, in the parish church at Lac Vert.

"Where he'd been baptized and made his first communion," Genny said. "Very boring and conventional."

"No wedding's boring," May said. "And being married to a hockey player isn't, either."

"That's for sure. How are you adjusting?"

"I miss him already, and it's only November. At least we have the holidays coming soon."

"Don't get your hopes up. Christmas falls right in the middle of hockey season."

"I know. I'm trying not to mind. Work keeps my mind off it."

"I hear people talking about their work, and I think, 'I want that.' I walk through galleries and wish I was an artist. At the bookstore I wonder how it would feel to write a book. I want to do something I'm *good* at."

"You already know what I think." May said, aware of Tobin

watching them from across the room. Why wouldn't she just join them for tea?

"My jams?"

"I'm serious, Genny. Brides love to spend money. We sell our own herbs here. We have our own label candles, soaps, all sorts of stuff. I keep imagining a basket filled with your jams and apple butter called 'Wedding Breakfast.'"

"I could write up cards about how the fruit comes from Lac Vert, the most romantic lake in Canada."

"The baskets would sell like mad."

"I don't know." Genny was starting to smile. "It sounds fun."

"It would be. Strawberries in June, blueberries in July—what comes next?"

"Peaches, nectarines, cherries. Blackberries. Then apples . . . you saw our orchard. But it's November now. Nothing till next summer." Genny laughed. "Which is good. My usual style is to dream about something forever and ever, then do nothing about it."

"Don't put yourself down," May said. She remembered her grandmother always saying to the women who came to see her: "Never diminish your own worth, not even in jest, or someone will start to believe it."

"Well . . ." Genny trailed off, as if she were done with the topic of Genny Gardner for the time being.

"Did Trisha work?" May asked suddenly. May's mother had always advised her second-marriage brides never to ask questions about the first wife, to leave the past alone, not to borrow trouble, but right now May couldn't resist.

"She 'worked it.'" Genny laughed. "If you know what I mean. She was out for herself—going to spas, taking trips, visiting 'friends.' Ray said she was having affairs all along. Serge introduced Martin to Trisha, you know."

"Really?"

"Trisha was much more Serge's speed than Martin's," Genny said. "Designer flashy, very tan, perfect body."

"Wonderful." May looked down at her scuffed boots.

"No—she was never right for Martin," Genny said. "Ray and I knew right from the beginning. Even Serge recognized his mistake. She's an L.A. girl—parties, show, and glamor."

"There must be a part of Martin that likes that," May said.

"For a little while," Genny said, looking May straight in the eye, "when he was younger, he only thought he did."

"I hope that's true. Because I don't seem to have much of it around here." May felt a blast of cold air blow through the owl's entry.

"You don't need it." Genny smiled. "You're elegant and raffish, remember?"

May shrugged, smiling back. "Oh, right. I forgot!"

"Even Serge regretted introducing them, considering how things turned out. He told me once he wished Martin had met a girl like me. Someone who'd love him for who he was. He'd be very happy to know Martin found you."

May was silent, listening.

"It's sad," Genny said thoughtfully. "I know Serge did some bad things. But he did love Martin in his own way. You should have seen the way he'd look at him, out on the ice—so much pride."

"I want to meet him," May told her.

"That will never happen. Martin hates him too much."

"I thought I hated my father one day," May said. "And then he died."

"I'm sorry."

"The circumstances were very different. I was only twelve. If he hadn't died, I might barely have noticed we'd had a fight. But he did," May said, remembering what Dr. Whitpen had said about the veil separating the living and the dead.

"Such a long time ago."

"In some ways it seems like yesterday. Oh, I wish we hadn't had that hanging between us. All through my life, I've felt there's something unfinished. I wish I could get that day back so much."

"I can't even imagine going through that." Genny touched May's shoulder.

May nodded, her thoughts sliding to Tobin, working at her desk. Tobin had known her father; she had helped May through many years of grief. Staring at the owls in the rafters, May thought of her father and Serge, of her growing feelings of distance from Tobin, of what it all meant.

~

The prison always got cold in November. Just when all the houses out there were cranking up the heat, when all the families were roasting turkeys and chestnuts and whatever nice families out there did, the boilers here broke down. So Serge would stand out-

side in the prison yard doing calisthenics, watching his breath turn white, haunted by memories of his days as a family man.

"Cold out here, Serge," Jim the guard commented.

"For lightweights," Serge said, doing push-ups on the tar.

"That's right. You playing hockey all those years."

"All those years."

"How many push-ups are you up to?"

"Two hundred forty, forty-one." Serge pumped harder.

"Well, don't want to make you lose count," Jim said, walking away.

Serge was almost sorry to see him go. Jim was about Martin's age. He was fit—looked as if he might run and lift now and then. "Hey!" Serge yelled after him, still doing his push-ups. "You ever play?"

"Play what?" Jim asked, half turning around.

"Hockey."

"Nah. Football in high school. Baseball."

Serge dropped his head slightly and began to push harder. He upped the pace by half. "Martin played baseball every spring. Once the lake thawed," Serge muttered.

"What'd you say?" Jim asked.

"Nothing." But his voice was still too low for Jim to hear, so the guard just kept walking on his rounds. Serge did his three-hundredth push-up, then got to his feet. He walked to the wall, leaned in to stretch his hamstrings.

Martin had killed Detroit last night, Chicago two nights before. He was hot this year. The papers were saying he was having the season of his life, that his marriage was the reason. Marriage hadn't tamed the Gold Sledgehammer; it had turned him molten, more powerful. Serge was keeping watch on Martin's eyes, ankles, and knees, though. Once you hit your thirties, injuries could blast a good season to pieces.

"Old man," greeted Tino, the kid with the shaved head. He exhaled a puff of smoke.

"That a cigarette?" Serge asked.

"Yeah, want one?"

"*Merde,* no. I don't touch those things. You sure it's not weed?"

"It ain't weed, ain't crack. I'm clean, I keep telling you."

"*Bien,*" Serge said. "This morning."

Tino laughed. Serge kept his face stern, but he couldn't stop the corner of his mouth twitching. "Cold out here, man," the kid said.

"For weaklings," Serge said.

"I ain't weak."

"You will be, eh? Just keep smoking."

"Aaaah." The kid took another drag, then hid the cigarette be-hind his thigh, as if he was ashamed.

"How old are you?" Serge asked.

"Twenty-four."

"Your father ever catch you smoking?" Serge was no longer shocked by the ages of the young men he met in here.

The kid exhaled out his nose, half laughing. "What father? He split before I came along. Later, Serge. I'm not weak, but I'm fuck-ing cold. Besides, my kids're coming to visit. I'd better wash up and get ready."

Serge watched the young man walk inside. The prison yard felt empty, and a great well of loneliness opened inside his chest. Win-ter always made him feel that way. Even before he'd come to prison. When the snow fell and the wind blew, people needed their families.

"My son's coming to see me soon," Serge said to the door the boy had walked through. He patted his pants pocket, where he now always carried the newspaper picture of Martin, May and Kylie—the wedding picture that had run before the season started.

A whistle blew, announcing visiting time. Serge ignored it, standing in the cold. Out here he felt a little alive. Closing his eyes, he could see his lake: nestled among mountains, its ice froze blacker than that of any other lake in Canada. He had taught Mar-tin to skate on that lake. They had had dreams of playing on the same team some day. Big dreams, that Serge had promised to make come true.

"If I ever caught my kid smoking," Serge said out loud, "I'd have made him quit." That's what good fathers were supposed to do: help their kids to do the right thing, what was best for them.

"Serge!" Jim called. "Aren't you too cold yet?"

"We're skating," Serge said, his eyes open now but still seeing the black lake. "My son and I."

He knew it was crazy to want to stay out in the cold, while in-side it was warmer and soon food would be served. But out here he was breathing real air, the same air that somewhere Martin was breathing. When Martin came, he would have to pass through those gates over there. Serge looked east, in the right direction.

Martin would have to come through those gates right there.

Serge closed his eyes again. The black-ice lake was gone, but

Martin was coming through the gates. With his eyes shut, Serge could see his son coming. With his wife and the little girl.

On his way inside, Serge walked the long way back to his cell. Lingering outside the visitors' room, he listened to the sound of women's and children's voices. They pulled him closer, almost through the door.

Tino sat at a long table. A small dark-haired woman leaned toward him, and one young child sat on his knees, climbing his body, and a second sat as close to him as possible, as if the terrible separation made them want to crawl right inside him.

Tino's eyes were shining, his smile wide, the closest thing to joy Serge had ever seen on his face. The boy had his grin, his build. Holding his breath, Serge watched as the boy grabbed his father's ears, kissed him right on the face.

Knowing how those separations felt, how the connection and need were no less strong for the father than for the son, Serge turned his back and walked quickly away.

May had started getting fan mail of her own. It amazed her, but women across America and Canada were intrigued by her love story, by the fact that she had spent so many years as an unmarried wedding planner. "It gives me hope," one woman wrote, "that there might be someone out there for me, too." Other women wanted help in casting a love spell or planning a wedding. May tried to answer all the mail, but she was overloaded both at work and at home.

One frozen night between games, Martin brought home two pairs of figure skates—for May and Kylie—and took them skating on the pond behind the Bridal Barn.

May hadn't been on skates in years. Feeling ungainly, she'd let Martin wrap his arm around her waist and glide her across the ice. He moved like the wind, fast and sure, holding her steady and whispering in her ear until she got her balance. Breathless, she sat down on a log to watch him skate with Kylie. Shrieking with joy, Kylie wanted to skate all night, and they did: or at least till all the stars came out and the temperature dipped below twenty degrees.

The first postcard arrived amid a batch of Christmas cards. Sitting at her desk, May had been staring out the window at the pond and wishing that Martin was home instead of in Montreal, that they could skate again that night.

"For you." Tobin placed the card on May's desk.

"What's this?" May asked.

"A mystery," Tobin told her. "I shouldn't have read it, but I did."

May stared at the postcard a long time, her heart racing. The photo was of a lake in summer, and the message read: "Take good care of him." The card was unsigned. Addressed to her, it bore the postmark of Estonia, N.Y.

"Who's from Estonia?" Tobin asked.

May knew: Serge Cartier. That's where he was in prison. She had read about him often enough. Glancing up at Tobin, she wanted to tell her. But knowing how Martin felt about his father, May had never talked in detail about him to Tobin, and she hesitated now.

"I don't know," May said, blushing as she told the lie. The desire to blurt everything out pressed against her chest. Tobin stood there, waiting, her expression guarded, hurt. They had really grown apart these last months. May opened her mouth to speak, but she couldn't. Instead, she just stuck the card into her purse as Tobin went back to work.

At the bottom of her purse, May saw the blue notebook: her diary of Kylie's visions and dreams. She hadn't been in touch with Dr. Whitpen since last summer, nor had there been any incidents to record. No more angel dreams, no more questions about Natalie.

But, her fingertips brushing the diary, May thought of what Dr. Whitpen had said about the veil: that Kylie could see through it, that perhaps she had been drawn to Martin because of a connection with his father and daughter. Shoving the notebook deeper into her purse, May tugged the zipper closed.

———

May didn't show Martin the card, but her thoughts wouldn't go away.

Late one December night, after the Bruins had lost at home to the Rangers, she and Martin pulled out of the players' garage. Recognizing his black Porsche, fans pressed forward with programs for him to autograph. Martin rolled down his window to sign them. Most were fathers and kids, but May saw a few beautiful women standing in the group too. Martin signed in silence, his face stern.

Even as they pulled away, he didn't speak. May had come to learn that this was his pattern after a loss: He would analyze the game in his mind, going over mistakes he had made, thinking of moves that might have made a difference. Boston was decorated for Christmas, with white lights everywhere, and in spite of Martin's quiet mood, May felt herself getting into the spirit.

"Our first holidays together," she said.

"Still no regrets about moving in from Black Hall?" he asked.

"No. I love your—our house," she corrected. "I can do most of my work here, and commuting down 395 two days a week doesn't bother me."

"Good," he said, holding her hand and placing it under his on his knee. "Don't want you having any second thoughts. Missing your aunt and Tobin too much."

"Martin, on the topic of family," she began as they approached the Boston Common. She held her purse, practically burning with the blue notebook and Serge's postcard inside. "I'd like to meet your father."

He didn't say anything. They had come to a red light, and Martin had stopped, but now it turned green, and he still didn't move. The car behind him blew its horn, and Martin pulled away fast.

"No, May," he said, still watching in the rearview mirror to see if the same guy was there.

"He's your father," she said. "I know what he did, but he's old. He's in prison, all alone, and I think—"

"You don't know him."

"But I'd like to." Dr. Whitpen's suggestion wouldn't go away.

"You don't know him," Martin said again.

They had zigzagged up the old brick and cobblestone streets, and came to a stop in front of their house on Marleybone Square. A beautiful old brick colonial, it had gleaming white trim and black shutters. May had made a wreath for the front door, and she and Aunt Enid had woven a length of laurel roping to hang above. Aunt Enid had come up for a few days and she was inside right now, baby-sitting Kylie.

"Listen," Martin said, rubbing his eyes. He looked stressed and tired from the game, his jaw tense and brow furrowed. "You think people are good and fair. That's the way you see the world, May. I love you for it."

"I know people make mistakes."

"Mistakes come in all shapes and sizes," Martin said. "My missing Ray's pass tonight was a mistake. You think not kissing

your father good-bye was a mistake. I don't, but you do. My father's mistakes were different."

"Don't you believe in forgiveness?" May asked.

"Ask me that," Martin said, looking her coldly in the eye as he opened his door, "when something bad happens to Kylie."

He walked into the house, leaving May behind. She felt hurt and shocked beyond words, in the pit of her stomach. Following Martin into the house, she looked around. Aunt Enid had been given one of the guest rooms; she and Kylie must be asleep upstairs. Martin's rooms were spare, arranged more like hotel rooms than a stately Boston home. Years of bachelorhood had left him with a leather recliner, a sectional sofa, and several cases full of hockey trophies.

Martin had told her to redecorate, rip the place apart, do whatever she wanted. So far, May had been so busy working at the Barn and helping Kylie get settled in her new school, she hadn't even started, and right now she felt the room's masculinity closing in on her.

May found him in the kitchen, pouring a glass of milk.

"I'm sorry," he said. "I shouldn't have said that about Kylie. I didn't mean to."

"I know."

"May, you can't imagine how it feels to lose a child. I pray you never find out."

"So do I."

"It's hell," he told her. "I am not exaggerating."

"I don't think you are."

"I saw her being born. I held her in the delivery room. Her favorite color was pink. She loved playing soccer. Her teachers said she was a good artist and dancer. She was beautiful . . . magic . . . *mine*. She had a whole life, May. And he took it from her."

"He is in jail, Martin," May said.

"But not for her death," Martin said. "I hope he rots in there."

"You don't always."

"What are you talking about?"

"You didn't want to let him down last season. You told me yourself—you thought he might be watching you from prison."

"*Mon Dieu.*" Martin leaned on the sink, shaking his head. "Don't have such a good memory, will you? I'll stop telling you things if you throw them back at me."

May watched snow falling outside the kitchen window. She had always found peace in snow, but right now the weather was stirring

her up. Martin was twisting her words, and she couldn't figure out how to straighten them out.

"You said," she began carefully, "that people think you've written him off, but—"

"Let it go at that. I have written him off, eh?"

"I don't believe you."

"Listen, May." Martin turned to face her. His eyes were tense and cold, his shoulders hiking up toward his ears. "Hockey and my father are linked forever. When I step out on the ice, he's there. His voice, telling me what to do. How to skate, how to shoot. He's just there."

"Your first teacher?"

"The great Serge Cartier," Martin said with hatred. "My father."

May watched the anger building. It reminded her of last summer, and her stomach tightened. His face was red, and the tendons on his neck stood out. Looming in the kitchen doorway, he pressed his arms outward, flexing his biceps as if he wanted to knock the house down.

"Sometimes I think I want to win the Stanley Cup just to shut him up. So I can retire and get him out of my head for good. You know how many Cups he won? Three. He got rich winning them, and he threw every penny away. He gambled the money while my mother and I scrounged to get by. We were hungry and cold up on Lac Vert, with him living high in the States."

"He didn't send you money?"

"Money?" Martin asked, as if he'd suddenly forgotten the meaning of the word. "He sent what he had to. Not enough."

May listened, wondering how it must have felt to see his father really living it up while he and his mother struggled. The disturbance that must have created in Martin was still in place, May thought, watching him pace.

"Gambling isn't really about money," Martin said, his voice getting lower. He sounded raw, and the way his voice caught reminded May of an animal. "It's about living on the edge. Getting close, pulling back before you fall. He did it with me—" Martin touched his chest. "And he did it with Nat. But he didn't pull her back in time. He gambled my daughter's life!"

"Oh, Martin." May reached out, but he wouldn't let her touch him. He moved to the corner, hugging himself as if he was afraid he'd punch through a wall if he let go.

"He said he was sorry," Martin said. "Afterward. That's what he told me."

"He must feel terrible remorse," May said, trying to imagine.

Martin released his breath, fierce and brutal as a blast of arctic wind.

"I want him out of my life, May, not in it. When I met you and Kylie, I knew it was a blessing. Something I never thought I'd have—a wife and a little girl. Leave him where he is, where he can't hurt us."

May listened, hearing his voice shake. His face was still red, but she saw him lower his arms, as if he wanted to give the house another chance. May had heard his voice shaking, and she thought he sounded afraid. Her hockey-playing husband, fearless on the ice, all muscle and the first to fight, was trembling.

"He can't hurt you, Martin. He can't hurt you anymore."

"I want to protect *you,* May. You and Kylie. You got that?"

"I don't need protecting from him," she said. "This is important to me! I don't want our family to have a rift like that. I don't want you to have that rift inside you. Won't you at least consider—"

"Jesus Christ!" Martin exploded. "I don't want to bring him into our lives. I won't do it—like it or not, I think you do need protecting. And you don't need to worry about me." He looked at her angrily, shaking his head. Then he checked his watch. "I have to leave for St. Louis first thing in the morning. I'm going up to get some sleep. You coming?"

May stood at the foot of the stairs, breathing hard. What was Martin talking about: *protect her*? That was the biggest crock, a lame excuse to avoid facing his own feelings. If he could stay estranged from his father all this time, who was to say he wouldn't turn against her someday? If Kylie let him down, would he shut the door in her face? Anger like that killed everything it touched, eventually. May felt wild inside, her heart pounding against her ribs, powered by bone-deep fear.

"He's your family! Just like me and Kylie!" she said.

Martin exhaled, shaking his head as he headed upstairs. His feet were heavy on the stairs.

"Go ahead, walk away," May said. Outside snow blew along the brick sidewalks and cobbled alleys, sticking to the slate roofs, swirling around the smoking chimneys of Beacon Hill.

She wanted Martin to turn around, but he didn't. She heard him go into the empty guest room.

Once again, May did something she had sworn over twenty years ago never to do: go to bed angry. In her short marriage, it had already happened more than once. Her chest felt like exploding, and as she stood in the hallway she felt tears streaming down her face.

She wanted to talk to Tobin. Picking up the phone, she dialed her friend's number. But when Tobin answered, she hung up. Instead, she dialed a different number, one in Canada, that she hadn't used for a long time. She heard Ben Whitpen's voice on the answering machine.

She hung up before the beep.

Before morning, Martin walked down the hall to his and May's bedroom. He had to travel in just a few hours, and he was wide awake and exhausted. He had wanted to make up with May, but he couldn't. Rage had gripped him all night. Directed at May, at first, for refusing to let go of something she could never understand. But soon he directed his rage in the right place, toward his father, for abandoning him as a child, for returning to his life only to destroy his beautiful daughter.

May didn't understand.

When Martin said he had to protect her, he meant it. He had promised to love, honor, and cherish her, and in his book, that meant keeping her away from his father—in prison or out. She was small and delicate, sensitive and idealistic. She actually thought there was a parallel between a twelve-year-old girl failing to kiss her daddy good-bye and a battle-scarred NHL veteran hating his crooked father's guts.

If Serge died, Martin would be glad. He'd feel relieved, to have the burden lifted. Hatred and guilt were heavy loads, and Martin carried his every day. Staring at the guest room ceiling, he had wished May would accept the situation. She didn't have to like it, but he wished she'd stop pushing him.

Thinking of her, Martin had finally gotten up the courage to go into their bedroom. He hoped she wouldn't start in again, asking him if he'd changed his mind. Christmas was coming, and he knew she had some fantasy about visiting the old man at the prison—hell would freeze over before that happened. Still shaking, Martin walked over to the bed.

By the light of the streetlight shining through the window, he

saw her facing the wall. Her shoulder looked very tense, and her breathing seemed a little short—as if she might be awake.

"May?" he whispered.

"Hi."

"I couldn't sleep."

"Neither could I."

He paused, touching her hair. His heart was pounding, waiting for her to ask if he'd changed his mind about his father. She didn't ask.

Rolling over, May opened her arms. She was warm, and when Martin slid under the sheets, so was their bed. He held her hard, knowing he had to leave soon, wondering why they'd wasted their last night together for a week in a fight.

"I don't want to leave you," he said.

"I'm just glad you came to bed."

"The snow's coming down. Maybe my flight'll be canceled."

"I hope so," she said, her mouth hot as she kissed him hard.

Chapter 13

THE ALL-STAR GAME WAS scheduled for February 10 in Calgary, with Martin playing right wing for the East. Kylie and May were supposed to accompany him, fly northwest into Canada, but Kylie had a sore throat that kept them home in Boston.

Bundled in the bedclothes, Kylie stared at the TV. Mommy sat in a chair across the room, cheering for Martin as if they were at the rink.

"Where's Ray?" Kylie asked. "Where are the other Bruins?"

"Martin's the only Bruin to be named an All-Star," Mommy said. "This game is different from all the others."

"Are you mad I got sick?"

"Why would I be mad?" Mommy asked, smiling over.

"Because you want to be there."

"I want to be right here, taking care of you."

Kylie nodded. It hurt to talk, so she was saving her voice. She wasn't used to having two parents, and sometimes she heard angry voices coming down the hall. Martin could yell so loud it shook the house. Mommy would sometimes yell, but mostly she kept her anger inside, her arms folded tightly across her chest, her lips a thin line. Kylie picked up on their moods, and she worried that they'd stop loving each other and get a divorce, like other kids' parents.

"Is Martin mad we're not at the All-Star game with him?" she asked.

"Of course not. Kylie, why do you keep asking these questions?"

"I just want us to stay together," Kylie said, her throat burning.

"We *are* together."

"What makes some families go apart?" Kylie asked.

"Oh, I don't know, honey," her mother said. "Sometimes no matter how hard people try, they just can't make it work. Two peo-

ple might want opposite things from life, or their values are too different, or they find they can't talk to each other."

"Can't they pretend?"

Kylie's question must have made Mommy sad, because her eyes filled with tears. She ducked her head for a minute, and when she came up she had a small smile on her face. "That's never the way," she said, holding Kylie's hand. " 'To thine own self be true.' Do you know what that means?"

"No, what?"

"It means that your feelings are as important as anyone else's. You never have to pretend you don't matter."

"Even to get along?" Kylie asked. Her throat was raw, and she held her mother's hand.

"Even then. You might compromise, but you don't have to pretend."

"Com-pro-mise?"

"Give a little," Mommy said.

Kylie closed her eyes. She knew that Martin had gotten divorced once, that he had lived apart from Natalie, that he never even spoke to his own father. What if he got really mad and decided never to speak to Mommy and Kylie?

The room was dark, except for the TV. Outside, snow was falling, and Kylie heard a big snowplow passing by. Boston was noisier than Black Hall but Kylie didn't mind. Living in a city made her feel like a girl in a storybook. Their house was big and beautiful, and last week a big truck had arrived, full of furniture Mommy had ordered, to decorate the big rooms. Martin bought Kylie toys on all his trips. The only bad thing was the fighting.

The best part was having Martin. Not because of the toys or the fancy house, but because she had always wanted a father. Sometimes he faxed messages from his hotel, and when they checked, there would be a fax for Kylie, too. Sometimes Martin would draw her a bear on skates, because he'd told her a bruin was actually a bear. Her favorite drawing had shown a mother bruin, a father bruin, and a daughter bruin with "Kylie" written on her bowl of porridge.

Although she couldn't call him "Daddy" yet, Kylie felt as if she finally had a father. He tucked her in and told her stories when he was home. Together they dreamed of rowing the whole length of Lac Vert, someday seeing the great-granddaddy trout. When she went to school, Kylie felt proud—not because she lived with Martin Cartier, the great hockey player, but because she had a father.

"Father, father, father," Kylie said out loud.

"What's that, honey?" Mommy asked, glancing over from the TV.

"Oh, nothing," Kylie mumbled. Her head felt hot, and she knew she was having a fever-dream. She drifted off into missing her old school. Kylie missed everyone, even Mickey and Eddie a little.

The kids in Boston were different. Every Saturday they all took lessons in everything: musical instruments, drawing, gymnastics, figure skating, horseback riding, art appreciation at the Museum of Fine Arts. Sometimes the mothers asked Mommy if Kylie wanted to join a class, but Kylie didn't and Mommy didn't make her. She understood that Kylie just wanted to play, not improve.

She didn't get fevers often, but when she did, she sometimes drifted off into a sort of waking sleep. Things that couldn't be real seemed *very* real. The stuff she used to talk to Dr. Whitpen about.

Like the laundry hamper across the room looking like a crouching gnome, guarding all the soiled shirts and socks and pillowcases inside as if they were a great treasure he had swallowed. And the alarm clock on Martin's side of the bed looking like a flat-headed creature with glowing red eyes.

"Promise you'll never leave me, Mommy," Kylie whispered, holding her mother.

"I promise," May said, smoothing her hair away from her sweaty forehead.

"Why do things have to change?" Kylie asked, her throat burning. "Why can't good things just stay the same? I wish they could last forever. . . ."

"I love you forever, Kylie," Mommy said. "Forever and ever and ever."

Mommy's white nightgown on the rocking chair moved, and for an instant, Kylie thought it was Natalie. Suddenly Kylie felt a message in her heart, as if it was coming straight from Martin's daughter: Bring them together, bring them together.

"Bring who together, Mommy?" Kylie asked.

The first day Kylie felt well enough to go to school, another postcard arrived. This one showed a city park in winter, children skating across a frozen pond. Turning it over, May saw that the picture had been taken at Estonia's Dexter Park. The message said:

"He's playing better than ever this year. It must be because you're rooting for him. So am I."

Like the others, the card was unsigned. May wondered whether Serge had bought the card at the prison store, whether someone had given it to him. The man was in prison, yet he was her father-in-law. She thought of the bad things he had done to get there—the lies he had told, the people he had harmed.

Last night, May had written in the blue notebook. She had recorded everything that had happened during Kylie's fever, the way she had called out "bring them together." Holding the diary and staring at the postcard, May picked up the phone and called Toronto.

"I was hoping I'd hear from you again," Ben Whitpen said.

"It's started up again," May said. "For a long time, I thought the dreams had stopped. But the other night—"

Dr. Whitpen was silent as she told him everything. At the end, she told him about getting postcards from Serge.

"Has Kylie seen them?"

"I don't think so."

"Has she heard you telling Martin you want to meet his father?"

"No. He gets angry, and I'm careful not to fight in front of her."

"You say that Kylie heard Natalie's words when she had the fever."

"She did." May's heart was pounding. " 'Bring them together,' Kylie kept saying. 'We have to bring them together, Mommy.' "

The doctor was silent, his computer keys clicking softly in the background.

"Did she tell you who she wants to bring together?"

"No. That was the entire message."

"Was it Kylie's message or Natalie's?"

"Kylie told me Natalie said it," May said, speaking quickly. "But there was no one else in the room!"

"To Kylie there was."

"I was there," May said.

"You don't see what Kylie sees."

"You're saying she saw Natalie?"

He paused. "It's not that simple."

"That makes her sound crazy," May began. "She's not, though. She just imagined it, I think. She has such a big heart; she's sensitive to people who are hurt."

"You're speaking of Natalie?"

"Yes."

"In fact, I think it's someone else . . ." Dr. Whitpen began, then veered into a different direction. "The metaphysical explanation centers around the arrival of those postcards. They have sparked something, Mrs. Cartier."

"In Kylie?"

"Not in her, no. *Around* her."

May drew a deep breath, covered her eyes.

"But I haven't told anyone about the postcards. I don't think Kylie has seen them."

"She senses the emotions in the air—in you—caused by them. Perhaps she even feels the power of Serge's longing."

"But why?"

"Just as the shock of seeing that hanging man, Richard Perry, was the catalyst for Kylie's gift to emerge, the postcards are now the catalyst for what she has been called to witness."

"What are you talking about?" May asked.

"Something concerning Martin and his father, from what you tell me," Dr. Whitpen said. " 'Bring them together' was the message, wasn't it?"

"Yes, but—"

"I believe it refers to Martin and his father."

"That's impossible."

"In the world of metaphysics," Dr. Whitpen said, "many things are."

"This is over Kylie's head," May said. "The troubles between Martin and Serge are too deep for her to understand."

"Are they?" Dr. Whitpen asked softly. "It would not be the first time a youth has set about to effect change in a troubled landscape. David comes to mind. Hamlet."

"This is crazy," May said. "Those are figures in the Bible, in literature. I'm talking about my little girl. She had a fever; she was sick."

"I know this is hard for you to comprehend, Mrs. Cartier. But you're doing the right thing. Keep writing everything down."

"I don't have any choice," May said. "If I didn't, I'd go crazy myself."

"When you're ready, I hope you'll bring Kylie back to see me again. I think our visits are of value to her. For children like Kylie, it helps a great deal to know that they are being understood."

May thanked him and hung up.

That afternoon, without telling Tobin or Enid where she was going, May went to visit her parents' graves. They were buried in a small cemetery on the bank of the Ibis River in Black Hall, surrounded by a stone wall and a circle of pine trees. All the snow had melted, and crocuses were poking up through the brown grass.

May walked up the stone path. She felt nervous, as if she were going to visit people she hardly knew. For several years, she had come here with her grandmother. Emily would tend the graves of her daughter and son-in-law, raking the leaves in autumn, planting flowers in spring, telling May stories about her parents. Sometimes Tobin had come along. But as May grew older, got busy in her own life, she had stopped coming.

This was her first visit in many years. Dead leaves had blown against the headstones, and the only plants growing were weeds. May bowed her head against the March wind and rested her palm on the headstone. It felt cold to her fingers.

Her parents' names were chiseled, along with the dates of their births and deaths. *Samuel and Abigail Taylor.* Touching the deeply cut letters, May wished she knew why she had come. The hills and woods spread around her, silent and empty. The Ibis River, a narrow tributary of the wide Connecticut, was edged with ice. Brown leaves and dead grass, frozen together, stuck to the grave. Kneeling down, she began to clear the leaves away.

As she did, her head touched the stone. She thought of her mother and father and deep feelings of love came bubbling up in her chest. So much time had passed since she had seen her parents; she had grown up, had a child, gotten married.

The wind blew, scattering leaves.

May bowed her head and cried. She thought of the years she and her parents had missed. It seemed so cruel and unfair. They had been right here in the ground, just a few miles from the barn, while other people went on taking the days and seasons and years for granted. She thought of Martin and his father, wasting time in a fight, whatever terrible things had passed between them.

With her eyes closed, May tried to conjure up her father's face. She remembered him handsome and smiling, with bright hazel eyes and a quick and brilliant smile. His face was full of love. Then she saw the look of hurt as she turned her back on him.

What had Dr. Whitpen said? That it helped children like Kylie to know they were being understood. May thought back twenty-four years and remembered how she had felt to have her father die without hearing her.

"I love you, Dad," May whispered, touching the stone. "That's what I want to tell you."

He didn't speak back. Unlike Kylie, May couldn't see or hear through the veil. But the strange thing was, she was filled with the belief that he could hear her now. She felt a shiver down her spine, as if he had touched the top of her head.

May felt her father's love, and she suddenly had no doubt that he was with her. He would have told her he loved her, too; he'd forgiven her a long time ago: She could almost hear his voice in the air. The March wind blew steadily through the trees, scraping branches against each other. May knelt where she was for a few more minutes, and then, feeling as if a burden had been lifted and knowing what she had to do, she drove straight home.

Chapter 14

ONE EVENING AS WINTER TURNED to spring, when Martin was home, they all took a walk down Beacon Hill into the Public Garden. The setting sun washed Boston's old brick buildings with rose pink light, and the bare branches in the park interlocked like black ironwork against the sky. While Kylie ran ahead to see the ducks, May and Martin walked slowly behind.

"Martin Cartier!" a bunch of kids called, surrounding him. He autographed their notebooks, whatever they had, but when a thirty-something couple approached him, he just shook his head and shepherded May quickly away.

As they walked, he had his arm around her shoulders. Passing behind a lilac bush, he couldn't keep his hands off of her. They stopped to kiss, and May felt how much he wanted her. Their time apart made their time together wild and passionate. He started tugging her toward the bushes, and she laughed, resisting.

"Let's go home," he said.

"Great idea," she said.

"I wish the season was over already, eh?"

"It almost is. You'll definitely make the play-offs."

"And then the Cup. I'll win it for you."

"I'll take it," May said, laughing. She found herself thinking of the conversation she and Kylie had had earlier. How she had casually asked Kylie about her dreams, whether she had dreamed of Natalie since the night when she'd been sick. Instead of answering the questions, Kylie had asked one of her own.

"Why doesn't Martin talk to his father?" she had asked.

"He's very mad at him," May had answered calmly, her palms sweating as Kylie herself made the connection Dr. Whitpen had theorized.

"Sometimes he gets mad at you."

"I know, honey, but that's different. Married couples get angry sometimes, and then they work it out."

"But what if he stops talking to you? What if he wants us to move out?" Kylie had asked, her face twisted with worry.

"We love each other, Kylie. I trust him not to stop talking to us, and I trust that he'll talk to his father when he's ready," May said.

"I wish we could bring them back together before something terrible happens."

"Something terrible? What do you mean?" May asked, the words "back together" ringing in her mind.

"I don't know."

An hour later, with Martin expected home from Toronto and Kylie playing outside, May had called Estonia. She had learned that Serge Cartier was in Unit C, Cell 62. That he could have visitors every other Monday, that she wouldn't need special permission to show up, that she wouldn't even have to tell him she was coming.

Now, walking through the Public Garden, May felt caught in a tangle of lies she hadn't even told yet. She knew she should tell Martin about the call, but she couldn't. She should show him the postcards. She should also tell him that she had gone through his dresser drawers, found an envelope full of pictures way in back.

That she had finally seen a photo of Trisha, that nothing she had heard had prepared her for the woman's startling beauty. She looked so at ease with herself, in her clingy sleeveless dress, looking utterly California and designer and charming all at the same time. The baby was tugging at the scoop neck, trying to get to her mother's large, perfect, half-visible breast.

He kept the picture because of Natalie, May told herself. His adorable daughter with his eyes and her mother's mouth: How could he throw out any picture with her in it? But May's attention was held by Trisha. Her sultry gaze, full lips, creamy skin.

There were other pictures.

More of Trisha and Natalie, many of Natalie alone, Natalie with Martin, and one of Natalie with Serge, showing them in a rowboat. On the back was an inscription: "Dad and Nat, summer at the lake."

May had stared at Martin's handwriting for a long time. It was the only picture he'd written on; the handwriting was careful, precise, telling May something tender about Martin's feelings on the subject.

Kylie had run to the pond's edge, to feed the ducks a roll she'd

brought from home. But now she trailed back, telling Martin about the birthday party she had attended last Saturday as he bent down to listen.

"It was a skating party," she said. "Ellen Linder can skate backward."

"Really?" Martin asked. "How old is she?"

"Seven."

"That's how old you'll be your next birthday, eh? I think we should rent the same rink, plan the greatest skating party Boston has ever seen."

"A skating party," she said, sounding doubtful.

"*Bien sûr*," Martin said.

"But I can't skate like that," Kylie said. "All Ellen's friends are expert skaters. They take ballet on ice, and all I do is fall down."

"Falling down is how you learn how to stand up, yes?" Martin said. "You do great when I see you on the pond."

"When you're with me."

"I'll come to the party with you."

"Honestly?"

"If I'm in Boston." He stopped, thinking for a minute. "When I was six, my father gave me a pair of new skates for my birthday. They were real hockey skates, my first pair, and boy, they felt different. I went out on the ice, and all I did was fall down. I was like a new colt, with wobbly legs."

"But your father helped you?" Kylie asked.

"Maybe he did," Martin said. "Just like I'm going to help you."

"That's what fathers do," Kylie whispered, her eyes shining.

"They're supposed to," Martin said.

Kylie stared into Martin's eyes for a long time, and then she put her hands on either side of his face. Her expression was troubled, as if she was trying to decide how to break bad news to him.

"Natalie's right," she said instead, and May's heart began to race.

"Kylie, honey—"

"What do you mean?" Martin asked. He started to straighten up, but Kylie held onto his collar. She stared him straight in the eye and said, "People need fathers. Even fathers need fathers. Daddy."

"What?" Martin asked.

"Daddy," Kylie said, throwing her arms around his neck. "People need fathers so much."

May waited for Kylie to ask more about Serge, but the child held back. This was May's chance to tell Martin that she had called

the prison and was thinking of going to visit Serge, but *she* held back, too. Kylie had just called Martin "Daddy," and all three of them were silently overjoyed.

———

Once Kylie began to call Martin "Daddy," she didn't stop. May had been unaware that so many sentences had the word "Daddy" in them. Such as, "Yesterday my teacher wore a blue dress to school, but Martha Cole spilled red paint on the floor and when Miss Gingras knelt down to clean it up, she got it on her dress and then she had two purple knee prints right in front—Daddy!" Or, "Charlotte sent me an early birthday card, Daddy, with a picture of a canoe on the front, and she said next summer she'll take me on an overnight canoe camping trip, but I have to wear a life vest. Right, *Daddy*?"

Martin seemed to thrive on Kylie's exuberant affection. His face lit up every time she said the name, and every night he was on the road and called home, he asked to speak to Kylie before hanging up the phone. The Bruins had made the play-offs again, and because of the schedule, Martin would probably be away the day of her party.

"Is she upset?" he asked.

"Disappointed," May said.

"It's weird," Martin told her. "I want to win, you know I do, but I want to be there almost more. I don't want to miss her party. Is she still nervous?"

"Well, she's a little afraid of being embarrassed," May said. "Some of these Boston kids have been taking figure skating for two years now. They're so much better than she is."

"Figure skating," Martin said, snorting. "Ballet on ice—ridiculous."

"They're little girls." May smiled.

"Girls can play hockey, too," Martin said. "Kylie's a natural—I can tell. Nat was, and so was Genny, as a matter of fact. I'll work with her when the season's over. We'll do drills, I'll teach her to shoot. Figure skating!" He laughed.

May, who had watched Kylie practicing pirouettes in front of the mirror, smiled. She had stood around the corner when Kylie didn't know she was there, watching her pretend to glide across the ice as if she were dancing *Swan Lake*. Up on her toes, twirling around, skating across her bedroom. Knowing that hockey was not

the stuff of Kylie's dreams, May smiled as she asked, "Natalie liked to play hockey?"

"She was damn good at it," Martin said.

"But she liked it?"

There was a long silence on the line. May waited for Martin to speak. She could almost see him sitting there, thinking about her, and she wished they were in the same room.

"Um," Martin said, clearing his throat. "I guess her preference would have been figure skating. She never told me, though."

"How did you find out?"

"Her mother let me know. She told me Natalie's dream was to someday skate in the Ice Capades. Her idol was Michelle Kwan."

"Trisha told you that?"

"Yes. We tried to get back together for a short while, but it would never work. She was always pointing out how far apart I was from Natalie. How I didn't know her likes and dislikes, how I didn't even know my own daughter. *Merde!*"

May was silent, taking in the information that Martin and Trisha had once tried to reconcile.

"Hey, don't think anything about Trisha, okay?"

"What would I think?"

"That I wish we had stayed together. That we have any sort of bond. It was over before it really started—you know that, don't you? This was back when my father lived in California, when I still had the idea that we should all be together, a family."

"I think that part's a good idea," May said.

"Meaning?"

"Your father sent me a postcard, Martin."

"No," he said. "Tell me you're joking."

"I'm not joking, and I want to meet him."

"Jesus Christ!" Martin said. "When will you drop that? How many times do I have to tell you—he's never going to know you, not as long as I'm alive. Leave it alone, for Chrissakes. Burn the goddamn postcard, May. Do you want to ruin us? I swear, that's what you're doing."

"Maybe it's what *you're* doing," May blurted out. "My reasons for wanting to meet him are just as important as yours for not—"

He hung up on her. Shaking, May walked over to the bureau. She stared for a long time at the picture of Martin and his father. And then she went to the phone to call the airline, her daughter's words ringing in her ears.

We have to bring them together.

Chapter 15

IN THE MIDDLE OF APRIL, when Martin left for his next away game, May asked Aunt Enid to come up and stay with Kylie overnight. She flew the shuttle to New York, rented a compact car, and drove north toward the Catskills. The route to see Dr. Whitpen had taken them over these mountains many times.

Estonia was a small city filled with old, abandoned brick mills. Set above falls on a wide river, it had once been a prosperous manufacturing center. The town park boasted a band shell, a soldier's monument carved from granite, and a reflecting pool now drained and filled with debris. Beautiful Victorian houses had fallen into disrepair, and the mansions on Main Street had been broken up into apartments and offices.

The prison crowned a western hill. May saw it from miles away. Driving up the road, she saw people trudging up the sidewalk, on their way to visiting day. She parked in the visitors' lot, followed the flow of people to the entrance. Coils of razor wire glistened in the sun. The brick walls looked thick and impenetrable, and the dents in the gray metal door made her think of rage and frustration.

Entering the waiting room, May smelled sweat, stale cigarette smoke, and fast food. The crowd was thick, mainly women and children, talking and laughing. Jostled on all sides, May had the feeling of being in steerage, at the beginning of a voyage to an unknown country.

A guard at the front desk took her name and asked who she wanted to visit.

"Serge Cartier," she said. "Unit C, Cell sixty-two."

"Wait over there," he said, without once looking into her eyes.

Sitting down beside two women who had obviously been here before, May heard them talking about their husbands' court cases,

their public defenders, chances of acquittal. Talk turned to violence, how an inmate had been stabbed over drugs last week, with a straight-edged razor, or a shank.

Twenty minutes passed. Then a different guard unlocked the double-thick inner doors and allowed the visitors to pass through. The gray corridor echoed with excited voices and the clatter of footsteps. May hung back. She felt afraid of what she was walking into. Her blood was pumping, thinking of the weapons the women had talked about. The anxiety came from knowing that she was going behind Martin's back, that this was her last chance to turn around.

But she kept walking. Passing through another metal door, she entered the large visitors' room. Many reunions were taking place, with guards standing everywhere to prevent kissing and hugging. May stood frozen in place, looking around. Just as she was about to ask a guard for assistance, she saw a man walking toward her.

He looked just like Martin. He was older and thinner, slightly stooped, but he had those brilliant blue Cartier eyes. His expression was guarded, hesitant as he approached May. Like all the other inmates, he wore a baggy orange prison jumpsuit, but the garment couldn't hide the fact that he was a handsome, commanding man. He stopped dead still, just staring at her, and May felt pressure rapidly building inside her chest. But then his eyes lit up, and the Cartier smile took over his face.

"You got my postcards," he said.

"I did."

"Your pictures don't do you justice. I've seen you in the papers—"

"You look exactly like Martin—you both have the same eyes."

"I'm glad to meet you. Serge Cartier—"

"May Cartier."

"My daughter-in-law." May heard the emotion in his voice just before he turned away to find them a place to sit. All of the chairs were taken by other inmates and their families, but May watched Serge approach one young Hispanic man and his female visitor, say a few words, and clear two hard plastic armchairs.

"One of the benefits of being old," he told her. "Occasionally someone decides he wants to respect his elders."

May nodded, sitting down. She had seen the exchange of smiles and words, the way Serge spoke to the young woman as well. Now that she was here, she didn't know what to say, what she hoped to accomplish.

"I was surprised when they said I had a visitor," Serge said in the same French Canadian accent as Martin.

"People don't come to see you?"

"Oh, lawyers. Reporters, sometimes. Hockey players once in a while. But no one who matters, eh? No family."

May nodded.

"How is my son?"

"He's fine," May said. "The Bruins are winning. It looks like the play-offs will—"

Serge shook his head. "He's got you thinking it's one and the same? Life and hockey?"

"No." May laughed. "But he tries."

"You see through that?"

"I try to understand him," she said slowly. "Hockey has been such a central part of his life. But I never played, never even watched it until I met him."

"The papers say you plan weddings."

"Yes," May said, laughing nervously. "Slightly different from pro sports."

"More important in the long run, eh?" Serge said. "What brought you two together?"

May found herself telling him about the plane crash, Kylie asking Martin to help them, the not-to-be-denied love that had happened so fast between them. How they'd gotten married just a month after meeting, how they had merged their lives without really even knowing each other. She left out Kylie's visions, Dr. Whitpen, the blue diary.

"And how is it going? You are happy together?"

"Mostly," May said, but the pressure in her chest increased. "We have some differences."

"Everyone does, *non*?" Serge asked. "The trick is in how you handle them. Maybe that's why this room is so full. Many, many differences of opinion. Does Martin know you are here?"

"No," May said. "That's one of the differences."

"Don't tell me I'm the cause of you two fighting."

May swallowed hard.

"It's hardly worth it," he said. "Martin wrote me off long before you married him. He has his reasons."

"I know them," May whispered. "He's told me."

Serge gazed toward the door, his eyes following a young girl running in circles around her parents. "He blames me for Natalie's death," he said.

"I know." May's heart kicked over. "But you never meant to hurt her."

"Never," Serge said, the word forceful and passionate.

May believed him. She knew about mistakes made in a moment that shadowed all the moments to come.

"Why are you here?" he asked, his eyes glittering with tears.

"Because you're Martin's father," she said. "Because you're so important to him." The blue notebook testified to deeper reasons, but she couldn't tell him.

"Did he say that?"

"He doesn't have to," May said.

"He hates me."

May stared at his hand. If the guards weren't standing there, she would have taken it. She cleared her throat. "I thought I hated my father," she said. "For a few minutes, I guess I actually did. By the time I realized I'd made a mistake, it was too late. I couldn't see what was right there until he was gone. I don't want that to happen to Martin."

"What's he missing?" Serge asked. "What doesn't *he* see?"

"I'm not sure yet." May was struck by the question, reminded of something Kylie had said to Dr. Whitpen. "He won't talk about it. Maybe this summer, when the season ends—"

"Martin keeps everything inside," Serge said. "He always has. When he was little, he got hit in the head with a puck. Didn't tell me, didn't tell his mother. We found him bleeding from his ear when we tucked him in that night. Later he told us he thought we'd be mad at Ray Gardner—his best friend—for hitting him, or we wouldn't let him play the next day."

"Were you mad at Ray?"

Serge shook his head. "Of course not. Ray was like a brother to Martin. Still is, from what I can tell. But Martin did have a concussion."

"A concussion?" May asked.

Serge exhaled. "The first of many. That's hockey for you. You've seen his scars, the scar tissue around his eyes. From what I read about him, he's in the line of fire every game. He nearly lost his eye a few years back, in a fight with Jorgensen. He talk about that?"

"Nils Jorgensen?" May asked. "Yes—his enemy."

"They hate each other, those two," Serge said. "I know how it is, eh? When Martin's mother divorced me, I took it out on a guy who played for Boston at the time. I couldn't wait to play the

Bruins. So I could beat the hell out of their right wing. The divorce was my fault, *bien sûr,* but I couldn't see it that way at the time."

"Why blame anyone, right?"

"*Non!* I thought it was Agnes's fault, her father's fault, even Martin's fault. Everyone's but mine, believe me. I was a mess. The Boston player was damned easy to hit—the rest of the time I tried to prove my worth at the roulette wheel, the craps table. See, I thought if I was lucky there, I must be a good person."

"How do you mean?"

"I believe in *le bon Dieu,* May. I believed that if I won at gambling, God was tipping the odds in my favor. He wouldn't do that for a bad man."

May smiled.

"I was a bad husband," he said. "And father. I was trying to change that, though. When Natalie came along . . ." his voice cracked. "I promised myself I'd be the best grandfather I could. I'd be there for Martin, help him not to make the same mistakes I did. I'd baby-sit, I'd love that little girl."

"You did love her," May said. "I can hear that."

"I let her die," Serge said, his eyes washed in terrible grief and pain. "No matter what else I felt or did, that part's true."

"But you didn't mean to."

"*Non,*" he said, bowing his head. "I did not."

A bell rang, and people began to move. "Time!" a guard yelled. The crowd was restless, and tension rose. People trying to embrace were thrust apart by guards. May wanted to hold Serge's hand, kiss his cheek. He was her father-in-law, and she could feel his love for Martin and Natalie across the space that separated them.

"I wish you didn't have to go," he said, wiping his eyes.

"I wish I didn't, too."

"You have a beautiful daughter, *très jolie.* I have seen her pictures. I'm certain—" he trailed off.

"What?" she asked as a guard gestured for her to leave.

"I'm sure she brings Martin joy. He loved having a daughter."

"Thank you for telling me that," she said, staring into his eyes. She thought of her own father, who would be just about the same age as Serge. If only she could have one last minute with him, say whatever she wanted . . . what would it be?

"Martin's balance, is it okay?" Serge asked suddenly. "I watch him on TV, and sometimes it seems to me he's off a little—that he favors his right side, as if he's having problems with his left."

"It seems fine to me," May said, surprised.

"Maybe he needs glasses," Serge said. "After all those hits to the head."

May nodded. Her heart hurt; the guards were telling her to leave. She had his postcards, the blue notebook in her bag. She couldn't believe the visit was over.

"Tell him something for me, will you?" Serge asked.

"Of course."

"Tell him I love him," Serge said.

"I will," May promised, her voice breaking. Her father-in-law had just taken the words out of her mouth. Because she couldn't think of anything better to say, she leaned forward and kissed him lightly on the cheek. A guard stepped forward to hurry her out. Serge protested loudly, but it didn't matter.

He went back behind one thick steel door, and May, looking over her shoulder, walked freely through another. She had intended to check her notebook, look up the words Kylie had said to Dr. Whitpen last summer, but in the emotion of the moment, she forgot.

———

May returned home and couldn't wait the four days for Martin to get home from his road trip. Driving down to Black Hall, she worked extra hours, helping Tobin prepare and send out a huge Bridal Barn mailing. While Aunt Enid baby-sat Kylie, they worked until midnight, watching Martin's game on TV.

"When I came in yesterday, Enid told me you had an unexpected trip," Tobin said, stuffing brochures from one stack into envelopes from another.

"I went to upstate New York," May said.

"Something to do with Kylie?" Tobin asked.

"Why?" May asked, surprised.

"I've seen you looking at the diary lately. The dream notebook. I thought you had finished with Dr. Whitpen."

"I had," May said, looking over at Tobin. Going through the notebook, she had found the entry from last July: "Some people can't see with their eyes," Kylie had said to the doctor. What could that have to do with Serge asking "What doesn't he see?" Probably nothing, but the connection left May feeling unsettled. May wanted so badly to tell Tobin everything. The barn was dark except for one circle of light over their work space and the TV's violet

glow. The owls were busy, hunting the fields outside. May leaned on the table, feeling tired.

"You can tell me, May," Tobin said.

"I know," May said.

"Have things changed that much? We never talk the way we used to."

"Kylie still has dreams," May told her, letting go. "She still talks about angels."

"Your imaginative girl," Tobin said warmly.

"Dr. Whitpen thinks," May began slowly, "that Kylie's sightings are all connected. The thing is, some of it involves Martin and his family."

"I know you think you shouldn't talk about Martin to me, but you can," Tobin said. "I swear you can. My marriage has been rocky before; maybe I should have talked to you more."

"We're not rocky," May said quickly.

"I didn't mean to say you are."

"It sounded . . ."

"Just, I want you to know that you can trust me."

The two women spoke fast, their words tumbling over each other as they tried to get the ideas out.

"I do trust you," May said finally, taking a deep breath. "You know I've been keeping track of Kylie's thoughts in the blue diary, and for so long—" May began.

"For so long, you've worried about her."

"I have," May said.

"What did Dr. Whitpen say?"

"That she wants to bring Martin and his father back together."

"The father's in prison," Tobin said, shivering. "John showed me an article in *Sports Today*. It must be horrible, trying to face everything that happened. For Martin *and* for you and Kylie."

May fell silent. She knew Tobin meant to be supportive, but suddenly, her defenses rising, she felt protective of the Cartiers. Wanting to tell her best friend about her meeting with Serge, the battle she knew she would have with Martin, May couldn't find the words.

Just then the camera panned to Martin, and May saw his face on the TV screen. She stopped in mid-thought, squinting as she tried to see what Serge had said about Martin favoring his right side.

When the camera zoomed in on Martin's face, she saw the wild rage in his eyes and she shivered as she wondered where it began

and ended. Tears flooded her eyes, and she knew she couldn't talk more about his private demons. It would betray some essential trust between them.

May heard Tobin make a sound, a moan of disappointment. Glancing across the table, she saw her best friend bowing her head.

"Tobe," May said, knowing that she had hurt her deeply.

"When you're ready," Tobin said, her voice choked up, "I'm here."

"I know," May said. She turned to watch her husband on TV, feeling a sense of dread building in her chest.

———

Four days and nights passed after her visit to Estonia. After midnight, lying in their bed, with the windows open and the spring breeze blowing through the room, she heard his key in the lock. May pulled on her robe and walked downstairs to meet him. He had played a game in Montreal that night, been traveling for hours, and he looked exhausted.

"Martin," she said, walking into his arms.

"Je t'aime, je t'aime," he said.

Dropping his hockey bag, he kissed her deeply, and she could feel that they were both breathless. When they stopped, he wouldn't let her go. She saw him staring at her hard, as if he'd missed her more than he'd expected. The lines around his face and mouth made him look tired, and she took him by the hand.

"Are you hungry?" she asked. "Want me to make you a sandwich? Some soup?"

"Let me look at you."

"Why?" she laughed.

"This trip seemed really long. We won all our games, and I wished you were there."

May swallowed, looked away. She knew she could have gone to all or some of his games, but her trip to Estonia had prevented that. Her secret felt like a stone lodged in her heart.

"Come sit down," she said. "I want to talk to you."

"It's late," he said, laughing and pulling her close again. "Forget talking—I want to take you upstairs."

His embrace was hot and rough, and May felt his hands sliding down her back, his arms wrapping around her. The secret scraped her insides, but she knew she could wait until tomorrow to tell him.

"I've been waiting days for this," he said.

"Me, too," she whispered.

He grabbed his bag, stopping by the hall table to drop off his car and house keys. As he did, he noticed May's small travel case sitting on the chair. She had been carrying it the day they'd first met: she always took it with her on trips because it held her plane tickets, guidebooks, and maps so conveniently.

"Going somewhere?" he asked, grinning as he glanced up.

"No," she said. He hugged her greedily, and the stone in her heart grew hard and hot. Not telling him was one thing; lying was another. "I went somewhere," she said.

"You did?"

May nodded, and Martin saw the truth in her eyes. She felt so guilty for going behind his back, but at the same time so hopeful for what she knew could happen between him and Serge. "Martin," she began.

He stepped away, shook his head. "I don't want to know."

"I have to tell you—"

"I am tired, May. It is time for bed, eh?"

May grabbed his hands and shook them, forcing him to look her in the eyes. His gaze went all over the entry hall: at the paintings on the wall, the keys on the small table, a package of invitations for Kylie's birthday party. May was shaking, and she jogged Martin's hands hard.

"Listen to me!" she said.

"*Non!*" he said, his blue eyes cold. "*Ecoutez!* You listen to me. I want you to burn his postcards, put all thoughts of him out of your mind. Don't tell me anything more. I don't want to know."

The truth was right there for them both to see. Fate had brought them together on that plane a year ago. Love was their destiny, and they had lessons to teach each other. The rift between Martin and his father had brought May closer to her own past, and she felt the healing of love, truth, and forgiveness. She had to find the words, she had to make Martin see. *It's so easy,* she wanted to tell him. *It's so incredible, so simple!*

Instead, she forced her thoughts to slow down and she made her voice gentle and steady. "I have a message for you," she said. "From your father."

"No," Martin said, his eyes bright and intense.

"He wanted me to tell you he loves you. He—"

But Martin didn't stick around to hear the rest. Grabbing his hockey bag and keys, he bolted outside. The door slammed behind him, so loud it sounded like the metal doors in prison. "*That's* what

you don't see," she cried after him. "How to understand and forgive!" May listened to the echo of her own voice, and she wondered if Kylie had heard it in her sleep. She stood rooted to the
floor, wanting to run after him, knowing she had to stay with her
child.

———

May waited for Martin to turn around and come back home.
When that didn't happen, she waited all night for the phone to
ring. She waited in the hallway, shivering in her nightgown while
the sun came up. She fixed Kylie's breakfast, dressed her for
school, tried to act as if everything was fine. She told herself Martin was just angry, that he'd be home as soon as he cooled down.

She made herself go to work. Aunt Enid asked whether she
was sick, coming down with something, and when May went to the
bathroom she looked at her face in the mirror and saw the dark circles under her eyes: She looked as if she'd had the fright of her life.

The entire day passed without any word. Driving home to
Boston, she was sure there would be a message on the machine, or
even that Martin would be waiting in their bedroom. Was what she
had done so unforgivable? Couldn't Martin see, finally, that she
had done it for him, for them?

But he wasn't there, and he didn't call. May made dinner for
Kylie, read her a story, put her to bed. She sat on Kylie's bed long
after the child had fallen asleep, after the sky grew dark and the
city lights came twinkling on. Her heart racing, she started every
time she heard a car door slam.

When the phone rang at one in the morning, May knew it was
Martin. She was terrified of what he was going to say. She hoped
she was wrong.

"Hello?"

"It's me," he said.

"Where are you?"

"I'm—" he paused. "I am at a hotel."

"In Boston?" she asked, feeling pressure in her chest, as if her
heart had just dissolved.

"Yes."

"Come home," she whispered.

"No, May."

She saw the lights outside the window. Beacon Hill sloped
down to the Common, with thousands upon thousands of lights

glowing in houses, offices, and hotels. Martin was somewhere out there—within sight, within walking distance. Her eyes filled with tears.

"You wouldn't listen to me," he said. "I tried to tell you how I feel about my father, eh? What he did was unforgivable, yet you've been determined to force something."

"Force?" May asked, wanting to laugh. The word was so hard for what she had been trying to do. Ease, maybe; heal, soften.

"Never mind," he said. "I'm staying here now. It's better, I think, that we are apart. You couldn't be happy with me, with things the way they are."

"You're wrong," she said. "We were trying, learning together—"

"But you refused to accept me as I was," he said. "You had to go see him. You wouldn't believe me when I told you that I consider some things unforgivable."

"I've learned that about you tonight," May said, gulping back tears.

"Tonight?"

"Yes," she said. "You can't forgive me for reaching out to your father, so now you've left me. You've closed the door on me, like you closed it on him."

"May—"

"It's true, isn't it?"

"Yes," he said. "I'll come pick up my things tomorrow while you are out. Good-bye."

May let out a cry, but Martin had already hung up. Holding the phone, she stared out at the lights of Boston and wondered which one was Martin. She asked herself why she hadn't listened to him, how she had let this happen. And she realized that perhaps she *had* forced something, that maybe some of this *had* been a test.

Her worst fear—and Kylie's—had been that if Martin could write off his father, who could say he wouldn't do it to them?

He was gone now; he had written them off. She had thought the bond they had felt from the beginning would protect her, protect their love.

She had been wrong.

Chapter 16

MARTIN SLAMMED THROUGH THE NEXT few games, a tornado of
human fury. He scored hat tricks in every one, and the papers called him a winning machine. Ripping face masks, slashing
his stick, pounding every opponent into the boards, he was berserk.
He wanted blood, and he got it.

His skating changed. He would run—not glide—down the ice.
In practice, the Bruins goalie told others that Martin looked inhu-
man, like a movie Cyclops with one eye closed, the other lit up,
flashing and glowing, as he flew toward the net with the puck on his
stick.

Ray tried to talk to him, and Martin snarled at him. Coach
wanted to discuss his increasing time in the penalty box and Martin stalked away. He swung at a reporter who wanted to discuss
May's absence from the latest home games, and his picture appeared in the next day's paper, looking like a killer.

Kylie called the Fleet Center, saying she hoped he would be
able to come to her birthday party. At the sound of her voice, Martin could barely talk.

"Kylie, you know I wish I could. But the schedule . . ." he said.

"I still want you to come," she said.

"Well, unfortunately my team has other ideas," he said.

"Are you and Mommy getting divorced?"

"You know, Kylie," he said, "you'd better talk to your mother.
As a matter of fact, I have to go now. They want me on the ice."

"I miss you, Daddy," she said.

Martin hung up, slamming the phone down so hard he broke
it. Her voice, her words reminded him of similar talks he'd had
with Natalie so long ago. He had broken his own daughter's
heart—what had made him think he wouldn't do it again to another girl?

April nights were soft and warm, and Martin spent them in his hotel room—in Boston or wherever he was playing—alone with the television. He'd order dinner from room service, watch movies while his teammates banged on his door and tried to get him to go out on the town.

"The Gold Sledgehammer is *back*," some of the single guys kept saying, wanting to tempt him into the bars and clubs.

"Fuck off," Martin said to them, ready to fight if they kept on.

The telephone rang a lot, but it was never May. What would he have wanted to say if she did call? His past was frozen inside him, a lake that would never melt. His memories of Natalie were sharp, untouched by time or words.

What May didn't—couldn't—understand, was that nothing would ever bring her back. Talking to his father, knowing the old man hadn't meant to let her die, that he hadn't ever intended to hurt her—none of that would change things, breathe life into Martin's little girl.

No matter how much he loved May or wanted to turn back time to the day before she'd betrayed him, he couldn't forget what she'd done.

"Betray" was a strong word, and it sounded as sharp as it was: a blade of a word, slicing Martin deep inside. By visiting his father, May had betrayed Martin. Lying on his hotel bed, he curled up on his side and wished he didn't hurt so much. His cheek was bruised, his lip was split, but he didn't even feel those injuries.

He hurt deeper inside his body, somewhere where he believed his heart to be, right where Natalie lived. The only person who had ever touched that spot was May. She had soothed it with her gentleness and love, and now Martin felt as if she had split it wide open.

Or maybe that was just easier to admit than the other part. If he wasn't speaking to May, he wouldn't have to tell her what was happening. Covering one eye, then the other, he stared at the picture on the wall. Testing his sight, Martin lay on his bed and tried not to think.

When Martin had been gone for two weeks, Genny came to the barn, ostensibly to bring May a batch of pineapple jam. They left the basket on May's desk and went walking outside through the rose garden.

"How are you?" Genny asked

"Bad," May said. "Worried about my daughter. Kylie cries a lot. She misses him terribly."

"And you?" Genny asked.

May shrugged, turning away to keep from crying. She felt shaky and numb. Unable to eat, she'd lost weight. At night she couldn't sleep, and during the day she didn't want to stay awake. The hours without word from Martin were long and terrible, and she couldn't stop wondering what he was doing.

"Talk to me, May." Genny touched her shoulder.

Shivering at her friend's touch, May buried her face in her hands. "At first I thought maybe he wasn't serious. That he'd come home once he'd cooled down."

"I know."

"It's been two weeks," May said. "He hasn't called once in all this time."

"The play-off schedule . . ." Genny said helplessly, trailing off.

"They're winning, and I can't even congratulate him."

"He doesn't deserve you congratulating him," Genny fumed. "I'd like to wring his thick neck."

"I just wish he'd cool down," May said again.

"Martin doesn't cool down," Genny told her. "It never stops amazing me—or Ray. He holds on to a grudge like a dog with a bone."

"This time I'm the bone," May said, her voice cracking. But the problem with Genny's analogy was that Martin didn't hold on; he let go. She felt empty inside and out, as if she'd been in an accident and lost one of her arms. At night she'd roll over to hold Martin, find an empty bed. She'd look at the clock and feel her heart skip because soon he'd be home, and then she'd remember he didn't live there anymore.

"Ray says he's impossible to be around," Genny said.

"Does he talk about me?"

"No. Ray says he refuses to talk at all."

"Believe it or not," May said, wiping her eyes as she walked through the rosebushes, "I wanted to make things better. I wanted to clear the air, help heal the rift between Serge and Martin."

Genny shook her head. "I know how much Martin adored his father. He has to face that someday. He felt let down, betrayed—and then murderous when Natalie died. More than you or I can ever know. He's full of rage at Serge, and I think it drives him on the ice, and everywhere else."

"I think so, too." May closed her eyes to picture Martin's face. She'd seen him on TV and in the papers lately, looking like a bear attacking prey, as if his own soft, human side was being eaten away.

"Don't give up, May."

"I'm not the one who gave up," she said. They were standing in the spot where Martin had proposed to her last year. She smelled fresh earth, coffee grounds, rosebuds. The scent brought back memories, and she felt her eyes burning with more tears.

"You know," Genny said, taking her hand, "when he told us he'd met you, we could see how changed he was—how happy. We hoped so much that he'd let himself be loved, that he'd let go of the fight."

"I wanted to help him let go," May said, her throat searing.

"Some people live for the fight," Genny said, squeezing May's hand. "It drives them more than love or anything else. We see it in the hockey world all the time."

May hugged her. "I'm really glad you came out today."

"So am I," Genny said. "And I wish I could take all the credit for it. You have a wonderful friend."

May stared, puzzled.

"Tobin is very worried about you."

"She called you?"

Genny nodded. "She did. Don't be mad at her."

May gazed across the barn. Tobin stood by the tea table, talking to a mother and daughter, showing them the old scrapbooks. Like May, she was thirty-six, married, a mother. But her eyes were as bright, her gestures as animated as they'd been as a young girl, when she'd first become May's best friend.

"Thank you," May said, hugging Genny with appreciation for the pineapple jam and more.

Once the clients had gone for the day, May went out to the shed. Light filtered through broken boards, turning the spiderwebs silver. May felt their threads on her face and hair, but she was a country girl and she brushed them away with barely a thought. The two bicycles were leaning against the wall, their tires flat from three seasons without use.

Hauling out first hers, then Tobin's, May filled the tires with air from an old hand pump. She could barely remember the last time they'd gone riding. Glancing up at the barn, she saw Tobin watching her from the window. Then May leaned them against the barn, walked through the door, and handed Tobin her jacket.

"Come on," May said. "Let's go for a ride."

"I have to get these orders in," Tobin said, riffling the stack of papers on her desk.

"Don't worry," Aunt Enid said. "Get on your bikes and have a good ride. I'll hold down the fort."

Wordlessly, Tobin followed May outside. Her handlebars were traced with dust and more spider silk, and May watched her brush them off with her bare hands. Pushing away, May pedaled down the driveway, gravel crunching under her tires, coasting down the small hill that took them through the meadow.

New leaves twinkled in the wind and sunlight, shading the narrow road. May pedaled hard, gaining speed, the exercise feeling good to her body. Tobin rode just behind, not speaking. They followed their ancient route, the one they'd been riding for thirty years: down the farm road, past the hidden creek, over the bridge and past the waterfall, up and over Crawford Hill.

May's eyes watered from the wind. She wondered how many hundreds of times she and Tobin had done this, and she thought of the ways they had changed and the ways they had stayed the same. She thought of the secrets they shared, the things they knew about each other that no one else alive could ever suspect.

They passed the fallen tree where they had once smoked cigarettes, the abandoned farmhouse where they had pricked their fingertips and become blood sisters, the hayfield where May had had her first kiss, the dead-end lane where Tobin had lost her virginity to John. When they got to the ice-cream stand, May signaled with her arm and wheeled into the sandy parking lot. Hitting a patch of sand, she skidded ten yards and wiped out.

"May, are you okay?" Tobin dropped her bike and ran to her side.

"I think so." May was examining her skinned wrists. She had torn her jeans, and sand was imbedded in her knees and shins. "Ouch."

"You're bleeding." Tobin was already pulling a tissue from her back pocket.

"I'll get it," May said, starting to take it from her. But Tobin wouldn't let her. Peering at May's wrists, kneeling next to her, she dabbed methodically at the cuts and scrapes.

"There," Tobin soothed. "There you go."

"You called Genny," May said.

"I was worried about you," Tobin told her. "You wouldn't talk to me, and I thought you needed someone."

May stared at the top of her friend's head. The dark hair was

short and full, and in the sunlight, May saw a few silver strands of gray. She thought about how time flew: Just yesterday, they'd been twelve years old. Shocked by the spill, and by everything that had happened, May felt a dam burst inside, and she started to cry.

"Everything's going to be fine." Tobin put her arms around May.

"It doesn't feel that way," May cried.

"You've wiped out before," Tobin tried to joke. "You've survived more skinned knees than—"

"My husband's gone, Tobin," May gasped. "I went behind his back to the prison, and he left."

"He'll come back," Tobin said. "He loves you. Who wouldn't? He's a good man, or you wouldn't have fallen in love with him."

"I fell in love with Gordon Rhodes," May reminded her.

"Married, I should have said. You wouldn't have *married* Martin. It's true, your record on love does include some lulus."

"As only you know."

"But now you talk to Genny . . ."

"She knows him from before," May tried to explain. "She knows his whole story. The details about his father, his first wife, Natalie . . . I don't have to feel guilty about telling old family secrets. Martin's so closed about it all."

"How am I supposed to know that stuff if you don't tell me? Talking to your best friend isn't betraying your husband."

"I'm new at this," May said. "And I married a man with a lot of baggage."

"I swear," Tobin agreed. "We've all got loads of it."

May nodded, wiping her bleeding knee. Then she looked straight into Tobin's eyes. "I don't want to lose our friendship, ever."

"Me, neither." Tobin stared back into May's eyes. "Can I tell you something?"

"Sure."

"He wants you back. No matter what happened, he doesn't want to do this."

"How do you know?"

"Because I was at your wedding, May. I heard him say his vows. He meant them. I know it. Go pull him home by the hair."

They hugged, then pulled apart and gazed over at Paradise Ice Cream, the small white building that had been there forever. The same family had owned it all that time, had been making ice cream since before they were born.

"Ready for a cone?" Tobin asked.

"First of the year."

"Let's go." Tobin helped May to her feet. Limping over, feeling her friend's arm around her waist, May stood at the window. The world seemed large with hope and possibility. Tobin ordered vanilla, May maple walnut with chocolate sprinkles. Some things never changed. And, luckily, May thought, some things did.

———

She had always been intimidated by the Fleet Center, with all the players, guards, and groupies, but two days after eating that ice-cream cone, May drove straight into the parking lot and took a deep breath. Locking her van, she strode across the lot. There was Martin's Porsche in his regular spot. The sight of it made her dizzy, but she just kept walking.

The security guard nodded hello, not very friendly, but at least he didn't turn her away. Did that mean Martin hadn't spread the word they were separated? Smiling, May said hi back.

She was struck by the similarity of her visit to Estonia. Signing in, she was allowed through the special entrance that led to the locker rooms. Walking down the long corridor, she felt alone and nervous. She rehearsed the words she would say to him—*I'm sorry, Martin. I shouldn't have gone behind your back. I didn't mean to hurt you*—and wondered what would happen. What if he refused to forgive her? What if he had found someone new? She thought of Tobin assuring her he wanted her back, that he had meant his vows, and she felt strong.

Rounding the corner, she met Ray Gardner in a pack of Bruins coming off the ice. Suited up and sweaty, he looked surprised to see her.

"May!" he exclaimed.

Music blaring from speakers overhead made it hard to hear.

"Is he here?" she asked, her lips dry.

"Out there." He gestured at the ice. "You sure you want to talk to him here? Why don't I tell him you're waiting, and you can meet somewhere more private—in a conference room?"

"I'm sure," she said, hugging herself. "I'll just wait."

Ray nodded, kissing her on the cheek. He walked into the locker room, and May faded back against the wall. Other players nodded as they passed. A few gave her friendly hellos, and May waved and tried to smile. Cold air poured off the ice, and she shivered in her spring cotton dress.

Martin was the last player to pass through the door. Standing in a shadow, May watched him come. His shoulders were enormous, his face angry and set. Still squinting his left eye, he reminded her again of a rageful pirate. Her heart pounding, May reached out her hand.

"Martin," she said, the loud music drowning out her voice.

He walked straight by, disappearing into the locker room without even a second glance. May stared with disbelief. It had all happened so fast: He was there and gone in two seconds. She stood in place, frozen for an eternity, then ran straight into the locker room.

"Martin Cartier!" she screamed.

"Excuse me," a guard said, coming forward, grabbing her arm. "How'd you get in here?"

Players stood around, some in their jerseys and others barechested, some in their jockstraps and some totally naked. She glanced wildly around, ignoring them all.

"Where's Martin?" she asked.

"Mrs. Cartier," the guard said, hauling her toward the door. "Wives aren't allowed in here. I'll give him your message and—"

May didn't wait to hear. Wrenching her arm free, she walked away. Martin's teammates were laughing nervously, calling after her, telling her Martin was already in the shower room. May's ears were buzzing. She thought of Tobin saying he wanted her back, and she shook her head. Best friends didn't know everything.

The third Saturday in May, May had given up on hearing from Martin again. He didn't want to talk to her: That was very clear. She and Kylie drove up to the Gardners' house in New Hampshire. They lived far out in the country, on thirty acres reminiscent of the land around Lac Vert, and the clear air smelled like new leaves and spring flowers.

"It's so peaceful out here." May stood on the front porch with Ray while Genny took the kids out back to fly kites.

"Genny and I are country people," he said. "Always have been."

"Like Martin."

"I consider him a brother," Ray told her, "but right now I think he's an idiot. I don't know what he's doing—he's not even acting like himself."

"Because he left me?"

"Especially that. But in other ways, too. He seems like a different person."

The memory of Martin walking by her at the Fleet Center, her chasing him into the locker room, was still so raw and painful, May cringed to think of it. The man May had married, loved for a year, would not have done that to her.

"He can't forgive me," she said.

"For going to see his father?" Ray snorted. "His father was everything to him. Let me tell you a story."

Spring was spilling over to summer, and as night fell over the New Hampshire hills, May listened to the peepers and watched the stars come out, waiting for Ray to begin. He was smaller than Martin, but broad in the shoulders and back. He was very dark, with almost black hair and eyes. Although May knew he was very gentle, when he was deep in thought, he wore a glowering expression that deepened as he started talking.

When Ray and Martin were fifteen, they had decided to hitchhike six hundred miles to Toronto to watch Serge play hockey. Martin hadn't seen his father in five years, and by then Serge was at the top of his fame. Toronto was leading the league, and Martin was convinced that if they could get to the door at Maple Leaf Gardens, he could get someone to take them to Serge.

"Agnes wouldn't even hear of us going," Ray said. "And who could blame her? You've seen the scars on his chest. Martin never talks about the details, but Genny and I have a pretty good idea of how they got there."

May nodded.

"Well, by that time she despised Serge. Martin wanted to respect her, but . . ."

"He was fifteen."

"And his father was the top scorer in the NHL. So we set out to hitch twelve hours from Lac Vert to Toronto, middle of January, during a thaw."

"Twelve hours," May said with disbelief.

"Well, the snow was piled high, but the sun was out, so we felt good and warm. Caught a trucker going all the way from Quebec City to Montreal, then another most of the way to Ottawa, then a few rides to Toronto. It wasn't till we arrived that it got hard."

Ray told of going to the Gardens, talking to someone in the ticket booth, being turned away. Trying to get in through the players' entrance, telling the guard Martin was Serge's son, showing him school ID, everything they could think of.

"We couldn't get anyone to believe us. Serge had the reputation of being a swinger, big single guy hanging out in Las Vegas. None of the news stories ever mentioned a son, because Serge knew Agnes would kill him if he ever brought attention to Martin. She wanted her son raised right—no fame and fortune . . ."

May nodded, sympathizing with the mother-in-law she'd never met.

"So the rink personnel didn't even know Martin existed. Later, we found out Serge had two people fired for not bringing us back to the locker room. But that day, we never got past the gate."

"I know how that feels. Martin must have been crushed," May said.

"To put it mildly, eh? We started back home, just as the weather turned. Got a ride as far as Belleville, where the wind whips off Lake Ontario, when the storm turned into a blizzard."

"A blizzard?" May asked.

Ray nodded. "Bad. Snow so hard we couldn't see each other standing two feet away. We were freezing. Never in our lives had we felt cold like that. Never."

May closed her eyes, thinking of the lengths Martin had gone to to meet his father. To go so far and then not see him!

"We had jackets and boots, but the snow was over our knees. The roads were deserted, no one passing by. It got dark. Our fingers and toes were numb, our faces frozen to the zippers of our jackets. We were bleeding, and the blood froze. I thought we were going to die."

"What did you do?"

"Martin never let me lose hope," Ray said. "I've always believed his faith kept us both alive that night."

May felt Ray staring at her, but she couldn't look up.

"Saved my life." Ray was glaring out at the low hills. "We knocked each other around, then we built an igloo and stayed there till the blizzard ended."

May closed her eyes, picturing a shelter made of frozen snow and ice. Martin lived in one still, she thought, wondering about her husband's faith now.

"Don't give up on him," Ray said, touching May's hand. May squeezed her eyes shut, trying to breathe. He had given up on *her*.

"What did he say about my coming to the ice that night? He walked straight past me."

"He didn't say anything."

"You're protecting him," May said, glaring at him.

"No, I'm not. I told him he's an asshole, and he said he agreed. One guy kidded him about you walking into the locker room, and he grabbed his throat so hard he left handprints."

"What's going on with him?"

"I don't know," Ray said, staring at Genny reeling in the kite. Dark against the darker sky, it dove and bobbed like a bat. "He's my best friend, and I don't have a clue."

Genny and the kids approached the house, and May heard Kylie talking about her skating party the next day. She was nervous because she couldn't skate well, and the Gardner kids were telling her to be fearless and go for it.

"Want to come?" she asked.

"I can't," Charlotte said. "I have to decorate for a dance at school."

"And I have a baseball game. Sorry, Kylie," Mark said.

May wrapped Kylie in her sweater and held her on her lap. Kylie hid her disappointment deep inside. It came out late at night, during her sleep, when she'd call out for Martin. She would wake up, sweaty and crying, mumbling those words that had started it all: "Bring them together. Natalie says we have to . . ." May wrote everything down in the blue notebook.

"First star." Charlotte pointed at the sky.

"Make a wish," Genny told her.

"I wish for the Bruins to win the Stanley Cup," Mark said.

"Good boy," Ray said, laughing.

"I wish . . ." Charlotte began, typical teenage girl, making her wish in silence.

Holding Kylie tighter, May kissed her hair. She leaned down, to ask what Kylie was wishing for on the eve of her birthday, and she heard the fierce, almost inaudible whisper her daughter had intended no human ears to hear:

"I wish for Daddy to come home."

Every night he was in Boston, Martin did the same thing: left the ice or the hotel, got into his car, and drove around. He told himself he needed air, space, to keep moving, but what he really needed was May.

He'd drive past their house in Boston, and if he saw her car parked there, lights on in the windows, everything was fine. He would just park down the street, find a dark shadow, and watch

until the lights went out. On weekends, when Kylie didn't have school, she wasn't there, so he drove all the way down to Black Hall, doused his headlights driving through the field, and made sure she was safe in the farmhouse.

Watching the windows of those houses, knowing that May and Kylie were inside, gave Martin the closest thing he had to peace of mind during those weeks without them. Sometimes he would see her close the curtains or pull a shade or move from one room to another, and he'd start toward the door, ready to take her in his arms and tell her he'd made the biggest mistake of his life, that all he wanted was to start over.

Pride was his worst sin, though. He couldn't imagine the words he'd say. Hugging May was a great fantasy, but if he knew his wife, that would be just the beginning. She'd want to sit up till dawn and beyond, hashing everything out. May loved talking and connection and making sense of life's mysteries. Martin would rather let them alone—especially now, when he was dealing with something more confusing and mysterious than he had ever faced.

Ray had told him about May's visit to the rink. How he had come off the ice, found May standing there by the locker room door. She'd been wearing a yellow dress, Ray had said, and had looked so strong, determined to see Martin. Ray had offered her a conference room, but May had said no, she'd wait to see Martin right then and there.

Martin must have walked right by her.

She had chased him right into the locker room. Getting into the shower, Martin had heard the laughter and catcalls, and some of the guys had had the bad judgment to tease him about it.

Martin had been thinking of her—of that he was sure. Wanting her, needing her, planning what he'd say to her, and she'd been right there the whole time. He could almost picture her now: smiling, small and determined and shy, holding out her hand to touch him.

But what she didn't know, what Martin couldn't tell her, wouldn't even quite admit to himself, certainly wouldn't tell Ray or the other Bruins, was that he had not seen her.

Peering through the darkness now, it seemed as if thick cobwebs were hanging from the trees. Covering one eye, then the other, he tested himself. The night sky was clear, but he was sitting in fog. His vision, especially in his right eye, had been getting blurrier for several weeks now. He hadn't told the team doctor, and he'd been afraid to tell May. When she had admitted her visit to

Estonia, Martin had found the perfect excuse to not tell her at all: He had just walked out.

Tonight, she wasn't in Boston and she wasn't in Black Hall. Martin had had the long drive from Boston to the Connecticut shoreline and back to worry about it. Her van was nowhere to be seen. Aunt Enid was alone at the farmhouse, playing solitaire in front of the TV, and the Boston house was dark and empty.

Martin felt panicked. He was burning to talk to her. This had to come to an end, this insane separation. Lately he found himself thinking of the first moment he saw her: on that plane to Boston, with Kylie by her side. He pictured her leaning over Kylie, giving him a look of suspicion, as if she could somehow see that he was bad, that she would have to protect her child against him.

What kind of man would just leave his family?

That was Martin—he had done it twice. Obviously, May's instincts had been right that first day. She knew how to love; Martin knew how to rage. Parked on Beacon Hill, he stared at their empty house, testing his eyes again. If she wasn't here, and she wasn't at the Bridal Barn, where was she? Tomorrow was Kylie's birthday. Had they canceled the skating party and gone somewhere far away to celebrate?

Chapter 17

THE BACK BAY SKATING RINK echoed with laughter and music. Many children attended Friday night classes there, and they had their own lockers and equipment. On that Sunday in May, the day of her party, Kylie stood behind the partition, watching girls glide past on graceful white skates, wearing beautiful short skating skirts, the boys flashing by wearing black skates and stretch skating pants.

Kylie wished she could disappear.

Martin was gone from their lives. He didn't live with them anymore, and he wasn't coming to her party. He was "away"—supposedly playing hockey. That's what Mommy and Genny had told her, wanting her to think he would be there if he could.

"Hi, Kylie! Come skate!" the rink monitor called.

"Happy birthday, Kylie!" his assistant called.

Kylie nodded, waving. Her mother stood off to the side, talking to the man in charge of birthday parties. Kylie had a pit in her stomach. The minute she stepped onto the ice, she'd fall down—just like she'd done at Ellen's.

"Martin Cartier's not here?" Jimmy Vance demanded, skating to a fancy stop right in front of her.

Kylie shook her head. Everyone had been asking her about Martin: At school last week, people had given her candy, gum, and Pokémon cards, just so maybe she'd invite them to her skating party, so they could meet and skate with Martin.

"Thought he would be," Jimmy said.

"He has a hockey game . . ."

"They won two nights ago," Jimmy told her. "The Bruins didn't play last night, and they don't play today. They play *tonight*. So he could be here if he *wanted* to."

"Oh," Kylie said, her shoulders coming together in front of her chest.

"She just wanted us to think he'd be here," Ellen said, twirling over. "So we'd all come. This is my riding day. I was supposed to be in Chestnut Hill on Silver Star right now, but I came to her birthday party instead."

"She's not even wearing skates," Jimmy said, looking over the rail at the sneakers on Kylie's feet.

"My mother's bringing them over," Kylie explained. "She has to help me get them on."

Kylie's heart was pounding, and she wished she had a fever so Natalie would come. If only this party would just be over, so Kylie wouldn't have to skate in front of all these kids. They'd be making fun of how she couldn't stand up by herself, and how Martin wasn't here.

Kylie closed her eyes. Wishes sometimes came true—she knew that for sure. She had wished for a father, and Martin had come into their lives. But now he was gone, and she wondered what she had done to drive him away.

Her mother seemed sad. She was getting skinny from not eating, and instead of sleeping, she read all night. Kylie knew because she saw her. She'd climb out of bed and walk quietly down the hall, then stand outside her mother's bedroom door and peek through the crack.

All of a sudden, Jimmy and Ellen gasped. Their eyes got big, and Jimmy said, "Wow! It's him!"

Other children and parents stopped skating and began to drift over—slowly at first, and then with great speed—to the gap in the wall where Kylie stood. As Kylie looked over her shoulder, she saw Martin coming toward her, a package tucked under his arm.

"Hi, I'm Tally Vance, Jimmy's mother." A lady wearing a red skating skirt was holding out her hand. "My son is such a fan, we all are! Thank you so much for—"

"Nice to meet you," Martin said, shaking her hand but turning away. "Excuse me a minute. I have to see my daughter."

Kylie's heart leapt. She put one hand to her mouth as Martin crouched down in front of her. He stared her straight in the eyes.

"You came," she whispered.

"I could never miss your birthday," he said.

"I thought you didn't love us anymore."

Martin shook his head. His eyes looked terribly sad, as if she'd just said the worst thing in the world. "I'm so sorry you thought that." He handed Kylie her present, a box wrapped in shiny pink

paper. But then he lifted his eyes and his whole face changed, and Kylie knew he was looking at her mother.

"May," Kylie heard him say.

⎯⎯

Walking across the crowded area, May carried their skates, hers and Kylie's, in her hand. They had last worn them on the pond behind the barn, skating that frozen day with Martin. May just wanted to get them on her and Kylie's feet, go out on the ice, and give Kylie the best birthday party she could.

"May."

Hearing her name, May looked through the crowd. Parents and kids were clustered around the bench where Kylie sat, and through them all, she saw Martin looking at her.

"Oh," she said, dropping one of the skates.

Martin came toward her, bent to pick it up. He was so close, she felt his hand brush the top of her right shoe. Her heart was beating so fast, she might have been running a race. When he stood to hand her the dropped skate, his face was nearly touching hers, and she felt his breath on her cheek.

"May," he said. "I made a mistake."

She stared into his eyes, trembling with wanting to hold him, unable to reply.

So did I, she wanted to say.

"I walked out because I couldn't take it," he said, taking her hand. "I stayed away because I had to figure it all out."

She gazed into his eyes. They were so very blue, surrounded by many more lines than had been there a month ago. Martin had aged in their time apart, and May was sure she had, too.

"Was it better without me there?" she asked.

"It was horrible."

She started to laugh, choked instead.

"I brought you something." He reached into his pocket.

All around them kids were jumping and yelling. Parents were buzzing, and Kylie was sitting alone on a bench. May wanted to go to her, but Martin held her arm. He handed her a small object wrapped in tissue paper.

Hands shaking, May opened the package. It was the little leather pouch she had given him last season, when they had first met, to help him through the play-offs. Untying the drawstring, she looked inside and saw the rose petals and tiny bones. Her

throat ached to remember how much hope she'd put into assembling it.

Martin put his arms around her. His mouth against her ear, he whispered, "Forgive me, May."

"Oh, Martin," she said.

Aware of Kylie watching them, she wanted to be careful, to make sure. There had been moments when she would have taken back everything she'd ever said about his father, thrown her principles right out the window just to get Martin back. And there had been other times when she had wanted nothing more than to see him just once more, to have the chance to say "good-bye forever" to his face, for what he'd put her and Kylie through.

"It's what you do so well. Please forgive me," he repeated.

"I do, Martin."

"We belong together."

"I've never stopped believing that," she said clearly, words from the blue notebook echoing in her mind: Bring them together, together, together.

———

Kylie watched her parents. Mommy had looked so upset at first. She had held back from speaking or hugging, her eyes glittering with tears. But Martin just kept talking, touching her hand, stroking her hair, until finally she flew at him with her arms open to kiss and hug him. When that happened, Kylie could breathe again.

Jimmy and Ellen wanted her to open the package Martin had brought, and the Tally Vance lady started to help her untie the bow. But Kylie just held on tight, bowing her entire body over the box to keep everyone away from it.

"Ça va, Kylie?" Martin asked, walking over with her mother.

"Daddy," Kylie said, putting her arms around him as he lifted her up. Mommy was right there too, and they stood together in a small family group. Kylie felt a huge jolt of joy, as if everything was going to work out after all.

"Happy Birthday, Kylie," he said.

"Thank you."

"What about your present, eh?" he asked, his blue eyes very serious as he tapped her box. "Aren't you going to open it?"

"I was waiting for you."

Kylie held it on her lap. The box was large and perfectly

square, neatly wrapped in pink paper. As she pulled the ribbon, undoing the big bow, her heart began to beat more quickly.

"Skates," Jimmy said, looking over her shoulder. "He got her hockey skates."

Kylie shivered. She felt thrilled and scared at the same time. The box seemed stuck as she tried to get the top off. She pictured hockey skates, like a miniature pair of the ones Martin always wore, brown and plain and, well, ugly, with that streamlined blade —she didn't care; she'd love them anyway. But what she actually saw took her breath away.

"A skirt!" she gasped. "Just like they wear in ballet on ice."

"For the prettiest girl in Boston," he said. It was silvery white, a lot like angels' wings, with diamond sparkles on layers and layers of tulle. Kylie slung her arm around Martin's neck, and he held the skirt steady while she stepped into it.

Now Kylie couldn't wait to get her skates on. Mommy pulled off her own sneakers and Kylie's, and while Mommy laced up her own skates, Martin crouched down in front of Kylie to slip her skates on.

Kylie had never noticed how beautiful they were before: white leather with silver blades, the jagged slant in front to catch the ice. They matched her skirt perfectly. As he laced the skates up, making them tight enough but not too tight, Kylie stared at the top of his head. His hair was brown and gray, and all she could do was lean forward to kiss it and whisper "Thank you, Daddy."

"You're welcome, Kylie," he said. Reaching into his canvas duffel bag, he whipped out his own hockey skates and got them on and laced so fast Kylie hardly had the chance to blink her eyes.

"You're skating?" Kylie asked.

"At your party? Yes, I am. But only with you and your mother. Are you ready?"

Gulping, Kylie nodded.

The ice was clear. Every single person had stepped aside, just to watch Martin Cartier skate—or Kylie fall down.

"Look straight ahead," Martin said quietly as Kylie's ankles wobbled. Mommy skated away, trying to get the feel of the ice. Kylie watched her, nervously wishing she'd take her other arm.

"Mommy's doing it," Kylie said, seeing her mother glide cautiously across the rink.

"She is. So are you." Her feet turned in, and she stumbled the second they stepped onto the ice. Martin caught her, holding her

up, helping her to stay on her feet. A few kids laughed; she heard
Ellen's voice above the others.

"I can't do it," she whispered, tears in her eyes.

"Sure you can," Martin told her. "Remember the pond? This
is just like that, eh? Just you and me and your mother."

"You're doing great," Mommy said, coming alongside.

"No!" she said, trying to stop.

But Martin wouldn't let her stop. "Brand-new skaters are like
newborn colts," he told her. One arm around her, he held her hand
in his.

"You said that once before," Kylie reminded him.

"That's what my father told me the first time I tried. Wobbly
legs and all," he said with a special look at Mommy.

"Your father," Kylie said, thinking of her dreams, of the message Natalie kept trying to give her, but then she tripped. "I *can't*,"
she said, feeling all the eyes watching her.

"But the thing about colts," Martin went on, holding her just as
tight, leading her around the ice so smoothly she hardly noticed
they had passed Mommy again, passed Mrs. Vance, Jimmy, Ellen,
and all the others, "is that they learn fast. Once their legs get the
feel of the land, they start to run and they can't stop. Just like walking, Kylie. Move your feet first, and your legs will follow. That's my
girl."

Swallowing, Kylie concentrated on her legs. Move one, then
the other. This leg, that leg. Martin slowed down, and all of a sudden, Kylie realized he wasn't holding her up. Supporting her, yes,
but her legs were moving on their own. Back and forth in short
steps.

"Don't scrub," he said. "Glide. That's it—long motions. Look
ahead, not at your feet."

"Perfect," Mommy said. "Oh, I'm so proud!"

Kylie tried to smile, but she had to concentrate on not falling
down. Was Mommy really as happy as she seemed, almost like her
old self, smiling and bright?

"I'm skating, Daddy."

"That's right. You are."

"I'm skating!" Kylie said again.

"Ballet on ice."

Now, for the first time, Kylie heard the music. Had it been
playing the whole time? It was beautiful, sweet ballet music. Kylie
could almost see the ballerinas dancing, telling stories on their
skates. She could see fairytale castles, princes and princesses, evil

sorcerers. The characters were dancing all around, but Kylie, Mommy, and Martin were the only people on the ice.

Now Martin let go of her waist, and Kylie gasped with fear. But she just kept skating. He had hold of her hand, and she didn't fall down. Kylie was the foal who had found its legs, and she almost wanted to run. But instead Martin swung around backward, taking her other hand.

"Look in my eyes, yes?" he said. "That's it, that's great. We're giving your friends a little show, eh?"

"I won't fall if I keep looking at you?" she asked, not even blinking.

"You won't fall," he promised.

"You're skating backward."

"You'll do that someday."

"I like this," she said, loving this moment, imagining herself skating backward in her sparkling skirt, in front of the whole Ice Capades.

"Oh, I like it too," he said.

"Am I doing it right?"

"Better than Michelle Kwan."

As if they were dancing together, with him skating backward and Kylie holding his hands, skating right along with him, they went around the rink, Martin twirling her in slow circles while the music played, everyone in the entire rink watching the father and daughter as they danced across the ice.

Kylie felt so happy she could almost forget that her parents had ever been apart, that Martin had been gone for so long, that she had cried herself to sleep every night. She could almost forget her dreams, of Natalie begging her to help, of not knowing how.

Then Martin signaled to someone in a rink uniform, and he allowed all the other kids to pour onto the ice. Kylie felt so proud. Mommy joined in, taking her hand. Martin had hold of the other. The children and some parents surrounded them in a pack, just so they could say they'd skated with Martin Cartier, but Kylie knew:

He was theirs alone—hers and her mother's and Natalie's. They were a family, and Martin was the father, and they were all back together exactly where they belonged.

Chapter 18

ONE HOUR BEFORE GAME 1 of the Stanley Cup finals—a virtual rematch against Edmonton—Martin Cartier sat in the locker room having his ankles taped. He knew May and Kylie were already in the stands. Music played, the team was pumped, Martin could feel the presence of Jorgensen right here, in the stadium.

Martin felt electric, as if this was his moment. He and May were back together. He was ready to crush Jorgensen, win the game, the series, and the Stanley Cup, and he was thinking he'd do it all for her when suddenly the window of his vision went completely black.

One minute the lights were blaring, his teammates were walking around, Coach Dafoe was standing there with one foot propped up on the bench, and the next instant everything disappeared into the dark. Martin heard their voices, but he couldn't see anything.

"Okay now, Martin," Coach was saying. "We're gonna feed you the puck. That's all you need to know. Just be waiting for the puck, and do what you do best. Last year you took us all the way. You can do it again, Martin. On defense, naturally—"

"Don't worry about defense, Coach," Ray said now. "Martin and I will take care of business there."

"Yes," Martin said, and it was as if the word "yes" flipped a switch in his brain: the lights came back on. His vision cleared, and everyone was still there—Coach, Ray, the trainer, his teammates—doing what they'd been doing before. "Defense will not be a problem."

"You're a married man now," Coach Dafoe went on. "The news shook me up last year, I have to admit. I thought, we lost because Martin was distracted. But what do I know? Who am I to say what's good, what's bad?"

"You can say it's good," Martin told him.

"Well, you've had a powerhouse year."

"So you can say it's good," Martin repeated. He was shaken by the blackness that had just descended on him. But it was easier to forget it, because his vision had cleared.

"It's good," Coach Dafoe said. "We're in the finals, aren't we?"

"Glad to have you notice," Martin said.

"Where's she been lately? These last games? I haven't seen her."

"She's here tonight," Ray said sharply. "Right on the ice with Genny and the kids."

Martin closed his eyes. He thought back to his first year in Boston. Not long after Natalie's death, his play had fallen far below his own and the team's expectations. Batteries can't make the lights work if the connections are corroded, and Martin was burned out, just going through the motions. Meeting May had changed all that—even during their time apart, she had totally driven his play.

"We're going to win," Coach said, shaking his hand.

"Give me Jorgensen," Martin roared. "That's all I ask."

"On a silver platter." Pete Bourque laughed.

Martin dropped his head. He'd suddenly had double vision. It was slight, as if each object within his line of sight had a shadow. A coach-shaped shadow, a Ray-shaped shadow. Martin shook his head, and the shadows disappeared. Everything looked normal.

"You okay?" Ray asked.

"Fine," Martin said, wishing Ray would say something about the lights flickering, anything to keep the thing that was happening in his brain and eyes at bay, but he could tell by Ray's demeanor that the locker room lights had stayed steady.

"What's wrong?" Ray asked, narrowing his eyes. Martin gazed at him. Ray was swarthy for a Canadian. His skin was dark, his hair darker. His eyebrows were thick and menacing, and when he concentrated on something, he always looked as if he was planning where to stick the knife. Yet whenever Martin looked at his face, he saw the boy he'd grown up skating with.

"You ever consider shaving your eyebrows?" Martin asked. "You're pretty scary looking."

"Works to my advantage on the ice."

"No one's looking at your face out there, my friend."

"No, they're too busy trying to outguess my fantastic stick work. I have to work double hard to make you look good."

"Save yourself the bother." Martin grinned, clapping Ray on the shoulder. "That I can do myself."

"Well, we'll see," Ray told him. "I have May to answer to now."

"She gave me this for you." Martin handed Ray a small leather pouch of rose petals. Martin watched Ray tuck it into his waistband, and Martin did the same with his own pouch. Other players passed by, and without speaking, Martin handed out the talismans May had made for every Bruin playing that night. He must have shaken his head again, because Ray leaned closer.

"Got a hcadache?"

"No," Martin said. "Just a pain in the butt. Now leave me alone, and let's win the Stanley Cup. *D'accord?*"

"*D'accord,*" Ray said, as they punched each other in the shoulder.

"What's that?" Coach Dafoe asked, passing by and seeing the small leather bag in Ray's hand.

"It's a good luck charm," Ray told him.

"One of your wife's?" Coach glared at Martin.

"Yeah." Martin flexcd his biceps. Dressed for the game, every muscle in his body showed, and if Dafoe was going to challenge him, Martin would rise to the occasion.

"Rose petals," Coach said derisively. "That's what the papers say. Rose petals from her wedding farm. Is that what's in there? You've got a little leather bag full of rose petals?"

"May made them," Martin said.

"She made them for the team," Ray added. "Solidarity, Coach."

"Where's mine?" Coach Dafoe demanded.

Martin's head was pounding, but he grinned. Reaching into his duffel bag, he pulled out another talisman. "Didn't think you'd want one."

"Solidarity," Coach said sternly, tucking the pouch into his breast pocket as he walked away.

———

With massive excitement and trepidation, the Boston Bruins entered the Stanley Cup finals against the Edmonton Oilers ready to take back last year's seventh-game loss. May and Genny sat with the children in their box, concentrating on every move as if they were coaches instead of wives.

After a scoreless first period in the first game, May could

hardly sit still. Having weathered the terrible time apart, she felt more connected to Martin than ever. She could feel Martin's frustration, every time Jorgensen blocked one of his shots.

"The old rivalry's alive and well." Genny watched Jorgensen make an obscene gesture as Martin missed another shot.

"They hate each other," May said. "Look at their eyes!" It was terrifying to see Martin attack the goal, his eyes electric and gleaming as he menaced his enemy.

"I'll say," Genny agreed, cheering as Martin skated by.

"Score, baby, score!" May yelled.

The crowd screamed for a goal, and Martin obliged with a blistering shot, but Jorgensen blocked it with a bulletlike dive. The fans booed, and Martin swore.

"Does Martin seem okay to you?" May asked.

"He's nervous," Genny told her. "So's Ray. It doesn't matter how many times they've been here. They'll say they're fine, ready to play, but they get butterflies every time."

"I wonder if he's getting the flu." May watched her husband wipe the sweat off his face with the back of his glove.

"He's got Game One nerves," Genny said. "That's all."

May nodded, trying to settle down. Martin got the puck again, and as he shot for the goal, the officials called him offside. The puck slammed into Jorgensen's right cheek, and he fell to the ice, blood pouring down his cheek. Jorgensen leaped up, flying across the ice at Martin. They rolled in a ball on the ice, fists flying and skates flashing.

May jumped up, wanting to run to Martin. The men were fighting right in front of her box, and she could hear the grunts and punches, see Martin's face twisted in rage, feel the energy pouring off him. Finally the refs pulled them apart, and Martin was as bloody as Jorgensen: he had a gash over his left eye, a new chip in his front tooth, and a split lower lip and chin.

"Oh, Martin," May cried.

Genny put her arms around May, trying to comfort her. Together they watched the two men being led off the ice. They would spend time in the penalty boxes, see their team doctors. The fans were on their feet, booing and throwing peanuts and popcorn, calling "an eye for an eye."

"What do they mean?"

"Four years ago, Jorgensen nearly put Martin's eye out," Genny reminded her. "They're saying his shot was justified."

"Martin wouldn't do it on purpose," May said, remembering that Serge had told her the same story.

"No, of course he wouldn't. And besides, Jorgensen's all right—see? This was just a fight that needed to happen," Genny said soothingly. "Now Martin's got it out of his system, and he can play hockey."

May clenched her fists. She felt the violence in her own body, as if she had taken blows herself. Martin sat in the penalty box, his head down in frustration, as the doctor tried to pry his chin up. May stared at him, but he wouldn't look at her.

The Oilers scored twice while Martin was out, and they won Game 1 by a score of 2–0.

The Oilers took Games 2 and 3, and then it was on to Edmonton. Martin refused to discuss the fight with Jorgensen, a point which proved moot, since there were many more fights with Jorgensen—and others—to follow. It was as if the violence belonged to him, that he didn't want to drag May into it.

Before the start of Game 4, May found Martin lying on the hotel bed with a pillow over his eyes. She sat beside him and took his hand. She was trying to remember her promise to be patient, but that was proving to be a challenge.

"Leave me alone, May," he said, pulling his hand away.

"What's wrong?" she asked.

"Nothing."

"Kylie called. She said good luck."

Martin grunted.

May stared down at him. Only his chin and neck were visible beneath the pillow. She gazed at the stitches in his lip and chin, the bruise on the side of his neck. His body was as tense as a board, but when she'd tried to touch him last night, he had flinched away. He seemed to have a constant headache; she had watched him gobble aspirin like candy, and sometime around midnight he had made himself an ice pack for his eyes.

"Martin?"

He didn't reply right away. But then he snatched the pillow from his head, sitting bolt upright. "I'm not sure you should be here."

"Why?"

"Because it's too hard on you. You don't like to see me fight-

ing, you're afraid I'm getting hurt, you know I want to rip Jorgensen's face off."

"Strange, but true," May said.

"That's hockey, May. It's why I didn't want you along last year. The finals are different from regular season. Very different."

"You think I can't handle it?" she asked. "Well, guess what? I can."

"Doesn't seem it," he grumbled.

"It's just that I'm worried about the way you keep squinting. Do you have a headache?"

"What's with everyone asking me if I have a headache?" he exploded. "You, Ray, Coach. Lay off me, May."

She thought of her meeting with Serge, how he had worried about problems with Martin's head, asked her whether he favored his right side. Last week's postcard had inquired what had happened to the backhand shot Martin used to fool rival goalies.

"So you don't have a headache?" she asked calmly.

"No." He exhaled loudly. "I don't."

"Good," she said.

"It's just the pressure." He bent his head so she could rub the back of his neck. She kneaded out some knots, feeling the tension in his neck and shoulders. "We have to win, May. I have to win. I've never wanted anything this much. And we're behind, three to nothing."

"You've come back from three-nothing before," she said. "Haven't you?"

He shrugged. "Yes, but it felt different than this . . ."

"But what?" May asked. "Did it ever feel easy? Did you ever think you could do it?"

He just kept staring at the ground, his eyes focused on the beige hotel room rug. But he was listening. May could tell by the tilt of his head, the fact he wasn't walking away from the sound of her voice. This is progress, she thought. They weren't running away from each other.

"Sometimes you have to be pushed up against the wall before you can find the door," May said.

"The door?"

"The way out," May said. "The door to . . ."

"Victory," Martin said, pulling her beside him.

In more ways than one, May thought but didn't say, embracing her husband and thinking of the card that had arrived that morning: "He's facing monsters inside him, and he needs to win."

Jorgensen, his past, his fears, his need to run away. Martin's father knew him so much better than he could ever imagine.

"You sure you're okay?" she asked.

"Fine. Twenty questions over?" he asked.

"No, here's one more." She slid her arms around his neck. "Do you love me?"

"*Bien sûr*, I do," he said, giving her a reluctant grin as he pulled her body against his. Smoothing back her hair, he kissed her on the lips. "But don't ask me again."

───

That night Boston blitzed Edmonton 3–0, with a hat trick by Martin Cartier. The following night was a repeat, 3–0, with another hat trick by Martin Cartier. The fans in Edmonton went berserk, and the question on everyone's lips was what had gotten into Martin? He was like a tiger on the loose, taking every shot that came his way, scoring every move he made. When Boston won the third game, tying the series score 3–3, the Bruins left Edmonton on a supercharged high.

The next game would tell the story. Papers ran stories about the great Serge Cartier, how history would compare father and son. Stories flowed about Serge's gambling and Martin's temper, about how love had changed Martin, how Boston had paid huge money for a hockey star, and they wanted their money's worth with a Stanley Cup victory.

The reputation of Nils Jorgensen as one of hockey's great goaltenders of all time was firmly established. Martin Cartier was already in the record books for most points by a right wing, most assists by a right wing; he had captured nearly every trophy known to hockey. But of the two rivals, only one had won the Stanley Cup.

Martin was going to change that tonight if he died doing it. Feeling his muscles tighten, he thought of everyone in his life worth winning for: May, Kylie, the spirits of his mother and Natalie, his Bruin teammates, his best friend Ray.

Deep down, in a place inside himself he didn't like to visit or acknowledge, he thought of one other person he would like to win for: his father. His wife had touched a place inside his heart, and now it was wide open.

Unable to tell May his thoughts, he pictured the man's face, thin and young, untouched by the ravages of living, victory, and wrongdoing. Serge had had a gentle, kind face, and Martin could

see it now, calling out for him to skate faster, keep a sense of his opponents, aim the puck at the cage as if he were shooting an arrow.

"I'm going to win tonight," Martin whispered to his father. "I'm going to take the Stanley Cup."

Serge Cartier couldn't speak back, but that didn't matter: Martin's eyes were closed, and he could hear his father's voice. Not the gravelly, rough voice of the gambling man his father had become, but the voice full of hope, love, and a particularly rural type of innocence. Martin had loved his father's voice at one time, and it gave him strength now.

"You can do it, son," that voice said. It was a voice of Canada, mountains, black ice, Lac Vert. It was his father's voice, but it came from deep within Martin's mind. That didn't matter, Martin knew. Tonight he was going to win.

"Got money on the game?"

"Cartier sucked the first three games."

"Hope you're bettin' on Edmonton, because they're gonna kill Boston tonight."

"Serge, man—two years in a row, Martin's gonna tank the last game."

"Game Seven, make or break . . ."

"Leave the old man alone," said Tino. "Just let him watch the game, okay?"

Serge sat still, tuning everyone out. The TV was on and working—that was all he cared about. He stared at the screen without blinking. Noise, chatter, cell doors clanging, nothing mattered. Only the game, only the camera panning across the crowd.

There, in the wives' box, was little Genevieve LeMay. Genny Gardner, now. Her kids were beside her, Charlotte and Mark, practically grown up. But Serge's eyes focused on the other two—May and Kylie Cartier. He felt tender and protective, and he wished he could keep the other inmates from seeing their faces.

"Hot mamas," Buford said.

"Shut up," Serge said.

"Real hot. Play hockey, you get girls like that?"

"That your granddaughter?"

"Nah, Serge don't have no granddaughter."

"Pretty girls, though."

Not even the nasty talk could distract Serge from watching the screen. He didn't have one word to say right now. Not in defense of himself, or of Martin, or to set anyone straight on the story of Natalie. That was no one's business here.

No words mattered now, except the ones Serge had inside.

Play, son, he thought. *Relax. Breathe. Aim true.*

The scoreboard flashed scenes from Martin's career. Now came a picture of Martin and Ray, age seven, after winning their first hockey tournament in Canada. There was Serge at Martin's side, helping him to hold up the enormous trophy, too heavy for the boy's small arms.

"Play, son," Serge thought, but he must have spoken out loud, because half the inmates were laughing.

Play son, play son, they said, mimicking him.

Serge didn't care. He glared above their heads, focused only on the TV screen. The words kept running through his head, and now he made sure they didn't leak out his mouth: *Play son, you can do it, you've got it won already, the Cup is yours. . . .*

And then, *Thank you, May.*

—

The face-off was played, the whistle sounded, the puck was dropped; Game 7 was under way. The capacity crowd at Boston's Fleet Center were shouting, stamping their feet. Police officers surrounded the rink, their backs to the ice as they scanned the crowd. There had been death threats called in for both Martin Cartier and Nils Jorgensen, and the authorities weren't taking any chances.

Two minutes into the first period, Martin assisted on a goal by Ray Gardner. Then Ray returned the favor, and Martin scored the next shot. As the puck zipped past Jorgensen, Martin raised both arms over his head and the crowd went wild.

Skating past May and Kylie, Martin saw them on their feet and waving. He grinned, tapping the protective glass as he went by. Kylie lunged toward him, trying to brush his fingers. But now it was time to play again. A pack of Oilers surrounded Martin, drawing his ire, and he got a two-minute penalty for slashing.

Taking advantage of the situation, Edmonton scored a fast goal against Boston; at the end of the first period, the Bruins were winning 2–1.

Martin's heart was pounding like the wings of a trapped fly. He could hear the crowd, and he felt the memories building. Last year

at this time, the Bruins had a shot at victory. Martin had had every chance; he'd scored like a champ, then choked at the end. Having May and Kylie here made all the difference. Skating past their box, he could hear their voices above all others in the stadium.

"Go, Martin!"

"Go, Daddy, go!"

At the second-period face-off, Ray won the draw and hit Martin streaking down the ice just as he crossed the blue line. Martin took his moment, shot, and scored. Coming around the goal, a shadow clouded his vision again: Every single player on the ice had a shimmering double right behind him.

"*Merde*," Martin said, ducking his head and covering his eyes. His hesitation gave Edmonton their chance as their center got the puck and skated down to the slot. Ray attempted to slow him down by hooking his stick across the center's arms, but the center made the goal anyway and Ray went to the penalty box.

A buzz went through the stadium, and Martin heard it. He could imagine everyone asking what Cartier was doing with his head down, and Coach Dafoe didn't waste any time calling him off the ice.

"What's wrong?" Coach asked when Martin came over.

"Nothing. Just a rush."

"What kind of rush? Over here, Doc."

The loudspeaker was blaring, announcing the fact that Edmonton had just tied the score, 3–3. The crowd was booing, throwing things onto the ice. Police in riot gear surrounded the players' box. Martin blinked, trying to clear his eyes. The doctor attempted to examine them with a small light, but Martin couldn't sit still long enough.

"Put me back in, Coach," he demanded.

"Not if you're dizzy."

"Dizzy, bullshit," Martin said. "It's gone, eh? All year you've been telling me 'wait till the finals.' Well, it's the finals, and this is our last game. Put me in."

The third period was under way, and time was running out. Martin skated back and forth, up and down the ice, trying for every shot he could. Nils Jorgensen blocked him every time. The shadows had disappeared, so Martin couldn't blame his eyes. He was up against a fierce goaltender, and Martin had the feeling they were fighting to the death. Both men bore scars the other had inflicted, inside and out.

The drama began to build. The clock was ticking down, and

every time Edmonton got the puck an eerie chill went down Martin's spine. But then Ray stole the puck and carried it down to the offensive zone, keeping it there while Edmonton tried every trick they had to steal it away.

Now time was running out. The Edmonton fans were chanting: "CARTIER CURSE, CARTIER CURSE . . ." The game was headed for overtime, and once again Martin thought of last year. *What's different now,* he asked himself? *What do I have this year that can help me? I'm another year older and more tired. But this year I have May. We're making it through, we're together, she loves me.* He felt his wedding ring under his glove, and he thought of the rose petals in his waistband.

May and Kylie were on their feet, cheering at the top of their lungs. Martin skated close, and he saw love in their eyes. It choked him up in a way he couldn't explain, and suddenly he couldn't hear the rest of the crowd. The time was ticking down, but for Martin, it suddenly stood still.

Ray fed Martin the puck, and the drive began.

The crowd rose as one and screamed louder. Their cheers shook the stadium, but Martin barely heard. He thought of his mother and father, his wife and two little girls. Thoughts so simple yet charged with fire. The energy shot through him, and he started to run, not glide from the left wing. A chorus of yells surrounded the rink, rising in a long crescendo of "GO, GO, GOOOO!"

It started the instant he hit the slot, the cloud of darkness overtaking his vision. Martin cocked his elbow and lost the puck. Someone had stolen it from him, an opponent he hadn't seen coming who took it straight down the ice.

He hadn't seen! The buzzer sounded. By the score of 4–3, the Cartier Curse had prevailed and the Edmonton Oilers had again won the Stanley Cup.

Serge filled out another postcard and addressed it to his daughter-in-law: "He played his best," Serge wrote. "So did you. Don't let him stay down." He knew how bad the loss had to be.

She had written back after the last card. She had enclosed pictures of herself, Kylie, and Martin. Serge wished she had said something about telling Martin about their meeting, but he accepted the disappointment. If Martin wanted to come, he knew where to find him.

"Hey, Serge." Tino was walking toward him in the prison yard. He pronounced the name the French way: Sairge. It was a sunny day, and the boy squinted into the light.

"Hello, Tino," Serge said, squinting back.

"Your kid lost the hockey game."

"He won more than he lost," Serge told him. "He took his team to the Stanley Cup finals."

"Yeah, whatever it is," he said. "I don't know much about hockey. But I saw him playing."

"You know the World Series?"

"Yeah, I know it."

"Know the Super Bowl?"

"Football, yeah."

"Well, the Stanley Cup is the World Series and Super Bowl of hockey. It's the top of the mountain, as high as it gets. And Martin took his team to the finals."

"Yeah? Wow. That's cool."

"I passed it on to Martin," Serge said. "Playing hockey. I just hope he's okay tonight. Not being too hard on himself."

The boy nodded. He seemed glad to be talking to Serge while the old man was in a quiet mood; he had a pack of cigarettes visible through his shirt pocket, but he hadn't reached for one.

"You've got kids," Serge went on, "I see them in the visitors' room."

"Maybe some day Ricky'll be a big-league pitcher," the young man said. "I'm good myself. I can strike out six guys in a row, no problem. Just like you passing on the hockey to your son, I'll do the same with baseball for Ricky."

Serge thought of Martin. He remembered endless drills, frigid nights on the lake when Agnes would have supper waiting while the moon rose high over the mountain and illuminated the ice with sharp white light. Martin and Ray had fired pucks at Serge in the pine-bough goal, and Serge had taught them how to aim true and straight. Then Serge's contract had taken him away, and his drills with Martin were over.

"I'll give him everything I know," the young man was saying. "My fastball, my slider, my best El Duque—" He wound up, pitching an imaginary fastball straight at the guard.

Serge felt the regret starting to flood in, the memories of being a young father and deserting his wife and son, the glory of the road, the hotels and women, the thrill of winning season after winning season. Lucky streaks, quick bets, good cards, bad cards: a tumul-

tuous life leading to this moment in the sunny yard of the prison. He should be there for Martin, telling him he had played a good series, that he would win the Cup next year.

Listening to this young convict dreaming of being a better father, making a difference in his son's life, made Serge hate himself so much, he stepped away.

"Quit that," Serge snapped.

"I'm striking the guy out." Tino retracted his bare arm, holding the invisible baseball against his chest. "So I can pass my pitching on to Ricky."

"You can't pass it on when you're in here," Serge said harshly, picturing Tino's little boy.

"Hey." The young man looked hurt.

"You're kidding yourself, you think it's any different."

"I can play—"

"You're in prison," Serge said.

The kid shook his head, sneering. He started to walk away, but Serge grabbed his arm.

"You take drugs, you steal cars—that's what you're passing on to your son."

"Shut up—"

"Maybe you've got the genes to play baseball, but your actions say something different. Otherwise you wouldn't be locked in here with murderers and thieves. With me."

"Yeah, with you," Tino said.

"I'm as bad as the rest of them." Overhead, the sky was so blue. Serge could see just a square of it: a window made of prison walls and razor wire, looking up at the blue sky. "I'm in here, aren't I?"

"It ain't forever," the kid said.

"It might be to your son," Serge said. "Who else is gonna pitch him balls out there?"

"Shut up," the kid said again, turning to leave.

Serge scowled. He shouldn't have gotten into the conversation in the first place. Talking never did any good in here. It took his pride and threw it back into his face. Better to think about Martin's pain in silence. Words brought ugly truths to light and made good memories a joke. Serge thought of fathers and sons, mysteries as deep and troubled as a northern sea.

"Dignity, kid," Serge called. "That's what you want to pass on. Forget the fastball. Dignity and living a good life. Get the hell out of here."

But Tino had already walked away.

Chapter 19

HEADING NORTH TO LAC VERT, May recognized landmarks—the road signs, the old abandoned Texaco station, the small suspension bridge, the distant hills. They made the same rest stops as last year, stocking up on juice and treats for the ride. At the Canadian border, when the guard greeted Martin, this time he had a big hello for May and Kylie as well.

May took Martin's hand while he drove; he had withdrawn into himself after Game 7, and he hadn't come out. Driving, he seemed distracted. He ran a red light on the way to the highway. A squirrel ran in front of the car, and he hit it without even swerving, as if he hadn't even seen it.

"Are you tired?" May asked. "Do you want me to drive?"

"I'm fine."

"That squirrel—"

"It came out of nowhere." Martin checked the rearview mirror to make sure Kylie was asleep and hadn't seen. "I didn't see it till it was too late."

"You didn't see it at all," May said.

Martin didn't answer. He just pulled his hand away, to keep both hands on the wheel, and focused on the road.

Last year, everything was brand-new. She hadn't known what to expect, what was going to happen. But now she could picture the small house nestled into the mountainside, the glittering lake, the starry nights. The Gardners would be waiting just up the shore. This summer May had the sense of returning home. But instead of feeling excited, she felt a growing sense of unease.

They spent the first few days sleeping, playing, and eating: a true vacation. Martin took Kylie rowing up the lake, and May lay out in the gazebo reading and writing. They all went swimming, and at night they sat in lawn chairs telling stories about the stars.

After midnight on their third night there, Kylie sleepwalked into their room. May and Martin had been making love, and suddenly they looked up to see Kylie standing beside their bed. While Martin pulled the sheet over himself, May leaned toward Kylie.

"Honey?" she asked.

"In the stars." Kylie pointed at the window.

"What do you see?" May asked.

"The Blind Man," Kylie said, her gaze directed at the stars. "He can't see."

"Is she awake?" Martin whispered.

"I don't think so."

"I'm supposed to tell him . . ." Kylie was blank-faced.

"Tell him what?" May asked.

"Where to look," Kylie said. Then, turning, she walked back to her room. Climbing silently out of bed, May followed to make sure Kylie was safe. Once assured she was fast asleep, May hurried back to record the incident in the blue diary.

"What was that all about?" Martin asked.

"I'm not sure." May said, trying to remember every detail.

"You're still keeping that notebook?"

"Yes," May said, laying down her pen.

"What good does it do?"

May stared at him. She thought about Dr. Whitpen's theory, that Kylie's dreams were connected to Martin's own story, but she kept it to herself. "It helps the doctors understand what's going on," May said.

"What was that bit about the Blind Man, eh?" Martin asked. "There's no constellation like that."

"I know," May said, gazing out their window at the stars.

⟜

Charlotte called to ask Kylie to sleep over the next night, and after thinking it over, May decided to let her go. She and Martin needed some time alone. Together they talked about their time apart, his Stanley Cup loss, what they hoped the summer might bring.

"What are you doing up?" Martin asked, when he found her awake the next morning. They had tried to make up for what they'd been through during the spring, and the late afternoon and night before had been filled with touching, swimming, and amazing ten-

derness. Now he reached across the bed to grab her leg as she walked over to open the curtains.

"It's nine-thirty," she said. "Do you know the last time I slept this late? It was—"

But Martin had a good grip, and he pulled her right back onto the bed, rolling on top of her as she tumbled down. "Nine-thirty's nothing," he told her. "We have a chance to be alone and you're not getting up till noon."

"But it's beautiful out." She pointed at the window where sunlight blazed through the crack between the curtains. "We should—"

"Should nothing," he said, smoothing back her hair and kissing her hard.

"I'll never be able to sleep till noon," she whispered, feeling his hands on her shoulders, moving down the front of her body.

"Who said anything about sleep?" Martin asked, kissing her neck.

They made love, then Martin brought her coffee in bed, then May opened the curtains, then Martin closed them. When he returned to bed, May noticed him squinting and covering his eyes.

"What's wrong?" she asked.

"I'm not ready for daylight yet," he said, lunging toward her. "Get back under those covers, woman."

May wanted to ask him more, but she found herself lost in passion. Martin was intensely physical. He was rough with his upper body and gentle with his hands, and May let herself surrender to sensations she had never even imagined. Once he kissed her hard, then whispered into her ear, "Is that good? Do you like it like that?" and May was shocked to hear words. She had so totally forgotten herself, lost track of where she ended and Martin began, that she had felt her voice and thoughts and feelings merging straight into his.

"It's incredible," she whispered.

"Tell me," he said.

"With my body, not my voice."

The light had brightened, even through the closed curtains, as the sun traversed the sky, and May walked across the room to pull down the shades and make the room darker.

"I thought you wanted sun," he teased.

"I don't want to see or hear," she said, shivering with excitement. "I just want to feel you."

"You're wild," he said.

"Only with you." She lay down beside him. Their separation had cleared the air, and now she felt closer to him than ever before. Kissing her lips, he placed his hand over her eyes. Unable to see, she felt his breath on her cheek, his arms surrounding her body—the sensations of his fingers on her skin, his lips on hers, were exquisitely intensified.

May felt overwhelmed with the simple thrill of making love with Martin. She had never believed this kind of intimacy possible. They didn't speak, and she couldn't see, and she knew that she had surrendered sight and hearing for touch, for the chance to experience this level of trust and risk in her own bed with her own husband.

As the days wore on, Martin and May got down to business as sort-of-usual. Reporters stopped calling to interview him. The memory of those terrible last few seconds in the game began to fade. Ray came over to talk, and the two men drank beer and had a postgame postmortem sitting on the porch.

While living in Boston, May had worked out a system with Tobin involving the telephone and a fax machine, and this summer they perfected it from Canada. They agreed that Tobin would handle any new clients from June through September, and May would oversee the in-progress wedding plans from Lac Vert.

One day, while Martin and Ray went fishing, May invited Genny and Charlotte over to visit. While the girls played outside, their mothers talked on the front porch.

"How's Ray taking the loss?" May asked.

"A little better every day. The name Martin Cartier was pretty touchy that first twenty-four hours."

"He blames Martin for losing?"

"They all do," Genny said. "He lost the puck instead of putting it away."

May frowned, wanting her friend to rise above blaming her husband.

"Athletes always need a scapegoat," Genny told her. "I'm sure you've noticed by now. Ray's been it plenty of times, and so have all the others. Everyone makes mistakes. But that one . . ."

"It was big." May remembered those awful last seconds.

"He just stopped in mid-ice," Genny said. "Ray said, if he wasn't so mad at him, he'd be worried."

"Why worried?"

"Well, it was as if Martin was paralyzed or something. As if he just went numb."

"I thought that, too." In her mind, May could see Martin driving down the ice, then just halting—his arm cocked and ready to shoot, with the puck already on its way to the Edmonton goal. "His father mentioned something to me the time I went to see him. He said Martin's been favoring his right side."

"They go back and forth." Genny laughed. "Depending on what's hurt. There's always something."

"So I shouldn't be concerned."

"Not unless he wakes up one morning and can't move. That's about the only thing serious enough to keep Martin off the ice."

"Okay," May said.

Then, offering Genny some tea, May headed for the kitchen. Following along, Genny stopped to look at some old pictures in the living room. She caught sight of Martin's mother's collection of needlework pillows, displayed all along the back of the sofa.

"Agnes always kept busy," Genny said. "Knitting, needlepointing, doing cross-stitch. She showed me how to make a sampler once."

"Did you make one?"

"I started it." Genny said, looking around the room. Her gaze traveled over all the walls, the mantel, and the bookshelves. "Hmm. That's funny."

"What?"

"There used to be a cross-stitch picture hanging in this room. Dark blue thread on fine muslin, I think. It showed two baby animals, and I loved it so much. It inspired me to try my own. Agnes made it when Martin was born."

"I wonder where it is," May said.

"I wonder." Genny scanned all the walls of the room as if the picture would suddenly reappear. "It hung here forever."

Martin borrowed Ray's uncle's truck and drove to the local nursery to buy up all their rosebushes. He wanted May to have her own rose garden up here, just like the one in Black Hall. The growing season was about a month behind Connecticut, so most of the bushes he picked out were full of buds.

Kylie had come along for the ride. While Martin loaded sixty

rosebushes into the truck bed, Kylie played with an old basset hound lying in the shade.

"Careful now, he bites," called the nursery owner, Jean-Pierre Heckler.

Martin put down the rosebush he was carrying and went to retrieve Kylie.

"He doesn't bite me," Kylie said.

"Well, he bit me," Jean-Pierre told her, pointing at his foot. "Last night he smelled so bad I kicked him right out the door. And he grabbed my foot—"

"What are you doing with a dog who bites?" Martin asked, staring down at the old hound. He was tied to a fence post, lying in a shallow hole he'd dug himself, his face creased with wrinkles. His fur was white around his eyes and muzzle, and when he panted, his tongue was so long it hung into the dirt.

"He used to belong to Anne's father," Jean-Pierre explained. Martin listened. He had gone to school with the man's wife, Anne Duprée, and Martin vaguely remembered that her father had owned a small farm southwest of the lake.

"Did Mr. Duprée die?" Martin asked.

"Yes, last winter. We sold the farm, but of course the new owners didn't want a mean old dog. He's bad for business, growling at all the customers."

"Poor old dog," Kylie said, squirming to pull away from Martin. He couldn't believe, looking into the hound's droopy eyes, that he would bite anyone, but Martin wasn't taking any chances.

"What do I owe you?" Martin asked, reaching for his wallet.

"Well, I'm going to give you a ten-percent discount," Jean-Pierre said. "On account of the honor you've brought Lac Vert. Anne is very proud of you. Next year, even greater victory! You'll win the Stanley Cup for sure."

"Next year," Martin said, letting Kylie go as he counted out the money.

She reached for the dog, and he licked her hand. Grabbing the rope, the nursery man yanked the dog away. "All I need is for this mutt to bite your girl," he said.

"He won't bite me," Kylie insisted.

"He's very old. Too old. The vet is coming soon, if you know what I mean," Jean-Pierre said. Martin felt ice in his veins.

"You mean you're putting him to sleep?" Kylie asked.

"He's got arthritis, bad teeth, a terrible disposition," Jean-Pierre Heckler said. "It's for the best."

"Can we adopt him?" Kylie asked.

"You don't want this dog," Jean-Pierre said. "Believe me. Now, you want a nice pet, I can give you a kitten from out back. Our big tiger just had a litter—"

Martin watched Kylie inch toward the old basset hound. He could smell the dog's breath from where he stood. Kylie reached out her hand, and the hound craned his neck so she could pet his head. He squirmed under her touch like a happy puppy, and Martin heard himself ask, "What's the dog's name?"

"Thunder," Jean-Pierre told them.

"Hi, Thunder," Kylie said.

"The kittens—"

"She wants Thunder." Martin watched the old dog slobber over Kylie's hand. Kylie laughed and stroked his long ears.

"He's a mess," Jean-Pierre said quietly, so Kylie couldn't hear. "Can't control himself—goes all over the house. We let him sleep outside, and then he howls all night. He's a one-man dog—turned mean and surly the day his master died. Believe me, Martin—let the vet do his work. It's best for everyone."

Martin thought back. One day Genny had taken her kids and Natalie to the Lac Vert dog pound, behind the municipal garage on Mountain Road. The Gardners adopted a young shepherd, and Natalie picked out an abandoned beagle, telling the woman in charge that she and her father would be back for him before the weekend.

She had begged Martin to let her get the dog. They could train him together, and he could keep Martin company when she went back to California. Martin had said no. The hockey season was long; the dog would be alone while Martin was on the road. His situation wasn't like the Gardners', with lots of people to play with the dog every day.

Natalie had been devastated. Sneaking away one morning, she had ridden her bike to the pound. She named the dog "Archie," and all that summer she never stopped begging Martin to reconsider. One morning he got a call from the woman who ran the pound. Obviously not a hockey fan, she spoke to him with venom in her voice, telling him to pick up his child.

"These roads are dangerous," the woman had said. "She has no business riding her bicycle up here by herself."

"I'll come get her right away," he said.

"Don't let her come back," the woman warned. "This dog has

been here all summer, and he's being put down tomorrow. She won't find him here again."

When Martin picked Nat up, she started to cry, clutching Archie's neck. Breaking her grasp, Martin had pushed the dog away, getting bitten on the hand in the process. With Natalie weeping inconsolably, Martin had driven away, aware of the woman's cold stare.

Remembering Natalie's sorrow and anger, Martin watched Kylie now. He saw her kiss the basset hound's ear, and he watched the dog's droopy-eyed gaze widen. The dog licked Kylie's face, revealing gray-pink gums missing lower teeth.

"How about a new puppy, Kylie?" he asked. "Or one of those kittens?"

Kylie shook her head. "I want Thunder."

"Okay, then," Martin said. Then, turning back to Anne's husband, "Would that be possible? I mean, it sounds as if you don't intend to keep the dog."

"We don't, but neither do you—honestly, it would be an insult for us to give you this mangy animal—"

"*He's not mangy,*" said the little girl, and although it was Kylie speaking, Martin could swear he heard Natalie's voice.

"I'll be happy to pay you for him," Martin offered.

"That's not necessary." Jean-Pierre was shaking his head. He helped Martin load the last rosebushes into the truck, as Kylie climbed into the cab with Thunder.

"Why is his name Thunder?" Kylie asked.

"He had a brother, Lightning," Jean-Pierre said. "Their names were sort of a family joke. All they liked to do was eat and sleep! Those big sleepy eyes, their short legs. They'd lie on the porch and birds would steal their food. Pigeons would sit on their heads."

"What happened to Lightning?"

"My father-in-law went to the hospital and never came home, and old Lightning refused to eat or drink. Wasted away and died. Thunder and Lightning. They were quite a pair."

"You miss your brother," Martin heard Kylie whisper to the old dog. "And your master. That's why you've been in a bad mood."

"Got quite an imagination, that one," Jean-Pierre said, pointing.

"She has a big heart," Martin said, keeping an even temper as he climbed into the truck and backed down the driveway. Next time he wanted rosebushes, he'd visit Green Gardens, north on the lake road. Anne Duprée had been a nice girl in school. Martin

couldn't picture her married to someone who'd kick her father's dog. No wonder the old hound had bitten him.

But then, a dog had bitten Martin once.

—

Overnight, May had a new rose garden and an old dog. Taking her coffee outside to watch the sunrise and walk through rows of just-planted rosebushes, she thought about life: how impossible it was to see around corners and up hills, how every day was filled with the unknown.

"Come on, boy," she said out loud to her companion, the elderly and as yet unknown basset hound Thunder. Thunder padded through the recently overturned earth, sticking his considerable nose into furrows and under leaves, huffing and puffing as he walked at May's feet.

The sun was peeking out from behind the mountain, spreading diamond light down the rocks and onto the lake's green glass surface. Deer grazed in shadows across the lake, unseen by Thunder. May walked slowly, to keep from scaring them. Rabbits scattered into the underbrush, and she found herself thinking about the missing cross-stitch picture, wondering which sort of animals Agnes had stitched.

Sitting in the gazebo, May looked around. The old dog stood by the water's edge, as if contemplating a swim. Martin had expected May to resist the dog: his bladder problems, his halitosis, his dandruff, his missing teeth, and his need for special food.

But May had seen only Kylie's love for her new dog and Martin's care for Kylie. It had touched her beyond words. Then Martin had told her about Natalie and Archie, how he had let the chance to let his daughter have a dog slip by once before. Thunder was a sweet old creature, saved by Martin from veterinary death, but what May found ineffable was how her husband and child had become a team.

"Here, boy," May called softly now. "Thunder . . . c'mere, boy."

Thunder looked over his shoulder, his eyes drooping and bloodshot. He had gotten stuck in the mud. Paw-deep and sinking to his knees, he gazed helplessly at his mistress's mother.

"You can do it, Thunder," May said, setting her coffee mug down on the gazebo bench.

The dog let out a mournful bay, then took a long drink of lake

water. He shook off his ears and jowls, soaking May from ten feet away. She kicked off her sneakers and wondered how hard it was going to be to pull a sixty-pound basset hound—with a reputation for biting—out of the mud. Looking around, she happened to glimpse the rose garden.

The sun, half hidden by pines on the mountainside, was striking the rosebushes. A thousand new buds, in scarlet, crimson, vermilion, pink, peach, and pearl, were straining toward the light. They were tiny flames licking the sky, ready to explode into bloom. Martin had started planting them the minute he got home, and he hadn't finished until after dark.

The smells of dirt, coffee, wet dog. May felt so happy, she couldn't contain the feeling. Dew covered every stick of wood, each blade of grass. She started to roll up the legs of her jeans, but then she found herself taking them off. Peeling off her sweatshirt and blouse, wearing nothing but her underwear, she stood alone on the steps of the gazebo where she had married Martin.

Walking down to the lake, she felt the cool mud between her toes. Thunder wagged his tail as she approached. Reaching her arms around his torpedo-shaped body, May eased him out of the mud. She started to turn, to place him on the grass, but he started to whimper and point his nose toward the water.

"Want to swim?" she asked.

Thunder didn't reply, but his front paws began to paddle. May slid him into the lake, and he glided forward with all the sleekness of a sea otter, a sailboat, or a very young puppy. May followed right behind.

She swam out from the shore, straight into the patch of diamond sunlight. The mountain lake felt smooth and cold, clean as dawn. Thunder stayed closer to land, paddling back and forth along the edge. When May turned, to look at her house and barns and rose garden, she saw her husband walking down the path.

She waved, but he didn't wave back. When he came upon the pile of her clothes, he picked them up and held them against his chest. She watched him looking around, moving his head from side to side as if trying to see where she had gone. At the sight of Martin, Thunder waddled into shallow water, and Martin hauled him out. Martin's shoulders were tense, and he never stopped scanning the lake.

"May!" he called.

"I'm out here," May called back.

He nodded, and she saw him relax. He was barefoot, but now

he undid his shorts and pulled his shirt over his head. May watched him place all the clothes on the steps of the gazebo. Standing there in his jockey shorts, he looked like a marble statue. The sun glistened on his skin, showing every scar, every muscle, every flat surface. He walked down to the edge, standing very still for a few seconds.

He dove in, and May thrilled with excitement watching him swim out. Could it be considered skinny-dipping if they were wearing their underwear? She opened her arms to embrace him, as he swam toward her. He grabbed her with such ferocity, it took her breath away.

"I couldn't see you," he said into her neck. "I found your clothes, and I saw the dog, but I couldn't see you."

"I didn't mean to worry you," she said, stunned by the intensity in his voice. "Thunder was stuck, and when I helped him I decided to swim."

Martin nodded. She felt him moving his head, and then he let her go and backed away, treading water. They were face to face, swimming in the sunlight. She tried to read the look in his eyes: It was filled with confusion, relief, and something else.

"You couldn't see me?" she asked.

"No."

"I was right here." They were just fifteen yards out; surely she should have been easily spotted from shore.

"The sun was in my eyes," he said.

She nodded, feeling something like relief herself. But relieved of what? They swam in a patch of glare, making her squint and look away from the sun. Martin brushed her bare leg with his own, and she drifted into his arms. They kissed, ducking beneath the surface. When they came up, they heard Thunder barking. He let out a long, joyful yip, and Martin said into May's ear, "He's happy to be alive."

As they kissed, the sun passed behind a tall pine tree, momentarily throwing the entire lake into shade. May shivered, holding her husband closer until the shade passed and the sun burst out again.

Thunder bayed, welcoming the sun back. Martin and May stopped kissing to look over. He had climbed the gazebo steps, and he circled once before stretching and settling down for a postswim nap on the pile of clean clothes.

"He's in trouble," May said.

"For what?" Martin asked.

May stared into her husband's eyes. He was smiling in the direction of the old dog's heartfelt call, staring straight at the gazebo. She felt suddenly cold in spite of the sun, and she found herself thinking of those last few seconds of the last game.

Martin couldn't see.

Chapter 20

I N THE YARD, OVERLOOKING THE lake and the mountains, were two old white chairs. Their cushions, faded by time and weather, had once been dark blue. May set the low table between them with rolls, butter, a bunch of grapes, a pitcher of juice, and coffee. After rinsing off in the outside shower, Martin sat down beside her for breakfast by the lake.

As they ate, May stared out over the lake. A heron fished the shallows, walking on yellow stick legs through the tall grass. A lone moose stood amid lily pads, his antlers glistening in the sun. When May pointed to him and Martin didn't get excited, her heart fell.

"I'm worried about your eyes," she said.

"Why?"

"Because you're not seeing things."

"Like what?"

"Like Thunder rolling all over our things this morning. Like that moose."

"I see it."

"Are you sure?" she pressed.

"May," he said, touching her arm. "I'm not as young as I used to be. I've taken a few hits to the head, you know? The day's coming when I might need glasses. Believe me, that's doom for a hockey player, and I don't want to face it."

"You've talked to the team doctor?"

He nodded. "You think they let me get away with anything physical? If I have a symptom, they send me for X rays. All I need is the summer off, to heal. It's beautiful out. We're alone together. Just enjoy it. Okay?"

"Okay." Unconvinced, May tried to eat her roll. She wasn't hungry anymore, so she broke it into crumbs and threw them on

the ground. A flock of sparrows darted down from the trees, eating hungrily.

She had brought the blue diary outside with her, to read over the summer's entries and write a letter to Dr. Whitpen. Worried about Martin, she found an outlet filling two pages with accounts of the last weeks.

"What's that?" Martin asked, looking over.

"A letter to Dr. Whitpen."

"Seems like you have a lot to say to him."

"Even when I want to resist, staying in touch with him has always been important to me. I guess I think having a psychologist overseeing Kylie's case, even from far away, is the best thing."

Martin gave her a long look, as if he had just understood something. He reached across the space between their chairs and took her hand.

"It must have been hard for you, going through that all alone."

"Well, I had Tobin and Aunt Enid."

"I hate her father for abandoning her," Martin said. "Does she ever talk about him?"

May shook her head. "No. She used to dream about him sometimes, telling me he'd come to take her riding, out for ice cream, things like that. But then we took that walk in the wildlife preserve and everything shifted."

"Shifted how?"

"All her dreams were about dead people."

"And that's when you started taking her to Dr. Whitpen?"

May nodded. "It seemed more unusual to have her dreaming of ghosts than of Gordon taking her for ice cream. Though I'm not sure why. Gordon spending time with her is far-fetched."

"Think she'll ever want to see him?" Martin asked.

"Yes," May said. "Probably. When she's older."

Martin shook his head hard. "We'll have to talk her out of that. Move to another country if necessary."

"That's not how I see it, Martin," she said quietly. "Someday Kylie will want to make the connection. And I'll support her totally. No matter what I feel for him, I want Kylie to know her father."

"I want to raise her," Martin said. "Help me be a good father to her."

"Just take care of yourself," May told him.

"What do you mean?" Martin asked.

"That's the example I want her to have." May was staring down

at the blue notebook. "I take her to Dr. Whitpen because I think he can help. And I'd like you to see someone because I'm worried about your eyes."

Martin nodded, but he pulled his hand out of May's. He resumed staring across the lake, through the golden haze of pollen and morning light, at the heron and moose she knew he couldn't see.

—

That night, after her parents had gone to bed, Kylie couldn't sleep. The moon was nearly full, and it spun a silver web through the pine trees, down the mountain trails, onto the lake itself. Kylie had pressure inside her chest, the feeling of Christmas mornings mixed with how she felt when a storm was coming. She tiptoed downstairs, Thunder thumping along behind her.

Very quietly, she walked into the dining room. There was a big closet beside the chimney, deep and dark. Kylie had discovered it last summer, when they had first come to Lac Vert. The door blended into the wainscoting. If you didn't know it was there, it would be easy to miss.

Turning the small brass latch, Kylie let herself inside. It smelled dry and musty, and her heart was pounding as she felt overhead for the long string that switched on the light. Thunder was waiting outside, afraid to come in.

Kylie turned on the light. She felt different in this closet than she did anywhere else in the house. Family secrets were hidden here, and if there were any ghosts or angels at Lac Vert, this was where they lived. Blinking at the bare lightbulb, Kylie was sure she saw the flash of some filmy white wings.

"Natalie?" she whispered.

But she heard only Thunder sniffing the air, his breath heavy and labored as if the whole thing was too much for him. Kylie looked around. Spiderwebs hung in every corner, shifting gently in the air.

Kylie thought of Richard Perry. She pictured him all the time, hanging from the tree branch, his dead body swinging in the wind. His knobby bones had been pure white, the tatters of his clothes and skin and muscles brownish gray. Kylie had looked up at his body, seen a man begging to be cut down. His lips had moved, his eyes wild with despair.

The police had come. While answering their questions, Kylie

had kept an eye on Richard Perry's body. Police officers had finished taking their pictures. She had watched the medical examiner approach the tree, decide the best way to proceed, raise a ladder and shinny out on the limb. Wielding huge clippers, the man had cut right through the thick rope, and a team of people had caught the body from below.

"Thank you," Kylie had heard the man cry. "Thank you for setting me free."

Kylie had come in here to look for something. She had heard her mother asking Martin about an old picture, and Kylie knew where it was. One rainy day last summer, exploring the house, she had found a bunch of things someone had hidden away. A silver baby cup, a toy carriage, a pile of children's books, and a cross-stitch picture.

Climbing up the shelves, using them as the rungs of a ladder, Kylie reached the top shelf. There, pushed toward the back, she found the frame. Inching her fingers along the boards, she caught hold and pulled it forward. Holding it under her arm, she jumped back down.

The glass was covered with thick dust. Kylie brushed it off, to stare at the picture inside. The background was cloth, white muslin that had yellowed like the antique wedding dresses in the Bridal Barn. Pulled tight, the cloth had been embroidered with tiny x's, all done in pretty blue thread, the x's adding up to a picture of two baby animals: a lamb and a leopard, sleeping together.

Around the outside was a message. Last year, Kylie had been just starting to read, but this year the words flowed easily: "The wolf shall dwell with the lamb, and the leopard lie down with the kid, and a little child shall lead them."

Kylie didn't know what that meant, so she read it again. With dust still on the glass, she wiped it more carefully. Beneath the dust was another substance, sparkling like tiny bits of mica. It was all over her fingers, making them shine with iridescence.

Her heart was beating. She had the feeling something was about to happen, that Natalie was about to appear. She could feel her presence in this hidden room, and somehow she knew the shiny matter was proof of her existence.

"Natalie," Kylie begged. "Let me see you."

Thunder whined outside the door, begging Kylie to come out.

"I know you're here," Kylie said. She stared at the picture again, reading the message over and over. Natalie had wanted her to find it. Kylie was positive. She had been fast asleep, and some-

thing in her dreams had told her to come downstairs and search for this old picture.

"Are you the little child?" she asked out loud.

You are, she heard. *Bring them together.*

Kylie wheeled around. No one had spoken.

A rustle overhead made her look up, and she saw a phalanx of bats roosting in the rafters, watching her from their upside-down positions. Kylie shivered with fear, and Thunder started to bay. Suddenly Kylie heard footsteps on the stairs.

"Kylie?" she heard her mother call.

"Natalie's here, I know she is," Kylie cried.

"She's dreaming again," she heard Martin say. "Sleepwalking."

"Natalie," Kylie whispered, letting her mother lift her into her arms.

But the presence was gone. Thunder had stopped baying and was gazing with great peace and comfort at the open window. His fur was glossier than Kylie had seen it, and his eyes were bright.

Her mother carried her over to the window. They stood there together, breathing the fresh air, and Kylie felt the intensity leave her, as if the last moments had been a dream. The hills rose majestically all around the lake. Kylie saw how the moonlight danced through the trees, struck the silver rock, rounded the soft knolls. It looked alive, magical.

"You're safe," her mother whispered. "You're awake now. I'm right here with you."

"I saved him, didn't I?" Kylie wept. "That man, hanging in the tree. I did what he asked. . . ."

"You did, honey," her mother said, her eyes wild. Kylie knew she was going to go upstairs and write in that blue book, probably call Dr. Whitpen in the morning, and the thought made her so sad she started to cry harder.

"What have you got there?" Martin asked, reaching for the frame Kylie held under her arm. He wiped his hand across the glass, and Kylie saw that his fingertips were covered with sparkles. It glittered like diamond chips, like moondust, and suddenly Kylie realized it had come from angel's tears.

"The cross-stitch picture," her mother said.

"My mother did this when I was born. I put it away . . ."

"Why did you put it away?" Kylie asked.

"Because it reminded me of Natalie," Martin said. "'And a little child shall lead them.' She did, too. She led us all."

"She's still leading us." Kylie knew she had to get Martin to un-

derstand that time was short, that he had to see his father. Natalie had drawn Kylie into the closet, to give her messages: the picture, the sparkles. But now it was up to Kylie: *You're the child; bring them together.*

"Something's going to happen," Kylie whispered.

"Let's all go to bed," her mother said. "It's very late."

"That's a good idea." Martin was frowning at the picture.

Kylie didn't reply. She just gazed long and hard into his blue eyes, brushing his lips with her fingertips as she kissed his forehead. When she drew back, she saw that she had left silver flecks on his lips, that her fingertips had transferred Natalie's tears onto his skin.

———

Serge couldn't sleep. Some idiots down the hall were trying to kill each other, screaming as if they were being torn to shreds. He clapped his pillow over his head, but the ungodly noise penetrated even through the hard foam. Sitting up, he checked his watch: two A.M.

Giving up on sleep, he sat on the edge of his bunk, his head in his hands. He had a dry mouth and a pounding heart; he felt as if he had a hangover, but he hadn't had a drink in some years. Vices had stopped working for him the day his granddaughter died.

His eyes burned. Someone was smoking close by, and it wasn't a cigarette. The prison walls smelled of drugs and piss and loneliness and death. Serge's cell walls stank of greed and guilt and selfishness and a lifetime without word from his son. Down the hall the screaming got worse, and Serge realized it wasn't just a standard prison fight.

"Hey," he shouted at the top of his lungs.

"Shut up," someone yelled back.

"Help," Serge called. "Guard, help!"

"Shut the fuck up!"

"You want some yourself? Keep out of it!"

"Help!" Serge yelled. "Jesus Christ, help!"

Time passed, the minutes ticking by on his wristwatch. Although he couldn't see a window anywhere, he felt a blast of fresh air blow through his cell. It sent shivers down his spine and made the hair on his arms stand straight up. It felt like arctic air, straight from Canada, and it smelled like the pines of Lac Vert.

Maybe someone was dead. Serge had been religious as a child,

and wondering whether a man had just died in the fight down the hall, he crossed himself. Footsteps came running, then more. He could hear the guards talking, calling for more help. Stretchers were brought; after a few minutes, they were carried away.

Huddling on his bunk, watching them pass by, Serge tried to see who it was. Sheets covered the bodies, so he couldn't tell whether they were alive or dead. But he caught a glimpse of one man's shaved skull.

"Tino," he said, then called it louder: "Tino!"

The guards carried him past without a word.

"Hey!" Serge yelled. "Is he all right? Is the kid okay?"

No one responded.

Serge thought of Tino's children, and something made him sink to his knees. He hadn't prayed in years, but he remembered the words. He said them by rote: *Our Father . . .*

When he was done, he reached under his bed. Pulling out the box of paper and pens, he placed one sheet in front of him. The blank space was daunting, as if there weren't enough words available to say what he needed to say.

The scent of pine was stronger than that of prison, and he found himself thinking of a small boy and a green lake, of ancient hills and twisting trails. He thought of black ice and hockey sticks, and he thought of Martin.

It was the ultimate defeat to lose in Game 7 in the championship play-offs, to have the puck stolen right off the end of your stick. On the other hand, what did winning actually mean? Serge had possessed the Cup three times in his lifetime, saw it sitting on a table in his own home, slept with the thing beside his bed. And what the hell did that matter now?

What mattered: Inside the box was a picture of Natalie, a picture of Martin, and the blurry newspaper photo of May and Kylie. Serge spread them on the rumpled bed before him. Still on his knees, he thought of Tino and his children. Clearing his throat, as if he were trying to speak instead of write, Serge formed the words:

"Dear Martin . . ."

They appeared on the blue paper before him, even though, Serge would swear, he couldn't remember picking up the pen.

Chapter 21

M ARTIN HAD AGREED TO PLAY an exhibition and lead—with Ray—a two-day hockey clinic in Toronto. Both families were going, the Cartiers and the Gardners, and they had booked adjoining suites in the grand and elegant King Edward Hotel.

"What do you think she meant, 'something's going to happen'?" May asked, looking over at Martin as they packed their bags.

"I think she was dreaming. I think you'll talk to the doctors at Twigg University and have them tell you she's fine."

"I wanted to be done with that," May said, checking to be sure she had the diary in her purse. "I just sent Dr. Whitpen that letter, and I hadn't planned to see him all summer."

She stared out the window at the lake. Martin came up behind her, and her eyes filled with tears.

"What's wrong?" he asked.

"I'm sorry," May said. "I can't stand it. Hearing her in so much pain, not knowing if I'm doing everything I can to help her. She's so tense. She really believes something terrible is about to happen."

"But there isn't," Martin told her. "We're together. It's a beautiful summer day. We're about to go to Toronto with our friends. We made it through a tough winter, and here we are at the lake."

"We'll be back in two days," May said, as if reassuring herself. Martin held her close. He smelled like soap and spice. She closed her eyes and felt her heart beating hard in her chest.

As they loaded up their car, May felt nervous about him driving—what if he lost his vision on the road? So she climbed into the driver's seat, joking that Martin had to hold smelly Thunder on the way to the kennel. Martin laughed, obliging. Just three hours later, after an easy flight, they had arrived at the King Edward Hotel in downtown Toronto. Everyone from the livery-clad doorman to the

manager greeted Martin as if he were a long-lost friend, welcoming May and Kylie with a bouquet of flowers.

"The King Eddy," Martin said, looking up at the great domed lobby ceiling.

" 'Eddie?' " Kylie asked.

"That's what we call it in Canada," Martin said. "Everyone who stays here has a soft spot for the old place."

May hung back, listening as the doorman told Kylie some Canadian history. When Martin asked if she and Kylie wanted to accompany him to the stadium, May shook her head.

"I'm going to take Kylie straight out to see Dr. Whitpen. He'll see us, even if we don't have an appointment."

"Want me to come with you?"

"No, but thank you," May said, remembering the last time he'd gone to Twigg University with them, how he hadn't even wanted to go upstairs. Besides, he had important work to do today.

Every year since becoming a professional hockey player, Martin had led a clinic for any young child who wanted to sign up. Money didn't matter—Martin arranged for the ice on his own, and he donated his time and equipment. He had learned his love of hockey very young, and he believed in helping less fortunate kids: He wanted to give back.

Last year, in the whirl of his unexpected marriage to May, for the first time in seventeen years he had canceled the clinic. Perhaps he could have done it all—gotten married, had a honeymoon, moved a family, staged a clinic—but somehow he had failed to follow through on the clinic plans.

Letters had been forwarded to their home—from disappointed kids, alumni of previous clinics and would-be first-timers who had lost their chance to skate with the great Martin Cartier.

This year, watching Martin check his equipment bag, May felt such tenderness for him. He had come to coach unknown kids, strangers' children who traveled from all over Canada to spend a few hours with him.

He was a good man, wanting to help others. A family approached him, asking for autographs. Martin said yes, and he signed his name and left room for Kylie to sign hers. Giggling, Kylie obliged.

Life had changed dramatically, but all the glamor paled beside the fact that Kylie now had a father who loved and wanted to spend time with her. Holding Martin, kissing him as he prepared to leave,

she closed her eyes and tried to ignore the fear she felt in the pit of her stomach.

The cab ride took about forty minutes, and when Kylie saw the familiar gates of Twigg University, she settled lower in her seat. May paid the driver and took Kylie's hand, leading her into the building. They walked down the dark hall, up the stone stairwell. By the time they reached Dr. Whitpen's office, May's heart was racing.

"My service gave me the message you called," he said, meeting them at the door. A shock of hair fell into his eyes. He wore khakis, a blue oxford shirt, and sneakers without socks. He wasn't smiling, but he seemed excited.

"Kylie, why don't you go play with the dollhouse?" May said, pointing her toward the playroom.

"I want to stay with you."

"Please, honey?" May asked, looking directly into her eyes. "I'll be right there. Just let me talk to the doctor for a minute."

Kylie shrugged, doing as she was told.

"Has something happened?" the doctor asked quietly. "Since you wrote the letter?"

"Yes." May removed the diary from her bag.

Lowering his wire-rimmed glasses from the top of his head, Dr. Whitpen took the notebook to his desk and began to read.

"She says Natalie hides in a cupboard by the fireplace," May said. "Natalie leaves tracks everywhere, evidence that she's been crying."

"Crying about what?" Dr. Whitpen asked, scanning the pages.

"She cries because she can't get her father to understand. Or because Kylie can't get him to understand. It seems we all know what's supposed to happen except for Martin. He's meant to go see his father. I went to visit Serge at the prison."

Dr. Whitpen lowered the notebook. "What did he say? Did he talk about Natalie?"

"He's filled with remorse," May told him. "It's weighing on him, so heavily, and he wants to set things right with Martin, as soon as possible."

"That fits," the doctor said, nodding his head. "That goes along with Kylie's sense of urgency." He read to the end of the pages, taking note of certain passages.

"But I don't talk to Kylie about it," May added.

"I'm not sure that matters."

"No?"

"You've never talked to Kylie about these things she sees. She

just . . ." he paused, gathering up his clipboard, a tape recorder, and the notebook, "sees them."

"I don't suggest them to her?"

"Not from what I've been able to discern," he said. "But let's go talk to her now." And they headed for the playroom to see Kylie.

⸺

Kylie watched her mother and Dr. Whitpen coming, and she turned back to the dolls. They all stared at her, the little beings that had seemed so alive on other visits to this office. They had whispered jokes and stories, they had laughed at her big hands coming through the small windows. But now they were just dolls.

"Hello, Kylie," the doctor said.

"Hi," she said shyly.

"Your mother tells me you've been spending the summer at Lac Vert."

Kylie nodded. "I got a dog."

"Thunder," he said, reading the blue notebook.

"I can read now," Kylie added, remembering the cross-stitch message. The hair on the back of her head stood up, but when she looked into the dollhouse, the little creatures were still just dolls. Something was gone.

"Tell me about the cupboard in the dining room," he said, crouching beside her.

"You know," Kylie whispered. "Natalie was in there."

"Natalie cried," he said. "You saw her tears."

"They stuck to my fingers," Kylie said.

"Why was she crying?"

"Because something's going to happen." Kylie had been feeling nervous all morning, kind of dizzy.

"What's going to happen?" he asked.

Kylie shrugged. She didn't like this new feeling inside. Something was missing. She hadn't told her mother yet, and she didn't want to tell the doctor.

"Who knows what's going to happen?" he asked. "Can you tell me that?"

Kylie just shook her head. "Let's play the card game," she said.

He nodded. He had funny hair that fell over his eyes, and sometimes she couldn't see what he was thinking. If she could see a person's eyes, really look into them, she could usually read their

thoughts. But right now, he was hiding his eyes. He handed her the deck, and she cut it. Then he shuffled, she did, and they started to play.

"Blue," she said.

He held up the first card, a look of surprise on his face. "Red."

"Next card, blue," she said.

"Red."

"Next one red." But it was blue.

Wrong, wrong, wrong. Kylie got them all wrong except one. She glanced back at the dollhouse: just dolls inside. Outside the window, birds were just singing. She didn't feel any magic inside her anymore—no magic at all.

When Martin walked into the Air Canada Centre, all the kids began shrieking with excitement. Although he had played here with the Bruins, this was his first clinic in the new arena; previously he had gathered everyone together at the old Maple Leaf Gardens, sacred ground to any hockey player—veteran or brand-new.

Looking around at the modern glass architecture, he thought about history and tradition and wondered what his father would think of the place. To the shouts of "Martin!" "Sledgehammer!" he waved and smiled.

The crowd was mainly boys from the ages of eight to fifteen, but from the very beginning Martin had always made sure that girls were welcome. Martin had had a daughter, and he had been coached for a long time by his mother.

Alone in the players' locker room, Martin saw no sign of Ray yet, and he was relieved. His hands shook as he laced up his skates. He hadn't been back on the ice since that last Stanley Cup game, and what May suspected was true: His vision had been steadily growing darker all through the early summer.

Back at Lac Vert, it didn't really matter. Everything was beautiful, and his work was slow and lazy. Planting the rose garden, moving rocks, Martin could see fine. He could pretend everything was okay. But here, at an ice arena, where every movement was precise and every shadow meant something, Martin felt afraid.

"So, you made it this year," Ray said, shaking his hand as he walked into the locker room.

"Last summer I was a little busy, getting married."

"Hard to believe."

"That someone would have me, or that I'd settle down?"

"Both, my friend." Ray laughed.

"Enough out of you," Martin said.

"This year I thought you might stay away for another reason," Ray said. "Five seconds to go, the clock ticking . . ."

"Enough," Martin said, closing his eyes. It didn't matter that Ray was only teasing, that they had already talked out the debacle of Game 7. Martin didn't even want to hear it mentioned.

When he and Ray took the ice, the small crowd went wild. Martin had always made one absolute clinic rule: no press, cameras, or paying fans. The stands were partially filled with parents, grandparents, family friends, and a few others. The lights were very bright. Martin blinked hard, darkness gathering in the center of his vision.

As he skated up and down the ice, fog formed and lifted. Now he could see clearly, now he was looking through a scrim. As if some dust or sand had blown into his eyes, he kept blinking, to try and clear it away. The kids cheered as he skated, and Martin knew he could make his moves blindfolded.

"Whoa, watch it," Ray said as Martin nearly tripped over his stick.

"Sorry," Martin said.

The skaters had been assigned to five lines of ten kids each: blue, red, green, yellow, and orange. They assembled on the ice, and Martin addressed them all and thanked them for coming. As he spoke, their silence was complete. In that vast cavern of ice-cold space, Martin heard his own voice echoing in the rafters.

"I know why you're here," he said, and although he spoke quietly, his voice boomed in his ears. "Every one of you, no matter whether you're from Saskatchewan or the East, from Quebec or right here in Toronto. You're here because you dream.

"All the time," Martin continued. "In July, when it's hot out and all your friends are swimming in the lake, you dream of winter when it freezes, when you can put on your skates and go out on the ice. At night, when you're supposed to be asleep, you dream of waking up nice and early, hitting the ice before anyone else, when the surface is clear and black.

"If you live on Nova Scotia or Vancouver Island, you look out at all that salt water, at the Atlantic or Pacific Ocean, and you dream it has frozen, that the rocks are goals. If you live downtown here in Toronto, you dream that you have the keys to the ice—the Air Canada Centre or better yet, Maple Leaf Gardens. That you could play your game better than anyone who ever played here be-

fore—Wayne Gretsky or Mario Lemieux or even Rocket Ray Gardner!"

Everyone cheered and laughed, and Martin swallowed with emotion. The kids were going wild, thrilled to be playing with him and Ray.

Gazing at the sea of children, he saw himself at their ages. He remembered being that young, of the dreams he had had of meeting a real hockey player. His dreams of playing with a professional, of being taught by his own father. Of playing with his idol, Serge Cartier.

"So let's do it," he said, his voice thick and low. "Let's make our dreams come true right now—let's play."

The kids took turns, line by line, shooting the puck and being coached by Martin Cartier and Ray Gardner. Martin talked about discipline and concentration. He corrected grips and postures. He talked about passing and defense, and he answered questions more intelligent and perceptive than any professional interviewer's.

Then the kids cleared the ice, to watch Martin and Ray show them practice drills. Martin's heart was pounding as he skated down the ice, waiting for Ray to fire the first shot. The two of them had been doing this for decades, beginning on the clear December ice of Lac Vert.

Wham! The puck hit his stick like a cannonball, and Martin returned it full force. The two friends skated back and forth, exchanging passes, slamming shots into the net, sending the puck away and gliding after it. The kids laughed and yelled. Martin knew Ray's style so well, he hardly had to look at all. He'd reach out his stick, and the puck would be there. He'd whirl around, and Ray would find him.

Eyes in the back of his head . . .

His father, marveling at Martin's superhuman peripheral vision, his incredible skill at anticipating passes from behind, had come up with the theory that his son, in fact, had eyes in the back of his head.

He skates like a blind man, his father had said once, giving Martin the ultimate compliment. His senses were so acute, so fine-tuned, he could find his man without seeing him, hit the goal without looking directly at it.

"Practice constantly," Martin heard himself saying to the kids right after scoring an easy goal on a perfect pass from Ray. "Find yourself a buddy, and do drills every chance you get."

"Buddy," Ray said, dropping the word over his shoulder as he skated by in search of his son.

"Every chance you get," Martin said, his voice filling the arena again as everyone fell silent to listen. "Others might skate faster, shoot better. But if you focus, if you put in two hours a day, if you really concentrate, hockey will become second nature. The worst that will happen is you'll make a really good friend."

Martin paused, aware of Ray watching him from the sidelines.

"And if you practice every chance you get, if you get a sense for where you are in the world, on the ice, in relation to the puck, your friend, and everyone else—well, one day, you might just get the skill you need to play like a blind man."

"A what?" someone called.

"A blind man with eyes in the back of his head," Martin said, staring through dark fog at the crowd of young faces.

The SkyDome was packed, the baseball game was exciting, and the Toronto Blue Jays beat the Chicago Cubs 4–2. From there they headed to the Hockey Hall of Fame. It stood in downtown Toronto, at the corner of Yonge and Front Streets, occupying a stately Beaux Arts building that had once been a bank.

At first the other tourists surrounded Martin, begging him for autographs. Some had their pictures taken with him. Although he complied, his shoulders were so stiff and his mood so dark that most people soon backed away.

"Are you okay?" May asked.

"It's one thing to bother me when I'm alone," Martin said, "but it's another when you and Kylie are with me."

"I like it," Kylie said.

They visited the goal scoring arena, where visitors were able to challenge the greatest hockey players of all time. Martin seemed strangely quiet as he led May and Kylie through the exhibits, showing them the photographs, archives, equipment of his game: retired jerseys, sticks, skates of revered players, and the exhibit showing how masks are made. When they came to the Honored Members Wall, they stopped to stare at the glass plaques.

"Are you up there?" Kylie asked.

"No," Martin answered.

"Not yet," May said, sliding her arm through his.

"Takes three years after retirement, if I make it here at all," Martin said. "And I don't plan to retire for a long time."

"Is your father here?" Kylie asked abruptly.

"Yes," Martin said, starting to walk away.

"Where?" Kylie asked.

Without even looking, Martin pointed at a plaque right in the middle.

"Serge Cartier," Kylie read.

"There was some talk about kicking him out." Martin was gazing down the long hall. "They should have."

"Did you ever come here with him?"

"Once or twice," Martin said. "We brought Natalie when she was little. Stood right here, in this very spot." He stared down at the floor, as if he could see her small footprints.

"All of you together?" Kylie asked.

"Yes."

"The strange thing about the Stanley Cup," Kylie announced, "is that it was donated in 1893 by the Canadian Governor-General, Lord Stanley, and he never even once saw a Cup game."

"How do you know that?" May asked, laughing.

"I dreamed about it when Martin was playing the finals. Someone told me in my dreams."

"Who?" May asked, but Kylie just shook her head.

"Didn't Lord Stanley like hockey?" May asked, going along with the story.

"No," Martin said, as if he already knew.

"But his sons did," Kylie said. "He created the Stanley Cup because he loved his sons."

"Yes, he did," Martin said, peering at her. "Who did tell you that story, Kylie? Not many people know it."

"Some people do," she said.

"Yes . . ."

"You know who loved it the most. Your father told her right here, when you were all standing in this spot."

"Natalie . . ." Martin was staring at Kylie as if he had just seen a ghost.

�097

For their last excursion before returning to Lac Vert, Ray surprised everyone by renting a minivan.

"We're going to Niagara Falls," he said when the Cartiers walked back into the King Edward. "Get your cameras—the bus leaves in ten minutes."

The actual drive took one and a half hours, but it turned out to

be not so much a day trip as a pilgrimage. There were many stops to be made along the way: at the Butterfly Conservatory because Charlotte loved butterflies; Kurtz Orchards so Genny could investigate alternate sources for fruit for her jams; the Inniskillin Winery so Ray could buy a few bottles; and MarineLand because Kylie wanted to see fish and animals.

As soon as they arrived at Niagara Falls, Martin wanted to take May and Kylie down the elevator at Table Rock House, on the Journey Behind the Falls. If they didn't go now, it would be too late. The elevator would close, and they'd miss their chance. The sun was bright gold, sliding into low purple clouds above the horizon. It spread buttery light over the rocks and rails, the buildings and falls themselves.

Martin herded his family through the gate. Whisked one hundred and fifty feet down through the rock, Kylie laughed as her ears popped. She couldn't get over the fact there was an elevator inside the earth, and neither could May. Martin loved showing them something new, feeling their excitement. He wanted to forget the pain in his eyes, the shock of hearing Kylie repeat almost verbatim that conversation he'd had with his father and Nat so many years ago.

"Ready?" he asked.

May and Kylie nodded, pulling on the yellow slickers handed to them by the attendant. Martin got his on, and together they stepped onto the viewing platform. A wall of water enclosed them as Martin caught his breath.

"We're standing inside Niagara Falls!" May said.

"It's like being inside a wave," Kylie called.

The water roared all around them, the spray soaking their faces and hair. Martin blinked, trying to clear his vision. The crowd was very thin, most people having left for the day.

"What's wrong?" May asked.

"I know it's not Kylie's fault, but her telling that story about Lord Stanley, the one my father told to me and Natalie. Jesus, it was as if Kylie had been there . . ."

May nodded, listening.

"I must have told her the story once," he said.

"Probably."

"But I don't remember it," he said. Then glancing up, "Is she still upset about her visit to the university?"

"She's confused because she got so many cards wrong. Out of fifty, she only picked the right one once."

"What does that mean?"

"It seems she's lost the gift," May said.

"I don't know." He was staring into space. "The way she talked about my father, as if she'd been there . . ."

"She used to dream about helping you find your way back to him," May said.

"That would be a nightmare, not a dream," he said.

"It felt important to her. To me, too."

"I know," he said.

"I'm a river!" Kylie sang out.

"Be careful, honey. Not too close," May warned her, stepping away from Martin.

Their voices were off to his left. Martin stepped back, drying his face. He squinted, but everything was dark down in this subterranean chamber. Backing against the stone, he felt condensation.

"It's slippery!" Kylie cried.

"Take my hand," May said.

"Mommy!" Kylie shrieked, her voice sharp and full of panic.

Martin lunged toward the sound of their voices. His hands found emptiness. The walkway seemed to end as he crashed into the rail. The roar of the water got louder, as if he had stepped right into the falls. It banged and rushed in his ears, so loud he couldn't hear May or Kylie's voices. Spray coated his face, and the more he wiped his eyes, the worse his vision became.

He bumped into the corner, the wall, calling their names. Right in the middle of his vision was a black hole. No matter where he looked he saw the black hole, the outer edges veiled and murky, and it was as if May and Kylie had been sucked in. He felt a sob well up in his chest, filling him until he wanted to explode, wild with the panic of being trapped and unable to save the only two people he loved.

He was alone in the world, everything crashing in around him. Then he felt May take his hand.

"It's okay, we're right here," she said. "We're fine." He felt her breath on his skin, her cheek against his, felt her arm slip around his waist. He tried to hold the panic in, but he knew she could feel with her own body the terror going through him.

"I thought I'd lost you," he whispered.

"That will never happen," she said.

Chapter 22

T HE TRIP HOME TO LAC VERT seemed endless. Martin refused to talk about what had happened at the Falls and they traveled in virtual silence.

When they reached home, their post box was overflowing with mail. They brought Thunder home from the kennel, but he wanted to return immediately—he had fallen in love with a French poodle in the next cage, and he bayed his heart out their first night home. By dawn, he had scratched a hole in the screen door and escaped.

A neighbor driving to work found him running along the road and brought him back. Kylie was overjoyed, and May found a length of clothesline to tie him to the porch. She and Martin sat on the steps, watching the dog strain his collar, howling in lovesick agony as he attempted to break the rope.

"He's wild for his woman," Martin said, squeezing May's shoulder. "I know how he feels."

"Don't flirt with me till you tell me what happened."

"Right now? Come on, Kylie's playing in the gazebo, we're all alone. Come upstairs with me, yes? Want to do that?"

"TALK TO ME! I know you couldn't see me at the Falls."

"My eyes were bothering me, *c'est vrai*. They're better now. It's traveling, May. And the spray. I get stressed, and I get a headache, and the next thing I know I can't see so well. Maybe I need glasses, eh? I'm getting old! I'm the old man on the ice, just ask the guys. Don't worry—it's nothing serious."

"You were afraid, I know you were."

"Don't remind me," he said, squeezing her harder. "Water in my eyes, that's all."

"You're full of it, Martin."

"Come on. Let's go upstairs. Kylie won't notice—she's all wrapped up in her doll or whatever she's doing out there."

"Please tell me you'll go to a doctor."

"I need you, that's all," he said, kissing her neck, feeling her breast. "The only cure is taking you to bed. Come on—"

The day was hazy and bright. The beautiful summer light shimmered across the lake, turning the water dark green. Flies buzzed over the shallows, and a bass jumped out to snap them. The concentric rings settled back into the lake, one inside the other, rings and rings of calm. Kylie was busy talking to her doll.

"Come upstairs with me, eh?" Martin whispered into May's ear.

She took a deep breath and refused to budge. Once he figured out he couldn't distract her with superior seduction techniques, he stormed away.

But he still wouldn't talk.

Thunder escaped again the next day. They found his rope chewed through, saw his tracks leading down the driveway. May took the car for a drive, searching the roads for the old basset hound. As she scanned the meadows and hills, tracing the route back to the kennel, she noticed how tense she felt and realized it was because she didn't want Martin to drive: She had been worried he would get to the car before her.

"Any luck?" Martin asked when she returned.

"No. He hasn't been to the kennel. I checked."

"Where is he?" Kylie asked.

"Just on an adventure," May said, trying to reassure her.

When the mail arrived, it contained a postcard addressed to Thunder. Kylie had written it from the King Edward Hotel and signed it "Eddy." When May tried to show it to Martin, he barely even smiled.

The mail also contained a blue envelope addressed to Martin. May saw him hold it very close to his eyes, examine the handwriting, then throw it right into the garbage without opening it. She was about to retrieve it when the telephone rang.

Their next-door neighbor, Vincent Dufour, had seen a police car picking up a dog that looked like Thunder; maybe they had taken him to the dog pound.

"You'd think in a town the size of Lac Vert they'd know where all the dogs live," Martin exploded.

"Thunder's new around here," she said. "I'm sure they'd have

brought him home if they knew he was ours. We'll have to get him a license—"

"So now he's at the pound?"

"That's what Vincent thinks."

"Give me the phone," Martin said, grabbing it out of May's hands.

It was painful to watch him snatch the phone book and try to find the right number. He slashed at the pages, ripping one. Bending close to see the names, he got so frustrated he swore at the top of his lungs.

"Would you let me—" May started to say, but Martin had already dialed information. Once he had the number, he had to dial twice before getting through correctly. May listened to him take a deep breath, then explain to the person on the line that he had lost his dog, a basset hound and that he had reason to believe the dog had been taken to the pound.

"My name? Martin Cartier," she heard him say. Watching his eyes narrow, she saw the anger building.

"He's there," Martin said, slamming down the receiver. "And the woman won't let me pick him up."

"What are you talking about?" May asked.

"She says Thunder bit her when she put him in the cage, and she's having him put down tomorrow."

"No!"

"He doesn't have a tag on, she said, so there's no proof that he's had his rabies shots."

"He bit her? He doesn't even have teeth!" May said, watching Kylie out the window. "He doesn't have rabies."

"I know. She didn't say any of that until I told her my name."

"Martin Cartier? I thought that cut through red tape anywhere in Canada."

"Not with her. She remembers that business with Nat. She's thought badly of me from that day on. Thinks I'm just a self-centered hockey player who couldn't make time for his own daughter."

"That was never true," May said.

"You weren't there," Martin told her. "She's right about me. She's a bitch, and she has no right to keep Thunder, but she's got my number."

"I see how you feel about Kylie, and I know how you feel about Natalie."

Just then the screen door squeaked open and they heard

Kylie's footsteps on the kitchen floor. Her face fell as she looked up at the adults. But Martin spoke first.

"That old Thunder must be having himself quite a time," he said, gazing out the window. "Probably searching far and wide for that pretty little poodle."

"Do you think he's safe?" Kylie asked.

"That old guy?" Martin asked, snorting with laughter. "Sure he's safe. He's a basset hound through and through. It's the wild animals I'm worried about with him around. He's probably up the mountain, rooting a badger out of his lair. Or chasing a fox up a tree, trying to gets its tail as a souvenir for Fifi."

"Who's Fifi?" Kylie asked, giggling.

"His girlfriend," Martin said. "The French poodle."

Kylie laughed, standing beside Martin and trying to catch a glimpse of Thunder charging along a mountain trail across the lake.

After dark, once May had taken Kylie upstairs to read her a bedtime story, Martin walked outside. He had the keys in his pocket, and he headed out back to where they parked the car. Although he knew every inch of the yard by heart, he tripped on a rut in the earth. He walked a straight line, knowing there was nothing tall or deep in his way, but when he got to the car, he decided not to drive to the pound.

He couldn't drive tonight.

His eyes had been better yesterday, and he could have driven then. But Thunder had been safe at home yesterday, tethered to the back porch, howling for Fifi for six hours straight. That was the problem with Martin's eyes. They were unreliable. One day he could see fine, the next day he couldn't. The trouble was, he couldn't predict or control when the crises would happen.

The pound was located behind the municipal garage—a collection of old trucks and plows and one bunkerlike concrete building—about six miles north on the lake road. Martin had traveled this route thousands of times throughout his life, often on his way to or from Ray's house. The night was warm, the breeze light. He started off walking, but soon he started to run.

His legs felt strong. Running felt great. His arms began to move with their regular rhythm, and he thought of the team workouts starting in the fall. Back to Boston, straight into the regimen

that had kept him fit and strong all his years as a professional athlete.

"Merde," he said, stumbling on a hole.

A frost heave or something—he hadn't seen it coming. The road crews around the area were lazy, sometimes letting three or four summers go by without repairing the damage left by winter's brutal storms. Martin remembered one winter when he was twelve, when a blizzard had snowed them in for three weeks straight. He and his mother had been stranded without fresh food or heat; they'd had to live by the fireplace, eating canned beans and roasting potatoes while his father lived down in the States.

"Don't think about it," Martin said out loud, running easily along the road. Mind control: one of an athlete's most important virtues. He was good at not thinking about certain things: the blue envelope that had arrived in the mail, the fact that Thunder was scheduled for execution, the fact that he could barely see where he was going.

His feet followed the pavement, and every so often he caught a flash that might have been starlight swinging through the trees. The stars were so beautiful, he felt something give inside. What if he couldn't see them anymore? What if he could never again see a dark night blazing with stars? Mind control, he told himself. Don't think about it.

The pound was just around the bend. He heard the dogs, their barking filling the summer night. Thunder's voice sounded above the others', wild and passionate and full of yearning. Tearing across the sand parking lot, Martin slowed down when he approached the solid brick building. He tried each of the two steel doors and found them locked.

Until he arrived, he hadn't known what he planned to do. Picking up a rock, he walked straight over to the front door. Although constructed of steel, it had a window lined with chicken wire inside. Throwing his arm back, he brought the rock forward with massive force and broke the glass. It took three more blows to break the cage wire, and then he reached inside and unlocked the door.

Stepping inside, Martin's blood pounded in his ears. He had never broken into anyplace before. He had just committed a criminal act, one they could arrest him for. Sweating, breathing hard, he stood inside the office and tried to get his bearings.

Right there, he thought, facing the spot. *That's where Natalie had stood. There's the old woman's desk, there's the place I stood telling Natalie she couldn't have a dog. Archie,* he thought. Down the

hall, the dogs barked madly, smelling his human scent. Thunder's baying changed to a begging, puppylike yelp.

"I'm coming," he said out loud.

He banged into the desk and a chair, and he came to another locked door. This one wasn't steel, but he wasn't going to waste time looking for a key that might not be there, so he applied his shoulder to the wood and heard it crack. Another shove, and he knocked the door right off its hinges.

You're just like your father. A criminal, a man who takes what he wants. You skate like your father, you play hockey like your father, you take what you want like your father.

"I'm not like him," Martin told the dogs. He stood in a long room lined with cages. In spite of all the noise, he was surprised to find only three cages occupied. Thunder, wagging his tail. A mangy-looking shepherd. A retriever mix, covered with mud. Without pausing, Martin opened all three cages.

The two strange dogs ran straight past him, bound for freedom. Thunder bayed with gratitude, jumping up as high as his stumpy legs would allow. Martin bent from the waist, to let him lick his face. He thought of how little it took to make an old dog happy, how easy it was to please a little girl. Kylie would be overjoyed to see him.

Natalie would be proud of him. If she were here, she'd tell him he'd done the right thing, running half-blind up the lake to rescue Kylie's dog. Martin should have let her have Archie. He had known that for years, but right now, in the very building where he had let her down, he felt it in his skin, his teeth, his bones.

Thunder trotted over to the door, leading Martin outside. Reaching into his pocket, Martin withdrew the length of rope he'd remembered to bring. He didn't want Thunder running off in search of Fifi, getting picked up by the cops again. Thunder pointed his nose into the air, breathing in the fresh night.

Martin did the same. He felt free, holding the other end of a long leash. Reaching into his pocket, he pulled out his wallet and found a loose check. He wrote it in the amount of five hundred dollars and left it on the woman's desk. The check had his name on it, and he knew he'd probably get a visit from the police tomorrow, at least a call, but he didn't care.

Setting the dogs free, bringing Thunder home to Kylie, was worth it. But when he stepped back outside again, something happened. The night had gotten darker. Or fog had blown in. Martin couldn't see. Thunder was pulling on his rope, but Martin didn't

know which way to walk. He was alone in blackness, and he couldn't see which path to take.

—

Martin was out there, but at least he hadn't taken the car. May sat on the sofa, wondering where he had gone. She tried to do some paperwork: Tobin had sent her last month's invoices, and May tried to go through them with her calculator and pen. But the more she tried to concentrate, the more her mind wandered.

Walking over to the window, to peer into the blackness for the hundredth time, she glimpsed the blue envelope. It lay in the trash among fliers and old newspapers, and May knew she should forget about it. But she couldn't. Maybe if her husband were home where he was supposed to be, if she weren't worried to death about him, she wouldn't be so distracted by a dumb blue envelope.

Not only did she pull it out of the trash, she opened it. She unfolded the letter—written on plain blue stationery—spread it out on the window seat beside her, and read it.

Dear Martin,
You deserved to win, son. I'm not saying that winning's the only thing, but we're both competitors and we both know we're in it for victory. You made it to the finals again. That in itself is great. There's always next year, if you have the team to back you up. The Bruins had better appreciate what they have, or I know plenty of other teams who'll still be fighting to have you.

It's been a long time, Martin. Yes, for you waiting to win the Stanley Cup, but other things too. Since we talked, saw each other. I read about you. Watch you on TV. I know about your marriage. Congratulations on that, too. She is a good person. She held up when the press wanted to turn on her, so I know she's got guts. And she has a little girl. You married a woman with a little girl. I smiled when I saw that. Does she make you think of Natalie? I see her pictures in the paper, and I think maybe she has the same sparkle in her eyes.

I miss Nat. I know you think I took her from you. Maybe you think that means I didn't love her. Believe me that's not true. Boy, I loved that one. Almost as much as I loved you.

I've been a bad father. A bad grandfather. People make mistakes, Martin. I wasn't around enough for you and your mother. I didn't take care of you the way I should have. Her, either. Neither of you deserved what I gave you. Will you let me tell you this in person?

What I'm telling you is, I want to see you. May has probably told you that by now. When she came to visit me, I told her to give you a message. I know that she would keep her word, so I know she told you. You hate me for what I did. But will you listen to what I have to say?

A young man died here tonight. He was very young, about the age you were when you first started playing for Vancouver. Someone stabbed him in a stupid fight. At first, all I knew was that he had been hurt. But just now the guard tells me he's dead. As young as he was, he was a father. In my own way, I cared about him. I wanted him to be a better father to his kids than I've been to you.

Whatever you decide, I'll live with that. But I hope you decide to come.

Love,
Dad

When May finished reading the letter, she realized her hands were balled into fists. Her cheeks were hot and wet. She read the words over and over. She thought of Martin reading this letter, wondering whether he would ever consider visiting the prison. She wondered whether he could even read the words.

"Mommy!"

At the sound of Kylie's voice, she tucked the letter back into its envelope and slid it into the desk drawer. Then she climbed the stairs.

"What is it, honey?"

"Is Thunder back yet?"

"Not yet."

"Where is he?"

"Roaming, I guess," May said. "Can't you sleep?"

"Not really. I'm trying, but—" she stopped as the phone rang.

May didn't say a word, didn't tell Kylie she would be right back or anything. She tore down the hallway, knowing she would hear his voice even before she picked up the phone.

"May, it's me. I'm at the dog pound. I have Thunder."

"I didn't know where you were," she said. "I was worried."

"I need you," he said.

Her heart was in her throat as she listened.

"I can't see," he told her. "I can't see where I am."

"I'll come to get you," May said. "I'll be right there."

Then, telling Kylie to put on sneakers and a sweater, May hurried out into the warm, starry night to pick up her husband and their dog.

The short drive seemed to take forever. Kylie was wide awake, totally focused on the fact Martin had rescued Thunder. When they pulled up at the pound, she opened the car door and Thunder scampered in. May's hands were shaking as she walked over to Martin, took him in her arms.

"We're here," she said.

"I can't see anything," he said, his voice thin and wild with panic.

Chapter 23

L AC VERT AND ITS SURROUNDING towns did not have any oph-
thalmology specialists, but May found an optometrist located in
downtown LaSalle. The drive along winding country roads took
about thirty minutes, with pine boughs and oak branches interlac-
ing overhead. Genny had come to pick up Kylie—no questions
asked—and Thunder was securely locked in the kitchen. The police had stopped by to ask about the break-in, to apologetically
issue a warning against it ever happening again.

"Well, my eyes are better today," Martin said.

"They are?"

"Let's not go."

"We're already on the way."

"It's too gorgeous a day to waste in town. Let's row out to the
island."

"Please, Martin."

"Ten kilometers to LaSalle," Martin said, reading the mileage
sign.

May felt relieved, although she realized he probably knew
every sign on this road by heart. She wanted to believe that a mi-
graine headache or a minor infection had temporarily affected his
sight, that it had cleared up on its own.

"He's going to say I need glasses," Martin said.

"That wouldn't be so bad."

"How would I play hockey with glasses?"

"You could wear contacts," she said.

"I've been lucky," he said, "never to need them. I always feel
sorry for the guys who have to wash them, get them in right . . .
when there's a problem on the ice, it's hard to fix a contact with
gloves, pads, the face mask on. You know the difference between a
good player and a great player?"

"What?"

"Great players have superior vision. It's just a fact."

"You're a great player."

"Who might need contacts."

"Maybe you won't need them," May said.

"I hope not."

LaSalle was a small town built on the top of a hill. It over-looked Lac Vert and the Ste. Anne River, a hundred small hills and valleys rising into the Laurentiens. Two Catholic churches anchored Main Street, one brick and one white clapboard. Development had left the town alone, with Victorian houses, an old movie theater, and a long row of two-story office buildings.

Maurice Pilote, Optometrist, occupied a second-floor office, just above Pierre Pilote, Accountant. When May and Martin walked into the room, they found the optometrist, his receptionist, and an elderly customer deep in conversation. But the talking stopped as soon as they recognized Martin.

"*Mon Dieu!*" the optometrist said, striking his breast. "Martin Cartier! It is an honor to have you here!"

"We don't have an appointment," May began.

"It is for you?"

"For me," Martin said.

"Come right in," Pilote said, standing aside.

Together May and Martin walked into a small back room. Making light of the situation, Martin explained what was going on, that his sight had been fading in and out, that last night—in the dark, without any lights at all, with haze all around—he had been temporarily unable to see. The optometrist listened, making notations on a clipboard. Then, leading Martin to a darkened cubicle, he positioned him facing the eye charts.

"I've always had six/six," Martin said. Then, to May, "In Canada, that's the same as twenty/twenty."

"Perfect eyesight," Pilote said. "That would explain your perfect shot. Well, don't worry. I can make you an excellent pair of glasses. My God, to have Martin Cartier in my chair! Are you ready? First line please."

Martin read the large letters across the first line of the eye chart right away: "E N Y I Z X." Then the next: "H L B T D A," and the third: "Q F R M C."

May felt so relieved, she wanted to laugh out loud. Maybe this was nothing at all. Maybe they'd be out of here, rowing to the island, before the morning was up.

"Very good. Now I am going to cover your right eye. First line, please."

May waited for Martin to start. She read the letters silently to herself: E N Y I Z X. The room was silent except for the buzzing of a wall clock. The optometrist cleared his throat nervously. In case Martin hadn't heard, he said more loudly, "First line, please."

"Try my other eye," Martin said, without reading one letter.

"It would be best for you to tell me what you see right now with your left eye, not worrying at all about how many letters—"

"My other eye," Martin said sharply.

"Very well." Maurice Pilote covered Martin's left eye instead.

"E N Y I Z X," Martin read. "H L B T D A. Q F R M C."

"Excellent," the optometrist said. "Now, again, let's try the other eye."

Martin stared at the chart, his right eye covered, trying to read with only his left. May watched him concentrating, as if he was setting up a shot against Nils Jorgensen. He squinted, leaned forward, frowned.

"Nothing," he said.

"Just the top line."

"I said nothing."

Pilote paused. He checked the chart himself, made sure Martin's eye was covered properly. He took away the card covering the eye, told Martin to read the chart with both eyes. Then with just the right. When he asked him to read again using just the left eye and got the same response as before, "Nothing," Maurice Pilote's face looked pale and grave.

"Have you had an eye injury?" he asked.

Martin tried to laugh. "I'm a hockey player."

"A particularly bad injury, I mean."

"One," Martin said. "Three years ago."

"When is the last time you had an eye exam?"

"Last year. During the team physical."

"Was it like this, or more intensive?"

"It was pretty basic."

"I would like you to see a specialist," he said.

"But I can read fine with both eyes," Martin told him.

"Your right eye is normal, or very close to it," Pilote said. "It is working for both your eyes."

"But I see fine with both," Martin said. "You heard me read the chart."

Pilote shook his head. "You see nothing with your left eye. It is virtually blind."

Blind . . . someone had said the word. May felt the room get very cold, and when she looked at Martin she saw that he was frozen as still as stone.

—

The first step was getting a referral, finding the best possible doctor. Maurice Pilote recommended an ophthalmologist in Montreal, but when May called, he was on vacation. Martin didn't want to talk about it, didn't even want to think about it. Feeling lost, she turned to the yellow pages, but how would she know who was good?

"I can do exercises," he said. "Strengthen my eye that way."

"Martin, can we call your team doctor and ask for a referral?"

"It's like any other part of the body, isn't it? Injure something and get it fixed. I work with a trainer for my ankles and knee—what the hell, I'll work with someone for my eye."

May stared at the yellow pages filled with listing after listing, and her own vision swam. She wanted to approach the problem from one angle, and Martin was taking it from another. All she could think of was getting him to a doctor as soon as possible, and he wanted to start doing exercises.

"I could ask Genny," May suggested. "Either she'll know someone good, or she'll know whom to ask."

"No, May," Martin said sharply. "I don't want anyone to know there's a problem. I don't want it getting around."

"Martin, Genny wouldn't tell anyone! She's our friend. We have to tell her and Ray—"

"No!" Martin said, so loudly it shocked her.

Staring at him, she watched him shake his head, try to pull himself together. He walked over to the sofa and sat down beside her. Aware that he'd hurt her by his tone of voice, he held her gently and whispered against her ear. "I'm sorry. I'm sorry, May. I didn't mean to yell. But I don't want anyone to know yet. Not even Ray and Gen."

"They'd never tell," May repeated. "We can trust them."

"I know we can. But let's keep it secret for a while. Just till I get a chance to see the specialist, do some exercises, whatever they tell me to do. Build up strength in my left eye."

She watched him cover his right eye, look from floor to ceiling

with his left. He squinted, blinked, tried all over again, as if he could make his left eye work by sheer force of work and will.

"I can do it," he insisted. "I know I can. I'll be fine by the start of the season."

May looked down.

"I will, you know," he said, embracing her and smoothing her hair as if she was the one hurt, in need of comforting. Or as if he thought she wouldn't love him anymore if he couldn't play hockey.

"The start of the season," she said, thinking of practice and training in August and September, the first game on October first.

"So don't tell anyone till then, okay?" he asked.

"Someone will have to watch Kylie while I go with you to the doctor."

"I don't want Genny and Ray to know," Martin repeated.

Staring at the phone book, May wondered how in the world to make an informed decision on choosing the right doctor from a list in the yellow pages, when the answer came to her.

"I think I might know someone." She reached for the phone.

"Who?"

"An eye doctor in Boston. She's very well known, almost famous. She must be quite old by now, though—I wonder if she's still practicing. Dr. Theodora Collins."

"How do you know her?"

"She was one of my mother's brides," May said.

—

Dr. Theodora Collins had an office in her home at the very top of Beacon Hill, overlooking the Public Garden and all of Back Bay Boston. The family had flown home right away, and Kylie was staying with Tobin and Aunt Enid. The day was hot, and the sun made all the colonial brick buildings look dry and red. Here on top of the hill a breeze blew, lifting flags just slightly.

Sitting in her waiting room, Martin was drenched with sweat. The air-conditioning was on, but he felt drops running down his back between his shoulder blades. Shaving that morning, he had nicked himself in four places. Coming into Boston in the middle of summer felt wrong. He didn't want to waste one day away from Lac Vert. Soon hockey season would start, and another year would pass until their return.

"She's late," Martin said.

"Our appointment is for two. It's five after."

Martin picked up a copy of *Boston Magazine*. It was hard to read, but as soon as he opened the cover, he saw a picture of himself. He was dressed in his Boston Bruins uniform, his arm around Ray, grinning at the camera. He had a vision of the Stanley Cup, how he'd lost it for his team. And he hoped he'd get one more chance to play another season, to finally win the Cup next year.

"There you are," May said, looking over his shoulder.

Martin nodded. He stared at the picture, trying to make it come into focus. The pit in his stomach was growing deeper. What was this doctor, this stranger he'd never met, about to tell him? He played games in his mind. If she comes out before two-fifteen, everything will be fine. If she's smiling, it means I'm going to be fine.

Glancing around the waiting room, he tried to make sense of it all. He saw leather chairs, a bright hooked rug, a low table covered with magazines. A blue vase filled with yellow flowers. Large black-and-white photos of lighthouses hung on every wall. The place seemed homey, less professional than the optometrist's office in LaSalle. What could she tell him that he couldn't? Martin had come because May suggested Dr. Collins, but was he on some endless merry-go-round, being shuttled from one specialist to the next?

The door opened, and an elderly woman stepped into the waiting room. Any hope that she might be the doctor's secretary was quickly dashed when Martin noticed her white coat and the way she regally crossed the room—smiling, he noticed as his stomach flipped.

"May, is it really you?" the woman asked.

"Dr. Collins?"

"Yes. Oh, my dear. You're all grown up. Oh, it's been such a long time . . ." The doctor embraced May. They held on to each other for a long time, giving Martin the chance to figure out how long it would take to be introduced, let her give him a cursory exam, and politely say good-bye.

"How is your husband?" May asked as they broke apart. "I remember your wedding so well. It was in the Old North Church, and you hung lights in the bell tower just like Paul Revere . . ."

"William died," the doctor said, her eyes wide and steady. "Just last year. We had thirty wonderful years together. How I miss him . . ."

"I'm sorry," May said. "I remember how he looked at you. I was only seven, but I've never forgotten." She had told Martin that

although her family had overseen so many New England weddings, from Greenwich, Connecticut to Bar Harbor, Maine, some stood out more than others.

The doctor turned her gaze on Martin and took his hand. He felt a powerful current flowing from her fingers into his, but even more, he felt the warmth of her gaze. He blinked, wanting to see her better.

"You're Martin," she said.

"Yes, Martin Cartier."

"I'm so happy to meet you. William was a great hockey fan. We watched you play many times. And now, to know that you're married to May."

"Nice to meet you, Dr. Collins," he said.

"Call me Teddy," she said. "May, you too. Your mother called me that. Your grandmother always insisted on Theodora, but that's just the kind of woman she was. Correct and formal on all occasions. Let's not stand on ceremony around here. Okay?"

"Okay," May said.

Martin stared at her. She had to be sixty-five years old. Her hair was pure white, swept up and twisted behind her head. She wore pearls at her throat and ears. Her eyes were bright blue, wise and youthful at the same time. Something about her reminded him of his mother. But wouldn't he want someone young, aggressive, at the top of what had to be a changing field for eye doctors?

"Come on inside," she said, holding the door so they could walk in.

Through the white door was another world entirely. Instruments and machines were everywhere. A massive microscope sat on one desk, a computer terminal on another. Martin felt as if he had walked into the inner sanctum of a top scientist, not a gentle old lady who wanted them to call her "Teddy."

"This is my research office," she explained. "I write most of my papers here at home, and I like to have the equipment I need right here."

"You do research?" May asked.

"Yes. I teach at Harvard, and I need to stay ahead of my students. My practice is affiliated with Boston Eye Hospital, and I see most of my patients there. But I thought, considering your high profile, Martin, that it would be more private for us to meet here first."

"I'm sure it's nothing," Martin told her.

Teddy didn't say anything, but she gestured for him to take a

seat. May and Martin sat side by side, Teddy across from them. She took a detailed medical history, from childhood diseases to torn ligaments. She paid special attention to allergies and medications, his surgeries to have his tonsils removed and ankles repaired.

"Ever had any head injuries?" she asked.

"About ten thousand," he said.

"Can you remember them all?"

"Every one."

"Name them." She smiled, starting a new page.

Concussions, a fractured skull, broken cheekbones, a shattered eye socket, a detached retina, a dislocated jaw, lacerations of the scalp, forehead, chin, and cheeks. He showed her his scars, and she seemed to admire them. He had a story to go with each one, the memory of various opponents in different cities. But especially, his eyes told the tale of Nils Jorgensen.

"Tell me what brings you to me," she said.

"Well, my eyesight's been a little blurry," he said.

"Blurry?"

"Yes. Not always. Sometimes it's fine. But sometimes it's like looking through . . ." He searched for the right word, as if by calling it the wrong thing he might make his problem worse. "Fog. Or a curtain."

"Both eyes?"

"It's worse in the left," he said, without looking at May.

"When did it start?"

"A while ago," Martin said, still avoiding May.

"How long? A month, two months?"

"A year," Martin admitted. "It started then."

He had first noticed a problem just before the play-offs last year, during a regular season game against the Rangers, a few weeks before he'd met May. It had seemed almost like nothing, especially compared with what had happened three years before, when Nils Jorgensen had clocked him and the world had gone dark.

Martin had had a shattered eye socket and a detached retina. He had missed half a season, but surgery had repaired the damage, and by the next year he was as good as new. At first he had been religious about his eye exams, but once he had his 6/6 vision back, he had started slacking off.

And, until a year ago, his eyes had seemed perfect. But one day his vision had blurred. It happened suddenly, for no apparent reason, and at first he'd thought he had something in his eye. Dis-

tracted from the game, he had caught a stick in the side of his head, Lefebre had scored for New York, and Martin had learned a lesson: Keep playing hard whether you can see straight or not.

That wasn't much of a challenge. Martin had discovered long ago that on the ice he could adapt himself to many things. He had skated through his father's abandonment, his divorce, his mother's and Natalie's deaths. Every day he hit the ice with pain in his ankles and knees—pain his doctors told him would cripple some others. So blurry vision in one eye was no big deal; it had slowed him down just long enough for him to learn to compensate for it.

But now, hearing himself say this had been going on for a year, Martin felt a kick in his stomach. Why had he ignored an obvious problem for so long? What if it had been fixable then, but not now? Teddy made notes without expressing concern or judgment. Martin didn't want to look at May, to see the dismay reflected in her eyes, but she reached over to touch his knee, and when he looked into her face he saw her smiling with encouragement.

Teddy had him face the eye chart, and he repeated the process he'd gone through with Maurice Pilote. Both eyes okay, right eye okay, left eye nothing.

"All right," Teddy said. "Come sit with me over here, and I'll examine your eyes."

"I can do exercises," Martin said, crossing the room. "Whatever you tell me. I know I should have started them earlier, said something at my last physical. I guess I thought, if the doc notices, I have a problem. If he doesn't, I must be okay. I've always had six/six vision."

"That's right, you're Canadian." Teddy was smiling as she gestured for him to take a seat across the exam table from her.

They faced each other with the Haag-Streit slit-lamp biomicroscope between them. Teddy directed him to lean forward, placing his face into a masklike contraption. She explained that she was going to project a beam of light onto and into the eye, thereby getting an optical cross-section under high magnification.

"Can you see what's wrong?" he asked after she'd been staring for a while.

She chuckled. "Patience."

"Not my strongest suit."

"No, I wouldn't think it would be. I've seen you play, remember."

"Right."

The air-conditioning hummed. Martin tried to sit still, but he

felt anxiety rippling through his body. He felt like jumping up, grabbing May, running out onto the street. He had never been any good at staying in one confined spot—an airplane seat, an easy chair, on the bench—for very long. His muscles ached, and his brain screamed for him to run.

Teddy told him to breathe deeply, and he did. The panic faded out.

"You've had some scarring," she said.

"I have?"

"Yes. I can see where your retina became detached in your left eye. That's where you suffered the blunt trauma?"

"Madame, I suffer blunt trauma for a living," Martin said.

"I suppose you do," Teddy said.

Now she explained that she was going to put drops into his eyes, to dilate his pupils. The drops stung, but he didn't even flinch. Using the Goldmann aplanation tonometer, she measured the pressure in each eye for glaucoma. Finally, using a high-powered camera mounted on the slit-lamp, she took a series of photographs.

Sitting up straight, she smiled at him, indicating that the exam was over. She made a few notes, and Martin glanced over his shoulder at May. She had been sitting quietly across the room, and Martin tried to bring her into focus. The drops and strange light in his eyes had temporarily clouded his sight even more, and all he could see was a dark shape sitting near the window.

"What did you find, Teddy?" he heard May ask.

"Well, there's evidence of the retinal detachment Martin told me about."

"That's the problem, then?" Martin asked, somehow relieved. "That happened almost four years ago—Nils Jorgensen getting me back for some damage I laid on him. I was playing for Vancouver at the time, and I had laser surgery up there. The doc told me he did 'spot welds,' and I'd be fine. I was—no problems at all. I got Jorgesen back, he got me again."

"A sort of endless cycle," Teddy said.

"Hockey." Martin shrugged.

Teddy nodded. With her hands folded in front of her, she reminded Martin of how his mother would stand there in the kitchen at Lac Vert, listening to one of his more far-fetched excuses about why he'd been playing hockey with Ray instead of doing his chores or homework.

"That's the problem?" May asked.

"I'm not sure yet," Teddy said. "I'd like to do more testing, but I don't have the equipment here. Can you come to my office at the hospital?"

"Sure," Martin said. "And just hope the GM doesn't hear about it."

"The GM?"

"Translate, Martin," May said.

"Oh, sorry. General manager of the Bruins. My contract's up this year, and all I need is for them to find out I'm having eye problems. They're already giving me a hard time about my ankles. I don't want to hand them more ammunition for the bargaining table."

"They won't hear it from me or my staff," Teddy said. "But I can't speak for everyone at the hospital. I'll tell you what. Come after hours, tomorrow night. Around nine? I'll see you then."

"Thank you so much," May said gratefully.

"Merci bien," Martin said.

He wished the drops would dissolve from his eyes. He remembered the photographs around the room, and once again he thought of his mother. She had taken great pictures. "Who took the photos on your walls?" he asked the doctor.

"My husband did," she said.

"He was a photographer?"

"That was his hobby. We loved to travel, especially to islands. We both adored islands. And everywhere we went, we'd find the lighthouse, and William would take its picture."

"Why lighthouses?" Martin asked.

"Because they're beautiful in their own right, and because William wanted to honor the work I do with the blind."

Blind: The word filled Martin with fear. But Teddy just kept talking, telling about the brick lighthouse on the bluff at Gay Head, the striped lighthouse at Cape Hatteras, the stone lighthouse on Block Island, the dark column on Gull Island.

"Photography was his passion," Teddy said.

"My mother took pictures," Martin said.

"Perhaps you inherited her talent," Teddy said.

Martin shook his head. "No, I got my father's. Playing hockey. Rough stuff."

"You might be surprised what you'd find out if you ever picked up a camera," Teddy said.

Martin's throat closed. His vision, blurred with eyedrops and whatever else was going on, would make it impossible for him to

take any pictures. He started to speak, but instead he just shook his head.

"So," Teddy said. "Tomorrow at my other office."

"Thank you for doing it that way," May said.

"It's the least I can do," Teddy said. "Martin is like Boston royalty. William wouldn't have it any other way."

"My mother would thank you, too," May said, hugging Martin. "I wish she could have met Martin."

"I have the feeling she knows all about him," Teddy said.

Chapter 24

THE SUMMER BREEZE BLEW THROUGH the prison yard and gave the prisoners a little relief from the heat. When Serge looked out through the bars of the yard, he saw a young boy standing there with a baseball glove. It wasn't visiting day, but even if it was, the person this kid had come to see was no longer there. Serge recognized him as Ricky, Tino's son.

"What's he doing?" Serge asked Jim, the guard.

"Sad case," Jim said. "Comes here every chance he gets."

"His father's dead."

"Tell him that."

"He doesn't believe it?"

Jim shook his head. "They had a funeral and everything, but the kid refuses to accept the truth."

"What does he do?" Serge asked, staring through the bars. The boy was about eight, small and wiry, dressed in a blue T-shirt and Yankees hat. He held his baseball glove on one hand, and he was thumping the ball into it, like a pitcher waiting for a batter to take his stance.

"Stands there. Throws his ball against the wall till I tell him to go home."

"What about his mother?"

"She's got trouble all her own."

"What does he want?"

"Who knows?" Jim asked, watching the boy. "Maybe he's waiting for his turn to come inside. Like father, like son."

"That's a lousy thing to say."

"I didn't write the statistics," Jim said. A skirmish across the yard attracted his attention, and he went to see about it.

Serge stared at the boy. What had he bothered asking Jim for? Serge knew what he was doing: waiting for his father to come play

ball with him. Reason didn't play any part in it. Even after Agnes had banished him and Serge had taken off for the big time, he had always plotted to return for a big father-son reunion.

But something always got in the way: the next game, the next party, the next horse race, the next woman. His kid hadn't deserved his abandonment. Martin had never stopped waiting and hoping, looking out the window or down the ice, wishing for Serge to come around the corner. Serge knew; no one had to tell him.

"Hey, kid," Serge called.

The boy was standing across the narrow street, and he pretended not to hear. He just kept throwing his baseball into the glove, staring at it with total and fierce concentration.

"Kid," Serge said again. "Ricky."

At that, the boy's ears perked up, but still he didn't look over. The ball kept whacking the leather glove, harder and harder.

"Good boy," Serge said. "Don't talk to strangers, especially cons."

Now the kid turned his back, so he wouldn't see Serge at all. His throwing got more intense.

"You miss your dad," Serge said. "I miss him, too."

The kid threw and missed, and the ball went bouncing down the sidewalk and hit a tree. Running for it, the kid might have been fielding a line drive down the left field line. He dug in, slid, came up with the ball. Then he returned to the spot where he had been standing and started throwing the ball into his glove again.

"Your dad was a good man," Serge said.

The boy said something under his breath, and although Serge couldn't swear to it, he thought he'd heard a correction: "Is," the boy said.

"He said you're a good ball player," Serge said. "That true?"

Instead of replying, Ricky just wound up and threw the baseball as high as it would go. It exploded out of his hand in a straight shot to the sky, then fell into his glove with a perfect "thwack."

"Excellent," Serge said.

Ricky resumed his private game of catch. The day was hot, a beautiful summer day. Serge thought of Lac Vert, wondered where there might be a nice lake or pond around here. Boys should be spending their summer days swimming, playing with friends, not haunting the prison gates for a glimpse of their murdered fathers.

Serge looked at the boy and thought of Tino. There was a strong resemblance: the sinewy build, the high cheekbones, the in-

tense dark eyes, the crew-cut hair. How old had Tino been when he had become more interested in the streets than in playing catch?

"My son played a lot of ball," Serge told him.

The child seemed not to hear.

"He never stopped. He worked and practiced, day in and day out. Now he's a professional athlete."

In spite of himself, Ricky glanced over. He broke his rhythm, and the ball rolled away. This time, when he retrieved it, he took a step closer to the bars and started playing again.

"Yeah, he's one of the greats," Serge went on. "Next year he'll win the Stanley Cup, plays hockey for the Boston Bruins."

Ricky glanced over, as if trying to discern whether Serge was lying or not. He'd probably heard plenty of lies from his father along the way. Serge had become expert at delivering half-truths and non-truths, telling himself it didn't matter, that what he did was no one's business, justifying every lie with a reason.

But he was a liar from way back, and he deserved the kid's suspicious look.

"Martin Cartier," Serge said. "The Gold Sledgehammer."

Ricky lifted his eyebrows as if to say "Maybe yes and maybe no." Then he began throwing the ball against the wall, catching it on one hop.

"He never stopped practicing," Serge said again. "He never took his eye off the ball, and don't you, either. Keep your eye on the ball, Ricky. Make your father proud of you."

Throw, hop, catch. Throw, hop, catch.

The guard came back from the melee, and he stood at the gate and clapped his hands, scaring Ricky. The boy caught his ball and faced the guard with a mixture of fear and defiance in his eyes.

"Go home, now," Jim said. "Don't make me call someone to come get you."

"I'm waiting for my dad."

"You know you're not," Jim said. "You know your father passed away. Now, I'm sorry about that, but you can't be hanging around here."

"I'm waiting for him," Ricky insisted.

Jim shook his head. "You're gonna make me call the cops to come get you."

Ricky's eyes widened. That had done it: the mention of police. Eight years old, and already he was afraid of the law. Serge felt sorrow for what Tino had done, left to his only boy. If only fathers could live life backward, take their sorry lessons and carry them

back to the early days, when their sons were small, when there was still time to make things right.

Scowling, Ricky started to back away.

"Kid, keep practicing," Serge yelled. "Don't ever quit."

"Won't make a difference," the guard muttered under his breath.

Ricky tilted his head, as if he'd heard, but he didn't say anything. He just kept walking backward, one step at a time, throwing the baseball into his glove.

"You a Yankee fan? Who's your favorite player?" Serge asked.

Ricky opened his mouth, as if he wanted to say something. Instead, wheeling around, he revealed the name emblazoned across the back of his T-shirt: MARTINEZ. Serge was proud of him for not speaking.

"Tino Martinez," Serge said. "Good man."

Ricky nodded: Serge saw his head bob up and down. He started to walk faster, and then run.

"Don't come back," Jim said.

"Practice harder than ever," Serge called. "And don't talk to strangers!"

He wondered whether the mail was in yet. Every day he checked. Writing that letter to Martin had given him something to dream about, to hope for. He had a new reason for getting up in the morning, and all it had taken was a stamp and an envelope. He started walking across the yard, to check his mail, and then he began to run.

———

The Cartiers had decided to stay out in Black Hall instead of the town house, because the country air was a little cooler, fresher, more like Lac Vert, and because it was easier to leave Kylie home during the day.

"Anything you need," Tobin had said, now that May had filled her in. "I mean it, May. Ask me. He has to be okay. An athlete like Martin . . ."

"I know," May said, breaking down. She hadn't wanted to cry in front of Martin. They still had hope. Teddy hadn't told them anything definite yet. "It's so unfair," May sobbed. "He's scared, Tobin. I hate to see him scared."

"He's got you," Tobin said. "You're going through it together."

They had a long ride up to Boston, and this time he didn't even

try to get behind the wheel, and she knew his vision had changed dramatically since the beginning of the summer.

Neither of them had slept the night before. May had lain awake, staring at the ceiling, knowing that Martin was awake and staring at the wall. She had watched the stars set one by one, into the western sky. By the time the neighbor's rooster crowed at dawn, she hadn't even been to sleep. She focused on Serge's letter. She had brought it from Lac Vert, and she still wished Martin had read it. Thinking about anything else seemed too terrifying.

Today had seemed endless. Neither she nor Martin had been hungry for dinner; en route to his after-hours appointment with Teddy, they had traveled northeast on 395.

"Are you okay?" she asked him now, driving east on Route 90. The Boston skyline was visible, the Prudential and John Hancock towers twinkling above the city, and she felt her stomach flip, wondering what they were heading into.

"Fine. You?"

"Fine," she said. She knew they were both lying.

It felt strange, driving Martin. May had gotten her license at sixteen, had been driving ever since, and she loved being on the road. But when they were together, Martin always drove.

To break the silence, she turned on the radio. She found a station playing good music, and they listened to a few songs. She felt herself relax and begin to feel as if everything just might turn out all right. Martin must have felt it, too, because he put his hand on her thigh.

"Thanks for driving me," he said.

"It's the least I can do," she said.

"Not just in the car," he said. "I mean in general. You've really been there for me, May."

"Thank you, Martin," May said, hearing Tobin's words of strength. She glanced over, saw him covering one eye then the other, testing his vision with his hands, as if somehow during their long ride the problem had corrected itself.

Following Teddy's directions, they pulled straight into the hospital parking garage and walked through the skyway to the office tower. Through the glass bridge, they could see the dark waters of Boston Harbor alive with ferries and tanker traffic. Party boats passed by, and faint orchestra music penetrated the glass. Outside, people were enjoying the pleasures of a summer night, but the Cartiers were entering the medical world of air-conditioning, disinfectant, and tension.

In stark contrast to her home office, Teddy Collins's office at the Boston Eye Hospital was sleek and modern, all gleaming white and chrome. She called them right in, the moment they arrived, to minimize the likelihood of their being seen by other people.

When May started to follow Martin into the exam room, Teddy stopped her at the door.

"I'd like to examine Martin alone," she said.

"Of course," May said, feeling sharply hurt. She didn't want to take it personally, but she couldn't help feeling a lurch in her stomach.

"Go on in, Martin," Teddy directed. "Just sit in that seat by the table. I want to show May something."

Martin nodded, moving inside. Teddy brought May into her inner sanctum and told her she could wait there. She laid a white leather album on the desk before her, placing one hand on the cover.

"My wedding photos," Teddy said. "With lots of pictures of you and your mother. I thought you might like to see them."

"Thank you," May said. She stared at the richly embossed leather, the initials "T & W" entwined in flowing script, and she looked questioningly at Teddy. Had they been wrong in choosing Teddy as Martin's doctor? To come to her at a time like this, when they were both nearly paralyzed with fear, and to have her show May her wedding photos?

But at the sight of Teddy's lined and compassionate face, the sense that she was completely present and focused, May's own eyes filled with tears.

"I love him so much," May said.

"I know."

May bowed her head, wiped her eyes.

"I understand," Teddy said. "He's facing something very difficult."

"Then you know already—"

"I suspect, but I'm not sure of the degree. We'll know by the end of the exam."

"I'm so worried about Martin," May said. "Please help him, Teddy. Please . . ."

"I'll do whatever I can," she said. Then, embracing May, she left her alone in the big corner office. The room had a view of Logan Airport across the black water, and there were planes taking off and landing. The office walls were covered with William's beautiful pictures of lighthouses all over the world.

But May didn't look at any of it. She stared down at the wedding album. It was filled with pictures of Teddy and William, Emily and Lorenzo Dunne, Aunt Enid and May herself, but most of all, Samuel and Abigail Taylor. Staring at the pictures of her father, May couldn't take her eyes away.

He looked just as May remembered him. Tall and strong, with curly brown hair and hazel eyes. He wore a gray suit with a blue tie—narrowing her eyes, May thought she could see tiny seagulls printed on it. She had given him a seagull tie for Father's Day once. Grinning at the camera, he had one hand on May's shoulder.

Staring at the picture, May's eyes flooded. She was six or seven, the same age as Kylie. In every shot, she was no more than two steps away from her father. She had adored him, and the feeling had been mutual.

Love mattered so much. Family and old friends helped even when they weren't there. Now May closed her eyes, shutting out even the pictures. She conjured up her parents' faces. There was her father, smiling out at her. Since her visit to Serge, May had gotten her father back.

She thanked God for Martin, that he wanted to be a father to Kylie. Tears rolling down her cheeks, May wished Martin had *his* father back. She wished that no matter what this exam would reveal, Martin would have the strength and love of his father to lean on.

———

Martin had never liked doctor's visits. As a kid, his mother had had to bribe him to go to the pediatrician. As he got older, his checkups had been restricted to team physicals and the aftercare for injuries sustained while playing hockey.

So, sitting in this high-tech doctor's office, he had butterflies in his stomach. He wished May had been allowed in with him. The equipment looked like instruments of torture.

"How are you feeling, Martin?" Teddy asked.

"I'm great," he lied.

"That's good. I'm going to do a few tests today, a little more involved than we did yesterday, and I'd like you to try to relax."

"I'm relaxed," he said, the muscles in his neck and shoulders tight and knotted as wet shoelaces.

"Good, dear." In spite of her motherly manner, the doctor's movements were all business. She checked the dials on the instruments, made notations.

"I'm going to do a fluorescein angiogram," she said. "It's going to test any changes in your retina, but to get the best reading possible, I have to inject dye. You're not allergic, are you?"

"No," Martin said. Having undergone a myelogram to check his spine after a severe altercation with several New Jersey Devils five years ago, he had experienced contact dye. The mere idea of it made him feel bad, and Teddy noticed.

"It's not fun," she said. "Makes some people feel nauseous."

"I remember."

"Well, it will give me the truest sense of what's going on—"

"Do it," Martin interrupted her. "Whatever it takes, anything you say. I'll do anything to get this over. Finish the tests, make the diagnosis, give me my medicine. I'll take it, all of it, just to be ready for practice next month. Exercises, surgery, anything."

"Martin—" she began.

Martin didn't like to plead or beg, but he wanted to state his case clearly, so she'd understand. She was a hockey fan; she had probably treated other players at different times. "I have to get better fast," he said. "This might be my last year."

"Your last year?"

"To play hockey." Now that he had started talking, he felt the words coming faster and faster. "I'm getting old for the game. My joints are giving out, but that's just what happens when you've played as long as I have. I didn't tell May this, but I'd been planning to retire this year."

"You mean after next season?" Teddy asked, frowning.

Martin shook his head. "I mean after *last* season."

"But you didn't . . ."

"I couldn't. I have to win the Stanley Cup first," he said.

"You're a great player, Martin. With or without—"

He shook his head hard. Maybe he'd been wrong; perhaps she didn't get it after all. "It's everything," he said. "I've been playing for it my whole life. My father won it three times. Yep, three times. These last two years, ever since I've had May, I've been so close. Right there, about to win . . ."

"I watched you on TV," she said.

"If I'd won Game Seven, I would be retired by now," he said, his heart pounding. "That was my plan, but it didn't happen. One more year, Doctor. That's all I need. I know I can win this time. I'm positive I can do what it takes, if I can just hang on for one more year."

Teddy stood there in front of him, her arms at her side. Mar-

tin's eyes were so blurry, he could hardly see her. "It's getting worse instead of better," he said, the words flowing out. "I wake up in the morning, and I can hardly see."

"I know," she said.

"Fix me," he said. "Give me one more chance to win—"

"Martin," she said gently. "We don't know what we're going to find here tonight. I promise to do my best, and it's wonderful to know what a willing patient you are. You have no idea how important that is."

"I'll do anything," he said.

When she didn't reply, Martin stopped talking. His face felt red, and his vocal chords hurt as if he'd been yelling. He closed his eyes, pulled himself together the way he did during the toughest games. The doctor was going to do her best. He felt her hand on his shoulder, and he looked up without blinking or smiling.

"I'm ready," he said.

The testing began.

Through keratoscopy, concentric rings of light were projected onto his corneas. Teddy then did corneal topography, explaining that she was using the newest equipment to make a map of any subtle underlying structural defects. To measure the cornea's thickness and any possible swelling, she used a pachymeter.

Martin willed himself to sit still, not move a muscle. He focused on the exam as if he was driving for the goal. He told himself this was the most important game he'd ever played, that if he got through today, he'd make it to the Cup finals next spring and have another chance. He felt sick to his stomach, and his eyes stung and ached.

Teddy explained that gonioscopy was the procedure by which the anterior chamber angle of the eye is evaluated, that ophthalmoscopy allowed her to view the optic nerve, retina, blood vessels, choroid, and a portion of the ciliary body—the point of attachment for the ligament of the lens as well as the cells which secrete the aqueous humor.

"The eye is a camera," she said. "But we actually see with the brain."

She explained that the clear forward part of the eye allowed light through the cornea, pupil, and lens. The retina acted as film—tissue covering the back. Containing cones and rods, the tissue transformed light into electrical impulses that carried data through the optic nerve to the brain. From the data, images were formed by the brain.

"My right eye's fine," Martin said, tightly holding the chair arm. "I know my left eye's weak, but I can see through my right—"

Teddy told him to breathe deeply as she injected the dye, and Martin felt waves of nausea. He pictured Jorgensen out there jeering, and it steeled him to get through Teddy recording the retinal changes with a special camera. The flashes startled him, just like photographers waiting outside the locker room when he least expected them.

The light bursts unlocked an ancient memory: Martin at four or five, walking down a long corridor with his father. It was after a game, and his father's team had won. Martin remembered a deep sense of pride, of knowing his father was the best hockey player in Canada. Carrying his father's skates, Martin had felt nothing would ever tear them apart. His mother had surprised them, snapping their picture.

Martin still had the photo. Years later, when Serge had won his first Stanley Cup, Martin had come across the picture buried in his bureau drawer. Estranged from his father by that time, Martin had felt the misery of rage mixed with pride.

Sitting there, he thought of Game 7, of how much he had wanted his father to see him win. He thought of May's visit to Serge, of the letter he had received and not opened. Martin exhaled, to get rid of the thoughts.

Images flashed on a computer, and Teddy printed them out. Martin had to use the rest room, and she pointed him down the hall. She asked if he needed help getting to her office. He said no, and she told him she would see him in a few minutes. He just wanted the news, to get started on a plan of action right away. To fix his eyes.

———

Waiting for Martin, May had continued looking through Teddy's old pictures. Her wedding had taken place one June morning at the Old North Church, and because she and William had had no young children in their lives, May had been the flower girl.

"Your family was very good to me," Teddy said, walking into the office.

May's stomach dropped at the greeting. Why hadn't she mentioned Martin? If it was good news, wouldn't she have said right away? "You mean my mother and grandmother for planning your wedding?" May asked slowly.

"All of them. All of you. You were such an important part of that day."

"Thank you. We didn't often attend the weddings we planned. Yours is one of the only ones I remember."

"Maybe that's why I'm so glad you came to me," she said steadily. "For this. So I can help you and Martin."

For this. Two words. Teddy didn't smile as she said them. She had an edge in her voice, as if she was warning May of something that had to be done. May heard the little sound escape her throat, and her mouth was dry. May questioned her with her eyes, but Teddy was settling herself at her desk, arranging a sheaf of papers and printouts, looking up as Martin came through the door.

Dr. Theodora Collins sat at her desk. There were two Windsor chairs set in front, facing her, with May sitting in one. Martin crossed the room and took his place beside her. Squeezing her hand, he heard himself breathing as if he'd just climbed a steep hill. His mind raced with questions, all of them elaborate and confusing. Teddy put on half-glasses, ready to start.

"I'm going to tell you straight out," she said. "We're facing a complicated situation."

Complicated, Martin thought, grabbing onto the word. It wasn't necessarily dire, or even bad. Just complicated. Teddy held up one of the pictures she'd taken during the tests, and to Martin it looked like a big red blotch with dark spots and jagged lines running through it.

"Your left eye," she said, "shows severe scarring. When the hole or tear developed in the sensory retina, some liquid vitreous seeped through, severing the retina from what's called the retinal pigment epithelium. Although I can see evidence of cryotherapy—the laser welds you mentioned—scar tissue has formed to tear it away again."

"So I have another detached retina?" Martin asked. Even as he asked, he was calculating the time it had taken last time: one day for surgery, a week to wear the bandage, two months before he could play again.

"Is that serious?" May asked.

"It wasn't too bad," Martin said, squeezing her hand, feeling a lightness all over.

But Teddy wasn't smiling. "Somehow, the macula—that's to

say, the central portion of the retina in your left eye—appears to have been detached for some time. You seem to have suffered an infection, perhaps at that same time, that caused retinal vein occlusion. Your left eye is without sight."

Martin let the words sink in. He heard May let out a small cry; her hand was so slippery, it almost slid out of his. Martin cleared his throat, tried to keep his heart from pounding out of his chest. "We knew that. Even the optometrist up in LaSalle told us that. Luckily, I can see with my right eye. I can see with both—just not with my left alone."

"Martin," Teddy said. "Your right eye is being affected as well."

"But I wasn't hit in my right eye."

"Never?"

"Nothing bad," he said. "Nothing that needed surgery."

"Did you ever receive high-dose cortisone treatment in your right eye?"

"In both eyes, yes. Cortisone," Martin said. "I remember getting injections way back then. Right next to my eyes . . . it wasn't fun."

"He's taken it for inflammation of his knees and ankles," May said. "For his hips and shoulders . . ."

Martin listened to her voice and wished he could see her better. He tried to swallow, but his mouth was too dry.

"What I see in your right eye," Teddy began.

"My good eye."

"Yes, your good eye. What I see there is a condition known as sympathetic ophthalmia."

"Sympathetic . . ." May said, and Martin knew she was seizing on a word that sounded gentle and kind.

"Sympathetic ophthalmia," Teddy said. "It is a rare inflammation of the eye that sometimes develops after penetrating injuries in the fellow eye. Its symptoms include severe light sensitivity, difficulty in focusing, and marked swelling—in the eye *opposite* the one that sustained the injury."

"But it happened years ago," Martin said. "Jorgensen hit me in Vancouver almost four years ago. . . ."

"The condition can occur within one or two weeks, or it might lie dormant for years."

"But how?" May asked, holding Martin's hand. "It sounds impossible."

"Exposure of some of the internal contents of the injured eye

initiates a sympathetic, immunologic process which adversely affects the same type of tissue in the opposite eye. The fellow eye."

"But cortisone helps?" Martin asked. "That's why you wanted to know whether I've had it?"

"Corticosteriods can sometimes work. But prolonged use can inhibit the body from producing its own, and, in some cases, build up a resistance."

"Then what?" Martin asked.

He could feel Teddy staring at him, and he could hear the small sobs coming from May. She sounded so hurt and afraid, and Martin wanted to take her in his arms and tell her everything was going to be all right. But he couldn't move, and the only thing he could say was directed at Teddy.

"Am I going blind?" Martin Cartier asked.

"Yes," she said.

Chapter 25

THE DIAGNOSIS WAS NOT WITHOUT HOPE. Teddy had given Martin a periocular injection of cortisone, numbing the area next to his eye before giving him the shot. Then she had prescribed a short course of high-dose Prednisone. After one week, she would check the inflammation and determine what to do next.

Surgery would most likely be indicated. Teddy described a "scleral buckling" procedure, in which she would suture a silicone material to the white of the eye behind the lids. Another option was intraocular gas injections: a minuscule inflatable balloon would take the place of the silicone buckle. If successful, the balloon would be removed after the retina had reattached.

May and Martin had listened, completely numb. Martin's hand was ice cold, and the look on his face was far away, as if he had escaped from the room. As Teddy talked, May knew she should take notes. She should pull her wedding-planner notebook from her straw purse and write it all down.

"The success rate for anatomic reattachment of the retina is quite high," Teddy said. "But regarding the macula, we'll have to see."

"The macula?" May asked dully. Hadn't Teddy just explained what that was? If she'd been writing everything down, she would understand, not make Teddy repeat herself.

"The retina's most sensitive, central section," Teddy said, not seeming to mind going over it again. "If the macula has been detached for too long, the prognosis for good central vision may be poor."

"Then what's not poor?" Martin said. "Forget that, and tell me what will work."

"For complicated detachments like yours," Teddy said, "we have multiple procedures, such as vitrectomy—removal of the vit-

reous. I need to study your case a bit longer before I can say for sure. Let's see how you do on the Prednisone, and when you come back in a week—"

"A week!" Martin exploded. "I don't have a week. Training starts soon, and I need to be on the road to recovery by then."

"Martin, I know this comes as a shock to you. But try to realize, we're trying to save as much of your sight as we can. We're not talking about restoration of your sight, but rather, stemming the deterioration and—"

"You're telling me I'm not going to play hockey? Ever?"

"Yes," Teddy said. Her arms were folded on her desk, her gaze direct and compassionate. May shivered as the word penetrated her bones, her very being, and she felt Martin rip his hand out of hers.

"Come on, May," he said, jumping up. "Let's go."

"Martin," May said, trying to calm him down. "Listen to her."

"I've heard all I need to hear. Let's go."

"Treatment needs to begin right away," Teddy said quietly, as if Martin was still sitting there, not poised to leap. "We shouldn't waste any time."

"Exactly," Martin snapped. "That's why I'm getting out of here." He grabbed his jacket, dropped it, picked it up again. Heading for the door, he went in the wrong direction and crashed into a bookcase. He turned himself around, strode to the exit. "May?"

"Sit down, Martin," she pleaded. "Please, we're talking about your eyes!"

"They're fine enough. I read the chart in LaSalle, didn't I? Are you coming?"

"Listen to me, Martin," May said sharply, tears filling her eyes. "I've done it your way all along. Your timetable, not mine. We can't pretend anymore. I won't let you. I love you too much."

"I'll meet you at the car," Martin said coldly, slamming the door behind him.

May buried her head in her hands and sobbed. Coming from behind the desk, Teddy patted her back.

"This reaction is normal for him," Teddy told her. "It is exactly what I would expect from Martin. Acceptance comes very hard after news like this."

"Hockey is his life," May cried.

"I have no medical answers for that," Teddy said. "I'll do everything possible to save what I can of his sight."

"He'll really never play hockey again?"

"No."

"You're sure?"

Teddy paused, taking so long to consider that May dried her eyes and looked up. The elderly woman looked beautiful, thoughtful in the lamplight. She had a light of warmth and humor in her eyes; there was nothing tragic in her expression at all.

"I would never presume to say 'never' about Martin Cartier," she said. "As his doctor, I will say that I advise against it, that it would be harmful to his eyes, that, frankly, I don't believe he is able to see the ice. But you saw him, and you know him better than I do. He's something else, that man."

"Yes, he is," May said.

"William was like that," Teddy went on. "He was an inventor, and we used to travel the world in search of ideas. Everywhere we went, he found things that he became passionate about. That lighthouse on the Isle de Ré," she said, pointing. "And that one on Corfu. The afternoon light on Block Island, in Brittany. And then one day, his cardiologist told him the risks of travel made it advisable for him to stay home."

"Did he listen?" May asked.

Teddy shook her head. "No, he didn't. He went straight home from the doctor's office and booked us passage on the Queen Elizabeth. A transatlantic crossing and two weeks in the Mediterranean."

"Did you try to stop him?"

"I tried," Teddy said. "But not for long."

"Why?"

"Because I loved William for who he was. Even the obstinate, stubborn side of him." She bowed her head, then gave a half-smile. "At least that's what I tell myself now. At the time . . . well, it wasn't easy."

"Did you go on the cruise with him?"

"I did," Teddy said.

May took a deep breath. She knew that when she reached the car, Martin would be furious about the diagnosis. He would want to see another doctor, someone who would tell him what he wanted to hear.

"He wants to win the Stanley Cup," May said. "More than anything. He says it's for him, but I think—"

Teddy waited.

"It's for his father," May said, the words tearing from her throat. "I think he wants to win the Cup for Serge."

"He's going to need your support, no matter what. I've worked with professional athletes before. The loss of control they feel associated with vision loss is terrible. He'll feel his entire identity at question, so be patient if you can. But keep in mind: There's no time to waste. He needs treatment immediately."

"I know." May wiped her eyes.

"It's a tall order for you," Teddy said. "But I know you're up to it."

"Did you have a good time together?" May asked.

"Excuse me?"

"On the cruise you took. The one William booked . . ."

"He died on it, dear," Teddy said gently. "Our third night aboard."

———

Martin had left Teddy's office without the keys, so he was leaning on the car when May came walking out. The night was hot and sticky, and the parking garage smelled like oil and exhaust. Down below, horns blared on the southeast expressway. The Fleet Center was just a few blocks away, and Martin imagined the team gearing up for the season.

"I'm sorry I took so long," May said.

"Don't worry about it," he said, waiting for her to unlock the door. They were both careful not to look at each other or brush hands. Once she got into the driver's seat, she fumbled the keys and dropped them onto the floor. She picked them up, stuck one in the ignition, couldn't get it turned. Martin just reached over and started the car.

"I'm nervous," she said.

"Don't be," he told her. "There won't be any traffic at this hour."

"Not about driving," she said, and he heard her voice catch.

Martin put his seat back and reached for a baseball cap over the visor. He stuck it on his head. Except for that Blue Jays game in Toronto, they hadn't seen much baseball that year. Usually he took in a few Expos games, and on his rare summer visits to Boston, he'd go watch the Red Sox play.

"You know what I love about summer?" he asked.

"No," she said, turning onto Storrow Drive.

"Baseball and fishing. I was just thinking, we haven't done enough of either."

"You and Kylie have fished a few times," she said carefully, holding her voice very steady to keep from screaming. "And we saw that game with the Gardners."

"Ahh, that's nothing. We should be up at dawn every day, rowing up the lake and giving Kylie her chance at the great-granddaddy. The hook filed down, just to say hello and let him go."

"She'll have plenty of chances," May told him. "It's you I'm thinking about right now."

"Don't worry about me," Martin said. "I'm fine."

"You heard Teddy," May said. "You're not fine."

As they drove along the Charles River, Martin rolled down his window. The breeze felt cool on his face, and he wondered whether the college teams had started training for the crew season yet. One of his great pleasures last year had been driving in for practice from the Barn and seeing the Harvard, MIT, and Boston University crews out on the lazy river, their sleek white shells gliding through the water.

"Hockey season starts—"

"I don't give a damn about hockey season!" May yelled.

"I do," Martin said.

"Listen to me!" May screamed. "I care about you. I love you! You have the chance to do something right now, to save your eyes. Your eyes, Martin. What are you telling me, that you're going out there on the ice to get run over and hurt by every—"

"No one runs me over," he said.

"You can't see! I know you want to play, but you can't see, Martin."

"I have one eye doing the work of two," Martin insisted, hanging onto the words of Maurice Pilote.

"Didn't you listen?" May cried. "Teddy said you're losing even that! You'll be blind. . . ."

Martin gritted his teeth, refusing to hear the word. Blind. If he didn't hear it, he could go on as before. "Shut up."

"Martin—"

"You wanted to force me to see my father, and now you're forcing me to accept a lie."

"You can't even hear me!" she said. "Seeing your father would be the best thing for you, but that's beside the point. Teddy says—"

"I won't be one of those cripples with a white cane and dark glasses," he ranted. "Sitting in the dark for the rest of my life. Do you think I'm like that? You think I could ever live that way? I'm a hockey player, and I'm not going fucking blind!" He smashed his

fist into the dashboard, ripping the glove compartment off its hinges. He roared so loud, his own voice was ringing in his ears.

May sobbed, swerving across the highway. Horns blared. Martin's heart was pounding. He felt like jumping out of the car. He estimated they were going sixty, and he wondered if hitting the pavement would be that much worse than catching some two-hundred-sixty-pound player's stick hard in the head.

"Pull over," he said.

"No, I want to get you home."

"Being blind would be worse than going to prison," he said. "I'm not an invalid."

"I know!" she screamed.

She gripped the wheel with both hands, tears streaming down her face. He saw them as he squinted through the bright highway lights. Reaching over, he touched her cheek.

"May."

"I don't want you to go blind," she sobbed.

"Pull over," he said, his throat closing as the feelings welled up from his heart. "Please. I need to hold you. Please, May. I'm sorry I yelled, scared you. I didn't mean to scare you."

———

"We're going home to the lake," Martin said the next morning. They had held each other all night, not letting go for a minute. May had lost count of how many times they had made love, fallen asleep, started all over again. It was as if they were afraid of the dark, fearful of drifting off into their dreams.

"Teddy's the best," she told him. "We can't leave. She wants to see you in a week, after you've taken the Prednisone."

"I'll take it," he said. "And I'll come back. But I need the lake."

"You promise?" she asked doubtfully.

"Yeah."

She didn't know whether to believe him or not. He was looking away from her as if he might be lying.

"I'm supposed to be patient," she said. "And get you to treatment right away. How can I do both at the same time?"

"It's summer," he said. "Fishing and swimming. We're going home."

"Okay," May agreed, giving in again. "As long as we come back."

The lake and mountains welcomed them home, and May knew that Lac Vert was the place they should be. The water was still and mysterious; she stared at it for hours, wondering what the future would bring. The sun rose and set behind the mountains, and the afternoons were filled with that wonderful hazy light, that yellow light sparkling with moisture and pollen, that made May believe that everything would be all right, that miracles could happen, that love could heal everything.

She, Martin, and Kylie swam every day, and May thought of the waters of Lac Vert curing Martin's eyes. She found her mother-in-law's Bible, and she found the story of Jesus healing the blind man. She rehung Agnes's cross-stitch picture on the living room wall. While Martin and Kylie played in the water, she sat gazing through the summer light, wishing this time could go on forever.

At night, Martin held her. They had made a silent pact to pretend nothing was happening. They had one week to see how the cortisone worked, and then they would return to Teddy and discuss further options. When Martin talked about the NHL, about recent player trades, who was coming back and who was leaving, what he believed about the Bruins' prospects for another championship season, she listened patiently.

When he lay on his back, drawing plays in the air, telling her stories of how he had scored his best goals, won his hardest games, she laughed and nodded and tried to see the plays in her mind.

Genny and Ray invited them to a barbeque, but Martin told May to make excuses. She thought Genny was beginning to suspect something—they had hardly seen each other all summer. May found that she liked it that way; denial worked best when secrets were kept, when fears were left unspoken, when the world didn't know what was going on. Only one other person knew—Tobin—but she was all the way down in Black Hall.

When Kylie came running in to tell May that Martin wanted to take her out fishing, to catch the big trout who lived in the hole near the island, her blood ran cold and denial ran out. Her husband couldn't see ten yards in front of him; there was no way May was letting her daughter out on the lake alone with him.

"I'm coming too," she said.

They packed a picnic lunch and started out before the sun had risen over the crest. May loved this time of day. The lake was sapphire blue, and the air was so clear she could see eagles circling a

mile up. Kylie sat in the bow, staring into the water for fish swimming under the boat. Martin and May faced each other—her in the
stern, him rowing in the center seat.

She felt so relaxed and safe, and she suddenly realized that
Martin didn't have to see to row. He knew where to go by instinct.
This was his lake, and he knew every rock, each bend, by heart. He
rowed backward, without turning around, staring straight into
May's eyes, hands on his oars.

She found herself wondering whether he could see her or not.
When she smiled, his face remained impassive.

"Floating branches," Kylie called out. "Go a little left."

Martin barely seemed to hear, but he pulled harder on the left
oar and they missed the gnarled root system of an old pine tree. As
they continued, they saw a family of deer swimming to the island.
May heard Kylie laugh, describing them for Martin: "Two parents
and two fawns," she said.

"You're my fawn," Martin told her.

"Me and Natalie."

"That's right," he agreed. "You and Nat."

At the fishing hole, Martin helped Kylie with her rod. She
threw her line into the water, satisfied that this would be the day
they'd catch the big old trout. Martin beckoned May over. She had
never been much of a fisherman, but she let him hold her from behind, teaching her how to pay out line and whip the pole.

"You want the fly to imitate what the fish are eating," he told
her.

"What are they eating?" May asked.

"Black flies, right?"

"Right, Kylie," he said. "That great-granddaddy's down there
waiting."

She nodded, cocking her head slightly. May watched, wondering whether she was listening for the fish, whether she could hear.
The blue notebook had been unused ever since that night when the
dreams and voices stopped. Kylie had had no new visions, and
the strange thing was, May missed them.

They drifted on the lake. As the sun rose higher, they pulled
their hats lower. May stopped worrying that anything might happen. Denial closed over her head, like water over a smooth gray
rock, and she let herself think this summer day would last forever.
They ate their lunch, and the light turned hazy. The air turned
gold, bathing the Cartiers in magic and hope.

Kylie caught two small trout, and Martin caught three. They

threw them all back. As Martin rowed them home, May felt as if they were back to normal. Rowing, driving, skating: he could do it all.

"There's a rock on our right," Kylie called. Then, a few minutes later, "Wow! Look at that loon diving for fish!"

Perhaps Lac Vert did have healing powers. Maybe a miracle had occurred in the blessed golden light, and Martin would see again. They would repeat this fishing trip for many, many summers to come. They would skate the lake when winter came, wondering whether the great-granddaddy trout was asleep in the mud below.

But once they were home, the sense of peace and insulation vanished. The telephone was ringing, and May ran to answer it.

"Hello?" she said.

"Hi, May. This is Jacques Dafoe."

"Oh, hello, Coach," she said. For a moment she thought he had gotten wind of Martin's visit to Dr. Theodora Collins, but his tone was too easygoing for that. They exchanged small talk about their summer, their children, and the rapidly approaching hockey season. Martin stood by, waiting for the phone, and May's stomach ached as she sensed her husband's tension. "I'll put Martin on the line," she said.

"Hi, Coach," Martin said. *"Ça va?"*

While Martin talked, May unpacked the picnic basket. She rinsed out the thermos and plastic containers, put the uneaten peaches and grapes in the refrigerator. Martin seemed to be listening more than talking, and May felt her heart pounding. When Martin hung up the phone, he leaned his head against the wall and didn't speak for a long time.

"Martin, what is it?" she asked, afraid of what he was about to tell her.

"Coach wanted me to hear it from him," Martin said finally. "He's calling a team meeting; we're getting together next Tuesday to meet our new goalie."

"Your new goalie?" May frowned, thinking of Martin's friend Bruno, the Bruins' goalie for the last seven years.

"Management traded Bruno and two minor-leaguers for him. We now have a two-time Stanley Cup-winning goalie on our team. Nils Jorgensen."

"You're kidding."

"I'm *not*"—his voice rose in a homicidal bellow—"KID-DING!" He punched the wall, sending his fist straight through the matchstick paneling. Thunder jumped up from his spot beneath

the kitchen table and started barking. Kylie just stood against the door, her mouth open and both hands pressing the door behind her.

May stepped forward, to somehow touch him, to let him know she was with him, but he burst past her. May saw him jogging down the path to the lake, but his pace increasing to a dead run. With Kylie and Thunder beside her, May watched her husband's back become a blur as he disappeared around the corner of the mountain.

When she turned around, she saw Kylie staring at the cross-stitch picture hanging by the window. Together they stared at the small animals sleeping peacefully side by side. May saw the words, neatly running all around the border: "The wolf shall dwell with the lamb, and the leopard lie down with the kid, and a little child shall lead them."

Kylie must have been reading them too, because she looked up at May, a frown on her face. "I was the little child," she said. "Natalie told me. I was supposed to lead him somewhere, but I was too late."

"No, you weren't," May said.

Chapter 26

THE BRUINS HAD SCORED THE trading coup of the decade: Nils Jorgensen was joining the team. With Nils the Knife and Martin the Gold Sledgehammer on board, the Bruins would take this year's Stanley Cup without question. "Expect fireworks at first," the sportswriters predicted. "The Jorgensen-Cartier rivalry is long and bitter, and it won't be resolved just because they're wearing the same jersey."

Preparing to leave for Boston, May knew she had some unfinished business. Martin kept talking about canceling his appointment with Teddy, but nothing on earth would make him miss the team meeting. He still wanted to call all the shots.

Packing for the trip, May took the letter Martin had thrown into the wastebasket out of her bureau drawer and smoothed out the wrinkles. Carrying it over to Martin, she held it up.

"You threw this away."

"I know."

"I opened it," she told him.

He shook his head as his face turned red. She watched his eyes narrow and felt a shot of fear. Maybe he would walk out on her again. But she grabbed his wrist and held him still.

"You shouldn't have done that," he said, trying to pull away.

"I knew you'd feel like that, but I disagree. You should read it."

"I have more important things to worry about."

May tried to smile. "I know you think that's true, but you're wrong."

"My worst fucking enemy is about to be my teammate," he exploded.

"Martin, read your father's letter."

"I'm going to forget you opened it, eh?" he asked. "We'll just drop it here and now."

"You left me once," May said, still holding his wrist. "That broke my heart. It really did, Martin. So much so, I've kept quiet all summer about something I know is *so* important to all of us. You have to read his letter. Please—"

"Drop it, May," he said dangerously.

"I won't," she told him.

He shrugged and went back to loading their things into the car.

The next day, Martin walked into the Fleet Center past a pack of reporters and photographers. Flashes burst all around him. Questions were shouted at him, but he ignored every one. One step in front of the other. May had dropped him off. She had volunteered to walk him in, but that would have looked suspicious. He moved slowly, deliberately, taking care not to trip on the TV crew's wires.

"Martin, is the rivalry over?"

"Are you going to shake and make up?"

"Forgive and forget?"

"Martin, are you going to give Nils a new scar today?"

Ignoring the journalists, Martin disappeared into the locker room. The lights were dim, but he could hear voices. The familiar banter of teammates, joking about last season and one-upping each other with stories of wine and women on vacation. Martin heard Ray laughing, and he headed toward the sound of his voice.

His mouth felt dry. He couldn't see where he was going, and he was terrified he was going to be found out. A dark veil covered everything in his path. He saw clusters of men standing around, but he couldn't make out faces. Everything in the room was imprinted on his brain: the lockers, the water coolers, the benches. Making his way around a bench, he crashed into someone crossing his path.

"What the fuck!"

"Sorry," Martin said.

But his apology was not accepted. He felt a shoulder jam his chest, fingers closing around his throat as he was shoved into the lockers. The metal crashed, and his teammates groaned. Martin swung on instinct, landing a punch that sounded like plates breaking. The two men were rolling on the ground, and even though Martin couldn't see the face, he felt enough hatred to know he was brawling with his new teammate Nils Jorgensen.

"Break it up!" Coach Dafoe shouted.

"Martin—" Ray was pulling him back.

"Get off him."

Half the Bruins yanked at Jorgensen, the other half pulled Martin. He felt his cheek, split and bleeding, already starting to swell. Someone was handing Jorgensen a towel, and the trainer went to get a few ice packs. Martin sat on one bench, Jorgensen across the way. Coach Dafoe stood between them, and the rest of the team circled around.

"Well, you boys get that out of your system?" he asked.

"He ambushed me!" Jorgensen complained.

"Just a warm Boston welcome, eh?" Martin said. "Can't you take it?"

"Nothing like a friendly icebreaker to start the season off right," Ray said, trying to make peace.

"I ought to fine you both," Coach Dafoe said. "But I'm in too good a mood. Boys, I'd like you all to look around. Take a deep breath and commit this moment to memory."

Martin felt the ice pack in his hand, and he held it to his cheek. He looked around the vast echoing space and saw shadows. He could taste the adrenaline, the aftereffects of the fight, and the anticipation of what Coach was about to say. Martin had sat through thousands of team meetings, and this one was charged with more electricity than he'd ever felt before.

"This is our moment," Coach said. "This is our shining moment. We're going all the way this year, boys. We're taking the Stanley Cup home."

"It's a good feeling," Jorgensen said. "Believe me, I know."

Martin felt the freight train in his chest, and he nearly crashed through Coach to knock the smugness out of the goalie's voice. Other Bruins booed, but a few laughed. Martin heard Ray chuckle, and he could almost see his friend shaking his head in that self-effacing way he had.

"Our greatest challenge," Dafoe went on, "as we have seen today, will not be the Edmonton Oilers. It will be ourselves."

"Him," Jorgensen spat. "Not me."

"Hockey is a sport of rivals, and you two have had one of the greatest competitions in history. When the books are written, kids'll be reading about the Cartier-Jorgensen rivalry long after you're both dead. The Knife versus the Sledgehammer. You'll be linked to each other more famously than you'll be to your wives."

"Just like Romeo and Juliet." Jack Delaney laughed.

Martin blinked. He made out the blurry shape of Nils Jorgensen, and he could taste the hatred. Jorgensen had ruined his vision, stolen his chance for two Stanley Cups. Listening to Coach say they'd be connected forever made Martin feel sick.

"So what I'm saying," Dafoe continued, "is that I expect you to put the past behind you. I don't care how you do it. Go into a field and fight till you knock each other bloody, go out on the ice and fire pucks at each other all day, go out to dinner with your wives and have a good time—hell, take them to the Ritz and charge it to me!"

"In hell," Martin muttered.

"Yes, for once I agree," Jorgensen said in his Swedish accent. "Hell will freeze over before we dine together."

" 'Dine together,' " Martin snorted, making fun of his prissy tone.

"Enough!" the coach yelled. "I've had about as much as I'm going to take from you. The both of you! Nils, welcome to the club. But when I give my players a suggestion, I expect it to be taken. And Martin, you know better. You're acting like a dumb kid, and you're not dumb and you're sure no kid. Do I have to tell you this might be your last chance to take the Cup?"

"You don't have to tell me," Martin growled.

"Getting old." Jorgensen chuckled.

"Hey!" Ray said warningly.

"The Ritz," Coach said thoughtfully. "I like that idea. Okay, men, listen up: This is what's going to happen. I'm making a reservation at the Ritz dining room, this Saturday night, table for four. To avoid controversy, I'll make it under my name: Dafoe. But I won't be there."

"You're kidding," Martin said.

"I'm not."

"Coach—" Jorgensen said.

"Shut up," Dafoe said. "A nice window table. You can look out over the Public Garden and bond over a nice bottle of Bordeaux. Maybe after dinner you can all take a ride in the swan boats."

"No way," Martin said.

"You two are going to be friends," Coach said. "Even if you don't know it yet. I have my doubts you'll manage on your own, so I've got to do my part. And I have great confidence in May and Britta. They've got the brains you two have knocked out of each other."

Martin stood. He knew May was waiting outside in their car, by

the players' entrance. His palms felt sweaty, and his stomach roiled.

"Shake hands," Coach Dafoe said. "We're going to get started practicing a week early, to all get used to each other, so shake hands."

Martin could feel the energy field across the bench. A thousand emotions were surging through his body, and he knew if he didn't get out of the locker room right away, he'd cause real damage. He began to walk away.

"I said shake hands!" Dafoe shouted.

Martin moved faster. He knocked into the end of the bench, then into someone's gear bag. Stumbling, he went down on one knee. He heard the silence as everyone watched him try to regain his footing.

"Got a problem?" Martin asked, glaring around the room. "What are you looking at?"

"Martin, man," one of the rookies said. "You okay?"

"No savoir faire," Jorgensen said, mocking. Martin stared over, saw the Swede standing there with his arm extended. Martin slapped it away.

"Cartier!" the coach barked.

Martin ignored him. With his name and his teammates' silence ringing in his ears, he left the locker room. He wanted to run, but he was afraid he'd fall. So he made himself slow down, move in a straight line down the hallway he knew so well. May was waiting outside. She had the car running and ready to go. Ray called his name, but Martin just kept going.

———

"What was that?" Ray asked when he called Martin later that night.

"I don't know," Martin said, not wanting to talk. He wouldn't have, but May had stuck the phone in his hand before he had the chance to say no.

"What's wrong with you?"

"Nothing. Why?"

"The way you were knocking into everything, acting like you were drunk. You weren't, were you?"

"You know me better than that. I don't show up to work drunk."

"And usually you're not an asshole to the coach. And the team."

"I'm sorry," Martin said.

"Look, I know the trade's a bitch. Getting used to Jorgensen won't be easy."

"He's an arrogant prick."

"Yeah, a real prima donna. Bragging about his endorsements and fame and fortune and what it's like to win the Stanley Cup two years running."

"From us," Martin said.

"Yeah, from us," Ray said. "But Coach is right about one thing—we have to put it behind us. Jorgensen's the best goalie in the NHL, and now he's ours. Look at it that way."

"That's hard," Martin said.

"Maybe so, but it's our best option." Ray paused. "You sure you're okay?"

"*Bien sûr,*" Martin said. "I'm great."

For support, May turned to Tobin. They talked on the phone five times a day, to make up for the fact that May was taking time off from work, that they weren't seeing each other all day at the barn.

"I'm so worried," May said. "He's completely isolated, won't talk to anyone. It's as if hc thinks everything will get better if he just sleeps through it.

"He's ashamed, I think," she continued. "That's the worst part. He didn't do anything wrong, but he's hiding out as if he can't face his friends."

"Just like when John lost his job," Tobin said.

"Sometimes I want to blame hockey," May said. "I see how rough it is, how they take their injuries for granted. I think about Serge and Agnes and wonder how they could have let him—Serge knew how bad it could be. He knew, Tobin."

"Like John and Michael in their race car," Tobin told her. "Believe me, I think about the possibilities. But fathers and sons . . . that's how they bond. How they communicate. Sometimes I think it's the only way they can say they love each other. In a sport so dangerous they know they could get hurt."

"Maybe," May said, and she could see Serge in prison, his face scarred from pucks and sticks, just like Martin.

"Your coach called again," May said, going upstairs to find Martin sleeping in the middle of the afternoon several days later. Just as she had told Tobin: All he did lately was crawl under the covers and hope the days would pass.

"Leave me alone," he said. "I'm tired."

"You've been sleeping for fourteen straight hours," May said, sitting on the bed. Thunder was asleep beside Martin's leg, and she had to push him aside. "You can't be tired."

Martin just rolled over.

"He reminded me we're having dinner with Nils and Britta Jorgensen on Saturday night. We're supposed to meet them at the Ritz at eight o'clock. Should I ask Aunt Enid if she'll stay with Kylie?"

"You know the answer to that," Martin said.

"He says it's an order."

"Tell him to fuck himself."

May checked her watch. It was nearly noon. Martin had an appointment with Teddy today at three. He had canceled the last two, and fifteen days had gone by since he'd started taking the cortisone.

"Teddy called," May told him. "She says she has to see you."

"Or what?"

"Or things will get worse."

"Do you really think they can?"

"For me," May said. "If you can't do it for yourself, don't you remember you promised you'd do it for me?" Placing her hand on his back, she began to rub in slow circles.

"I don't want to go."

"I know," she whispered, leaning over his back to kiss the side of his face. "But for me and Kylie. Do it for our family."

They walked into Boston Eye Hospital in the middle of the afternoon. Martin held May's arm, and she carefully steered him down the corridor. The guard called "Hello, Martin!" and various patients and doctors stared as he passed. One young boy wanted his autograph, and Martin silently gave it.

When they got to Teddy's office, May waited while Martin had his exam. Teddy was friendly, happy to see them; she didn't give

Martin a hard time for taking so long to come in, and for that May was very grateful. Martin was operating on a hair trigger, and anything could set him off, send him storming back to the refuge of his bed.

The exam was over quickly. May stood as Teddy beckoned her into the inner office, where Martin was already seated. Today Teddy looked very professional across the desk in her white lab coat. But in her inimitable style, she wore her white hair piled on her head and diamond earrings dangling from her ears. Her expression was filled with compassion, and May felt her own heart breaking.

"The cortisone isn't working," Teddy told them. "Not in the way we'd hoped."

"No," May whispered.

Martin stared straight ahead. He was so handsome, his blue eyes sparkling with life, and May had a sudden memory of falling in love with him: that very first day, when he had carried Kylie from the smoky plane.

"Complicated detachments, giant retinal breaks and traction detachments, sometimes require a different sort of treatment," Teddy said. "The best course being a vitrectomy." May listened, her head buzzing, as Teddy went on to describe the operation: removal of the vitreous humor, to evacuate the blood from his right eye—his good eye—before more retinal nerve damage occurred, in an attempt to save what sight remained.

"My left eye—" Martin said.

"There is nothing to be done for your left eye," Teddy told him gently.

"Will my right eye get better if I have the operation?" he asked.

"No."

May's eyes filled with tears. She was temporarily unable to see herself, and she heard Teddy gently push the box of tissues across the desk. Martin sat perfectly still. When May was able to see, she looked over at him. His back was so straight, and his face was full of courage. There wasn't a trace of fear in his eyes as he turned to May.

"I'm sorry," he said.

"Oh, Martin—" she replied, her voice catching.

"I'd like to schedule the operation as soon as possible," Teddy said.

"Okay," Martin agreed.

"Next Tuesday. First thing in the morning."

"That's fine."

May gathered her bag and jacket, listening to Teddy give Martin directions on where to go, how long to abstain from eating or drinking the night before. As she spoke, her kind voice full of confidence, May looked around the room.

William's lighthouse pictures shone down from the walls. May remembered when she'd first seen them, how their torches had seemed so full of hope and inspiration. Right now she knew Martin was entering the darkness, and she prayed for the strength to help him through whatever was about to happen. She closed her eyes and imagined a beam sweeping the horizon, showing them the way.

Chapter 27

B EFORE, HE HAD WANTED ONLY to sleep; now, Martin wanted nothing more than to stay awake. Holding May, he stared at her beautiful face, the curve of her body, the look in her eyes. Would he be able to feel her love if he couldn't see it?

Boston was a blur of lights. He stared into them, remembering the lake. He pictured the mountains, sharp against the sky. He saw thin, white moonlight spreading over the fields and barn, over Lac Vert itself. He thought of how Lac Vert moonlight was the most beautiful anywhere.

"What are you thinking?" May asked, coming to stand beside him.

"I don't want to lose it," he said. They were naked, facing each other. He gazed at the liquid light on her soft skin, and he took her face in his hands and kissed her deeply.

"Come to bed," she said, pulling his hand.

"I don't want to forget," he told her. "I want to remember it all."

"Remember . . ." she began, a question in her voice.

"How it all looks," he said, his throat aching. "How the world really is." He had fire inside, and he went to the bureau where he had laid his wallet, and began to ransack it for pictures. Natalie, Kylie, and May.

Staring at the photos, he couldn't make out the features. Already the faces were beginning to fade—he couldn't remember the shape of his daughter's face, the exact color of her hair and eyes, the way she could never hold back her smile.

"I can't see her," he said, panicked.

"Martin," May said, trying to hold him, but he pulled away.

He stared at his daughter's picture, every feature blurred. Bringing it close to his face, he couldn't make it come into focus. He felt terror run all through his body, and he knew there was no

escaping this. It was like falling through the ice, not being able to climb out. Freezing, suffocating, drowning. It was like being trapped in his own coffin.

"I can't see her face anymore," Martin said, shaking.

"I know," May said, her voice breaking. Martin could no longer recognize his own child. May didn't even try to console him. She couldn't, and Martin was glad she didn't even try.

On Friday, the day before he and May were supposed to go to the Ritz-Carlton, Martin phoned Jorgensen.

"What the hell do you want?" Jorgensen demanded.

"To talk," Martin said, his mouth dry.

"Can't you wait till tomorrow?"

"Forget dinner," Martin said. "Meet me at the Fleet Center."

"Where?" Jorgensen asked in disbelief.

"Your home ice," Martin told him. "In case you've forgotten."

The drive into Boston seemed to take forever. May was against the meeting, but she drove him anyway. They listened to the radio so she wouldn't be tempted to try to talk him out of it, and he wouldn't feel the need to defend his actions. When they got to the Fleet Center, he kissed her good-bye and grabbed his stick and skates from the backseat.

"Am I allowed to say be careful?" she asked.

"Not today." He grinned.

"I'll say it anyway."

"I'll do my best," Martin promised.

Although he and Jorgensen hadn't advertised their meeting, many of the other guys had somehow decided to show up. They milled around, saying hello as Martin suited up. Ray walked over, and Martin could feel his disapproval before he opened his mouth.

"Don't say it," Martin said.

"You're being a jerk," Ray said. "Whatever the hell you think you have to prove, put it aside. He's your teammate now."

"Maybe."

"No maybes about it. He's making more than anyone here, and the fans are in love with him. So suck it up and move on. You have your big dinner tomorrow night."

"There's not going to be any big dinner." Martin had pulled on his Bruins jersey for the first time that year, and now he finished lacing up his skates. He felt the rush he always felt before a game,

and it didn't matter that he couldn't see where he was going. On the ice he was king, he could skate blind. Hadn't his father always told him that?

But rising from the bench, he bumped right into Ray's arm.

"You're doing it again," Ray said.

"What?"

"Walking like you're drunk."

"Yeah, I had a few on the way over."

Ray was silent, shocked.

"Martin, he's waiting for you," Jack called.

"*Bien*, okay." Martin moved through the room on autopilot. The rubber flooring felt solid and eternal beneath the blades of his skates. Stepping onto the ice, he felt alive and powerful. The cold surrounded him, and once again he felt invincible. He flew down the rink, blind to anything in his path. But he knew he and Jorgensen were alone out there, that no one was going to get between them today.

"You ready?" Martin called as he flew past the goal.

"To kill you," Jorgensen yelled back.

"Try," Martin said.

He caught the blur of black and yellow, and he shivered to see his eternal enemy wearing the Bruins' colors. The two men had agreed to a private face-off, a sort of sudden death. Coach Dafoe had told them to go at it—in a field, on the ice, or at the dinner table. Well, there was only one place on earth Martin wanted to meet Nils Jorgensen, and it wasn't at the fucking Ritz-Carlton.

"You done sightseeing?" Jorgensen shouted.

"Just giving you a chance to back out," Martin called to the goaltender. He found his heart rate nice and steady. The ice felt like home to him; he loved to skate, and the feeling of his stick in his hand gave him pure confidence. He wasn't going to crash into anyone, and he wasn't going to miss. This was one-on-one, and Martin knew he could do it.

"Hey, Martin," Ray called, and Martin followed the sound of his voice.

"What?"

"Put your damn mask on."

"What are you, my mother?"

"No, you've got May to mother you. She's up in the stands watching. But do it anyway—"

"She's here?"

"Yeah, watching you from the nosebleed seats."

Martin didn't smile, but he sort of liked thinking of May watch-

ing him today. He felt as if he was on the edge of something, that this might be his last time skating on this ice. It was fitting his wife should be here to see it. Ray skated over to hand Martin his face mask, and with deliberation, Martin put it on.

Ray started the clock. Martin Cartier and Nils Jorgensen had ten minutes to show who was best. If Martin scored one goal, he would win. If Jorgensen shut him out, the goalie would prevail.

Dangerous from anywhere on the ice, today Martin Cartier was a sniper. He fired cannon shots from inside the blue line, nailing Jorgensen with all he had. Jorgensen refused to yield any goals, and Martin was determined to see that he did. The first minute was a slick blur. Martin came around again and again. Twice he drilled the puck straight at Jorgensen's head, and twice he was blocked.

He heard May call from the stands.

Martin steeled his spine and took a spin across the red line. His heart was pumping, and he remembered days on the ice with his father, practicing penalty shots until after dark. It was like that now, amid the glare of Boston's gleaming rink, shades of black blocking his sight. He clutched, nearly skating off the ice.

"You can do it!" May yelled.

"Come and get me," Jorgenson snarled.

Martin thought of his father, and he could hear him saying the same words on the vast mountain lake: *Come and get me.* His father had taught him everything he knew about competition. Hockey was a blood sport, and it could make bitter enemies of best friends, of father and son, if they were on the opposing team.

"Come and get me," Jorgensen shouted again, and this time Martin thought of their worst fight, Jorgensen's stick to the eye, his own shattered eye socket. He felt the howl beginning in his gut, and it roared out of his mouth as he started down the ice.

Martin Cartier advanced like a departing jet on the runway, achieving velocity he'd never experienced before, cocking his arm with blinding force. As he fired the puck toward a goal he couldn't see, he felt the sweet spot.

"Score!" Ray Gardner yelled a fraction of a second after the puck slammed past Jorgensen's glove. The small crowd broke into cheers, May's voice louder than anyone's.

Grinning, Martin pumped his fists in the air. His stick waved around, and he heard his teammates' skates clicking the ice as they came to greet him. Suddenly he was being swarmed, and he felt the panic of being unable to see. They were all around him, shaking his hand, punching his shoulder.

He hunched over, protecting himself from what he couldn't see. Ray gave him a bear hug, then skated off. The other guys zigzagged in front, trying to punch his fist with theirs in a salute of victory. Martin felt dazed by the motion, and he felt the rush as Jorgensen skated over. Activity ceased, and Martin could feel Jorgensen waiting for something.

"Okay, I'm extending my hand and you're still so fucking rude you won't shake? You won, is that what you want to hear?"

Martin heard his voice, but he couldn't see him.

"Martin . . ." came Ray's voice.

Turning toward where Jorgensen had spoken, Martin wheeled around, but the goalie had moved. Nervously skating around, he was everywhere, swearing about Martin's bad manners.

"Jorgensen," Martin said, putting out his hand.

"Yeah?" The goaltender stopped short.

Okay, Martin had him now. He had his back to the locker room, a halo of rink light silhouetting him from behind. Martin's hand was shaking as he moved forward. The goalie laughed, backing up, making Martin work harder just to shake his hand. Wanting it to be over, to get out of there, Martin put on the speed.

He crashed straight into Mark Esposito, who had crouched down to tie his lace. The men tumbled over each other, and when Martin looked up he couldn't see a thing. The rink was black, as if night had closed in on the lake, as if there wasn't a moon or a star to light his way. Mark scrambled to his feet, but Martin just sat there.

"Martin?" It was Ray's voice.

"Help," Martin heard himself say.

A hand came out of the darkness. Martin took it, felt himself pulled to his feet. Suddenly his skates felt unfamiliar, and he thought he'd lose his balance again.

"Steady, Cartier," came Jorgensen's voice, and Martin felt the goalie's arm around his waist. "You all right?"

"Yes, Martin," Ray said, standing so close Martin could feel his breath on his cheek. "Are you okay?"

"No," Martin heard himself whisper into the vast and empty darkness of the rink that had been his home.

⎯⎯

"How long have you known?" Genny asked the evening before Martin's surgery. The Gardners had come down to Black Hall, and

she and May were walking through the rose garden as the sun began to set.

"Most of the summer," May admitted.

"Why didn't you tell me?" Genny asked, hurt.

May thought about it. The breeze was chilly, and she had her hands in her jacket pockets. Autumn was just around the corner. She and Kylie had seen the first red leaves that morning, a crimson vine slashing through a pine tree behind the barn. Kylie would be starting school soon, and Martin would be recovering from surgery.

"I could say it was because Martin told me not to, but that's not the real reason," May said.

"Then what is?"

"Because I didn't want it to be true," May said. "That he's going blind. If I had told you, you'd have told Ray, and we'd have had to face that it was happening. We just wanted the summer . . . even with the accidents and the doctor's appointments, we just wanted the summer to last a little longer."

"I can't believe it," Genny said. "I love Martin, too, you know. I've known him my whole life. I can't imagine him not able to see."

"I know."

"He's an athlete, through and through. He can do anything in sports—there's no one like him. When we were kids, his father would coach us and tell us we were lucky to know Martin, that he was the best hockey player he'd ever seen."

"Serge said that? In front of Martin?"

"I'm not sure," Genny said. "But certainly to me and Ray and the others. Why?"

"Because I'm not sure Martin knows it," May said, her heart aching.

"Are they in touch at all?"

"Serge wrote a letter. Martin was furious I opened it."

"He would be."

The first stars had come out in the purple sky, and summer's last fireflies darted around the rose garden. May picked one perfect white rose to go with the one she had brought down from Lac Vert when they'd left two weeks ago. She placed it in her pocket and thought about tomorrow.

"Why do I think that if he would forgive his father he could open his eyes and see?" May asked her friend.

"Because you're a healing woman," Genny told her through tears. "You know how everything in life goes together. You've done so much to make him whole."

May gazed up at the stars, at the constellations she could see. She thought of the myths, of all the lovers separated by time and tragedy. "That's what I believe about marriage," she said. "That two separate people come together and make a whole. That's what Martin's done for me."

"Look how much you believe in love," Genny said. "You've made it your life's work."

"I know."

"You've helped Martin so much, more than you know. Let us help you, May. That's what friends are for."

"I always knew that." May embraced her friend as she let out a sob. She couldn't hold any of it inside anymore. "I just didn't want to believe we needed it. Oh, Genny—why can't summer go on? Why can't it last forever? Why does Martin have to go through this?"

———

At the hospital, May stayed with Martin for as long as they would let her before he was taken down to surgery. They held hands as she huddled over his gurney, waiting till the last possible minute. He was covered with a white sheet, and his arms and shoulders looked so strong and powerful, the rest of the scene seemed like a ridiculous joke.

Two orderlies moved in to take him away. They both were Bruins fans, and they promised they'd take excellent care of him. May thanked them, but Martin asked them to wait for just a minute more. Respectfully, they backed off and gave the Cartiers a moment of privacy.

"I feel like I'm going to the firing squad," Martin joked. "My mouth is so dry, I can't talk."

"Teddy's the best. Everything will be fine," May said, trying to believe it.

"No matter what happens," Martin said, staring into her eyes with an intensity that made May tremble, "I've loved every minute with you."

"And I with you," she said, confused about his meaning.

"Every minute." He smoothed back her hair, as if he wanted to see every inch of her face so he could store the memory of it forever.

"There'll be so many more," she told him.

When he closed his eyes, she realized that he didn't believe her.

"There will," she said.

"I know," he said without feeling. But suddenly he opened his eyes, and she saw that wonderful familiar glint. A smile started slowly and spread across his face. "I won, though. Didn't I?"

She must have looked blank because his grin kept getting bigger.

"I beat Jorgensen."

"And I was there," she said, trying to grin back.

⬤

Serge read about his son's eye surgery in the paper. Martin had suffered blunt trauma to the head and eyes, resulting in a detached retina and ophthalmia, leading to the operation he'd had on Tuesday.

"Jesus Christ," Serge said under his breath.

He read about Dr. Theodora Collins, the distinguished ophthalmologist from Harvard and the Boston Eye Hospital. He read how, by using the most sophisticated microsurgical techniques, she had performed a vitrectomy.

"Results vary greatly," she was quoted as saying. "Each case is different, and they cannot be generalized."

The paper went on to say that despite advancements in the field, the success of the surgery was unlikely. A surgeon from New York, one of Dr. Collins's former students, told reporters, "Many physicians would consider Martin Cartier's to be a hopeless case. But Teddy Collins is an innovator in the field. And a Bruins fan to boot."

The article concluded with a few quotes from Martin's coach and teammates: "We're praying for him," Dafoe said. "We want him back as soon as he's ready."

"There'll never be another Martin Cartier," Alain Couture, a young wing, said.

"No comment," said Ray Gardner.

"He was a great opponent, and I was looking forward to having him as my teammate," said Nils Jorgensen.

Serge crumpled up the paper and threw it against his cell wall. He sat on his bunk with his head in his hands for a long time. When the bell rang to go outside, he filed through the bleak corridor with fear in his heart.

Outside, the air felt crisp and fresh. It smelled like apples, the sharp scent drifting up the hill from all the orchards in the valley. Serge drifted over to the wall. It was too thick and high to imagine

getting past, but all he wanted was to escape and get to Martin. His son was suffering, and Serge couldn't help. He had at least another three years to go in this place.

Hearing the thump of a ball, his attention was drawn to the young boy standing outside the wall. It was Ricky, Tino's son, playing catch against the building. He wore his Yankees hat and dark blue jacket, and his face was streaked with mud. Serge noticed his grip, how he threw with a bend in his arm. Looking up at the sight of Serge, he smiled.

"You're not supposed to talk to me," Serge said gruffly.

"I know," the boy said, his dirty face shining.

"You need to extend your arm when you throw."

"Huh?"

"Like the pitchers do it," Serge said. "Like this," he said, demonstrating.

The boy did his best.

"One more time," Serge said. "But straighter."

Again the boy tried.

"Better," Serge said.

Encouraged, the boy flew after the ball and brought it back. He tried again, and damned if his form hadn't improved a little.

"Looking like a big-leaguer," Serge said. "Like Tino Martinez."

The boy grinned, and Serge went reeling back in years. He pictured Martin on the ice, beaming as Serge told him he'd be another Bobby Orr, Maurice Richard, Doug Harvey. Serge thought of his son now, and his chest tightened.

Ricky just kept playing, improving his throw with every try. Serge threw out comments and suggestions, keeping it up. He didn't know why, but coaching Tino's son was about as close as he could get to praying, to asking that Martin's sight be spared, that his own boy would get the chance to play again.

"Looking good," Serge said through the prison bars. "Looking real good, son."

Chapter 28

WHEN THE BANDAGES CAME OFF, Martin discovered that he could see less than before. Teddy had warned them of the possibility, but the reality sent shock waves through their home. Martin held his feelings inside most of the time, unwilling or unable to share any of them with May, and she missed their connection more than she could believe.

They moved back into Boston in September, so Kylie could start school. Martin spent his days sitting in the dark, staring into space. Whenever May would suggest a walk along the Charles, he would tell her to go alone. When Kylie had a spelling bee, he told her he was too tired to attend. Thunder was his most constant companion, sitting at his feet most of the time.

When hockey season started, it was the first time in fourteen years that Martin hadn't been playing professionally for one NHL team or another. He refused to listen to games or allow them on his TV. May offered to read him stories from the paper, but he shut her out. He told her hockey was part of his past, that she should know enough to leave it there.

The Gardners wanted to see him, but he said no. May would meet Genny for lunch or coffee, but always away from home. Martin didn't want anyone to visit, and although he forbade May from discussing the details of his recovery, in one case she went against his wishes.

"There's no improvement at all," May said. Tobin had come into Boston one early November day, and they rode their bikes along the river. Brown leaves rustled along the sidewalk, and the college crew teams slipped through the dark steel water in their sleek white shells.

"None?"

"He can't see us at all anymore. And he won't talk to anyone—

not even me. I can feel him wanting to drive me away." As she began to talk, the truth came pouring out. "He won't sleep with me. He stays in one room, I sleep in another. He tells me it's because his eyes hurt, but I know that's not it. It's because he doesn't want me."

"He must be in shock," Tobin said.

"So am I," May told her.

"Don't let him get away with it."

"I'm trying not to," May said. "But Martin's will is incredible. When he wants something, he makes it happen."

"So do you, May," Tobin said. "I know you, remember?"

They had been best friends a long time, and May knew her friend's words were true. Pedaling along, she reached out; they rode their bikes holding hands. The wind whipped up, making them pull their coats tighter around them.

"What do I do?" May asked.

"Make something happen," Tobin urged.

One December night, as the snow covered Beacon Hill, angels came tapping at Kylie's window, asking to be let inside. Kylie rubbed her eyes, thinking she was asleep. Thick snow blew across Louisburg Square—or was it something else?

Jumping out of her bed, she padded over to the window to see ghosts and angels flying through the snow. Her hands pressed against the mullioned window, Kylie felt the cold spread up her fingers into her body. The beings were moving so fast, calling out as they went by.

"What are you saying?" she called frantically, wanting them to stop.

And then she saw Natalie.

Kylie drew a sharp breath, her forehead leaning on the glass. The little girl hovered just outside their house, right outside the window. Kylie hadn't seen her in so long, but she would have known her anywhere. Natalie smiled and nodded, beckoning her to follow.

Feeling wide awake, Kylie watched all the angels disappear. They were there, and now they were gone. Had she been dreaming? Staring outside, she saw sparkles on the glass. It wasn't ice or snow, but something else. Kylie thought of the glitter she'd found in the closet at Lac Vert . . . Natalie's tears.

Which way had the angels been flying? Kylie looked across the

slate roofs, past all the brick buildings and white steeples of Boston. She gazed toward the Old North Church, and there she saw a great white cloud. It might have been more snow, or it might have been a flight of angels flying north: over the church, out of Boston, north to the land of mountains and lakes. Home to Lac Vert.

"Mommy!" Kylie yelled, tearing down the hall.

—

May stared at the blue diary. After so many months of leaving it untouched, she had just finished filling it with pages of Kylie's latest vision. Riffling through, May remembered how worried she had been at the beginning.

"The angels were flying to Lac Vert," Kylie had told her, wild with excitement. "They want us to follow them! Something's going to happen there."

"What, honey?" May had asked.

"I don't know," she'd said. "But I think it has to do with helping Martin."

It had taken a while for that to sink in. May remembered it now, along with the words Tobin had spoken on their bike ride in November: *Make something happen.*

For Christmas, the city of Boston was dressed in white lights. The Boston Bruins were having a mixed year, trying to recover from the loss of Martin Cartier. Mentally exhausted from the season so far, Ray had decided to take the family up to Lac Vert for the holiday. Usually the Cartiers remained in Boston until spring, but Kylie had gotten May thinking.

"Martin," she said. "I want us to go away for Christmas."

"Where?"

"Lac Vert."

Stony silence filled the room.

"Did you hear me?" May asked.

"The answer is no."

"But Martin—"

"No!" he shouted.

He sat in his chair by the window, doing what he did all day: nothing. Staring into the dark, growling at everyone who passed, banging into furniture as he tried to make his way to the bathroom.

Teddy had suggested that they hire a physical therapist, but Martin had refused. "No white cane, no dark glasses," had been his promise, and he was keeping it with a vengeance.

"How much do you love me?" she asked on Christmas Eve day.

He didn't reply. He lay still as their dog made a nest in the bunched-up bedclothes beside him. Thunder smelled of wet snow and the Charles River. He must have been dreaming of a good chase because he bayed in his sleep, one loud, long, and plaintive call. Waking himself up, Thunder looked from Martin to May.

"Tell me," she said. "Tell me how much?"

"May," he said. "Stop."

Sunshine poured through the bedroom window. It flashed in the mirror and burnished the maple chest and carved bed. Hitting May's diamond ring, it split into a million rainbows that danced across the ceiling. The dog watched the sparkles as if they were birds, as if he were considering chasing them.

Martin stroked the dog's back with big, broad hands, and he didn't blink when the sunlight hit him full in the face. May found that it hurt to talk.

"I can't stop," she said, taking Martin's hand from Thunder's back and holding it in her own. The dog ambled over to the window, and Martin's expression revealed that he felt betrayed by his friend. "Answer me."

"What's the question?" he asked bitterly. "I can't remember what you asked."

You don't listen to me anymore, May wanted to scream. *You don't care, you've given up on us, you've given up on yourself.* Instead she took a deep breath and repeated her question. "How much do you love me?"

"You know I love you," he said. "I love you enough."

"Enough to keep your vows?"

"Vows?"

". . . For richer, for poorer," she said. "In sickness and in health."

"May," he said, the anger building like steam in a geyser. "I'm the one who's blind. All right? I'm the one who's ruined, not you. If I want to set you free, then feel grateful you don't have to waste your life taking care of me. You must hate it; you're going to hate me, if you don't already. Leave, May."

The sun was extra bright that winter day, with no leaves on the oak trees to block the rays. Light flooded every inch of the room, showing the lines and scars on Martin's face. May glanced in the mirror and saw that she herself had aged: she saw starbursts of white lines around her eyes and mouth. They reminded her of how much

time she had spent smiling in the sun with Martin. He had given her a life she'd never known existed, beyond her wildest dreams.

Stunningly bright, sitting on top of Martin's bureau, was a big silver trophy. He had won many awards, cups, and trophies, but this particular one dated back to Martin's childhood—his first hockey trophy, won his first season skating as right wing on a team that played on mountain lakes in the Canadian woods. Sunlight exploded off the trophy, right into Martin's face.

"I want us to have Christmas at Lac Vert. Kylie needs it, and so do we. But I have to know. How much do you love me?"

Their bags were already packed, but Martin didn't know. He couldn't see. These weren't idle questions. May waited.

"Tell me," she said, her hands shaking.

He let out a sigh so violent, the dog exploded out of the room. "I will," he said. "I'll tell you. Are you sure you want to hear?"

"I'm positive," she said through chattering teeth. "Tell me."

"It's more than you can take," he said. "I'll bleed you dry, May. I'll take the life right out of you. I can't walk on my own, can't feed myself, can't get to the bathroom to take a piss."

"I don't care."

"You have to care! You didn't fall in love with a cripple!"

"No, I fell in love with *you*." May grabbed him and climbed onto his lap. Feeling his strong arms around her back was so unexpected—it had been so long—that she moaned into his neck.

"I'm not the same."

"Yes, you are, Martin."

He shook his head, and she could feel his sorrow and shame. "When I sit in here," he said, "and I can't see, I start thinking I don't exist. I feel you holding me right now, and I want to tell you I'm just a ghost. A shadow—you're holding air."

"I'm holding you," May said, kissing his neck, his forehead, his lips. "You're right here. You're real and alive, the same Martin Cartier you've always been. And you're taking me to Lac Vert. Right now."

"No," he said, but she could tell he didn't mean it. He wanted to go. She could almost hear the hope in his voice.

"Yes," she said. "I'm making it happen."

And so they went.

They arrived so late, Kylie had been asleep for hours. May had

worried about deep snow, about how they would get up their long driveway in the Canadian woods, but her concerns were put to rest. Genny had anticipated May's powers of persuasion, and Ray had plowed the drive and shoveled the walk.

Waking Kylie up, May had her walk inside on her own. It was little times like this—knowing that Martin would have carried her sleeping into the house—that made May long for how things had been. But she felt Martin take her arm, and leading him up the snowy path, she reminded herself to be grateful.

The house was warm and cozy. Genny had hung a wreath on the door, set up a small Christmas tree. Good friend that she was, she had left it undecorated for Kylie to do later. She had also left a basket of fresh home-baked muffins and a jar of ginger jam for Christmas breakfast.

Snow had fallen during the last few days, covering everything outside with a thick mantle of white. May wished there was a moon, so she could see the mountains and lake, but all she could see was one bright star in the sky. It hovered just over the northern hills, glinting in the dark blue night.

Kylie peered out at the lake, scanning with purpose.

"Are they here?" she asked.

"Who?" Martin asked.

But Kylie didn't reply. Still looking for the angels she'd followed north from Boston, she stepped off the path into deep snow, wanting to run down to the lake. May had to lift her up, carry her into the house.

"They didn't come," Kylie cried. "I was wrong."

"Wait till morning," May advised. "I'm so happy we're here, and it was all your idea."

"It was?"

"Yes." May kissed her good night, tucking her under the warm winter quilt. May was exhausted from the long drive. She wanted to sit up, smell the evergreens Genny had left and feel the peace of their home, but she couldn't keep her eyes open. Martin and Thunder were sitting downstairs in the living room.

"Who didn't come?" Martin asked when he heard her enter. "What was Kylie talking about?"

"A dream she had last week," May told him. "Of old ghosts."

"Too many of those here," Martin said bitterly. "We shouldn't have come."

"Maybe you'll feel differently tomorrow," May said.

He grunted. That might have been because he was still trying

to drive May away, or it might have been weariness from the long drive. Kissing her husband hard on the lips, May chose to believe the latter. "Come to bed soon, okay?" she asked. He didn't answer, and May didn't press.

———

Martin didn't know how much time had passed. Had he fallen asleep? If so, what had woken him up? His mother's clock ticked across the room. His elbow leaned on the small pine table, a gift from his father's grandmother in Alberta. Had something happened to May or Kylie?

Kylie's dream of old ghosts . . . it had somehow entered Martin's head, and he realized he'd been dreaming of the past. Other Christmases, long ago, in this same house. The sound of his mother's knitting needles clacking, the feel of a baby in his arms.

"Natalie," he said out loud.

Something moved across the room. A skirt swishing along the floor, an animal brushing past the table. He leaned forward with a start. Listening intently, he heard only the sound of his own heart beating. Or was that Thunder's tail thumping on the floor?

"Who's there?" he asked.

Thunder let out a small whimper. It sounded like fear, and when he did it again, Martin knew for sure there was someone else in the room.

"Who it it?" Martin asked again.

"Look at me," came the voice.

Martin was dreaming. He shook his head, thinking of ghosts again. He hadn't heard that voice in many years. Kylie's gift for dreaming of the dead had rubbed off on him, and he strained himself listening. The lightness of it, the sweetness and joy. He knew her voice as if it hadn't been silent all these years, as if she had never died.

"I'm dreaming," he said, wanting never to wake up.

"You're not," Natalie whispered.

"I have to be; this can't be real."

"But it is. Go on—look at me."

"I'm blind."

"Daddy," she said.

"I can't see you," he said. "Even in my dream."

Then he felt her fingers on his face. She must have touched him hundreds of times in her lifetime—grabbed his nose or ears,

tickled his chin, rubbed his scratchy beard with her tiny hands—
and he would have known the feeling anywhere.

"Open your eyes," she said.

And Martin did, and he saw. His daughter stood before him,
dressed in white, gazing into his eyes.

"Oh, my sweetheart," he said, feeling the tears come to his
eyes.

Her dress looked like a child's first communion dress, and she
had wings that glimmered when she moved. Her face was radiant,
as if she couldn't believe they were together again. Stretching her
arms out, she stepped forward.

"How have I lived without you?" he asked. He reached for her,
but she backed away.

"The same way I've been without you," she answered.

"I miss you so much," he whispered, his voice breaking.

"Too much, I think."

"That's impossible," he said. "You're my beautiful child. My
life changed forever the day I lost you."

"Daddy, it changes every day. That's what life is. A million
changes, one right after another."

Thunder bayed, waddling over to stand by Natalie. Glancing
down at the dog, Martin raised his eyes back to the girl. She returned his gaze, as if she knew what he was thinking.

"Archie," she said.

"I should have let you have that dog," he said, his eyes flood-
ing with tears. "It was so little to ask. I think of it every day."

"But you let Kylie have Thunder," Natalie said. "Do you know
that when you let her keep him, it was like giving Archie to me?
You gave us a second chance."

"I don't understand."

"I think you do," she whispered, sounding too wise for the tiny
girl she had been.

"I loved you so much," he wept.

"Don't say 'loved,' Daddy," she said. "Love never dies."

"I never thought I'd see you again."

"I had to show you," she said. "That love never dies."

She reached out her hand and he started to take it. She pulled
back slightly and said words that chilled his heart. "This will be the
end. Once I hold your hand, I'll never be able to come back again.
This will be my last night on earth."

"No, Natalie," he started to say. But he couldn't seem to stop
himself. He took his daughter's hand, just as he had when she was

alive. He hugged her tenderly, not believing it could ever end—no matter what she said. "Tell me what to do. Anything, Natalie. I'll do anything."

"Get our skates and mittens, Daddy. Will you, please?" she said—and in her voice he recognized his own and his father's before him—things kids had said to parents here at Lac Vert for generations. So Martin went to the kitchen shed and grabbed his old brown skates and Kylie's new white ones. He took his mittens and a jacket from the mudroom.

They walked out into the cold night, Thunder galloping after them. Natalie led the way down the snowy path, straight toward the lake. They stopped in the gazebo to lace up their skates. One section of the surface was clean, as if Ray had plowed it, and following Natalie, Martin skated onto the ice. They held hands, flying up the lake.

The night was so dark, with just one bright star piercing the velvet sky. Was he blind or could he see? Holding his daughter's hand, he forgot to care. They skated north over the fishing hole where he had spent so much time with Kylie these last two summers, and he ached to think of how poorly he had treated her recently.

"I sent her to you," Natalie said, as if she could read his mind. "I knew you needed a daughter to love. Kylie was the one; she could see and hear me, and she helped me to find you again. See, Daddy, this night is as much for me as for you."

"How, Nat?"

"I need to find a way to say good-bye."

"Sssh," Martin said.

They passed the island, skated around it, and came to what Martin remembered as the Green Cove. This was where he and Ray had learned to play the game of hockey. Martin remembered his father setting up a goal of pine branches, teaching Martin, Ray, and Genny to shoot with precision and power and accuracy.

Suddenly, as if his vision had not only returned but become extrasensory, Martin could see them all playing. A dark winter day thirty years ago, with the light dying and night falling, his father shouting out commands and encouragement. The look in his father's eyes! Martin stared with disbelief: It was bright with love, with adoration for his only son.

"He left us the next year," Martin said.

"It hurts to be left," Natalie said.

"I hate what he did to you." As Martin said the word "hate," the scene disappeared, and he was back to the present, in this dark

night of Christmas thirty years later. Natalie shimmered beside
him, holding his hand.

"He hates it, too," Natalie said. "He would never have done it
on purpose, not for anything in the world."

"Forgive me," Martin whispered. "For leaving you with him,
for not being able to protect you. Please forgive me, Nat."

"I don't need to, Daddy," she said.

"I can't believe that."

They began to skate home, very slowly, and Martin felt fear
and dread growing in his chest. She'd be leaving soon. The dream
would end, and Natalie would be gone and he would be blind
again. When they were in sight of the house, they saw Thunder
waiting on the ice.

"Don't go," he whispered. "Never leave me again."

She didn't reply, but held his hand tighter. He remembered her
baby days, when he had skated with her in a backpack all the way
up to Ray's house, just to show her off.

"It's almost time," she said.

"Don't say that."

"I have to know what you know," she said. "It's the reason I
came back, that I've been among the living."

"What I know?" he asked, confused.

"You're my father," she said solemnly, "but I've learned some
things that most people, even adults, don't learn until—"

"Until it's too late," Martin said, guessing her last words.

And then her voice filled the air with a sweetness so piercing it
brought tears to his eyes: "The truth."

Listening, Martin trembled, feeling the bitterness in his heart
suddenly give way. It broke like a dam, pouring out of him like a
river.

"You saw, didn't you, Daddy?" Natalie asked. "Back there, at
the old goal?"

"I saw my father," Martin said, his voice breaking. "Me and my
friends, when we were young."

"Not just who," Natalie said tenderly. "But what?"

"Love." Martin answered, again picturing the look in his father's eyes. He held the word in his mind, a thousand images filling
his sight: his mother's arms, his father's eyes, May's embrace,
Kylie's constant warmth.

"Prisons don't all look alike," Natalie told him. And her words
were so deep, Martin had to look twice to make sure it was really
her. A huge icicle fell from the barn roof; it crashed and tinkled,

and the falling ice became the sound of bells. The bells rang loudly, and Thunder bayed.

"Prisons don't all look alike," Natalie said again, as if the words were very important. She was crying, but she had an expression of love and happiness on her face. When she kissed Martin, he saw her tears sparkling on his skin, and remembered that summer night when Kylie had left glitter on his cheeks.

"My darling child," Martin said.

"Go see your father," Natalie said.

Martin felt himself nodding, agreeing to something he didn't quite understand. Natalie threw herself into his arms, and he hugged her with everything he had. His heart was pounding, and he knew that although he never wanted to let her go, it was the only way she could ever be free.

"I love you forever, Daddy," she said. "Tell Kylie thank you."

"Nat . . ."

"For everything. Everything!"

"Natalie . . ." he whispered.

But she was gone. The ice bells were still ringing, and the first light of Christmas morning began to fill the sky. It was dark gray, but as Martin stared it turned silver. The star hung low over the hills, and Thunder bayed until his voice was hoarse.

Still seeing clearly, Martin walked back into the house. He wanted Natalie to be waiting inside, but she wasn't. He looked all around the room, and his gaze fell on the old embroidery picture his mother had done before he was born.

She had made it for Martin, with her husband still at her side. Martin stared at the animals, at peace in the manger, and at the words: "The wolf shall dwell with the lamb, and the leopard lie down with the kid, and a little child shall lead them."

Martin had been that little child once, and then Natalie, and now Kylie. She had been trying to lead him all along. His eyes filled with tears, and he looked around the familiar room for the last time. He went to the window, to be gazing at the lake when it happened.

When the sun came up, it turned the world light even as Martin's sight went dark again, but he was ready.

Blindly, he felt his way up the stairs. The banister showed him the way, even though he knew every step by heart. May stirred when he climbed into bed beside her. His hands and feet were cold from his trip up the lake, and her body felt so warm beside him.

"I love you," he whispered to his sleeping wife. "I love you."

"I love you, too," she whispered back.

"Something happened," he said. "Just like Kylie said it would."

"What?" she asked, trying to wake up.

But Martin wasn't ready to tell her yet. He felt the pounding of his heart, remembering the trip he'd just had, up the lake with his daughter. He had another journey to make, and he wanted his family to make it with him. But right now he wanted to rest and remember.

So they fell asleep together until Kylie woke them up, calling Merry Christmas at the top of her lungs.

Chapter 29

ANOTHER CHRISTMAS PASSED IN ESTONIA without word from Martin. Serge had just about given up on hearing from him. He lay in his bunk, arms folded behind his head, staring at the concrete walls. Reading no longer distracted him. He hadn't worked out for several weeks now. What was the point in keeping his body healthy and fit? He had started wishing only to die.

When he went out into the yard, he stayed far away from the west gate. Since winter had hit hard, Ricky hardly ever came anymore. Serge felt a combination of emotions about that fact: He worried when he didn't see the boy, and he felt defeated when he did. The guards were probably right. What chance did a kid like that have? His father's legacy had been drugs and violence.

Sometimes Serge remembered his conversations with Tino and recalled the young man's pride in his son. It had been so disgustingly similar to Serge's own. How many years had passed—throughout so much of Martin's youth—with Serge promising that next week he'd visit, next month he'd bring Martin out to Detroit or L.A. or wherever the next game was?

He would show Martin's picture to his teammates, tell them what a great son he had. He carried a lock of Martin's baby hair, and it had been his lucky charm at the casinos: He would pat his pocket before rolling the dice, and he had sworn it brought him luck.

But it hadn't brought him family.

The day they had come to the apartment and hurt Natalie, Serge had touched his lucky charm—as if a lock of hair meant more than a living child. Thinking of Natalie, Serge bowed his head. Christmases were the worst for that. He was haunted by regret and sorrow, by all the things he had left undone and unsaid.

Serge had chased his son away on his own. Wherever Martin

was, whatever he was going through, Serge had deprived himself of the opportunity to help. He could love Martin from afar, but Martin was too smart to open a door to his father.

Now, standing in the prison yard, he happened to glance over at the gate. The boy was there. Wearing a too-thin baseball jacket, throwing his ball into the air and catching it again, he was checking to see whether Serge saw.

Serge narrowed his eyes—the sun was bright on the piles of dirty snow. He watched the kid's form: much better, as if he'd been practicing his throw. To see better, he took a step closer. The boy pretended not to notice, but he put on a little extra power as he fired the next one.

Little kids had no business hanging around a prison, Serge thought bitterly. Bad things happened around bad men—just look at Natalie.

"Where's your mother?" Serge asked.

Ricky didn't answer, but just kept throwing.

"It's cold out here. You should be home where you belong."

The boy shrugged. Serge noticed his grimy face, his filthy sneakers. He'd been walking through mud and rain and snow since summer in those things. His glove was the same old one, his baseball was brown. No one had combed his hair that day.

Serge cared about him, and that was a sorry state of affairs. Look what had happened to the last child he had been left in charge of. Thinking of Natalie, Serge tensed up all over.

"Go home," he called to Ricky.

Ricky stopped playing, shocked by Serge's tone of voice.

"Find somewhere better to go. You want a teacher, a coach. Not a bunch of criminals. Hear me?"

Ricky's mouth was set tight, his eyes wide.

"I'm a killer, kid. You don't want me telling you how to throw a ball, and your father's not here. He's gone from this place, got that? Go find a coach. Go to school, Ricky. Right now—"

As the boy's eyes filled with tears, he began backing away. He stumbled over his dirty sneakers and dropped his ball. It rolled over to the gate, and as he crouched down to pick it up, his hand nearly touched Serge's shoe. Looking up, his terrified eyes met Serge's.

"Go," Serge said.

And the boy grabbed his ball and ran away.

A long row of icicles hung along the cell block's western wall, and a sudden gust of wind blew them off. They crashed to the pave-

ment, tinkling one after another, sounding to Serge like church bells.

Watching Ricky disappear down the hill, he held the bars and listened to the bells. They reminded him of home, of the old church in Lac Vert, of how the mystical bells would peal at Christmas. They would play carols and hymns. Serge had listened to them with his wife and son, sitting in their pew on Christmas morning, celebrating the birth of the child.

Serge should have done more of that, he thought now: celebrated the children of his life. He had scared Ricky away, and he was glad. He hoped the boy wouldn't come back.

―

Something had come over Martin. May didn't know what it was, but she gave thanks from the bottom of her heart. On Christmas morning, he had climbed into her bed. After months of staying away, he wanted to hold her, whisper to her, make love to her body and spirit.

He had held her so tenderly. She had listened to him whisper how wrong he'd been, how much he loved her, that Kylie was right and something had happened. May had whispered back: "What happened, Martin? Tell me."

"We're in this together," Martin had replied, but that was all he'd say.

And for the next few days, that is what happened: Suddenly, they were in it together. No Christmas present could have made her happier. Martin had asked her for help in taking a bath, getting his clothes. He had let her tie his shoes. When he bumped into a chair, he had asked her to help him make the way clearer. At breakfast, he had asked her to show him where everything was on the table.

May had guided his hand.

"Your coffee, your plate. Muffins in a basket."

"Butter," Kylie had said, carefully pushing the covered dish closer. "And here's a knife . . ."

They had decorated the tree. Genny had gone into the attic and brought out old cardboard boxes filled with Agnes's ornaments. Sitting back, Martin had listened to Kylie describe them to him: "A red ball with a glitter snowman, a gold reindeer, four white snowflakes."

"Are they paper?"

"Yes."

"I made those in second grade."

Kylie had hung them right in front, in a place of honor. She had found ornaments shaped like hockey skates, a puck, and a stick. There were six tiny crystal angels. But the ornament that captured her attention most was one small silver bell.

Made of papier-mâché, it had rough edges and a sideways tilt. Kylie examined it inside and out. She saw that the artist had painted it with garlands of green, signed it with the initials "N.C." When Kylie held the bell over her head, it rang with a distinctive twang.

"Natalie's bell," Martin said.

"I can tell," Kylie said. "She painted her initials on it."

"She sent it to me when she was five," Martin told her. "I missed that Christmas with her."

"Where was she?"

"With her mother, far away from here." Martin was smiling slightly.

"You saw her, didn't you?" Kylie asked. "She was here."

"She was here," Martin said.

May couldn't breathe. Martin's eyes were shining, as blue as she had ever seen them, as if he could see everything in the room and beyond. And Kylie could barely hold herself still.

"What did she say?" Kylie asked.

"She told me you were right all along. That—"

"You believe me?" Kylie asked him, the words tearing out. "That I really saw her, I wasn't making it up?"

"Yes, I believe you," Martin told her.

May's gaze fell on the blue diary. She could write this down, add Martin's experience to the pages. Instead, she looked over at Martin and Kylie, at a father who needed a daughter and a daughter who needed a father.

"What's wrong, Mom?" Kylie asked when she saw May's face.

"I'm sorry," May said, wiping her eyes. "I wish I'd seen her, too. I'd like to see Natalie."

"I wish you had," Martin said, holding out his hand until she took it.

May watched Kylie ring the old bell, laughing at the funny click it made—the clapper was a twisted paper clip, the bell itself formed of old newspapers soaked and painted. But when she stopped, the strains of a different bell drifted through the window.

The sound of bells pealed brightly across the hills and lake.

They echoed off the mountains, whispering through the bare
branches of sycamores, maples and oaks, through the soft boughs
of tall dark pines. They rang over the ice, amplified by the lake's
deep holes and softened by its shallow coves.

"Listen!" Kylie said.

"What is that?" May asked.

"The bells of Sainte Anne," he said.

"Playing a Christmas carol," May said, listening to the clear
tones. But she was wrong; it wasn't a carol, but a hymn, and Martin recognized it before she did.

"'Amazing Grace,'" he said.

"How sweet the sound," May whispered. She remembered the
words. They had sung the hymn at her father's funeral, and she'd
never forgotten it: "That saved a child like me; I once was lost, but
now I'm found, was blind but now I see."

They listened for a few minutes more, until the bells stopped
and the only sound was icicles rattling in the trees. A gust of wind
blew off the frozen lake, swirling down the chimney. Thunder
jumped up to investigate, his tail wagging as he stood by the fire
screen. May shivered in the breeze, in anticipation of what was
coming.

Whatever she was expecting, it didn't come from outside. Martin pushed himself up out of the chair. May and Kylie watched him,
wondering what he was about to do.

"Is there a star in that box?" he asked.

"Yes." Kylie reached inside the carton of ornaments. She
pulled out a bent and battered cardboard star, covered with foil
and painted with red and gold glitter. The sparkles came off on her
fingers as she held the star aloft.

"C'mere," Martin said, bending down as he opened his arms.

Kylie knew just what to do. She slung one arm around his neck,
holding the star in her other. Martin lifted her up, stepping toward
the tree. Holding his hand, May guided him closer, until he could
feel the branches and know where he stood. She watched Kylie
examine the star, looking for a signature.

"Natalie made it?"

"I did," Martin said. "With my father, a long, long time ago.
When I was about your age."

"He helped you?" Kylie asked.

"Yes."

Then, hoisting Kylie even higher, Martin leaned forward so she
could place the star on the tree's uppermost branches. Kylie made

sure to secure it in place. Martin didn't flinch, letting her take as much time as she needed. When she had finished, she said, "Okay," and he let her down.

"How does it look?" he asked.

"Perfect," May said.

"He helped me," Martin said again.

"You did a good job together," May said. "It's a perfect star."

"I'd like to see my father."

May's heart pounded, and she felt Martin take both her hands. "On the way back home," he said. "Do you think it would be too far out of the way to take the New York Thruway? We could stop at the prison, then take the Connecticut Turnpike home."

"I don't think it would be too far out of the way," she said steadily.

"No," Martin said, as if he had a road map spread out before him. "I don't think it would, either."

Chapter 30

CLOSING UP THE LAKE HOUSE, May went back inside for a minute because Martin had forgotten his bag. There it was, right by the door. May walked through the rooms, making sure she had left the heat on low to keep the pipes from freezing. The truth was, she needed this time to herself, to prepare herself for leaving.

For several moments, she stared down the snow-covered yard to the gazebo. She could picture that summer day, with her and Martin surrounded by Kylie and their friends and family: their tribe. They had tried to elope, but how could they, when they had people who loved them so much?

During her long years alone with Kylie, when May felt that love had failed her, she had never stopped believing in it for other people. She had watched her mother, grandmother, and aunt plan the weddings of women in love. She had stood up for Tobin, watched her best friend's family grow; but deep down, no matter what Tobin said, May had never expected such things for herself.

Then she had met Martin. Saying her wedding vows had been the biggest promise she'd ever made. She had meant them then, and she meant them even more now, when they counted most. Martin needed her; even more, she needed him.

She reached into the big pocket of her wool jacket and pulled out the blue notebook. Sometimes she was tempted to send it to Ben Whitpen, let him keep it in his research file, so she'd never have to see it again. But May knew that it held their story. If Kylie never had another vision, never recounted another dream, May knew that every page in the diary led up to this moment.

She opened it, read a few words, and felt her heart break open to her husband and their two daughters, to love and confusion, to the mystery of it all. Her daughter had seen through the veil,

listened to the dead, shown them how not to be afraid. May thought of Richard Perry with gratitude, and she thought of Natalie Cartier with love.

Now, May lifted Martin's bag by the door. That's what a married couple does, she thought: love each other through sickness and health; for richer, for poorer; in good times and bad. They love each other's children and try to honor each other's parents—even when the whole thing seems impossible.

Through it all, they carry each other's bags. And so, slinging the strap over her shoulder, May locked the door of their lake house and carried her husband's bag out to the car. December's sunlight was thin and pale, and she knew that the next time they came, the summer light would be back, filled with gold, pollen, and hope.

They were on their way.

Somewhere during the week between Christmas and New Years—he had lost track—Serge was lying on his bed, listening to hockey on the radio. Boston was playing New Jersey, and they were losing 4–2.

"You need Martin," Serge said out loud.

The Devils were playing great, in a zone where they could do no wrong. The Bruins, on the other hand, were missing shots, allowing goals, throwing the game away. It gave Serge a small, wicked satisfaction to know the Boston club was struggling without his son.

"Visitors, Cartier," the guard said, stopping by his cell door.

"Funny," Serge said. "Go screw yourself."

"Okay, fine," the guard said, starting to walk away. "But you'll be sorry. The kid's cute."

Serge felt a chill go down his spine. Who could it be? Deciding it would be easier to go see than wait and wonder, he climbed off his bunk and followed the guard down the long hall.

His stomach flipped, as if he had eaten something bad. His palms were sweaty, his jaw tightly clenched. Serge Cartier hadn't been this nervous in a long time. He didn't know what he was going to find, and stepping into the unknown felt terrifying.

Maybe it was someone he owed money to.

Maybe it was one of his old running buddies, one of the few who hadn't written him off.

Maybe it was Tino's son.

Or maybe . . . Serge wouldn't even let himself think it.

Martin sat in the visitor's room, with May on one side and Kylie on the other. He was aware of clanging doors and shuffling feet, the smells of food, smoke, and sweat. Something about the place reminded him of certain locker rooms he'd been in, vast concrete caverns echoing with violence and aggression.

"Kylie, you okay?" he asked.

"I'm fine," she said.

"I wonder where he is?" May asked.

Martin nodded. Maybe they should have told his father they were coming. Or perhaps they shouldn't have come at all. His heart was racing, his nerves on fire. This was probably the biggest mistake he'd made in years. Visiting his father had seemed like such a good idea back in Lac Vert, but right now it felt like sentimental stupidity.

But Martin had promised Natalie. Not for one minute had he doubted their time together, dismissed it as a dream. He had seen his daughter. She had restored his vision in a way Teddy Collins, the greatest doctor in Boston, never could. Natalie had shown him things locked deep inside, the secret to life he had been missing all along.

And so, when the inner door opened and Martin's father walked into the room, Martin felt his presence although he could not see him.

Standing tall, Martin said, "Dad."

"Martin," Serge said.

They stood several feet apart. Other prisoners sat nearby, talking to their wives, playing with their kids. Martin could hear their voices buzzing, but the words faded into the background. Much louder, almost like the beat of a drum, was his father's breathing.

"I'm glad to see you," Martin said.

"Oh, son," his father said, and he grabbed Martin in a hug. A guard came forward to push them apart, but Serge wouldn't let go. Martin felt his father's strong back with his hands, and he remembered being lifted and carried as a child.

"Dad, I know you've met May—"

"Hi, dear," he said.

"Serge, I'm glad to see you."

"Mommy likes your postcards," Kylie told him.

"Well, that's good," Serge said. "That makes me happy."

They talked for a while, about Christmas at the lake, holiday food, life at the prison, traffic in downtown Estonia, and Kylie's school. His father asked whether she liked sports, and Kylie said figure skating, swimming, and fishing.

"Fishing on Lac Vert," Serge said. "Is that big old brown trout still there?"

"The great-granddaddy," Kylie said.

"Must be the great-granddaddy's great-grandson by now," Serge said. "Boy, I remember how he used to hide out under that flat rock, poking his old trout nose out just far enough so I could see him laughing at me."

"Saying 'you can't catch me!' " Kylie added.

"That's the truth of the matter," Serge said. "The simple truth. No one'll ever catch him."

"I have a dog," Kylie boasted.

"Yeah? What kind?" Serge asked.

"A basset hound. Named Thunder. His brother died."

"His brother wasn't named Lightning, was he?" Serge asked, making Kylie squeal, reminding Martin of what a funny and present grandfather Serge had sometimes been, how Natalie had loved him.

"He was!" Kylie breathed. "How did you know?"

"Intuition," Serge said, and Martin could almost see him tapping his head.

"Wow," Kylie said.

"Yeah, Martin has it, too. That's what makes him a great hockey player."

"Dad," Martin said, wanting to steer the conversation anywhere but there.

"He had it even as a little kid," Serge said, not getting the hint. "Brilliant at any sport he played. I knew he'd go straight to the top. He had a real love of the game." Martin opened his mouth to change the subject, but his father shifted it on his own. The conversation turned to some kid Serge had seen around, the son of a man who had died in prison.

"The boy loves baseball, just like you did," Serge said. "With a passion."

"Why does he come here," Martin asked, "if his father died?"

"Because this is the closest he can get," Kylie whispered in his ear, sending a shiver down Martin's spine.

"He makes me think of you." Serge's voice was low and rough. Martin felt his father take his hand, and he had to fight the urge to pull back and run as fast as he could.

"Well, playing sports, I guess," Martin said.

"More than that," Serge said. "It's the way he plays his heart out."

Silence fell on their little group, and after a few moments, May said she thought she'd take Kylie for a walk. She thanked Serge for his cards, and for seeing them. Then Martin heard his father kiss her cheek, and he felt May's hand on his shoulder. "I'll be right outside," she whispered.

"Good girl," Serge said when she had gone.

"She's the best," Martin agreed.

But without May and Kylie, there seemed to be nothing to say. The two men found themselves back to small talk: the cold weather, tomorrow's forecast, hockey. Martin tensed when his father mentioned listening to the game on the radio just before, but he found himself actually curious about the score. He hadn't heard a Bruins score all year, and he was disappointed to learn they were down 4–2 after one and a half periods.

"They need you, son." Then, as if he'd realized what he'd said, he drew in a deep breath. "I'm sorry, Martin."

"Yeah, well," Martin began, lowering his head.

"Martin, you deserve—"

Martin cut him off. "I have an excellent doctor. She's doing all she can. It's not easy, but being with May makes it better. I can be a real jerk to her sometimes."

"Cartier men are good at that," Serge said.

"Speak for yourself," Martin heard himself say, the edge of his voice razor sharp.

"You're right," Serge said. "I had no right to say—"

"I'd never leave her," Martin said. "Or Kylie. Never again. I'd never forget about them while I lived my life, going wherever I wanted, spending money as fast as I made it."

"In Vegas," Serge said. "L.A., New York, Chicago."

"While they lived alone at the lake, hungry and cold half the time."

"No, you wouldn't do that."

"And I wouldn't put my little girl in danger," Martin said, feeling his chest tighten. The aggression was building inside, and although he couldn't see his father, he had the urge to knock his head off. "I wouldn't let her be hurt."

"I did that," Serge whispered. "I know I did. God, Martin—I'm sorry. I'm so sorry, I wish I could trade my life for hers. Do you know that? Do you think I'm kidding?"

Martin bowed his head, shaking so hard he thought he'd come apart. But then he saw Natalie's face, heard her voice telling him Serge hated himself more than Martin ever could, that there was more than one kind of prison.

"Martin," Serge begged. "Answer me."

"I know you're not kidding." Martin wiped his eyes.

"I'd die myself," Serge said. "If she could live. I have, in my mind, a thousand times. I don't suppose that will ever stop."

"Make it stop," Martin said.

"I can't," his father said, raw with grief.

Martin took a deep breath. His eyes were open wide, though he couldn't see a thing. "I forgive you, Dad."

Serge broke down. He cried while Martin listened, feeling his own heart beat hard in his chest, tears rolling down his own cheeks. Martin saw his daughter's face, felt the ice beneath his skates as they flew over the lake, witnessing that scene from the past. He saw his father's eyes as clearly as if his vision were perfect, and he remembered the childhood excitement of spending time with the father he had loved so much.

"Forgive yourself, Dad," he said.

Serge blew his nose, and some of the prisoners laughed.

"Natalie would want you to."

"I've always known that," Serge said after a moment. "She was an angel, one in a million. But knowing you hated me, well, that made it kind of hard. Not that I ever blamed you for a minute."

"I don't hate you anymore," Martin said.

"Thank you, son."

"May's done that for me. I'm lucky, Dad."

"I know you are."

"When do you get out?"

"Three years," Serge told him. "That's okay, though. It'll make it easier being here knowing how you feel."

They sat quietly for a few minutes, listening to people talk around them. There were young kids visiting their fathers, fathers visiting their sons, wives with their husbands, sisters talking to their brothers. Martin let the conversations wash over him, knowing he was where he belonged. When the guard announced visiting hour was over, Martin felt a deep pit in his stomach.

"I'm glad you came," Serge said.

"I'll come again," Martin promised.

"Can I do anything?" Serge said. "I'd give you my eyes if I could."

"Thanks," Martin said, trying to smile.

"I meant what I said to Kylie. You were great, Martin. *Great.*"

"Not great," Martin said. "I never won the Stanley Cup."

"You think that matters?" Serge whispered.

Martin nodded his head. "Yeah," he said. "I do."

"Well, it doesn't. Not a bit. If anyone deserved to win it, you did. You're better than anyone playing today. That cup's just a hunk of metal. That's all," Serge said.

"Two years in a row," Martin said. "I was this close—Game seven, seconds left to play. I let my team down."

"Never. Don't say that."

"I did."

"Just watch," Serge said. "They won't even get to the play-offs without you this year. Jorgensen can't stop the puck to save his life. The Cartier Curse works both ways."

The two men laughed through their tears, but then Martin shook his head. "I don't want him to lose."

"Want it or not, he's doing it."

"Not that it matters," Martin said, "but I'm going to call him tonight. Tell him to get his ass in gear and start winning. The Bruins should win the Stanley Cup. This year. Ray deserves it."

"Ray Gardner," Serge said, shaking his head. "You took him right to the NHL with you."

"We used to be so proud of you," Martin said, slashing the tears from his eyes, "just to know you. And when you won the Stanley Cup, you made us believe we could win it ourselves."

"Misplaced pride," Serge said. "That's all I can say."

"No, Dad," Martin said. "I don't see it that way."

His father stepped forward, crushing Martin in a huge hug. The guards seemed to know they should keep back, and they did. Martin felt his father's chest rising and falling, and he could have sworn he smelled pine and lake in his father's hair.

"Take good care of yourself," Martin said.

"You, too. And of your family."

"I will." He turned to leave, but suddenly he stopped himself and asked, "Can I do anything for *you*?"

"As a matter of fact, you can," Serge said.

Epilogue

B Y LATE MAY, BOSTON WAS ELECTRIC, charged with the disbelief of watching the Bruins squeak into the play-offs, barely beat New Jersey in the seventh game of the series, and—in an uncanny repeat of the last two years—inch their way through the championship finals to Game 7 against Edmonton.

Playing for the Stanley Cup, the team was pumped and ready. Once again they had wound up at the Fleet Center, the capacity crowd on their feet and screaming for blood.

Martin stood in the locker room.

He had stayed away most of the season, even after his holiday call to Nils Jorgensen. He and the goalie had exchanged tentative greetings, but to Martin's surprise, he began getting calls back from the Swede, venting his frustration about the team, the coach, his lack of defensive support.

"Dafoe might seem tough and unfriendly, but that's just his style. Stand up to him, but don't be afraid to listen. He knows what he's talking about," Martin advised.

"The team thinks I'm the enemy," Jorgensen complained.

"You were." Martin laughed. "For years!"

"It's a lousy match," he said. "I'm looking to get traded."

Slowly, Martin had started calling some of his old friends. Every player, to a man, was happy to hear from him. They were tentative, asking about his health, but Martin just told them about his excellent doctor, waiting for advancements in the treatment of his condition, not giving up hope that one day he would see again.

He had listened to his former teammates' gripes about Jorgensen, what a conceited idiot he was, how disloyal they felt playing with him. Martin had laughed at them all, saying they didn't know a good thing when they saw it, telling them to take advantage of the best goalie to pass through the NHL in decades.

Then, with the help of May and Kylie, he had made up a couple of gifts. One was for the Bruins in general, the other for Jorgensen himself. Delivered by Ray, the team's gift was a sign saying "ONLY GOD SAVES MORE THAN NILS JORGENSON." To the goalie from Martin, Ray presented a stick, hand-painted by Kylie with the slogan: "THE PUCK STOPS HERE."

Now, visiting the locker room for the first time all season, Martin learned that the sign was hung above the door to the rink, and that since Jorgensen had started using his stick, he'd won five times as many games as he'd lost.

"You okay?" Ray asked.

"I'm okay," Martin said.

"Game Seven," Ray said.

"Been here before."

"Feels different without you."

"Without me, nothing," Martin said. "I'm here, aren't I?"

The coach called all the players together for one last pep talk. He had his typical tough tone, used his fighting words. In his mind's eye, Martin could see him squinting, chewing on his yellow pencil. The team stood there, listening intently, nervously shifting.

"You can do it, and I know it," Coach Dafoe said. "You're talented, and you're ready. I said it last summer, in this exact same spot: This is our moment, this is our year."

Remembering, Martin cleared his throat, feeling that old familiar rush of sorrow and regret, a strange shame that came from being blind and not able to play.

"We have everything it takes," Coach continued.

Martin bent his head, facing down at the ground so no one could see his face redden. They didn't have him. They had gone this whole way without him playing wing and, it turned out, they hadn't missed him a bit.

"We've got Ray Gardner, we've got Jack Delaney, we've got . . ." Dafoe ran down the roster. "We've got Nils Jorgensen, the goalie who stopped us cold our last two tries, with more saves in the play-offs than even I could believe—"

"Only God saves more than Jorgensen," Ray said, and the team laughed.

"But maybe more than any of you, we have the heart and soul of our team—Martin Cartier. With us today, just like last year and the year before."

Martin raised his head. His face was red and his eyes were streaming, but he didn't care.

"Thanks, Coach."

He felt his teammates slapping him on the back, ruffling his hair. But the moment was short-lived, as Coach Dafoe cleared his throat.

"What's going on, Cartier?"

"Coach?"

"You're in your street clothes."

"Yeah, I'm going to go out, sit with my wife and daughter—"

"The hell you are. Suit up."

"Coach—"

"Now, Cartier. We're going to win, and you're going to be with us."

"With us," Jorgensen echoed.

"All the way," Martin said, feeling someone press his jersey into his hands as he stripped off his shirt and got ready to take the ice.

———

May's voice hurt from yelling. She stood in the old familiar box with Kylie, Genny, Charlotte, and Mark. Tobin and Teddy had come as their guests, and so had Ricky Carera, the young boy from Estonia.

Serge had asked that Martin and May help him to save Ricky from the fate predicted by Jim the guard and others, to do right by a lonely, fatherless boy. Tonight, they had flown him to Boston, and they had picked him up on their way to the game.

"That one's the goalie," she heard Kylie explaining, and "that's the forward."

"Center," Mark corrected.

"Which one's your dad?" Ricky asked.

"The right wing," Mark said proudly.

"My dad played baseball."

"Cool," Mark said.

"Ricky's in Little League," Kylie explained. "My father and grandfather helped him."

"I like it," Ricky said.

"Well, this is hockey," Mark reminded him. "Watch the game."

The score had been tied 0–0 for three periods, and now they were in overtime. May had watched Jorgensen block every shot, throwing himself into the puck, using his body as a human shield.

She gasped with awe, just like everyone in the stands, wondering how much longer he could hold out.

"Martin looks good out there," Genny said, smiling toward the bench.

"He does," May said. She smiled back, but inwardly she felt a catch, as she watched her husband cheering the team on from the sidelines, talking quietly to individual players. She couldn't help remembering last year when he had skated so fearlessly, dominating everyone else on the ice.

"I thought he'd be sitting here with us," Tobin said.

"So did he, I think," May said.

"He's a powerful man," Teddy said.

May nodded.

She had been thrilled to see him skate out with the team. Wearing his old jersey, number 10, and his regular skates, he had looked so right and happy. But that was nothing compared to what the crowd had felt. Spotting Martin, their murmurs had turned into a roar: "Cartier!" "Martin!" "Gold Sledgehammer!"

The cries had filled the stadium, and Martin had waved his stick in recognition. But then all eyes were on the game, on the action at center ice, as the players were introduced and the national anthem sung.

May had thought back, over the last two years. She had made up those packages for Martin the first year and for the whole team the second: rose petals, owl feathers, and tiny bones from the barn. How superstitious and stupid they would seem to some people, but not to May.

She was a woman who had witnessed miracles. The blue diary was full of them. Her daughter talked to ghosts; her husband had skated up the lake and back with an angel. Martin had forgiven his father, and May had been there to see it. Giving talismans to a professional hockey team—that was nothing.

May was expecting a baby.

He was due in September, right around the time when summer gives way to fall. If only Kylie didn't have school, May would have liked to have him in Canada, by the lake where Martin had grown up, where their son had been conceived.

Their baby was a boy. He was already so precious to her, May

wanted every advantage medicine had to offer; the early tests had revealed his health, his size, and his gender.

"A boy," Martin said.

"A big boy," May told him.

"You really think we conceived him at the lake?"

"I know we did," she replied. "That last day, right after you saw Natalie."

"She told me she wouldn't be back," he'd started to say.

"But we've been sent a little boy to love," May had finished. "Can we call him Nate?"

Martin nodded, holding her with all his might, knowing that she was carrying his son.

"Go RAY!" Genny shouted now.

"Bruins!" May yelled, watching Martin.

The clock was ticking. Ray had the puck, and he passed it off. Genny screamed with all her might, joined by everyone in the box. Martin was on his feet by the bench, shouting his lungs out. The crowd was wild, yelling for a goal.

The Bruins lost the puck, and it was taken by Edmonton. Jorgensen blocked the shot, but Edmonton retained possession. Out of nowhere, streaking from behind the blue line, came Ray Gardner. He stole the puck right off the Oilers' stick, passing it off to Delaney.

"Give it to Ray!" Martin yelled.

"Go Bruins!" Kylie yelled.

"Yeah, go Bruins!" Ricky called, his eyes bright with joy.

"Ray, Ray!" Genny shouted.

"Martin, Martin," May shouted louder, holding her belly.

Delaney passed the puck to Ray, and the drive began. He darted between the defensemen, and watching from the box, May would have sworn the Oilers had stood aside to let him through. His way was clear. The crowd roared.

Ray Gardner swung his arm back, and with one straight shot, he put the puck into the net. The Boston Bruins had just won the Stanley Cup by the score of 1–0.

"Ray!" Genny cried, and the entire crowd joined her.

"Oh, Genny," May said, embracing her. The two women held each other, jumping up and down as everyone went crazy. The announcer was talking, the music was playing, policemen in riot gear

had ringed the ice to keep spectators from spilling over. Kylie was jumping on the seat so high she nearly fell off, and Ricky leapt up to join her. May watched a dozen Bruins smother Ray in a huge hug. They were in the middle of the ice, carrying Ray and Nils on their shoulders, and then an amazing thing happened.

The two men wriggled down, and the entire team turned as one. They moved in a swarm toward the bench, and the crowd knew what was happening before May did. The chant began: "MAR-TIN, MAR-TIN . . ." Shaking Martin's hand, crushing him in a group hug, they hoisted him onto their shoulders.

Coach Dafoe was grinning, swept along with the team. The Boston fans were jubilant, joyously out of control as they clambered over the boards.

"MAR-TIN, MAR-TIN!" Kylie sang, and May found herself chanting along. Mother and daughter held hands, jumping up and down. Tobin, Teddy, Genny, Charlotte, and Mark were doing the same thing.

Bedlam reigned at the Fleet Center. The officials were trying to clear the ice, to stage the Cup ceremony. May could feel the thrill in her veins. She ached with mysterious emotion, as if she needed to cry but couldn't stop laughing.

"We're not supposed to jump on the seats," Ricky said as he jumped higher.

"It's a special occasion." Kylie laughed.

His teammates carried Martin right over to the box where May and Kylie waited, and Martin jumped down to take May into his arms. Ray did the same with Genny. Kissing her husband, May was bent over backward. The crowd was wild, cheering as if they had won the game all over again.

"They did it," Martin said.

"You did it," she told him.

He laughed, holding something toward her. May leaned forward to see better, and there it was: Martin had the little leather pouch she had made him two years before.

"You took it back," she said.

"From your drawer," he said. "It brought me the best luck of all. It brought me you."

"Oh, Martin."

"You and Kylie," he said.

"And Nate," she whispered.

Now the actual Stanley Cup had appeared, carried onto the ice by men in dark blazers. The trophy was as tall as Kylie, and it

gleamed like treasure in the stadium lights. The team was yelling for Martin to come out, for the traditional parade around the ice, and Martin leaned down to Kylie.

"Got your skates?" he asked.

"Not on," she said, with one arm slung around his neck.

"Then you'll have to ride," he said, hoisting her onto his shoulders.

May swallowed hard, watching Martin skate away with Kylie held high. He was blind, but it didn't matter. His skates found the way, as if he could follow the path in his sleep. Ray and Coach Dafoe handed him the Stanley Cup, and Martin held it over his head. The crowd exploded in cheers, with May yelling louder than anyone.

Coming around, Martin blinked his gray-blue eyes, seemed to look straight into May's face. He held the Stanley Cup in his arms, exactly the way a person would treat his dream come true. The lines in his face were deep, and scar tissue showed around his eyes and chin in the blazing lights.

"Can you say a few words?" a reporter asked as Martin came near.

"Yes," Martin said, clearing his throat. "This is for you, May."

"Hear that?" Tobin asked, turning to May.

"Yes," May said, wiping tears from her eyes.

With Kylie on his shoulders, her husband held the Stanley Cup high, and as she listened to thousands cheer, she hoped Serge was watching on TV. The microphone must have been very close to Kylie's mouth, because May heard her words broadcast throughout the stadium:

"Lord Stanley had that cup made because his sons loved hockey so much."

"He did?" the announcer asked.

"Yes, he did."

"How do you know that?"

"My sister told me."

May strained her ears, trying to hear the next words, but Kylie's voice was drowned out by all the cheering fans and May gave up trying to listen. She knew all she needed to know. This was a moment for the blue diary, but she didn't reach for it. Some truths were too pure to be written down, or even said out loud.

About the Author

LUANNE RICE is the author of *Firefly Beach, Dream Country, Follow the Stars Home* —now a Hallmark Hall of Fame feature presentation—*Cloud Nine, Home Fires, Secrets of Paris, Stone Heart, Angels All Over Town, Crazy in Love*, which has been made into a TNT Network feature film, and *Blue Moon*, which has been made into a CBS television film. She lives in New York City and Old Lyme, Connecticut, with her husband.